Munich
IV

Munich 10

by
LEWIS ORDE

ARBOR HOUSE
New York

Library of Congress Catalogue Card Number: 82-72076

ISBN: 0-87795-423-2

Manufactured in the United States of America

10 9 8 7 6 5 4 3 2 1

This book is printed on acid free paper. The paper in this book meets the guidelines for permanence and durability of the Committee on Production Guidelines for Book Longevity of the Council on Library Resources.

TO MY PARENTS,
BLESS 'EM . . .
WHO ARE STILL SURPRISED BY NOTHING.

PROLOGUE

W ITH knuckles gleaming whitely on
the steering wheel, George Tokvarian drove the battered red Volkswagen
Beetle recklessly fast along the northbound side of the Rue de la Repub-
lique, past the UNESCO compound, across the Boulevard Saëb Salam
and onto the Rue Verdun in the western section of Beirut. Every few
seconds he glanced agitatedly into the rearview mirror as he tried to
identify one particular car from the many behind him.

The Volkswagen raced through red lights and Tokvarian closed his ears
to the curses in Arabic and French from pedestrians who scurried to
safety. The driver of a shiny new Mercedes, crossing with the signal, saw
the Volkswagen too late. Tokvarian swore viciously as he jammed his right
foot on the brake and jerked the steering wheel to the side. There was
a tremendous echoing bang, a shuddering, slamming collision, as the
Volkswagen ploughed into the Mercedes. Then the grinding, tearing
sound of tortured metal as Tokvarian reversed and slammed the Volkswagen into first again. Foot pressed to the floor, he surged forward,
shaken, but relieved that his tires had withstood the impact. Behind, he
left a headlight and front wing, mementoes of the accident for the Mercedes' furious driver.

Finally, outside a tall apartment block near the Rue de Baalbeck,
Tokvarian braked to a halt, jumped out and ran into the building with
such urgency that he left the key in the ignition and the engine running.

The building's sole working elevator was on the third floor. Tokvarian
held down the button, all the while staring fixedly at the indicator. Thirty

7

seconds passed before the elevator descended with an agonizing slowness, a full half minute in which the stockily built, dark-haired Syrian-Armenian could fret with unconcealed impatience.

As he stepped into the elevator and the door began to close, he spotted an elderly Arab woman weighed down by two loaded shopping bags. She gave Tokvarian a beseeching look, but he had no time to wait. He shrugged his shoulders in the helpless gesture of a man who does not understand how to keep the door from closing, and he hoped that the old woman would forgive him. She would not, of course; not if she ever chanced to learn the reason for his haste.

On the top floor of the building he let himself into the one-bedroom apartment he had rented for the past two years, double-locked the door and barricaded it with a heavy couch. Through the open window he glimpsed the blue expanse of the Mediterranean, the dirty smudge of smoke on the horizon that signified a ship. Briefly he wondered where the vessel had started its voyage, where it would be bound. Then he closed the blinds and forgot all about it.

He strode to the television console, turned it around and unscrewed the back. Hidden inside was a miniature radio transmitter with a permanent aerial on the roof disguised as one of the many television antennas. He turned on the power, twisted the dial to the correct frequency and waited for the all clear.

In code, he started to send the message: "Plans to reactivate Black September—"

A staccato hammering sounded from the double-locked door. Tokvarian broke off and looked around. How long would the locks and barricade hold? Fighting down fears for his own safety he turned again to the transmitter and continued sending: "No target yet. I am blown."

Those were the last words Tokvarian transmitted. The hammering at the door ceased. For an instant there was silence. Then a burst of automatic fire erupted.

Wood splintered. The locks were driven from their settings. Bullets sprayed across the apartment, gouging plaster from the walls, shattering the window. Tokvarian felt a burning hammer blow in the right shoulder that slammed him back into the television console. He could only watch powerlessly as the couch was shoved aside and two men carrying Kalashnikovs burst into the apartment.

A day earlier—no, an hour earlier—these two men had been Tokvarian's trusted friends. Now they had murder in their eyes.

8

One man, with graying hair cut so short that his sweaty scalp gleamed through, trained his weapon unwaveringly on Tokvarian. The other man rushed across the room, brown eyes blazing in his smooth, unlined face. He stood over Tokvarian, spat, and then smashed the butt of his Kalashnikov into the face of the wounded man, breaking his nose, knocking out teeth, tearing open his right cheek.

Hands grabbed at Tokvarian, half lifted him off the floor and dragged him roughly out of the apartment to the elevator, down to the ground floor and a waiting car.

The elderly Arab woman with the two shopping bags was still downstairs. When the elevator had returned for her after Tokvarian had gone up, the two men with rifles had pushed her aside; and she had been prudent enough not to argue. Now, as she watched those same two men drag Tokvarian's bleeding, battered body out of the building, she wondered what he could have done.

There was no way she could know. But she hoped for Tokvarian's sake that he was already dead.

Part One

CHAPTER ONE

A chill February rain gusted across Paris as Samantha Sutcliffe returned from her shopping expedition and found Alan Tayfield waiting for her in the foyer of the Plaza Athénée hotel.

Watching Samantha walk toward him, Tayfield played the game he loved—observing the observers. Heads never failed to turn when Samantha passed. Those who recognized the English actress experienced a certain thrill to be so close, even in a hotel where celebrities were commonplace. And those who had never seen Samantha on the screen, or who did not remember her from her heyday of international swimming ten years earlier, admired her uncontrived elegance. Eyes followed like magnets to take in the tall, striking woman with the thick brown hair that cascaded in soft waves onto her shoulders, the wide, startlingly blue eyes and the erect, graceful deportment that any top *haute couture* model would have envied.

And then those same following eyes would blink in amazement as Samantha stooped slightly to kiss the balding, paunchy man who was her escort, Alan Tayfield.

"All ready to cross swords with the press?" Tayfield greeted her. His accent was an odd mixture, difficult to place with any certainty. One moment there was a trace of New York, a slight inflection, the lengthening of a vowel; and the next instant he had slipped into the lilting, singsong brogue of Wales. Tayfield had an easy explanation for anyone who queried the origins of his accent. Born and brought up in Cardiff, he had spent twenty years in the United States before returning to Britain. Along the way he had managed to pick up the worst speech traits of wherever he had lived.

"I've been honing my blade all morning," Samantha responded.

"Good girl." While he spoke, Tayfield smiled at men who stared at him with unconcealed envy. He was enjoying the moment to the full. This was how Carlo Ponti must feel with his Sophia, an ugly duckling in a rumpled brown tweed suit with a beautiful, famous woman on his arm. Tayfield knew what the gossip was—that he, a middle-aged, divorced man was managing Samantha's career in exchange for a place in her bed. He wished! But he would never dare even to contemplate it. Their relationship was strictly business—a business far too important to jeopardize for personal desire.

"Ditch your shopping and we'll grab a cab," he told her. He waited while she arranged for her purchases to be sent up to her suite; then he helped her into a waiting cab and gave the driver instructions for La Tour d'Argent restaurant.

As the taxi moved off, Samantha seemed to lose the composure she had shown in the hotel foyer. She closed her eyes and expelled her breath in one long sigh. Tayfield gripped her hand comfortingly. "Relax," he told her. "You'll be a winner. You'll knock them dead."

The words, spoken so softly that even the driver could not hear, had a soothing effect. Samantha opened her eyes and gazed at Tayfield. The quiet confidence she found in his lined face was contagious. Any doubts about her ability to carry the press conference were swept away.

Tayfield continued to hold her hand, dry inside his own, while he reviewed the time he had spent as Samantha's manager. It was through his contacts that she had been given the lead role in the film premiering that night. Tayfield had convinced the producer that Samantha was perfect for the part. The screen test that had followed was merely a formality.

Called *La Maquisarde*, the film was as controversial as the left-wing causes Samantha had chosen to champion. The Second World War had ended thirty-seven years earlier and films about the German occupation of France were no longer fashionable; the structure of the Common Market was too fragile to risk a squabble between its members over deeds done and best forgotten. Yet the theme had been too compelling to ignore: a young German-Jewish woman escaping from a Nazi death train, reaching France and fighting in the Maquis until she finally sacrifices her

14

own life to save the French resistance fighter with whom she has fallen in love. Additional fuel had been poured on the fire by the film company's decision to look outside France for the female lead and to select Samantha Sutcliffe. In Europe and the United States, Jewish organizations had protested vigorously—but to little avail—that an actress who cried out for justice at Palestinian rallies should play a Jewish heroine.

The taxi pulled up on the Quai de la Tournelle. Tayfield and Samantha got out and entered the restaurant. The producer, director and members of the cast were already present. So were the journalists. Samantha prepared herself for her grand entrance.

The producer, Paul Hechter—a stylishly dressed man in his mid-forties, with dark brown hair and horn-rimmed glasses that lent him a studious air—came swiftly across the restaurant to welcome his star. "You look more radiant than ever," he said, kissing Samantha lightly on the cheek. "Ten million women would happily emasculate their most exciting lovers if only they could learn the secret of your beauty."

Samantha knew she should be immune to the producer's constant flattery by now, but the humor glistening in his hazel eyes was irresistible. "Paul, you're such a con man," she answered in perfect French. "Next, you'll be trying to sell me the Eiffel Tower."

Hechter grinned. "How many times did you read those reviews?" he asked. "Come on now, the truth. I want to hear the truth."

Two days before there had been a special press showing of *La Maquisarde*. Without exception the critics had been enthusiastic. One had even declared Samantha's depiction of the heroine to be the most emotionally wrenching portrayal he had seen since Susan Strasberg's performance in *Kapo* twenty years earlier. Paul Hechter had been vindicated in both his choice of subject and female lead. And Alan Tayfield had spent the entire previous day in his London office talking to American producers, lining up his client's next role. With *La Maquisarde* Samantha had moved from her British base to Europe. Now America, also, would be hers for the taking.

"I only read them once." Samantha tried hard to look serious, even a little bored. She lost the fight. "All right," she admitted, laughing now. "I read them a dozen times.

Hechter screwed up his face. "Ha! The conceit of an actress!" Then he kissed her again before guiding her to a seat of honor at the "royal table," at the very center of the windows that overlooked the Seine and

Notre Dame. Tayfield sat away, content now simply to watch. This was Samantha's day of triumph to be shared by no one else.

Taking the seat next to Samantha, Hechter clapped his hands to gain attention. "Ladies and gentlemen . . . we are privileged to be sitting in one of the finest restaurants in the entire world. To ask questions of Mademoiselle Sutcliffe now—or to even think of anything but the gastronomical delights that await us—would be an unforgivable insult to La Tour d'Argent. Question time is adjourned until after lunch." Amid a short burst of approving laughter and applause, Hechter bowed his head and picked up his drink.

Lunch was served. Pressed duck, the restaurant's specialty, followed by *poires en soufflé charpini,* an incredibly rich soufflé containing kirsch, pears and zabaglione. Napoleon brandy and coffee finished the meal. Then the press conference began in earnest. Paul Hechter spoke about the film, the criticism which had been leveled against him initially, the danger of opening old wounds and the decision to choose Samantha for the role. Some of the reporters raised their hands while Hechter was speaking. He brushed aside their queries politely with the promise that Samantha would answer everything.

Mostly the questions posed to Samantha were routine. Diplomatically she stressed how much she had enjoyed working in France, how she had benefited from the experience, and she outlined her plans for the future. From time to time she glanced at Tayfield, accepted his approving smile; she was charming them into eating out of her hand.

As the conference showed signs of petering out, a man with sandy hair and glasses raised his hand for the first time. "Monsieur—?"

"Reynard. Pierre Reynard of *Le Monde.*" He coughed discreetly into his hand to clear his throat and then asked: "Mademoiselle Sutcliffe, what religion do you follow?"

Samantha did not seem surprised by the question. "I was born a Catholic—but I don't practice," she added quickly.

"I understand. Tell me please, as a Catholic—and as an actress who has publicly aligned herself with the Palestinian struggle for freedom—what were your feelings, your emotions, about portraying a Jewish woman fighting against the Germans?"

"No—not Germans," Samantha was quick to point out. A slight trace of tension crept into her voice, two red spots appeared to accentuate her high cheekbones. "The heroine in *La Maquisarde* was fighting against the Nazis. The enemy was not the German people; it was fascism."

"Excuse me. I stand corrected." Reynard smiled apologetically and sat back to await Samantha's reply.

She took her time answering. She looked past Reynard to Tayfield who sat directly behind the man from *Le Monde*. Then she glanced down at Paul Hechter who watched her attentively. "My feelings were very mixed, I suppose."

"Oh?" Reynard's interest quickened. "In what way?"

Something had happened to the pleasant, easy atmosphere of the press conference. There was an abrupt surge of electricity, a current that seemed to dart between Samantha and Reynard. Even the other patrons of the restaurant had picked it up and were waiting to hear how Samantha would answer.

"I was proud to be asked to play such a role," she replied at last, "both as an actress and because of the film's significance, its theme of fighting against fascism. And at the same time I was very frightened."

Tayfield sat up in the chair, lips compressed into a thin, straight line. He could see exactly what was happening. Reynard was baiting her, and Samantha was unable to resist snapping at the line. Paul Hechter also moved, dropping his hands out of sight below the table where they rested on his suddenly tense legs. How could she do this? he screamed silently. He had given her the most important role of her career, offered her the opportunity to establish herself internationally, and now she was about to nail him to the cross of her own crazy left-wing political convictions.

"Frightened?" Reynard prompted gently. "Could you elucidate?"

Samantha's eyes narrowed for an instant, altered. The blue that could be so vivaciously warm turned to chips of Arctic ice. "I was frightened that this film would be used as a propaganda vehicle by the Zionists in the same way they use history to justify their illegal occupation of a land which rightfully belongs to the Palestinian people."

"Samantha!"

The horrified yell came both from Tayfield and Hechter at almost the same time. The producer, a member of a long-established Franco-Jewish family, jumped up from his chair and grabbed Samantha by the arm. Tayfield rushed toward her, his face panicky. The reporters scribbled furiously.

Samantha seemed to notice none of it. Not even Hechter's painfully tight grip on her arm could stop her as she continued talking to the man from *Le Monde*. "Monsieur Reynard, you have to understand that this

17

is a very real fear. All you have to see is how the Zionists manipulate the Western press and you'll realize exactly what I mean."

"Then why did you agree to go ahead with *La Maquisarde?*" Reynard wanted to know.

"It was an important step in my career, a wonderful opportunity. And at the same time it was a cry of protest against fascism."

Reynard appeared puzzled by the answer. "Mademoiselle, at the risk of offending you I feel that you were, perhaps, more interested in further-ing your career than in protesting fascism when you accepted the role," he said. "Is your career more important to you than your beliefs?"

"Not at all." Samantha's voice rose a fraction. "If it's any of your damned business—and I'm not very sure that it is—half of the money I make from this film will be donated to relieve in some small way the squalid conditions of the refugee camps in which the Palestinians are forced to live." A stunned gasp went up around the table and Samantha allowed herself a brief smile of triumph. "In *La Maquisarde* I portray a young woman fighting fascism. In real life I can do no less." With a violent motion she shook off Hechter's hand, picked up her bag and walked quickly from the restaurant. Behind she left an astonished audi-ence.

Tayfield was the first to recover. He chased after Samantha and found her looking up and down the rain-swept street for a taxi. "Are you bloody daft?" he hollered, his native Welsh accent and slang taking over from his years in the States. "Do you realize what you've just gone and done?"

"What have I done?" she snapped back fiercely as she continued to search for a taxi. "Tell me exactly what I've done."

Behind Tayfield the reporters gathered, eager for more. There was no sign of Paul Hechter, though; he had remained upstairs, unable to collect his shattered feelings. "What have you done . . . ?" Tayfield's face turned scarlet. His breath rasped out in short, furious bursts and his heart ham-mered wildly. "You've just taken a bloody great swipe with an ax at your career, that's what you've done! Who do you think controls the film industry in the United States? It's the Jews . . . "

"You're missing the point entirely, Alan." She continued to speak in French, directing her words to the reporters. "I've got no animosity toward Jews. If I had, I would never have accepted the role in *La Maqui-sarde*. I just loathe Fascists, and that's exactly what the Zionists are." At last a taxi came along. Samantha flagged it down, jumped in, slammed the door and told the driver to take her to the Plaza Athénée. Tayfield was

18

left on the sidewalk to face the reporters. They clustered around him like vultures.

"Do you have anything to add to that?" Pierre Reynard from *Le Monde* asked.

Tayfield shook his head as he stared numbly after the cab. "What the hell would you like me to add?" he barked angrily at the man.

"Are you surprised that Mademoiselle Sutcliffe chose this particular moment to make such an emotional display of her feelings?" Reynard persisted.

"Of course I'm surprised. This was hardly the time or place for a political speech."

"But you've managed her long enough," Reynard said. "Surely you could have seen her using an opportunity like this to air her views."

Tayfield forced himself to be calm. He had to rescue something from the debris of the press conference, perhaps undo some of the damage that Samantha's outburst had surely caused. But as hard as he tried, he could think of nothing to say.

"What about the money she said she would give to the Palestinians?" All the questions were coming from Pierre Reynard. The other reporters seemed content to let him represent them.

"What she does with her own money is her own concern, no one else's," was Tayfield's answer.

"Will you continue to manage Mademoiselle Sutcliffe? Only a few moments ago you pointed out that the American film industry is controlled by the Jews. Would you act for her and risk their powerful anger?"

Tayfield did not have an answer. "If you'll excuse me, I have other things to do." He swung around and went back inside the restaurant. The reporters followed close behind.

Paul Hechter was still sitting at the royal table, alone now. The other members of the cast had left, embarrassed by Samantha's outburst. Tayfield pulled up a chair and sat down next to the producer. "I'm sorry," he said, barely loud enough for the reporters to hear. "I had no idea she was going to pull a stunt like that."

"Jesus Christ!" Hechter suddenly exploded. "You know something? I don't even feel in the least offended on a personal level, although she promised me faithfully that she'd keep my picture and her lunatic opinions apart. I'm a Jew who gives plenty of money to those people she calls Fascists, and even that doesn't bother me. What really burns a hole in my gut is that I may have just seen a very talented actress slit her own throat."

"Would you hire her again, Monsieur Hechter?" Again it was Pierre Reynard who asked the question.

Hechter looked up, surprised, as if noticing the reporters for the first time. "I'd have to think about it half a dozen times." A slight grin stole across his face as he, too, realized that he had to salvage whatever he could. "Maybe I'd only have to think about it once if *La Maquisarde* breaks a few records at the box office. I guess there's no chance of buying you all a drink and asking you to forget what just went on, is there?"

No one answered.

Hechter's grin faded as suddenly as it had appeared. "Goddamned stupid bitch," he muttered scathingly. "And you can all quote me on that."

CHAPTER TWO

PIERRE Reynard, the journalist who had baited the hook for Samantha to snap at, was a free-lance political writer who contributed regular columns to *Le Monde* in his capacity as a specialist on the Middle East. Those columns were always slanted toward the Arab side of the dispute. Rarely did Reynard touch on the Israeli viewpoint; and when he did, it was only to launch an attack on their policies by stating that there could never be peace in the area without justice for the Palestinians. The other reporters had not been surprised to see Reynard at the press conference for *La Maquisarde*. In the past Samantha had voiced support for the Palestinians. Even as an actress she fell well within Reynard's sphere of interest.

From La Tour d'Argent Reynard took a taxi to the offices of *Le Monde* where he spent half an hour writing up the story for the next edition. Finished, he pulled a cigarette from the pack of Gitanes on the desk in front of him, lit up, and then telephoned the Plaza Athénée to ask for Samantha. He said he would like to interview her about the remarks she had made. She agreed to meet him for dinner.

They met early that evening in the Plaza Athénée restaurant where Reynard mutilated his expense account to buy dinner. He did not waste any time. Even before the waiter had appeared, he said to Samantha, "I feel that I'm responsible for your comments at lunchtime, for the commotion they created. I handed you a loaded gun which you promptly used."

"Don't feel so guilty," Samantha replied. "You provided me with an opening, that's all. I'd planned to make a statement. Everyone expected it of me, didn't they? It was just a matter of selecting the appropriate moment." For the first time she had the opportunity to examine Reynard closely. His name fascinated her. Reynard meant "fox," and Samantha decided that the man from *Le Monde* suited his name admirably. He had a thin face with a long, slightly pointed nose, and the light brown eyes behind his glasses were quick and intelligent. The classic cut of his double-breasted Cerruti suit failed to disguise the sharp-witted predator. She guessed from the slight lines around his eyes and mouth he was in his late thirties.

"Obviously I was flattered that a producer of Paul Hechter's standing would offer me such a prestigious role," Samantha continued. "But the last thing I wanted was for the film to become yet another propaganda piece for the Zionists. Another *Exodus*, if you like. So I had to speak out, to make my feelings known before it could happen."

"You may have harmed your career," Reynard pointed out. "Your manager was correct when he said that Jews who support Israel are very powerful in the American film industry."

Samantha nodded slowly in reluctant agreement. "I know. But I would hope that my career stands or falls on my professional ability as an actress, not because of my political beliefs."

Reynard lifted his glass toward Samantha. "Here's to your being right. You have a talent that is far too precious to be exiled. Have you ever seen those refugee camps you spoke of?"

"Only on films."

Reynard was saddened by the answer. "Films can never do them justice. How can you capture with a camera the stench, the feeling of bitter hopelessness that passes as a legacy from one generation to the next?" His face grew taut, his voice quiet yet forceful. "And to add to the suffering of these unfortunate wretches, the Israeli military establishment continually harasses them on the flimsy pretext that the camps are bases for guerrillas. For terrorists."

"You've been to the camps?"

"Frequently. I visit them because they are newsworthy, and to constantly remind the world of their existence. But I also go for a purely personal reason—to cleanse my soul, to purge myself of the false values that being a Parisian can produce."

Samantha nodded thoughtfully, "I see."

"Do you?" Reynard asked, his voice suddenly brittle with cynicism. "Do you really see? I doubt it. Believe me, the *fedayeen* who sacrifice their

lives in battle are the fortunate ones. They are dying for a reason, martyring themselves so that one day others may live with dignity. Their sudden,
bloody death is far better than the lingering end imposed by camp life.
That is like a cancer, first of the mind and then of the body." He lit a
cigarette and flashed Samantha a feeble half grin, as if abashed at becoming so carried away. "You should have been a journalist instead of an
actress," he finally said. "I wanted to interview you, and you have skillfully
reversed the situation."

Samantha accepted the compliment with a demure smile while suspect-
ing that Reynard was employing a long-practiced technique. The short,
intense delivery, the apparent moment of embarrassment, followed by the
unexpected words of praise, all designed to lower her defenses and make
her more susceptible to his questions. "What do you want to know?" she
asked.

"You were at Munich in '72, weren't you? At the Olympic Games?"

"Yes." Samantha had been expecting the interview to take this turn.
Reynard did not have to phrase the question any more directly. She knew
exactly what he meant: how, after being peripherally involved in the
Munich Olympics massacre, after attending the memorial service for the
murdered Israeli team members the following day—and shedding tears
like the other eighty thousand people crammed into the stadium—she
could speak up so strongly for Palestinian rights. "I swam for the United
Kingdom there."

"Well?" Reynard waited patiently, aware that he was treading on
extremely sensitive ground.

"I cried," Samantha admitted simply. "Death always makes me cry.
But the greatest tragedy of Munich was that the deaths of the Israelis—
and of the men who carried out the operation—were so totally unnecessary. Munich, more than anything else before or since, made me realize
that all this senseless bloodshed could be avoided if only the Israelis would
recognize the rights of the Palestinians to exist in their own land. To exist
in peace . . . like the Israelis claim they want the Arab countries to
recognize their right to live in peace."

Reynard stared thoughtfully at the wisp of smoke spiraling up from the
tip of his cigarette. "I was in the stadium on the day of the memorial
service," he said softly. "And I also wept. For those very same reasons you
just stated."

Samantha believed him. Reynard appeared to be the type of man who
would not be ashamed to display emotion, even grief, at the deaths of

people from a nation he constantly criticized. It was a facet of his character that Samantha found appealing.

"Where are you from originally, which part of England?" he asked suddenly.

"The Midlands. A university town called Loughborough, just north of Leicester. But I live near Bath now, on a small farm with my young son, David, and a housekeeper."

Reynard's interest picked up. "How old is your son?"

"He'll be nine in June."

"Are you divorced?"

"No. Are you?"

Reynard shook his head and smiled. "I never found the time to get married." Then he turned serious again. "Widowed?" he asked uncertainly; they had spoken too much of death already.

"No."

"Am I prying too much?"

"Not really. I had what the newspapers delight in labeling a love child."

"One of our failings, I'm afraid; we stick labels on everything," Reynard offered. "Would you like to tell me about your son?"

Samantha saw no reason not to. "I was having an affair with a man. When I became pregnant I realized that I dearly wanted to have the baby, but I wasn't very sure that I wanted the man."

Now it was Reynard's turn to say "I see," accompanying the words with a quick, spontaneous grin. And Samantha wondered if he really did see. Men never seemed to. It was always a laugh when a girl got knocked up. But Reynard might be different. He was personable, intelligent. And he seemed to possess a depth of feeling, a sincerity, that Samantha had not discovered in many men. Perhaps he really did see.

All through dinner Reynard continued his questioning in a conversational tone, eliciting information. Over coffee and a Havana cigar, he asked Samantha if she would be attending that night's premiere of *La Maquisarde*. She answered no, explaining that she was uncertain whether Paul Hechter would be pleased to see her after her lunchtime outburst.

"Be pessimistic for a moment," he asked her. "What would you do if your career ends right here and now? If you were blackballed so successfully that no one would touch you?"

Samantha bit her lower lip pensively. "I suppose I could always give swimming lessons," she answered with a bright smile. "Or do you have any better ideas?"

"Perhaps." But that was all Reynard was prepared to say.

The bill came and he paid. Then, to Samantha's disappointment, he said he had to leave; he had work to catch up on. She had expected a pass, and Reynard had not made even the slightest gesture. She was more attracted to him than any man she could remember for a long time. He had mesmerized her with his description of the refugee camps, his anguish at their unjustness. And he had charmed her as well, when he had switched to other, lighter topics.

"*Au revoir,* Samantha." It was the first time he had used her given name and she was enchanted by the way he pronounced it. Softly, almost —she hesitated before completing the thought—seductively. "It was most gracious of you to give me so much of your time."

"Thank you for dinner."

"*Mon plaisir.*" And then, to Samantha's delight, he bowed slightly from the waist and kissed her hand. She watched him leave the restaurant, disappointed that the evening had ended so abruptly.

Before picking up Samantha at the Plaza Athénée the following morning for their return flight to England, Alan Tayfield stopped off at Paul Hechter's office on the Rue Marbeuf. With him, he carried copies of every newspaper he had been able to buy.

Hechter cleared his desk of everything but a framed photograph of his wife and young daughter. Then he and Tayfield started to check the newspapers. Samantha's harangue at La Tour d'Argent was carried everywhere, in French papers, German, English, American. It was even given editorial space in one of the British dailies where it was noted that "among the power elite of the film industry which, due to its disproportionately large percentage of Jews, is notoriously pro-Israel, the Palestinians have finally found a friend."

Both Tayfield and Hechter agreed that the damage done to Samantha's career was grave. American producers to whom Tayfield had spoken only two days previously were now quoted as having reservations about using her. On the other side of the coin, however, the premiere of *La Maquisarde* had aroused tremendous interest. Provincial and foreign circuits were rushing to book it.

"Paul, I have to go, I have a plane to catch," Tayfield said, checking his watch. "Many thanks for all your help."

"Did you accomplish all you wanted to?" Hechter asked as he saw Tayfield to the door.

"I think so. We'll know more in a few weeks."

"I'm glad I could be of assistance." Hechter held out his right hand. "Have a good trip. *Shalom.*"

"*Shalom.*" Tayfield shook Hechter's hand before walking away quickly.

Ten minutes later he was in a taxi at the Plaza Athénée, sitting back while Samantha's baggage was loaded into the trunk. Neither spoke during the drive to the airport. Only when they had checked in and were waiting in a quiet corner of the passenger lounge did Tayfield say, "Your two performances yesterday deserve an Oscar."

"What happened after Reynard left me?"

"At eleven-twenty he met with a man in a bar on the Avenue Jean Jaures, in the slaughterhouse area." Tayfield recited the facts with meticulous precision, like a policeman reading off a report. "They talked for ten minutes. We identified the other man as Salim Maazi. He's listed as an information officer with the Palestine Liberation Organization office in Paris, but that's a position he's held in several countries. We think he's far more important than that."

Samantha's eyes turned cold as she digested the information. "How much more important?"

"Before he started doing this public relations work, he always seemed to be on the periphery of the biggest terrorist actions," Tayfield answered. "We now believe that he may have been loosely tied in with Munich, but it's difficult to prove with any certainty because he covers himself so well."

"What's his background?"

"Money," Tayfield answered simply. "Salim Maazi comes from a very rich family. They owned a lot of land in Palestine when the British were there, even when the Turks were in control. When Israel was created, Maazi's family fled along with all the others. But instead of hanging around some refugee camp while they waited to get back home, the Maazis settled in Kuwait. Salim's father opened a small shop there which he eventually worked up into a pretty luxurious store."

Samantha could not help smiling at the story. "I thought only the Jews could do that sort of thing."

"Don't believe everything you read about us in trashy paperbacks," Tayfield said, patting her knee in a paternal gesture. "Anyway, the old man died when Maazi was in his early twenties, twelve years or so ago. Maazi persuaded his mother to sell the store; then with his share of the money he went to Beirut—"

"Where he hooked up with the hard core of the Palestinian resistance movement," Samantha finished.

"That's right. Because that's what he was. He despised his father because he felt that the old man had settled for comfort in Kuwait instead of purgatory in the camps, but he didn't object to using his father's money to lead the high life. Salim Maazi's a playboy, throws his money around, especially on women. He's a charmer . . . and at the same time he's a vicious, cold-blooded bastard who believes one hundred percent in the ideology of terror."

They boarded the British Airways Trident. Samantha took a book from her bag and began to read. Tayfield leaned back and closed his eyes, grateful to finally drop the facade he had worn for the past two days. He felt tired from the playacting and found himself wishing that the aircraft would fly him, not west to London, but east to Israel so that he could visit Petah Tiqva where his daughter, son-in-law and two young grandchildren lived. Nine months had passed since he had last seen his family, hugged them, kissed them. It was too long, far too long.

Only vaguely was Tayfield aware of the Trident taxiing to the runway, gathering speed and taking off. He was too busy thinking, questioning whether his work—no matter how important he knew it to be—was worth all the sacrifices. It might be different if his family understood what he did. Then they would be able to appreciate his lengthy absences. But he dared not tell them. They had to continue believing that he was sales manager of an electronics firm in Tel Aviv, traipsing around the world eleven months out of the year to win vital export orders for his company. Postcards and letters with his handwriting arrived regularly at Petah Tiqva, mailed from Frankfurt, Vancouver, Copenhagen, New York City. And each time he returned to Israel, his arms would be full of gifts from those distant places. It was sound thinking. If you could deceive your own family, you would have no trouble fooling the other side.

Alan Tayfield was not a Welshman who had spent twenty years in the United States, but an Israeli citizen named Gershon Shual who had been born in Tel Aviv forty-eight years earlier when Israel had been called Palestine and was ruled by the British. He spoke English with a Welsh accent only because a young soldier from Swansea—spending his national service time in Palestine—had liked him enough to teach him the language.

Nor was he divorced. He was a widower whose wife had died fifteen years earlier at the age of thirty-one, a blistering shock from which he had still not fully recovered.

Most important, he was a senior field agent in Israel's Institute for Intelligence and Special Assignments. The Mossad.

Tayfield dismissed the thoughts of home and goaded himself back into the character of Samantha Sutcliffe's manager. It seemed now as though he had lived the part forever, establishing himself in London after allegedly spending those twenty years in the States. There were records of him in America, even a woman in Los Angeles he had never met who possessed a wedding certificate and divorce decree with Alan Tayfield's name on them. The Mossad was nothing if not thorough.

He concentrated on two men he had known through the Mossad, brought their faces to his eyes. Both men had been brilliant agents. Wolfgang Lotz, the vehement ex-Nazi owner of a fashionable riding school in Cairo who had become the friend and confidant of top-level Egyptian soldiers and statesmen. And Eli Cohen, who, as Kamil Amin Taabes, had almost been appointed as Syria's minister of defense.

Tayfield shuddered involuntarily as he recalled the photographs of Cohen hanging in Damascus's El Marga Square. Lotz had been caught and imprisoned, eventually traded for half the Egyptian general staff after the Six Day War. Cohen had been caught and executed. But neither man had been apprehended until he had caused tremendous damage.

Turning slightly in the seat, Tayfield opened an eye and looked at Samantha as she read her book. She, also, would cause tremendous damage. Not because of any birthright or heritage. She was not an Israeli. She was not even a Jew. But she would act because of a young man who *had* been an Israeli and a Jew. A young man called Asher Davidson who had suffered the misfortune to represent his country at the Munich Olympic Games.

Tayfield remembered Davidson well—a tall, rangy long-distance runner who had been given leave from the army to run in the Mexico Olympic Games of 1968. That was where Samantha had met him. There had been consternation at first among the Israeli security officials about Davidson sneaking away from the team's quarters to keep a secret tryst with the British swimmer. The anxiety had soon turned to patronizing amusement as the relationship proved to be nothing more sinister than two young, healthy people enjoying each other while convinced they were keeping their affair such a wonderful secret. And their future meetings, those stolen hours during international athletic meets around the world, were allowed to remain secret too. There was no need to disrupt Davidson's life by telling his wife about his intermittent affair with the British swimmer. But it was good to have such information on the files. Just in case . . .

Then came 1972, and Munich. When Palestinian commandos had broken into the Israeli quarters in the Olympic Village, Davidson had been seriously wounded while escaping. Six weeks later, in a Jerusalem hospital, he succumbed to those injuries. Ever efficient, the Mossad kept tabs on Samantha Sutcliffe in case her relationship with the runner could ever be of use. The Mossad knew about the birth of Samantha's child nine months after the Olympic Games and could guess the identity of the father, especially when she named the boy David. And when the boy was seven years old and Samantha had established a successful acting career, the Mossad made its approach.

Vividly, as if it were only yesterday, Tayfield remembered his first meeting with Samantha. He had telephoned her from Bath, claimed he had been a friend of Asher Davidson and asked if she would meet him for lunch. After her initial surprise at hearing Asher's name, Samantha had agreed warily.

When Samantha entered the restaurant, Tayfield was sitting at a table for two in the corner. He had no trouble recognizing her; the pictures in the Mossad files were recent. After introducing himself, he asked, "How is your son, little David? Asher's boy?"

The pallor that flooded Samantha's face was evidence enough that the Mossad files were, as usual, scrupulously correct. "How did you know?" Samantha asked. "About Asher and me? About my son?"

Tayfield tried to look regretful. "I'm afraid that I'm in a line of work where I have to know such things. I know about every meeting you ever had with Asher. Dates—times—where you went."

"How?" she demanded. "No one knew. Or—" She pointed a quivering, accusing finger at him. "Did his wife get you to spy on us?"

He shook his head. "I never knew his wife. For that matter, I never knew Asher either. I saw him run but I never knew him personally. I'm afraid," he admitted, his face blushing slightly with shame, "that I was not entirely truthful with you over the phone."

She regarded him quizzically for a moment. "That line of work you mentioned. Are you with the Israeli government? Security?"

"Of a kind."

"You didn't do much of a job at Munich, did you?" she said in a voice that was suddenly hard and choking. Before Tayfield could protest that

Munich had been the responsibility of the Germans as host nation and the Israeli security officials who had traveled with the team, Samantha's tone softened, became misty, as she explored the paths of memory. "Did you know that Asher and I planned to marry?"

That was startling news to Tayfield. Obviously Davidson's relationship with the British swimmer had gone far deeper than anyone had realized. "What about his wife? Did she know?"

"Yes. He'd already told his wife that he was leaving her. After Munich" —Samantha choked back sobs as she mentioned the name of the city and recalled what it had stolen from her— "after Munich, we were going to announce that we would marry once his divorce came through. I was going to live with him in Israel."

"Why didn't you go to Jerusalem when he was in hospital?"

"I suppose I knew he was going to die," Samantha said wearily. "As much as I wanted to see him, I couldn't bring myself to go."

"Because his wife would have been there?" Tayfield asked gently.

"Yes. I couldn't face her. Perhaps—perhaps it would have been better if I had gone, but . . . " Her voice trailed off and tears glistened wetly in her eyes. Shame and guilt tore through her as she imagined how Asher must have lain there in his hospital bed, waiting for her to visit. Waiting in vain until the very moment he died. All because she had not had the courage to face his wife.

"But you carried his child?"

Samantha nodded weakly. "When Asher died I wanted to kill myself, can you believe that? I loved him that much. We'd planned so much; we had so much happiness to look forward to. Without him I felt that I had been destroyed. Then, when I learned I was pregnant, I knew I had to live. I had to bring Asher's child into the world, create and mold a life of which Asher would have been proud. That way something of Asher would still be alive. And I'd have a reason for living."

Tayfield said nothing for a while, content to sit back while Samantha regained control of herself. Finally he spoke. "I'm going to propose something which you are to consider very carefully before replying. I want you to think about working for us."

"For the Israeli government?"

"Yes."

"You're with their intelligence department, aren't you?" Tayfield saw no point in denying his association with the Mossad. "Asher used to talk about it," Samantha said. "He always boasted that it was the most efficient intelligence service in the world, and it was hopeless for the Arabs to continue fighting because the Israelis knew what they were planning even before they thought of it." Her blue eyes softened as she traveled back in time to a tender moment. Then, with an abrupt swiftness, they turned hard. "What is it you want me to do?"

Tayfield was surprised by her forthright attitude, until he remembered whose child she had carried and how the father of that child had died. "We want you to become a friend of the Palestinians."

"You what?" she asked in hushed horror. "You must be joking."

"No, I am not joking. Far from it. In your position as an actress, as a celebrity, you would make a wonderful spokesperson for them. You would be a welcome friend."

Samantha thought it over for a while. "You want me to—to infiltrate them, is that it?"

"Not at first. You will have to earn their confidence in the beginning. Once you were well entrenched we would know what we could or could not ask you to do. It might"—he hesitated, aware that he had reached the crucial stage of the recruitment—"conceivably become dangerous."

"For me? Or for my son, Asher's son?"

Tayfield did not answer.

"Where will you be?" Samantha asked. For some reason she found herself trusting this pudgy, middle-aged man she had known for only half an hour. He had known her for much longer, of course. But she could feel no resentment because he and his colleagues had spied on her during those precious all-too-few moments with Asher. If anything, that knowledge made her feel close to Tayfield. They shared something. The rest of the world might have forgotten, but she and Tayfield remembered a man called Asher Davidson.

"I'll be with you all the time," Tayfield replied. "As your manager."

"My manager?"

"Believe me"—his face softened into a gentle smile—"I can help your career. I know many people." He did not bother to tell Samantha that his contacts in the film industry were those people classified as sympathetic by the Mossad.

"Whether you can help my career or not is unimportant," Samantha replied, her voice turning hard again. "Let me explain something to you. Two days are burned into my memory forever, the fifth and sixth of September, 1972. Whenever I hear the "Funeral March" from the *Eroica* or the Overture to *Egmont,* I shiver," she said, referring to the two pieces

31

of music which had opened and closed the memorial service for the Munich dead. "Because of what happened on those two days, my son never knew his father. Nothing can bring him back, but if I can help in any way to settle up with the murdering bastards who killed him, I will."

Tayfield leaned across the table and rested his hand on her wrist. "Samantha, don't make the mistake of hating all Arabs," he advised. "My wife died when a terrorist bomb exploded in a Tel Aviv marketplace shortly after the 1967 war. I only hate the men who planted that bomb and the men who were responsible for its manufacture . . . the men whose fingers were on the trigger. To arouse hatred among the Israelis for all Arabs is what the terrorists want. Once they do that will they have succeeded in their quest."

Tayfield heard a whine, felt a slight bump as the Trident lowered its landing gear. He straightened the seat back, made certain the belt was done up and turned to Samantha. "Home, sweet home."

She closed her book and popped it into her bag. "I hope my car's still in the parking lot," she said.

"It will be," Tayfield assured her. He looked out of the window and recalled how willingly she had been recruited. It was as if she had been waiting all those years since Davidson's death, expecting to be asked. On Tayfield's instructions she had started to mix with members of a disorganized Trotskyist group in London called the Workers' Unity for a Democratic Britain. Within a couple of months she had moved to the forefront of the party and, in a series of rousing, well-reported speeches, had established herself as the darling of the Left and a champion of Palestinian justice.

And then, when Tayfield decided the time was right, he had visited some of those contacts in the film industry whom the Mossad classified as sympathetic, seeking a role for Samantha that would arouse the conflict and controversy he needed. Paul Hechter had just the vehicle, *La Maquisarde*. Samantha was given the part. And the result had been her internationally reported attack on Zionism at La Tour d'Argent.

Yes, Tayfield decided with satisfaction, Samantha would surely wreak havoc.

She would destroy those men who had destroyed her love.

CHAPTER
THREE

Ａ T seven-thirty in the evening, traffic in Tel Aviv was unusually light. Most of the cars were heading into the city and Joel Rosen enjoyed the infrequent luxury of almost empty lanes as he drove toward Gav'atayim.

The drive gave Rosen the opportunity to think. The subject he chose was death—the death of a very close friend. It sickened him, and at the same time it filled him with a terrible fury. He just prayed that he was actor enough to conceal his true feelings when he reached his destination.

Parking outside a modest house, he walked through the neatly laid-out garden and pushed gently against the front door. As is the custom in a house of mourning, the door was open. He took a *yarmulke* from his jacket pocket and perched it on his thick gray hair; then he entered the house, feeling the veil of grief that persisted there reaching out to grasp him. Along one wall of the living room was a row of six low wooden chairs, occupied by the widow, two sons, a daughter and two brothers of the man who had died. Rosen walked along the line, shaking hands with the mourners. At last he came to the widow, a woman in her late forties with tinted brown hair pulled straight back from her face, and brown eyes that were red-rimmed from crying.

"Hannah—I'm sorry." Rosen felt powerless as he clutched her hand, and he wished for some of the strength and certainty he displayed daily in his work. "If there's anything I can do—"

The woman squeezed his hand fondly. "Why couldn't I see him, Joel?" she asked plaintively. "Why wouldn't they let me see my Shlomo? Why wouldn't they let me take one last look at him?"

"There was an autopsy, Hannah. They wanted to learn why Shlomo died so suddenly. You understand."

Slowly the woman nodded, and for an instant Rosen's fury grew wild. He loathed himself for the lie he had just told, but mostly for the job he had to perform. No matter how intricate the planning, how solid the cover, something could always go wrong. Just as it had gone wrong for Shlomo Berger, this woman's husband. And then family and friends were left behind to grieve, and in some cases to ask why they had not been allowed to see the body.

Rosen looked from the widow to the other members of the immediate family. Then to the cousins, the aunts and uncles, the nieces and nephews, the friends who filled the room. How many of these people had known Shlomo Berger as well as Rosen had? None of them, Rosen decided with a grim certainty.

He stayed in the house for more than an hour, long enough to participate in the service conducted by the rabbi from a local synagogue. At nine-fifteen he began the journey back to his office in the Kiria, which housed the headquarters of Israel's military and intelligence services. He would not be going home that night. There was work to be done; he needed to prepare.

While he drove, he thought about the lie he had told the woman. There had been no autopsy on her husband. Even if there had been one, the scars it would have left could have done nothing but improve Shlomo Berger's appearance in death. That infuriated Rosen the most—the senseless savagery, the work of psychopaths who dared to call themselves freedom fighters. Only psychopaths would cut off a man's penis and testicles and stuff them into his mouth, gouge out his eyes, hack off his fingers and ears and then cram the mutilated carcass into a crate that would eventually find its way into the trunk of a stolen car parked outside the Israeli embassy in Rome where embassy staff would discover it.

Whatever sins Hannah Berger might have committed during her lifetime, she had never done anything to deserve seeing the body of her husband. It was better that the coffin had been sealed. Shlomo Berger had died from a heart attack was all his widow knew; the death certificate signed by a government doctor attested to that.

Rosen thought about Shlomo Berger and surprised himself that after all these years he could still shed a tear. The two men went back a long way together. They had both been part of the Wrath of God, the Mossad hit squad, the eye-for-an-eye revenge unit created after the Munich Olym-

34

pics to track down and exterminate those responsible—and disbanded the following year after the disastrous killing of an innocent man in the Norwegian town of Lillehammer.

Before that they had worked together on Operation Damocles, the bloody terror campaign against German scientists employed in Egypt by President Nasser, which had culminated in the resignation of the Mossad's legendary chief, Isser Harel, after his confrontation with Ben-Gurion.

And before that . . .

Rosen found himself using the drive back to his office to relive his time in Israel, his arrival in 1952 from Cape Town, the Sinai campaign four years later, his choice of military intelligence, and from there to the notice of Isser Harel's Mossad. No wonder Harel had never smiled, Rosen thought as he pictured the little Russian with the big ears and cold blue eyes. The work of the Mossad did not encourage humor. Neither did sending your friends on assignments that caused their deaths.

Shlomo Berger's death and the blood-chilling manner of it were still very much on Joel Rosen's mind the following morning when he boarded a helicopter with General Benjamin Avivi, chief of the Mossad. Around Rosen's waist was a thin, strong chain which secured the briefcase he carried.

The helicopter lifted off and headed toward Jerusalem. General Avivi lit a cigarette and gazed out of the window. Slender and delicate-looking, with the high forehead of a professor, Avivi resembled anything but the dashing armor officer he had once been, a man who had spearheaded the drive across the Suez Canal in 1973 to cut off the Egyptian Third Army. Now he occupied the *memuneh*'s chair at the Mossad, manipulating the institute's men and resources as adroitly as he had ever jockeyed tanks into advantageous positions on the battlefield. Above all he relied heavily upon the cold, calculating skill of a man who was virtually unknown outside Mossad headquarters—his director of special operations, Joel Rosen.

"Terrible thing with Berger," Avivi said, turning from the window as he sensed Rosen looking at him. "You two were good friends, weren't you?"

Rosen nodded. "I went to the *shivah* last night."

"His family knows nothing of what really happened, do they?" Avivi asked as he stared into Rosen's sunburned face. Despite his understanding of human nature, Avivi could rarely tell what was taking place behind

Rosen's mask. The hard features, barely softened by middle age, seldom revealed any emotion; neither did the steady dark brown eyes.

"The family believes it was a heart attack. Hannah, Berger's widow, wanted to know why she couldn't see the body. I told her there had been an autopsy."

"What went wrong, Joel?" Avivi suddenly asked. "We've got to have something to tell the prime minister."

"Berger was too damned good at his job. He sent too much too often," Rosen said gruffly and lapsed into silence. Avivi did not question him further. The general knew that when they met with the prime minister, Rosen would have his facts and information ready; and at the same time Avivi found himself worrying that Rosen seemed so affected.

At two-thirty that afternoon, Rosen and Avivi were shown into the prime minister's office. The prime minister did not bother with any preamble. His first question was the same as that which Avivi had asked, and he expected an immediate answer.

"What went wrong?"

Rosen opened his briefcase and extracted a bulky folder. There was no name on it, just a number which he studied for several seconds as if realizing that Shlomo Berger was indeed nothing more than a number now. He opened the folder and scanned the top sheet. "Berger succeeded in penetrating Al Fatah two years ago under the cover of being a sympathetic Syrian-Armenian named George Tokvarian—"

"That was what went *right*," the prime minister interrupted. "I asked you what went wrong."

"Fatah had plenty of reason to be suspicious," Rosen answered. "In the last six months, Berger warned us of four separate operations. Each time we were waiting for them. So they started looking. They might have picked up his signal with a mobile detection unit, or he might have made a mistake somewhere along the line. His final transmission from Beirut was two weeks ago. He reported, 'Plans to reactivate Black September. No target yet. I am blown.' End of transmission."

"And three days ago his body was delivered to our embassy in Rome," Avivi concluded.

"What do you think they learned from him?" the prime minister asked.

"Nothing," Rosen said with a certainty tinged with pride. "Not even his real name. If they had broken him we would have received one final transmission, either with gloating or misinformation. We've heard nothing." As he spoke, Rosen formed a mental picture of Berger, a strong, chunky man with sallow skin and an unruly shock of thick black hair that seemed to explode out of his skull. Berger would not have broken, even if he had still been alive when they started to hack him up.

"And what did *we* learn?" the prime minister asked.

"Only that final message."

"Black September," the prime minister murmured. He removed his glasses and wiped the lenses with a tissue. Without the glasses he looked less formidable, more like an old man who found the strain of his position difficult to bear. Rosen felt an involuntary twinge of pity. He understood what tremendous pressures the prime minister was under, from both his own right-wing party which wanted Israel to enjoy the borders it had known in biblical days, and from the opposition which called for moderation. That conflict was particularly evident now, although no word of it had been allowed to reach the press. The Americans were leaning heavily on the prime minister, certain that they were on the verge of a real Middle East peace . . . if only the Israelis would be less intransigent about the Palestinians. If the prime minister showed good faith by promising total autonomy to the West Bank and Gaza Palestinians, the Americans claimed they could pull the Jordanians and Saudi Arabians into a face-to-face meeting with the Israelis and Egyptians. And from there—and this, suspected Rosen, was the Americans' prime concern—the formation of a multinational force of its allies to stand as a strong bulwark against the increasing Soviet presence in the Middle East. Rosen understood what a gamble it would be on the prime minister's part to accept the terms, both for the country and for his own political career. Yet the old man could not afford to reject out-of-hand this opportunity to sit down with his lifelong foes.

Satisfied that his glasses were clean, the prime minister replaced them. Immediately, his face resumed its normal shrewd expression. "So, like humpty-dumpty, they want to put Black September together again. How long has it been since they operated?"

Avivi had the answer. "They were disbanded in 1974 because Arafat could not afford to be linked to a particularly murderous bunch of killers when he was parading around at the United Nations as the potential leader of a sovereign state."

"Fatah always denied any association with Black September," the prime minister pointed out.

"No one believes that lie anymore," Rosen said. "Black September was Fatah's brainchild from the moment of its first bloody act when Wasfi

37

Tel was murdered in '71. And they were backed to the hilt by the KGB as we learned from the files we took from Fakhani Street in the Beirut raid." He replaced Berger's file in the briefcase, finished with it. "The last anyone heard of Black September was in October, '74, when Abu Iyad —Arafat's second in command—led them in the attempted assassination of King Hussein at the Rabat summit meeting."

"You might recall that it was our tip-off to the Moroccan authorities that averted the tragedy and led to fifteen arrests," Avivi added.

"Some thanks we got," the prime minister muttered sarcastically.

"What else is new?" Avivi could not resist saying.

While Rosen listened, he recalled the raid on the Iraqi nuclear plant at Osirak. The Syrians, Saudis and Jordanians had been having nightmares as they envisioned the nuclear weapons the Iraqis might produce in their bid for undisputed supremacy of the Arab world. Yet when Israel had taken care of the problem with a clinically precise bombing raid, after being kept informed of the Iraqis' progress by an agent within the plant, the Arab states had ganged up and bayed for blood. The French knew better, though. When they contracted to rebuild the plant they specified using caramel, a low-grade fuel that could never be converted to bombs. *And* they demanded permanent inspections just to make sure. Maybe all that had something to do with the Saudis and Jordanians suddenly coming to their senses, Rosen thought; not that the same could ever be expected of the Syrians. And they were throwing in the West Bank and Gaza issues just to appear to keep faith with the Palestinians.

"Black September," the prime minister mused. "What are your people doing about it?"

Avivi glanced at Rosen as he answered. "Joel's started Samantha Sutcliffe."

"Are you really happy about using an illegal?"

The Prime Minister's use of the word *illegal* grated badly on Rosen. He had never cared for that description of an agent who worked for a country other than his own. Rosen preferred to think of such agents as surprises. After all, nothing in espionage was ever strictly legal. "Samantha Sutcliffe is perfect for the part," Rosen said, defending his choice of the English actress. "She's spoken at Palestinian rallies. And after that business in Paris she's a damned heroine to them. She'll be able to go where no one else can go, and other, more experienced agents can ride right in on her coattails." Recognizing the doubt that remained etched on the prime minister's face, Rosen turned to Avivi for assistance.

"We've invested a lot of time and effort in her," the general pointed out. "What are we saving her for? Some courier job that any first-year man could carry out?"

"She has a son." The prime minister spaced out the words for emphasis. "The boy has already lost a father for our nation. I would hate for him to lose a mother as well. Or, even worse, for the child himself to be harmed."

"We've already taken that into consideration," Rosen said. It was like seeing Berger's widow all over again, the people on the sidelines who got injured. He felt sick with guilt. "If necessary, I'm prepared to go back into the field myself on this case. I'll see Samantha Sutcliffe and her son have plenty of cover."

Both Avivi and the prime minister turned to gaze at Rosen. "How old are you, Joel?" Avivi asked.

"Fifty-six," Rosen answered, surprised by the question.

"So am I," Avivi said. "And I know that a fifty-six-year-old man only gives up the comfort of his desk to return to the field because a dear friend has been killed. Don't let the tantalizing scent of vengeance cloud your better judgment."

Rosen's face went tight. "This mission comes under special operations, right?"

Avivi nodded.

"I'm director of special operations, right?"

Again Avivi nodded.

"Then don't let your concern about my motives cloud *your* judgment. If I feel it's right to return to the field, I'll damned well do so."

Rosen returned alone to Tel Aviv, leaving General Avivi in Jerusalem where he had other business.

Late that night, Rosen sat in his office, brooding. Fifty-six, how old was that? He was at his peak, and Avivi was critical of him for wanting to return to the field. What did a man like Avivi know anyway? He was a soldier, brought in to administer the Mossad, to ensure it ran smoothly. Men like Avivi thought that intelligence work was the meticulous collection and analysis of information. In part it was, but there was also that area called special operations. And there, Rosen had the decided edge.

Was it revenge? Was that why he was prepared to return to the field, to pursue a personal vendetta against the killers of Shlomo Berger? Or was it because he knew he could do a more professional job than anyone else?

Rosen did not know which reason to choose, which one was the truth.

Gradually, the period of meditation passed and Rosen concentrated on the work at hand. He knew he had to speed up the Palestinians' total acceptance of Samantha. He had to push her so hard into their arms that they would welcome her as if she were the second coming of Mohammed. No matter how much he despised the idea, he had to transform Samantha from an actress with strong political convictions into a woman pilloried for her beliefs. He had to turn her into a suffering martyr. And he thought he knew how . . .

In longhand, Rosen scribbled a letter to Alan Tayfield, giving him instructions. The letter would be carried on the following day's El Al flight to New York which stopped in London. Tayfield would receive it the morning after, in another envelope which bore a British stamp.

Finished, he stood in the center of the office and looked around at the parquet floor, the four straight-backed chairs, the wooden desk, the gray steel filing cabinets. The only luxury was the thermos full of hot tea and the jug of milk on a collapsible table. He went to the table, poured himself a cup of tea and sat down, trying to collect his thoughts. This promised to be one of the most sensitive missions since he had taken over as director of special operations. To send an illegal—damn! he was using the prime minister's terminology now—into Lebanon. Not only an illegal but a respected British actress. Did he really have the right? Of course he did! He had every right to use every channel open to him to stop whatever butchery was being planned.

From one of the filing cabinets he took a blank folder. Across the cover he wrote in thick black capital letters: OPERATION ASHER. At least he had a name for it now. Next, he picked up one of the two telephones on his desk and placed a call to Zurich. After three rings a woman's voice answered in German.

"I want Hunovi," Rosen said, using the Hebrew word that translated into "the prophet."

"Who is this?"

"Joel." Rosen drew a heavy circle around the two words he had written on the folder.

"I'll call you back." The woman hung up and Rosen replaced his own receiver. Ten minutes later the telephone rang. Rosen answered quickly.

"Joel?" It was the woman's voice. "Hunovi will contact you within the hour."

"Thank you." Rosen sat back in the chair and thought about the man for whose call he now waited. Like Shlomo Berger, Hunovi had worked with Rosen for the Wrath of God. The three men had comprised a select, tightly knit team that joined up and moved in once the target had been located and assessed. And then, when the mission was over, they would split up again, return to their respective bases.

If only, Rosen mused, the three of them had gone to Lillehammer in 1973 instead of the bungling idiots who had been sent. The Mossad had used rank amateurs that time, fools who had botched the job by killing an innocent Moroccan waiter when they thought they were executing Ali Hassan Salameh, one of the masterminds behind the Munich Olympics massacre. Nearly six years elapsed before the Mossad finally caught up with Salameh—blowing him into a thousand pieces in Beirut.

But at the time of Lillehammer, Hunovi had been lying low. Less than a month earlier he had participated in the killing of Mohammed Boudia, the Algerian manager of the Théâtre de l'Ouest in Paris. Not only had Boudia been one of the leading Arab terrorists in Europe, he was also the mentor of Ilich Ramirez Sanchez . . . Carlos. Hunovi had eliminated Boudia in Paris by leaving a pressure-activated bomb under the seat of his car. And when the Mossad had got the lead on Salameh being in Norway —the false lead—others had been sent.

After the debacle of Lillehammer, the Wrath of God had been put on hold. And then wound up when those same bungling imbeciles had admitted everything at their trial, revealing full details of the Mossad counterterror campaign. The world's press enjoyed a field day publishing stories about the international assassination operation. Instead of looking under their beds for Communists, frightened people searched for Mossad killers.

While Rosen had ascended quietly within the Mossad, men like Shlomo Berger and Hunovi slipped into obscurity, perfecting their covers, waiting until their talents were required again. Berger's call had eventually been to Lebanon. Hunovi's earlier summons had been quite different— to lose himself completely, to become the most concealed deep-cover agent the institute had, unknown to all but a minute handful of those he worked with. His name was removed from all records. No one ever mentioned him. Rosen ran him as he had run Berger, as he now ran Tayfield and, through him, Samantha. But he could never contact Hunovi directly; he always went through the control in Zurich. Hunovi could call into Tel Aviv, but never the other way around. His total anonymity was his most effective weapon.

41

The telephone rang. Not the one through the main switchboard but the direct outside line. Rosen snatched at it eagerly.

"Joel? Hunovi here."

Rosen knew Hunovi was speaking on an open line. He usually chose a booth in a bank of international telephones at an airport or train station. Somewhere public, a place where he could constantly see what was going on around him.

"Berger's gone." Rosen chose his words with care; you never knew who was eavesdropping along two thousand miles of cable and airwaves.

"What?" There was an instant of shocked grief in Hunovi's voice. Rosen had expected it. News like this would break through even the hardened veneer of a man like Hunovi. "Who sent him away?"

"Our old friends—the ones who sent Baruch Cohen on a permanent vacation." Rosen did not want to use the name of Black September over the telephone. Hunovi would understand whom he meant, though. Baruch Cohen had been an Israeli intelligence officer gunned down in Madrid in 1973 by Black September in retaliation for the killing of two Fatah leaders in Europe by Wrath of God teams.

"So, they are up to something. Did Berger find out what?"

"No. But we are going ahead with the actress and her manager. I'm arranging the finishing touches to her cover right now. In the meantime, keep an eye on the situation. And for God's sake, don't let anything happen to her or her son."

"Leave it with me, Joel." Hunovi hung up and looked around before leaving the booth and walking to the cashier's window to pay for the call. Anguish tore through him, choking him so badly that he could not even manage to thank the woman at the cashier's desk when she handed him change.

Berger had been his friend. To Hunovi it felt as if a part of his own body had been torn away—an arm amputated, a leg ripped off.

As he walked slowly to where he had parked his car, his grief turned to black, crippling rage. He knew he would find those responsible. He was Hunovi, wasn't he? The prophet? Once it had been a silly childhood name given to him by his superstitious mother who claimed he could see into the future. When he had gone underground he had remembered the sobriquet and taken it for his code name.

Hunovi would find the murderers of his friend. And when he did, the streets—like the Tiber—would flow with blood!

CHAPTER
FOUR

EACH time Samantha looked at her son, she could not help but see his father. David had inherited none of her physical characteristics. The warm brown eyes under long, thick curling lashes that were almost feminine came from Asher, as did the wild black wavy hair and quick impetuous grin.

She did not know where David had inherited his appetite, though. She sat at the oak table in the farm's breakfast room, watching in fascination as David ploughed methodically through a second large bowl of corn-flakes; and while she watched she wondered how long it would be until she could tell him the truth about his father. And what would be his reaction when he finally had the solution to a problem that had plagued his childhood? Often David had asked about his father, especially after he had started to attend school in the nearby village and had heard other children boasting of the marvelous feats performed by their fathers. Once he had come home and brought Samantha close to tears by demanding in a high, indignant voice to know where his father was.

"Why don't I have a daddy who can lift a car with one hand?" he had pestered her. "Why don't I have a daddy to show off to my friends?" Taking advantage of his youthful innocence, Samantha had answered simply that his father had gone away.

A year later, when he first came across the meaning of that dreadful word *death*, David asked Samantha if his father had died and gone to heaven. She told him yes, and that had satisfied him for another two years. Until he was almost eight years old and had come home crying after

43

another boy had called him a bastard because his mother was not married.

While Samantha tried to comfort him she had cursed the cruelty of people. It was not the other boy who was at fault, she understood that. It was his parents. It was always the parents who filled their children's minds with their own blind bigotry. Too much had been made in the press about the British Olympic swimmer becoming an unwed mother for people to forget easily. A photograph in a popular daily newspaper had even shown her holding David in the water when he was two years old, with the headline "Love Child Trains for 1992 Olympics."

David was only three when Samantha had bought the farm, and the local community had been cautious in its acceptance of the newcomers. Eventually when her acting career blossomed and she became involved in politics, the locals had come to regard her as something of a novelty. David had been forced to bear the stigma of his mother's fame, though. When he came home crying, she told him that his father had been the kindest man who had ever lived, and that the other boy was only jealous. After that she spoke to the school's headmaster and there had been no trouble since. But she would be glad when he was old enough to attend a good public school where all that mattered was a parent's ability to meet the annual fees.

Samantha looked across the table as David finished off the second bowl of corn flakes and started to attack a pile of toast and marmalade. "Trying to get into the *Guinness Book of World Records* as a trencherman?" she joked.

"Leave the lad alone, Mrs. Sutcliffe," an Irish-accented voice said from behind Samantha. "He's growing every day, needs all the sustenance he can get."

Samantha swiveled in the chair to look toward the kitchen entrance where Mrs. Riley, the housekeeper, was standing. She could never think of the robust, gray-haired bustling Irishwoman by any name other than Mrs. Riley. When she had hired her four years earlier, Samantha had tried calling her Eileen. It had not felt right, a woman old enough to be her mother, so she had stuck with Mrs. Riley.

Oh, that everyone were like Mrs. Riley, Samantha suddenly wished. Minded their own business and appreciated it if other people did likewise, thank you very much. Even if the housekeeper did insist on calling Samantha "Mrs. Sutcliffe" because she was old-fashioned enough to believe that any woman with a child had to be a Mrs., regardless of the circumstances.

44

"What does trencherman mean?" David asked between mouthfuls of toast.

"Your mother's trying to say that you're eating her out of house and home," Mrs. Riley answered as she wiped her red, coarse hands on the apron tied around her ample waist. "Would you be wanting me to take young David to school, Mrs. Sutcliffe?"

"No, that's all right. I'll run him down. I want to do some shopping in the village."

"Make sure he wears a sweater, Mrs. Sutcliffe. It's a mite chilly out there today."

Samantha turned away to hide her own smile, and she was just in time to catch the impish grin which flitted across David's face. The Irish-woman was like a mother hen clucking around her chicks; she would make sure no harm befell them.

Leaving the breakfast plates for Mrs. Riley to clear away, Samantha walked across the flagged floor to the front door of the farmhouse which faced the road leading down to the village. The mailman was cycling along the drive and handed Samantha a single letter. It was for David, from a philatelic company in London. Stamps were the latest rage in his class at school, and David had sent away for a special offer of American issues. She returned to the table, handed David the envelope and watched with fond amusement as he shouted, "Great! Fantastic!" and promptly forgot about the toast and marmalade in his rush to open the treasure.

Telling David to hurry up with his breakfast, Samantha went upstairs to her own bedroom which looked out over the farm. Heeding Mrs. Riley's advice about the temperature, she dressed in jeans and a heavy roll-neck sweater, while through the window she watched two of the dayworkers taking hay from the barn to feed the livestock. When she returned downstairs David was still sitting at the table, exploring the stamps, his face growing steadily longer as he discovered more and more duplicates. Gently but firmly Samantha took away the stamps and told her son to get ready. Then she went outside and opened the door of the double garage attached to the stone farmhouse. Two cars were inside, her own green Range Rover and Mrs. Riley's ancient black Austin A35.

Samantha took the three-mile trip along the wooded road slowly, enjoy-ing the companionship of her son. "What lessons do you have today?" Samantha asked.

David reeled them off on his fingers. "Two periods each of math and English. Then this afternoon we've got history and sports."

Samantha envisaged the washing machine going full blast that night as Mrs. Riley laundered David's sports kit. Even on a sunny day her son would find a muddy puddle to fall into. "Have any of your teachers said anything about me?" she asked lightly. "You know, about what happened in Paris." Often she wondered how her son felt about his mother's publicized link with a world that was far removed from the tranquility of rural Somerset.

David mentioned the name of a teacher who had commented that his mother had made the headlines again. Samantha nodded and thought: they all probably got together in the staff room and muttered about that stupid, eccentric bitch running off at the mouth again. If they only knew . . . She looked at David, saw Asher more strongly than ever in the boy and spontaneously leaned across to kiss him. The Range Rover wobbled ever so slightly as David clung to his mother's arm.

They reached the school where David pointed out two boys who were his friends. Samantha recognized them as having been to the farm and waved. David opened the door and prepared to jump out. At the very last moment he turned to give his mother a kiss on the cheek, very fast and hardly making any contact at all, so that his friends would not see. Then he slammed the door and ran to join the other boys.

Normally Samantha would have smiled good-naturedly at his obvious embarrassment. This time she did not. She was too busy looking in the rearview mirror at the black BMW parked fifty yards behind the Range Rover. The car had followed her from the farm, appearing from nowhere, making no attempt to pass. Now it was waiting. Suddenly frightened of the unknown threat that the BMW represented, Samantha put the Range Rover into gear and continued on toward the small row of shops. The BMW also moved.

Half an hour later she was back at the farm. As she turned into the driveway the BMW roared past, accelerating. She caught a glimpse of the driver, a dark man with a moustache and a cigarette dangling from the corner of his mouth as he hunched over the steering wheel. She wondered whether to call the police.

As she walked through the front door, Mrs. Riley called out from the kitchen that there had been a phone call. "Mr. Tayfield. He wants you to call him back right away."

She would not call the police after all, she decided. She would tell Tayfield. She dialed his number in London, but before she could mention the BMW he asked urgently, "What night is your housekeeper off this week?"

"Thursday. Why?"

"I want you and David out of the house that night as well. Take him to the pictures or something. And don't get back before eleven."

"What's going on, Alan?"

"You're going to have visitors, Samantha." Tayfield talked for another thirty seconds while Samantha listened intently. The hair on the back of her neck began to rise; despite the warmth of the house she started to shiver.

"Alan, do you already have someone watching me?" She told him of her suspicions about the BMW, the dark man with the moustache and the cigarette.

"Are you sure about that, Samantha?" Obviously, Tayfield knew nothing about the BMW.

"Of course I'm sure. Could your people be doing something without telling me?"

"Not a chance."

"Alan, I'm frightened. I'm going to call the police."

"Don't," he said brusquely. "Let me handle it." And he hung up.

Long after the conversation was over, Samantha continued to clutch the dead receiver, staring mesmerized at it. If she had not realized before what she had let herself in for when she agreed to work for Tayfield and the men he represented, she knew now. The visitors who would be coming on Thursday night—the man in the black BMW. . . .

She had agreed to be a spy. That's right, a spy, she repeated to herself. And she was just starting to get her first terrifying glimpse of the world of darkness and deceit to which she had exposed herself and David.

For more than thirty years, Mrs. Riley had owned a battered fur coat of indeterminate origin and a broad-brimmed beige hat trimmed with feathers which she kept for special nights out. Nowadays, those big nights out were usually to the village church hall once a week to play bingo until ten o'clock, and then slipping into the public house next door with her friends for a pint of stout which she nursed until closing time. Unless, of course, her luck had been at bingo. Then she would stretch to two pints of stout, followed by a painfully cautious drive home in the rickety Austin A35, petrified with fear that the local bobby would appear and order her

47

to blow into a plastic bag which would immediately turn as green as the Emerald Isle.

She slipped into the fur coat and, with a feeling approaching reverence, took the feather-trimmed hat down from the top shelf of the hall closet. Samantha watched while Mrs. Riley brushed the hat lovingly before placing it firmly on her head. The housekeeper would have looked perfectly at home in prewar London, Samantha thought. Samantha remembered photographs of her own mother wearing such styles.

"Off to bingo, Mrs. Riley?"

"I feel lucky tonight, Mrs. Sutcliffe. Watch me come back staggering under the big prize." For the first time, the housekeeper noticed that Samantha and David were also dressed to go out. "What about yourselves?"

David replied: "We're going into Bath for dinner and a film."

"Special treat," Samantha explained. "David came first in an exam at school."

"Did he now?" Mrs. Riley's florid face beamed with as much pride as if David were her own flesh and blood. She opened the clasp of her handbag, fished inside and gave David a tenpenny piece. "Buy yourself some sweets. If that's all right with you, of course, Mrs. Sutcliffe," she added quickly.

"It's perfectly all right with me, Mrs. Riley. And thank you." Obviously the housekeeper had not yet come to grips with inflation. Samantha decided to buy some chocolate for David and make sure there was enough left at evening's end to offer to Mrs. Riley. That was if anyone would be in the mood for accepting chocolates when this particular evening was over.

Samantha drove with David into Bath, a trip of twenty-five minutes. All the time she kept glancing in the mirror. The BMW was there, holding its station patiently. Whoever it is, he's not trying to keep it a secret, she thought. It's as though he's trying to reassure me—or spook me. Whatever the reason, Samantha did not like the BMW's continuing presence.

She parked the Range Rover close to where the movie was playing. In a small Italian restaurant, David went through a bowl of spaghetti large enough for two adults. Samantha could only pick at her food, though. She was worried about the black BMW, and she tried to imagine what was happening back at the farm. Nothing yet, probably. It was not dark enough. The deeds that she envisaged needed darkness. Wasn't that what Tayfield and his associates worked in? Darkness? Once she had thought it ridiculous that an inoffensive-looking man like Tayfield could really be a spy. He was a favorite uncle, kind, gentle, even sometimes given to sentimentality. Now, after the appearance of the black BMW, and the phone call, Samantha could believe anything of him.

When they emerged from the restaurant, Samantha noticed that the BMW was parked a few spaces from her Range Rover. There was no sign of the driver. An idea formed in Samantha's mind and she felt a flush of excitement. "David, stand in line at the cinema, will you? I left something in the car."

She watched her son walk toward the line for the movie, then turned her attention to the BMW. Where the hell was the driver? Where was he watching from? She looked around. All the shops were closed. Two men wandered out of a public house and strolled past her. A young couple perused the window display in a jewelry store. The driver of the BMW was nowhere to be seen.

Her mind made up, Samantha went to the back of the Range Rover and took out two empty milk bottles she had forgotten to return to the store. After insuring that no one could see what she was doing, she wedged a bottle on either side of the BMW's front left wheel, where they were hidden by the high curb. And I hope your spare's flat, she thought vindictively as she stood up and dusted her hands symbolically.

She joined David in the line. Two young men in front of them recognized Samantha and asked for her autograph. Welcoming the momentary distraction, she obliged.

Inside the cinema David sat hunched in his seat with excitement as the film began. Looking at him Samantha wished she were his age again, totally oblivious to everything but what was directly in front of her eyes.

Stop it, she told herself. You knew damned well what you were getting into. You wanted to do it because of Asher. And because of David. It was your duty.

Slowly she forced herself to relax and watch the movie with David.

Mrs. Riley had been prophetic about her luck being good that night. Sitting in the church hall, still wearing the feathered hat but having removed the fur coat, she won the first two games of bingo and the grand sum of four pounds and fifty pence. The first time, she yelled out "Bingo!"

49

and raised her hand triumphantly in the air, the other players applauded her good fortune. The second time, they good-naturedly shouted "Fix!" The next three games went to other players, but by the sixth game, with an outsized pot of eight pounds and change at stake, Mrs. Riley had persuaded Lady Luck to sit beside her again. This time, a groan of painful disbelief soared up to the rafters.

The excitement of winning proved too great for Mrs. Riley. She removed her hat as it began to weigh heavily on her head, and she realized gloomily that she was getting a headache. She searched through her bag for an aspirin, swallowed it with a cup of tea and concentrated on her card again.

The aspirin did not help. The headache steadily worsened until it centered itself painfully over her left eye.

Perhaps being so lucky did not agree with Mrs. Riley after all.

At nine-thirty, as Samantha and David were engrossed in the film and Mrs. Riley accumulated money and a migraine, a late-model Vauxhall Cavalier moved slowly along the dark tree-lined road leading toward the farm. Inside the car were two men, faces illuminated eerily by the dashboard light.

The car doused its headlights a moment before it turned through the opening in the stone wall that fronted the farm, and coasted to a halt by the house. The two men got out, pushed the doors and checked around the house and nearby barn. Satisfied that the premises were deserted, they set about their task with a swift professionalism, fully secure in the blackness of the night as heavy clouds obscured the moon.

One man, tall and angular, with cropped black hair, took an aerosol spray can from the pocket of his sheepskin coat. He sprayed it once in the air to be sure it worked; then he helped his partner—a square, heavy man with a hat pulled low over his forehead and the collar of his dark raincoat turned up around his face—to carry two five-gallon cans of kerosene from the car to the barn.

The main floor of the barn was full of machinery and farming tools. A ladder led up to the half floor above. The tall, angular man in the sheepskin coat climbed the ladder and looked around. The upper floor was full of hay. Grabbing a pitchfork he started to push bales of hay over the edge. His partner maneuvered them around the walls of the barn. Footsteps sounded on the ladder as the man in the sheepskin coat descended.

"Is that enough?" The question was asked in Hebrew.

"Should be." The second man inspected his work, moved a couple of bales closer to the wall. "Let's get the rest set up."

Each man took a can of kerosene and started to soak the bales of hay. Finished, they met in the middle in the barn where the man in the sheepskin produced an incendiary device no bigger than a cigarette pack. "Forty-five minutes?"

"Make it thirty," the other man said.

The man in the sheepskin set the timer and placed the firebomb under a bale of kerosene-soaked hay. While the second man returned the empty cans to the car, he took the aerosol can and stood in front of the house, spraying bright red paint in huge block letters across the stonework, the windows and the door.

"Sorry, dears, but as much as I'd like to have a drink with you all I'm calling it a night," Mrs. Riley said to her friends as the bingo session ended just before ten o'clock and everyone prepared to adjourn to the public house. "My head's just splitting."

"Serves you right for winning all our money," one elderly man joked, and Mrs. Riley shot him a stern, disapproving glance.

She went to her car, climbed in carefully and started to drive home. There was no need to worry about the local constable and his breathalyzer this time—she was not even sure he had been issued with the kit—but her head ached with enough force to make her believe she had consumed three times the legal limit and was paying the penalty.

The Austin's headlights picked out the barrier of trees which lined the road and Mrs. Riley steered the little car toward the center line. She came abreast of the low stone wall, changed down and flicked the indicator in preparation of making the turn. Then, as she rolled slowly through the gateway, she jammed her foot on the brake pedal and brought the Austin sharply to a halt.

An unfamiliar car was parked in front of the farmhouse, and Mrs. Riley's first reaction was that she had interrupted a burglary. But as the heavy clouds parted for a moment and the moon shone through, she saw a man standing in front of the house, moving his arm up and down, back and forth, as if he were spraying something.

"Vandals!" Mrs. Riley muttered ferociously. Incensed, she forgot all about her headache as she forced her way out of the car and started to march toward the house with a determined step that augured ill for the man in the sheepskin coat.

The two men had heard the Austin's whining change-down, had seen the headlights flashing over the low stone wall. While the man in the sheepskin coat continued to spray, his partner melted away into the darkness.

As the Austin came through the gateway, the man with the hat pulled low over his head loped behind. He saw Mrs. Riley climb out, heard her furious roar of: "How dare you? I'll teach you a lesson you won't forget, you bloody hooligan!"

Then he was on her, an arm crooked around her neck, a hand pressed over her mouth to stifle her screams. "Please, no noise and you won't be hurt," he whispered in accented English.

Mrs. Riley struggled to break free from the grip of the man with the hat and dark raincoat. She lashed out with her elbows, her feet. She wriggled. But it was like trying to fight a tank barehanded. Gradually her resistance diminished. The man eased his grip a fraction and guided her toward the garage. His comrade in the sheepskin coat fiddled with the garage lock. When Mrs. Riley saw the door swing open her struggles ceased completely and she became paralyzed with terror.

They were going to rape her! They might even kill her afterwards, but the prospect of a violent death was nowhere near as frightening as the thought of rape. Oh, dear Christ! she cried to herself. These animals were going to—to force themselves on her. And she'd had nothing to do with a man for twenty years, not since her husband had died.

Her fears proved baseless. Inside the blackness of the garage, the tall, angular man in the sheepskin coat flicked a lighter and looked around. He found a piece of rope and bound the housekeeper's hands and feet. He used his own scarf to form a gag. Finally, as Mrs. Riley sat on the stone floor, her back against the wall, he wedged a rolled-up sack behind her head to form a pillow.

"You'll be safe here," he said. "Soon you'll be released. We have no wish to harm you." He closed the garage door and followed his comrade into the car.

The Vauxhall moved away from the farm, turned toward the M4 motorway and from there east toward Heathrow Airport where the car had been rented.

Fifteen minutes later, when the Vauxhall was speeding at seventy miles an hour along the motorway, and Mrs. Riley tried to free herself in the garage, the firebomb left in the barn exploded.

The movie ended at ten-forty. Among the first out was Wadi Hassan, the driver of the black BMW. He had spent the entire time of the movie sitting near the door where he could keep Samantha and David under surveillance. Now he looked for a good vantage point to continue his watch. He hoped they would go home, so that he could return to his hotel and sleep.

How much longer was he supposed to tail this woman? Her life was a series of banal repetitions. In the morning she left the farm to take her son to school. Then she went to the shops, after which she returned home. In the afternoon she drove to the village to collect her son from school. What kind of report was that to send to Salim Maazi in Paris? And why did Maazi want to know anyway? It was typical of Maazi to give orders without explaining their purpose, Wadi Hassan thought bitterly. Was he supposed to protect her? If so, from what?

From a doorway Hassan watched Samantha and David emerge from the cinema. The moment they were inside the Range Rover, Hassan darted to the BMW and started the engine. He put the car in first, let up on the clutch and heard in horror the sound of glass being crushed. Cursing, he changed to reverse. Again the sound of breaking glass. The car's front left corner sagged noticeably.

"Sharmuta!" Wadi Hassan spat out as he leaped from the car and inspected the shredded front tire resting amid the debris of the two broken milk bottles. Frantically he ran to the back, snapped open the trunk and looked inside. The spare was there, fully inflated. But—"May she be fucked by a syphilitic camel herder!" Hassan yelled in impotent fury—there was no lug wrench.

He could only turn and watch helplessly as the Range Rover sped past him. Even in the darkness he could swear he saw a smile on the woman's face.

Samantha was, indeed, smiling. Despite the apprehension she had known on first noticing the BMW tailing her, the sight of the Arab—she assumed he was an Arab—gesturing in frustration at his misfortune made her laugh. And it made her admire her own initiative and nerve. Booby-trapping the BMW like that; perhaps she was not such a novice at this game as she had originally thought.

Beside her, David was fast asleep, head dropping onto his chest as the wide safety belt held him securely in the seat. With only the driving to concentrate on, Samantha thought about what she would find when she reached the farm. Very soon she would be in the public eye again. Not as an actress or a political activist, but as a martyr. She needed time to work herself into the mood of righteous anger that would be so necessary for the ruse to work.

At eleven-ten she passed through the village, eerily quiet as if it, too, were a part of Tayfield's conspiracy. On the sidewalk she spotted an elderly man and she wondered if Mrs. Riley's post–bingo party had broken up yet. She concentrated harder on creating her mood, digging into her experiences to build the necessary emotional stress.

By the time she was clear of the village, covering the last stretch of the journey, she was ready.

Flashing lights winked at her from the darkness of the narrow road as she approached the farm. She slowed down and David started to wake. "Are we home?"

"Almost." The Range Rover's headlights picked out the figure of the local policeman. Samantha stopped. "Is everything all right, officer?"

The constable peered into the Range Rover. "Miss Sutcliffe, I'm sorry but there's been an accident at your place. Fire in the barn, but it's out now."

Samantha steered the Range Rover off to the side of the road. Leaving the still drowsy David in the constable's care she ran into the farmyard. The lights from a fire engine and police car illuminated the smoldering ruin of the barn. A lone fireman played a hose across the area. A man Samantha had never seen before walked around the farmhouse taking pictures. In the glare of the lights Samantha could read the huge words spray-painted across the front of the house: ARAB WHORE BURN IN HELL!

And there—oh, my God! Samantha felt her stomach lurch, her heart begin to pound—was Mrs. Riley's little Austin. In vain, Samantha whirled around to look for the portly figure of the housekeeper, the old-fashioned fur coat, the absurd feather-trimmed hat. She was nowhere to be seen. Samantha started to curse Tayfield and his whole damned organization. They were just as bad, just as vicious as the Arab terrorists who had broken into the Israeli team quarters in Munich. If anything had happened to Mrs. Riley . . . ! Suddenly the outrage and fear Samantha had worked so hard to cultivate were alarmingly real.

"Miss Sutcliffe?"

She spun around, genuine tears of anger and anxiety springing to her eyes. Behind her stood a middle-aged, earnest-looking man holding a notepad and pen. He looked vaguely familiar and she finally placed him as a local newspaper reporter who had visited the farm when she had returned from Paris. "What do you want?"

"The police and firemen think it's arson, Miss Sutcliffe. Who do you think did it?"

Beyond the reporter, Samantha could see David. Standing alongside the local constable the boy was staring avidly as if the entire episode were an exciting extension of his night at the movies. "Why don't you ask the police who they think did it?"

"They say they don't know—yet."

"Oh, yes they do. They know just as well as I do!" Samantha shot back. "The Zionists, the enemies of the Palestinian people. That's who. They think they can shut me up. Well, they're wrong!"

"Have you ever been threatened before?"

"Crank letters, that's all. I never thought they'd go to these lengths. It just shows how scared they are when someone tells the truth." A camera flash exploded in her face and she blinked in surprise, all the while thinking about Mrs. Riley. Where the hell was the damned woman? What had Tayfield's men done to her?

A police sergeant came over. "Would you like us to look inside the house, Miss Sutcliffe?"

"Please." She seemed shaken now. The first moment of outrage had worn off and she was frightened. She handed the police sergeant a key. "My housekeeper—that's her car, the Austin. She was out for the evening but she must have come home early . . . " Her voice trailed off.

"Don't worry yourself, Miss Sutcliffe. We'll find her," the sergeant said soothingly. "Will you be staying here tonight?"

"I don't know. Will it be safe?"

"We'll leave a car."

"Thank you." She looked abstractedly at a police technician who was trying to make casts of tire tracks in front of the farmhouse. She did not think he would get very far. The car would be back at Heathrow by now, and the two men who had visited the farm would be on their way out of the country.

Just then a furious yelling erupted, accompanied by the hammering of a fist on wood. All heads turned toward the garage. Forgetting all about searching the house, the police sergeant raced toward the garage, opened the door and assisted an indignant, but unharmed, Mrs. Riley, who had finally freed herself from her bonds, into the cool night air.

Samantha let out an enormous sigh of relief when she saw that Mrs. Riley was all right. The housekeeper was still wearing that atrocious hat, and never was Samantha so glad to see it. "What happened to you?" she asked as she ran over, embraced and kissed her. "I saw your car. I was having fits."

"I came back early, didn't feel well," Mrs. Riley answered, embarrassed by Samantha's display of relief. She pushed Samantha away and straightened her hat. "Two men were here. Foreigners!" The single word, so full of distrust, bounced from Samantha to the police sergeant, and then to the reporter who had joined the small group. "One of them was spraying something on the house. The other one grabbed me. They tied me up and locked me in the garage. And then . . . " She sniffed the air distastefully and turned toward the burned-out barn, noticing the fire engine for the first time. "Did they do that?" she gasped. "Good God! Whatever next? What's this country coming to, I ask."

"They also did that." Samantha pointed toward the front of the farmhouse. "That's what the man was spraying."

Mrs. Riley strode away to stand in front of the house, hands on her hips as she surveyed the message. "Well, I never," she kept repeating softly. "The nerve of some people. I'll get that off for you, Mrs. Sutcliffe. Good elbow grease, that's all it needs."

"Leave it for now, Mrs. Riley. I'll have it removed tomorrow." Samantha turned back to the police sergeant. "Would you check the house for me now?"

The sergeant touched his hand to his hat and walked toward the front door. Samantha looked back to Mrs. Riley and wondered why on earth the Irishwoman had chosen this particular night to feel unwell. It was just as well that Tayfield had sent two men. One on his own could never have handled an irate Mrs. Riley.

David, who had enjoyed his fill of watching the barn being damped down, joined his mother. "Who's an Arab whore? What does whore mean, mummy?"

Samantha took his small hand and held it tenderly in her own. "I'll explain later," she said, relieved to see the police sergeant emerging from the farmhouse. He returned the key and said the house had not been entered.

"I think for your own safety, Miss Sutcliffe, you might be a lot better off not living in such an out-of-the-way place. They might not be happy with just burning your barn the next time."

Samantha threw back her head and glared at the police officer with an angry pride. Now came the moment for that mood. "No one," she said in a loud, clear voice that attracted the attention of all around her, "is going to victimize me for my beliefs. This is a free country. I can live where I want and I can believe in what I want."

"Miss, with all due respect, we live in an age of—" The police sergeant broke off as a large station wagon pulled into the farmyard. Two men clambered out. One held a television camera. Samantha turned away from the police sergeant to face the camera, the floodlights which suddenly blazed. She was ready to put on as gripping a performance as she had ever done.

By the time the press, the police and the firemen left the farm, it was past two. David was asleep upstairs while Samantha and Mrs. Riley—still wearing her fur coat and feathered hat—sat in the breakfast room, drinking tea. The telephone was off the hook, disconnected after half a dozen calls from London newspapers.

"Mrs. Riley, I'm very sorry about what happened here tonight. I never wanted to involve you in my personal life, but then I never expected this to happen either." Samantha had still not recovered fully from the shock of seeing Mrs. Riley's little car at the farm.

"Are you trying to tell me something, Mrs. Sutcliffe?"

"What I mean is, if you don't want to stay here with David and me, I'll understand perfectly."

"Go on with you!" the housekeeper exclaimed. "Do you think a little shenanigan like tonight would scare me off? I just wish I'd come back earlier. I'd have shown them a thing or two with my rolling pin." She collected the dirty cups and took them through to the kitchen. Her voice trailed back into the breakfast room. "Mrs. Sutcliffe, you almost suffocated me before with all that hugging and kissing when you saw I was all right. Now that means something to me. You and David are the only family I've got. I couldn't leave you even if I wanted to; there's no place else I can go."

The words brought tears to Samantha's eyes. She wiped them quickly and waited for the housekeeper to return from the kitchen. "Mrs. Riley, what's your opinion of my—"

"Your support for the Arabs? It's not my business to have an opinion on what you do." Mrs. Riley closed her mouth in a firm line.

"You just said that David and I were the only family you have. You're entitled to an opinion."

"All right, Mrs. Sutcliffe. I think you should consider your son first and foremost. What if he'd been here tonight? What if some lunatic victimizes him because of your convictions?" The housekeeper regretted her harsh words instantly when she saw the sheen of tears in Samantha's blue eyes. "I'm sorry, Mrs. Sutcliffe." She put her arms around Samantha's shoulders. "But all of your convictions, all of your sincere beliefs, aren't worth a hair on that boy's head. Now you'd better go on up to bed; otherwise neither of us will be awake to look after him in the morning."

While she finished clearing up, Mrs. Riley thought about the two men who had bundled her into the garage. Rape, she had thought at first. Silly old cow. Those men did not have rape on their minds. They were two professionals who had visited the farm to perform one particular job. Anyway, what would any man in his right mind want with an old bag like herself?

Foreigners! What were they? Jews—Israelis—who else would have burned down the barn and painted that disgusting message all over the front of the house?

Still, Mrs. Riley could not get over the way they had acted. Why had they not just bashed her over the head and been done with it? Lord knows, there was enough of that kind of senseless violence going around these days. Why go to all the bother of tying her up, gagging her and locking her in the garage? And sticking that rolled-up sack behind her head to form a pillow?

If was as if—as if they had known the house would be empty for their visit. And then—suddenly—there she was and they had been forced to take care of her. Reluctantly.

It made no sense at all to Mrs. Riley.

CHAPTER
FIVE

As the No Smoking signs flickered off, flight attendants rose from their seats and started to pass out plastic trays with coffee and croissants. Pierre Reynard accepted only the coffee and lit a Gitanes cigarette. Belatedly, he offered the pack to the swarthy man who occupied the adjacent seat on the early-morning Air France flight from Paris to London.

"Would you like to try one of these for a change?"

Salim Maazi shook his head in refusal. Despite having lived in Paris for two years, he had not become accustomed to the strong taste of French cigarettes. Putting aside the newspaper he had been reading, he took a pack of Winstons from his jacket pocket and accepted only the light which Reynard offered.

"You'll die by the time you're fifty if you continue to smoke those coffin nails," Maazi remarked lightly once his own cigarette was alight.

"Are you trying to tell me that your American *merde* is any better?" Reynard responded. "They'll kill you just as quickly."

"If that were the case, my dear friend, the Israelis would send me a carton a day—gratis," Maazi said, and both men laughed.

As Maazi returned to his newspaper, Reynard decided that the Israelis could be forgiven for not believing this particular Palestinian was worth killing.

Salim Maazi was only thirty-five, but his appearance was that of a man ten years older. The once flourishing black hair had thinned to the point where it was parted low on the right side and draped carefully across the scalp. Sagging pouches partially concealed his dark brown, restless eyes. His chin, as he slouched in the seat, spread itself across his shirt collar. Maazi appeared to be exactly what he was—an information officer, a desk jockey. But then, Reynard reminded himself, Arafat had looked much the same way when he had interviewed the Fatah chairman in Beirut. Appearances, as always, could be dangerously deceptive.

The two men had become firm friends a year earlier when Maazi had arranged for Reynard to visit a Palestinian refugee camp in southern Lebanon, which had been blitzed by Israeli jets. Maazi had accompanied Reynard, arranging for him to meet not only civilian leaders but also guerrilla commanders. After that each man had carefully cultivated the other. To Reynard, Maazi was a valuable contact. And to the Palestinian, in his public relations work, Reynard was just as priceless—a respected, widely read writer who could always be trusted to air a sympathetic viewpoint.

Maazi finally lost interest in the newspaper and stuffed it into the seat pocket. "I see the British police still haven't arrested anyone for vandalizing the Sutcliffe farm. Five days and all they can say is that they're following a line of investigation."

"A line that would lead straight to Tel Aviv if they followed it thoroughly," Reynard commented sourly. "The Israelis are far more efficient at discouraging international opposition than the Soviets could ever hope to be."

"What's she like?" Maazi asked.

"Who? Samantha Sutcliffe?" Reynard estimated this was the fifth time Maazi had asked the question. He understood exactly what was passing through the Palestinian's mind. Despite wanting to enlist Samantha as a propaganda weapon, Maazi would never be able to view her as a true supporter of the Palestinian struggle. He would see her only as a possible conquest. Perhaps that was what made him seem so dissipated, Reynard thought—the constant screwing as if he were trying to establish some kind of a record.

Reynard questioned how much success Maazi would have with women if it were not for the money he so liberally threw around. But, in truth, notwithstanding the flabbiness, the Palestinian did possess a certain style. He moved with a degree of grace, almost like an out-of-shape boxer who still remembered all the moves. There was something of the swashbuckler about him as well. The large hooked nose above the thick black moustache gave animation and character to his face. Even if it did—to Maazi's everlasting chagrin—give him the profile of a Julius Streicher stereotypical Jew.

"Did you get anywhere with her that night at the Plaza Athénée?" Maazi pressed. "Did you even try?"

"How could I?" The deep chuckle that accompanied Reynard's response served to disguise his true feelings. He felt uncomfortable talking about women in this manner, as if they were merchandise at a market. "I'd arranged to meet you immediately afterward, remember?"

Maazi smiled lewdly. He would have broken an appointment with Reynard for a chance with the English actress. She had spirit, that one —milk bottles all around the wheel of Wadi Hassan's car. There was no need to punish Hassan for his incompetence; being fooled by a woman was humiliation enough.

Maazi closed his eyes for an instant and brought to mind the movie he had seen in Paris. *La Maquisarde*—a stupid story. Who cared about the Jews and the Nazis? But he had enjoyed the film because it had whetted his appetite.

Salim Maazi had never made love to an English actress before.

Like most mothers, Samantha viewed school vacations with mixed emotions. She loved having David around but when he tracked in mud from the farm, she wished he were back at school.

To her credit, Mrs. Riley never uttered a word of complaint as she mopped the dirty floor after David had gone back outside. Samantha would not have blamed the housekeeper if she had moaned. Mrs. Riley was the epitome of patience, a veritable saint. Even the incident the previous week had failed to ruffle her composure once she had recovered from the initial shock and indignation. The next day she had supervised while the handyman from the village removed the offensive words from the front of the house, and after that she had never mentioned the incident at all. God bless her, Samantha thought warmly.

"Better answer the phone, Mrs. Sutcliffe," the housekeeper said as she caught Samantha watching her.

Samantha snapped awake, "Hello?"

"Vera, is that you?" a man's voice asked.

"Sorry, you must have the wrong number," Samantha said and hung up. She returned to the housekeeper and said she had to go into the

61

village. Making sure she had an adequate supply of tenpenny pieces to call Alan Tayfield from the pay phone, she put on a raincoat and left the farm in Mrs. Riley's little Austin.

The wrong-number-call-back system had between initiated by Tayfield after he had learned of the black BMW. If the Palestinians had already gone to the trouble of watching Samantha, they might even be listening in on her phone conversations. He did not want to take the chance.

There was no sign of the BMW, or any other car that might be following her, as Samantha stepped into the pay phone in the village. The man with the moustache must be watching out for the Range Rover, she reasoned, but not the Austin. She dialed Tayfield's number in London and pressed in the coins. "Alan, it's Samantha."

"Listen carefully. Pierre Reynard and the Palestinian Salim Maazi arrived at Heathrow Airport a short time ago. They hired a car and headed west toward you."

"Reynard?" Samantha's heartbeat quickened. Often she had thought about the French journalist, whether she would ever see him again. Reynard was charming, attractive in his intense manner. Nonetheless, he championed the cause of Asher Davidson's murderers. Reynard did for real what Samantha did only as a cover. She felt pangs of guilt because she knew she wanted to see him again despite his political beliefs. "How do you know?"

Tayfield ignored her question. "I'll take the train from Paddington. I should be at your place around midday. You can tell Reynard and Maazi that you're expecting me on business."

Upon her return to the farm, Samantha mentioned to Mrs. Riley—in a tone that suggested she had forgotten all about it until that very moment —that Tayfield would be coming for lunch. Then she almost blundered by telling the housekeeper to prepare food for Maazi and Reynard whom she could not know were coming. Damn . . . she had to stay alert.

Ninety minutes later the car bringing Reynard and Maazi from the airport turned into the farm. Samantha was outside, jeans tucked into gum boots, raincoat fully buttoned and belted, a silk scarf tied around her head to protect her hair from the drizzle. At first she stared curiously at the car. When she saw Reynard get out, her face reflected surprise before breaking into a warm, genuine smile of welcome.

The Frenchman shook her hand formally before introducing Salim Maazi and explaining his position with the Paris office of the PLO. Then Reynard led the way across the yard to the ruined barn. The smell of damp burned wood and hay was still unpleasantly strong. Reynard sniffed distastefully while he poked around with his foot, not seeming to care that he was ruining an expensive handmade shoe.

"You made some rather vindictive enemies," he finally commented.

"I'm just glad neither my son nor I was here when it happened."

"Where is your son?" Reynard asked.

"David? In the cowshed." One of the cows was giving birth and David was an excited firsthand witness.

"Where were you when this happened?" The question came from Maazi who was more intent on looking at Samantha than he was at inspecting the damage. The scarf around her head and the muddy gum boots suited her. She had the healthy, vibrant appearance of a country girl, tempered by a degree of city sophistication. Maazi found the combination sexually arousing.

"At a film," Samantha replied.

"One of your own?"

"No. Not one of my own."

"How's your manager these days, Tayfield?" Reynard asked. "Is he still upset with you over Paris?"

"Why don't you ask him yourself? He's supposed to be here around midday."

From the ruined barn Reynard walked alone to the farmhouse where he studied the front. The drizzle fell onto his sandy hair, flattening it against his scalp, smearing his glasses. He appeared not to notice as he continued his tour of inspection, his entire manner more formal and aloof than at their last meeting.

"Would you like to come inside where it's dry?" Samantha asked Maazi as they stood watching Reynard. "I can make you some coffee or something to eat."

"That would be very nice, thank you." Maazi elected to capitalize on Reynard's preoccupation with the farmhouse. "There was no time for breakfast on the plane, the flight was so short."

"You've just come from Paris?" Samantha feigned surprise. "Right this instant?"

"We live in an age of immediacy. We needed to see you, so we came." Maazi accompanied the words with a brief smile that reached no further than his partly hidden eyes.

Samantha stared into those eyes, recognized the seductive expression that lurked there. She could feel him undressing her and she found the

63

sensation unpleasant. "What was your urgency that you couldn't even let me know you were coming?"

"We'll explain inside." Maazi took Samantha by the arm and guided her toward the farmhouse. He held her a fraction more tightly than was necessary and felt the muscles of her arm tense.

When Samantha brought her two guests into the breakfast room, Mrs. Riley was cleaning the kitchen. The housekeeper's immediate feeling was one of distrust, especially for the dark-skinned Maazi, and when Samantha introduced both men, Mrs. Riley's deep-seated dislike of foreigners stretched itself to Reynard as well. A wog *and* a frog, she thought darkly. Nonetheless, they were Mrs. Sutcliffe's friends; therefore, it was her duty to treat them with respect and courtesy.

Samantha made omelets, toast and coffee for the two men. When she carried a tray into the breakfast room, she was acutely aware that they were watching her closely. She welcomed Reynard's attention. Maazi's stare, though, was repugnant to her.

"Why are you here?" she asked when all three sat around the oak table in the breakfast room.

Maazi answered. "We Palestinians are very rich in many areas." Again that brief, flirtatious smile as if he wanted to put Samantha totally at ease, win her over before he had even presented his case. "We are rich in culture, in our feeling of national identity, our history, our courage. But in one area we are extremely poor."

"Go on," Samantha said encouragingly. She glanced at Reynard who sat back in the chair, apparently content to let Maazi speak.

"Everyone makes propaganda films about the Israelis, about the Jews," Maazi continued. "You said so yourself in Paris. But no one makes them for the Palestinians. Therefore, much of the world sees us only as the Israelis and their allies want us to be seen. As butchers, as conscienceless murderers of old women and small children."

Samantha could feel her eyes begin to burn at Maazi's hypocrisy. But she remained outwardly calm, and in that moment she realized what a convincing actress she truly was. "What are you proposing?" she asked in a quiet, level voice.

"We are asking—no, we are begging you to support your sentiments with firm action. Believe me, your courageous stance on our behalf—particularly what you said in Paris—is welcome. It gives us the strength for our battle. Now we are asking you to enlarge that help. We want you to make a documentary film for us."

"What kind of a documentary?"

"On the camps. On the interminable suffering of my people."

Samantha raised an eyebrow at the statement. "You don't look to me like you're exactly suffering."

Maazi ran a hand over the custom-made Harris Tweed sport coat he wore, the fine cashmere sweater. "I am fortunate that my own family had money." For once he was embarrassed by his wealth.

At last Reynard spoke. "Samantha, much of Salim's wealth has been used to alleviate the misfortune of his people. You do him an injustice by mocking. Such behavior does not become you."

Samantha found herself blushing under the softly spoken reprimand. "I'm sorry. Please continue."

Maazi accepted the apology with a wave of his hand. "Whatever attempts we make to demonstrate the truth to the world are sneered at by those who befriend Israel. But if you—an accomplished actress, a humanitarian—would join with us, we would achieve a major victory."

Samantha stared down at the cup of coffee in front of her. "I'm afraid that's not something I can give you an immediate answer on."

"Why not?" Reynard wanted to know. "Are you still more concerned about harming your career than pursuing your beliefs?"

"My career will stand or fall on my own ability as an actress," Samantha replied stiffly. "I told you that once before."

"Then what is the problem? Is it Tayfield? Do you have to ask him for his blessing?"

"Yes, I do. He's entitled to be consulted."

Reynard fell silent as he remembered Tayfield's anger after Samantha had spoken out at La Tour d'Argent. He looked at Maazi and an understanding glance passed between the two men. If it all depended on Samantha's manager, they might as well go home now. Tayfield would be firmly against any involvement by his star in a Palestinian documentary.

"What could be your manager's objection?" Maazi asked. "If it's money he's worried about, we're willing to pay well for your professional services. Extremely well." He questioned briefly whether Samantha could be having an affair with Tayfield. Was it more than just business between them? Was that why she was so dependent on him?

"I don't support your struggle because I want your money," Samantha fired back. "I also give—remember?"

"All right, you also give. Then *you* talk to Tayfield. If you are really sincere in your support—and by that I mean you're not just using the

65

suffering of my people as a convenient publicity gimmick for yourself—you can persuade your manager that making this documentary is right."

Samantha decided that she had delayed long enough. Her two visitors were already pessimistic. Any further and they would be totally deterred. "I'll talk to him, Mr. Maazi—"

"Salim," the Palestinian cut in swiftly. "Please call me Salim."

"Salim." She experimented with the name. It felt strange to her tongue, uncomfortable. It was a name popular among the people who had murdered her love. "All right, Salim. We'll wait for Alan. We can talk over lunch."

"Good. I look forward to meeting Mr. Tayfield," Maazi said, pleased with what he considered his opening success with Samantha.

The Palestinian's feeling of triumph did not last long. The door burst open and, with a loud, excited yell, David burst in. "The cow's had a baby! The cow's had a baby!"

"David!" Samantha forgot all about her visitors and yelled angrily at her son as he tracked mud and dung across the flagged floor. "How many times have I told you to take your boots off before you come into the house?"

Reynard looked at Samantha, unable to stop himself from grinning at her sudden outburst of temper. Then he swung around to face the boy. "Cows have calves," he said gently. "They don't have babies."

David glared at the stranger defiantly, daring the Frenchman to intrude adult fact upon his childish excitement. Reynard recognized the expression—the thrust-out chin, the gritted teeth—and made himself look suitably apologetic. "All right, your particular cow had a baby. What was it, a boy or a girl?"

David just shrugged, still uncertain about the unfamiliar face. "I don't know."

"David, these are two friends of mine from Paris," Samantha explained. "Mr. Reynard and Mr. Maazi."

"Paris? France?" Immediately the boy forgot all about the calf. "Have you got any French stamps on you?"

Maazi regarded the boy awkwardly, unaccustomed to dealing with children. Reynard seemed more at ease. From his wallet he produced six uncanceled stamps. "Will these do?"

David's deep brown eyes opened wide as he studied the stamps. "Can I have them? To keep?"

"Of course you can. I don't think I'll be needing them to mail any letters from here."

Witnessing the interplay between her son and Reynard, Samantha experienced an uneasy twinge. Despite her own ambivalent feelings toward Reynard, she had no business letting him befriend David. "Come on, David," she said more brusquely than she intended. "Show me the cow's baby."

"Well, what do you think?" Maazi asked Reynard when Samantha and the boy had left. He spoke in French so that Mrs. Riley, if she could overhear, would not understand. The use of a foreign language in her home made Mrs. Riley resent the two men even more.

"Think about what?" Reynard replied. "About Samantha Sutcliffe working for us? Or about your overtures to seduction?"

"Do I detect a little animosity, *mon cher ami?*" Maazi asked, unable to stop the grin which spread across his face.

"I'm only concerned that you might let your *couilles* influence your brain," Reynard replied before turning away. At first he had been amused by the way Maazi had acted up to Samantha. Then, very quickly, he had become irritated by it. Even, he had to admit, somewhat jealous. She might be able to see and appreciate, as Reynard could, the raw, active power that simmered below the Palestinian's surface, like a volcano ready to erupt.

Alan Tayfield arrived shortly after midday. The moment he entered the farmhouse and spotted Samantha with Reynard, Maazi and David, who had returned from the cowshed, he became antagonistic. "What the hell do you think you're doing here?" he demanded of the Frenchman.

"Visiting Samantha. With a proposition."

"What kind of proposition?" Tayfield muttered suspiciously. "And who are you?" he asked of Maazi.

Samantha introduced the Palestinian and Tayfield literally bristled. "Alan, they want to know if I'll make a documentary on the refugee camps in Lebanon. And do you think," she added, looking at David for a moment, "we could continue this discussion somewhere else?" She led the three men from the breakfast room into the living room and closed the door.

Tayfield stood on the heavy rug in front of the fireplace and glared angrily at the two men. "I can tell you both right now that you've wasted your time coming here. Samantha will not make such a film."

"No?" Maazi took close stock of the middle-aged, balding man. There could not possibly be anything between him and Samantha. The idea was ludicrous. Maazi recognized the kind of man Tayfield was; he had encountered many of the same type. An opportunist. A leech. "What makes you so certain, Mr. Tayfield?"

"Yes, Alan. What does make you so certain?"

Tayfield spun around to face Samantha. "Is this what we've labored for? So that you can waste your talent, throw away your career for a cause that has no sympathy."

"There is plenty of sympathy for the Palestinian cause," Reynard was quick to point out.

"Not where it bloody well counts there isn't!"

"Where? In the United States? Where you and your glittering product hope to find the most lucrative market?" Reynard managed to impart so much derision onto the comment that Samantha winced; and for that instant she hated him.

"Mr. Tayfield, please listen to me." Maazi's was the voice of conciliation. "I would be more than glad to compensate you financially from my own pocket if that is what's troubling you."

"Money doesn't enter into it. I only care about protecting Samantha's interests. Her career is—"

When Samantha saw Tayfield about to explode again, she cut in swiftly. "Alan, will you please let Salim and Pierre explain what they have in mind?"

Tayfield sighed as he recognized defeat in the way Samantha referred to the two men by their first names. It was obvious to him—and he knew it was just as clear to Reynard and Maazi, which was far more important —that Samantha had already made up her mind. It was pointless to continue the argument.

"All we want is for Samantha to be the narrator for a documentary concerning the plight of the Palestinian refugees who have been robbed of their country," Reynard explained.

"Where will this documentary be aired?"

"We will try everywhere," replied Maazi. "Obviously, those countries which are friendly to us, sympathetic to our struggle, will carry it."

"Wouldn't that be a bit like taking coals to Newcastle?" Tayfield asked.

Maazi inclined his head in acknowledgment. "We will also offer it to British and American networks. Samantha will have the opportunity for great exposure in all the right places."

"And where do you come into this?" Tayfield demanded of Reynard.

"Mine is an auxiliary function. Following Samantha in Lebanon will provide fascinating copy. I'm sure that my readers will be interested in how one woman with a social conscience is doing her best to redress wrongs that others choose to ignore."

"Bullshit!" Tayfield dug into his repertoire of American slang as he made no attempt to hide his dislike of both the idea and of Reynard. He turned to look at Samantha. "Well?"

"Alan, I want to do it. I feel it's right, it's just. But first I want to hear your approval."

Tayfield looked away from her to catch both Reynard and Maazi in a tight, cold stare. The two men watched him expectantly. "I can't stop you," he said at last to Samantha. "You know that. I wouldn't want to stop you from doing anything you felt in your heart was right."

"Thank you, Alan." She threw her arms around his neck and kissed him. Then she turned to the other men. "I'll be waiting to hear from you."

"When I return to Paris I'll begin making the arrangements," Maazi promised.

Tayfield walked away and stared out of the window. He could hear the staccato drumming of his heart, feel his face burning. The sensations had nothing to do with the heated argument, nothing to do with Samantha's enthusiastic kiss.

Tayfield was frightened. The trap had finally been sprung. He had placed a woman he had grown to love into more danger than he would willingly face himself.

CHAPTER
SIX

T wo weeks after Maazi and Reynard visited Samantha with their proposition, Joel Rosen heard again from Hunovi. The deep-cover agent called in early one morning to demand an immediate meeting with the Mossad director of special operations.

Shortly after midday Rosen was passing through immigration at Rome's Leonardo da Vinci Airport with a South African passport made out in the name of Roy Chappell. The passport was genuine, one of a dozen the Mossad owned as payment for information shared with South African intelligence. From the airport Rosen took the forty-five-minute bus ride to the Via Giolitti terminal in the city, then caught a taxi to the Casina Valadier restaurant in the Villa Borghese where Hunovi had made reservations for lunch.

As he sat back in the taxi, Rosen wondered why Hunovi had picked Rome for this urgent meeting, dragging him halfway across the world at such short notice. But then again, Hunovi could not come to Israel; his cover was too complex to allow him that particular journey. At least, Rosen knew he would get a good meal out of it. He was glad that Hunovi would be paying for lunch. The head of the Mossad finance department would not quibble about the cost of the flight to Rome—that was legitimate business—but he might raise a querying eyebrow if Rosen, yes, even Rosen, presented him with a bill for a meal fit for royalty.

The taxi let Rosen off. He found Hunovi seated on the restaurant terrace, comfortable in the warm, clear air. Before sitting, Rosen gazed past Hunovi, down the Pincio to the magnificent view of the city.

"Do you know something, Joel?" Hunovi remarked as he watched Rosen admire the view. "Each time I am fortunate enough to be in this city, I think of the words of Henry James: 'At last, for the first time I live.'"

Rosen smiled at the sentiment. Rome had the same effect on him, not that he could have ever hoped to express it in Hunovi's literary style. Nor could he afford to spend as much time in the Eternal City as Hunovi managed to; he did not have that kind of money.

"You look well, Joel. Have you lost some weight?"

"Maybe a kilo, that's all." Rosen knew better than that. As of that morning he had dropped precisely four and a half kilos, the result of an intensive fitness program in case he needed to return to field work. He felt better for it, tighter, even though this lunch with Hunovi would probably set him back a few days. "What do you want to see me about?"

"Afterward we can talk. First we'll eat. You must be starving after your journey."

The answer went against Rosen's grain of business first and foremost. For Hunovi, though, he was prepared to make an exception. He did not see his old friend and partner often enough.

Over *filetto di tacchino*—sliced turkey breast sautéed in butter and served with truffles—they discussed general topics. Hunovi asked about events in Israel; he had not been home in five years. Rosen told him what the Americans were trying to do, and how the prime minister was prepared to risk his career on the gamble that the Jordanians and Saudi Arabians were dealing from the top of the deck. Then the conversation shifted to Shlomo Berger. A short, awkward silence developed as both men remembered their friend.

They finished the meal without a word of business being spoken. As they stood up, Hunovi glanced at the city spread out below them. "Can't you just see it burning merrily while mad Nero plucked at the strings of his fiddle?"

"I think we're also fiddling," Rosen said. "What's happening on Operation Asher?"

"In a minute." Hunovi led the way out of the restaurant. As Rosen followed the younger man he felt a momentary pang of jealousy for Hunovi's grace, the languid elegance. The man was a tailor's model. Even the cheapest mass-produced suit would look marvelous on him. The stylish, custom-made clothes he chose to wear made him look like a millionaire or a film star.

71

They took a horse-drawn carriage, riding leisurely like two tourists through the maddening bustle of Rome's traffic. Vespas and Harley-Davidsons, Fiats and Alfas roared past as Rome returned to work from its midday siesta period. Rosen swiveled in the seat to look closely at a traffic policeman whose white-gloved hands flashed this way and that as he kept the wild mass of traffic moving and—by some miracle—apart.

"Wonderful, isn't it?" Hunovi remarked. "If one solitary man can organize some semblance of order out of this chaos, why cannot all other men learn to live in peace with their neighbors?"

"You didn't *schlepp* me all the way from Tel Aviv to give me a lecture on how the world's nations could learn from watching Roman traffic. What's on your mind?"

"Maazi and Reynard have made arrangements for Samantha to visit Lebanon."

"With Tayfield?"

"Of course. Samantha will be going there in a month's time. Here"—Hunovi produced a sheet of newspaper from his jacket—"there's even a short piece about it in the American publication *Variety.*"

Rosen took the page. Under the headline "English Actress to Tour Lebanon" was a four-paragraph story about Samantha visiting Lebanon for the first two weeks in May to make a documentary on the refugee camps. Salim Maazi was quoted as saying the documentary would be the first of a series. Rosen fought down his annoyance at learning that *Variety* knew of it before he did. It was not that important; there was a month to go.

"A series?" he asked. "That should raise the hackles of a few American producers."

"A film producer's hackles rise and fall in tune with his bank balance," Hunovi observed dryly.

"Philosopher," Rosen muttered sarcastically. "You'll be in touch with them, of course."

"Naturally. Hunovi knows what he must do."

Rosen could not resist a smile. It intrigued him the way Hunovi occasionally referred to himself in the third person as though he found certain aspects of his own life too unpleasant to become personally involved.

Hunovi reached up and tapped the carriage driver on the back. "Please take us to the terminal on the Via Giolitti." Turning again to Rosen he finally came to the real reason for the meeting. "Joel, I want you to bring Tayfield home for a while. Let him rest, let him see his family before

72

Operation Asher really starts. Who knows when he might see them again. Or if . . . "

"Home? Family? What the hell are you talking about?"

"Tayfield isn't like us, Joel. We have no children, no grandchildren. We have no one but ourselves because we chose it to be that way. Think about it and you will see I am right."

Rosen could not believe what he was hearing. This was a side of Hunovi he had never seen before. Was Hunovi going soft on him? "Are you sure that's all?" he asked softly, fearing what the answer might be.

"No, Joel, it's not. When was the last time Tayfield had a medical examination?"

The question so amazed Rosen that he sat with his mouth hanging open. "What do you mean?"

"I'm very worried about him. I think he's a sick man."

"But—Jesus Christ! We can't pull him now. We've put too much into this thing!"

"I know, I know. But at least let us understand what we are dealing with."

Rosen lapsed into a period of silence, his mind working frantically. There was no time to replace Tayfield, no time to set up an alternative plan. And they could not let Samantha go in on her own; she would not know what to do, what to look for, how to deal with it. She was only the key.

"Well?" Hunovi pressed.

"I'll tell him. I'll tell him to come home immediately."

"Good, Joel. It's the right thing to do."

The carriage stopped at the terminal. Hunovi remained seated while Rosen prepared to get out. At the last moment Rosen turned around, grasped his friend around the shoulders and kissed him fondly on the cheek. "Look after yourself," he said in a choking voice. "I want to see you again."

Samantha saw Tayfield off from Heathrow Airport. The baggage tag on his single case proclaimed that he was traveling to New York on the 5:00 P.M. Trans World Airlines flight. He was ostensibly to meet with an American producer. In reality he would be in New York only long enough to catch the evening El Al flight to Israel under his real name of Gershon Shual. Ironically the flight would stop over in London.

Tayfield had received word only the previous day that Rosen wanted

73

him in for a briefing before he went with Samantha to Lebanon. Tayfield was not in the mood to question the summons; he was just grateful for the opportunity to see his family. He knew there would be a second case waiting for him at the El Al desk in New York. It would contain gifts for his daughter and son-in-law, his two young grandchildren, souvenirs from the United States, Canada, Mexico and South America where he had allegedly been working in his capacity as sales manager for the electronics firm in Tel Aviv.

"How long will you be gone?" Samantha asked. She knew Tayfield's true destination and felt happy for him; she understood how much he missed his family.

"A week. No more."

"What if something happens here while you're away?"

Tayfield had thought about that. Rosen's summons to Tel Aviv could not have come at a more awkward time. Would Samantha be all right if he were not there? Would she know how to act, how to continue playing her role without his direction? Of course she would, he assured himself. She had played the role perfectly so far; why should she go astray now? "Nothing should happen," he told her. "There will be people keeping an eye on you anyway. We're very thorough."

"You and the man in the black BMW."

"They'll be keeping an eye on him as well. Don't worry about a thing," he said, kissing her on the cheek in farewell. "Just think of Asher and you'll know what to do."

A Mossad agent met Tayfield the moment he stepped off the El Al flight at Ben-Gurion Airport, bypassed customs and immigration and took him straight to a safe house on the outskirts of Tel Aviv where Rosen was waiting. On the following day Tayfield would be returned to the airport to coincide with the arrival of the flight his family believed him to be on. But his first day back in Israel, as always, belonged to the institute.

Rosen congratulated Tayfield on his progress so far. Over tea and sandwiches prepared by the agent who had been waiting at the airport, the two men discussed the impending trip to Lebanon. Rosen stressed that no matter what Tayfield saw while with Samantha in Lebanon, he had to remember that his priority was Operation Asher.

"You're going there for two weeks, and in that time you have to learn the score regarding Berger's last message. I don't give a damn what else you see, we've got other people to take care of that. Your sole mission is to collect information on the revival of Black September. I don't want to hear from you until you've got that information." He paused long enough to sip his tea. "And another thing: I don't want you exposing Samantha to any more danger than is absolutely necessary. Once you've found out what there is to know, get the hell out. Don't take a chance on sacrificing her for one more piece of news."

"You know damned well I wouldn't place her in any danger!" Tayfield replied hotly. "I value her welfare more than my own!"

"Good. I don't want any mistakes," Rosen said, taking careful note of the flush that bloomed across Tayfield's face. What was it, high blood pressure? Tayfield looked overweight, but then he had always been pudgy. He was a nonsmoker. He did not drink, either, and that was a trait Rosen had frequently thought to be totally uncharacteristic in an agent with a British cover.

"What about the tag Samantha spotted?" Tayfield asked as he touched his flaming cheeks with his hand. "You know, the man in the black BMW."

"That's all taken care of. He's a Palestinian named Wadi Hassan, staying at the Mendip Hotel in Bath where he's registered under his own name. The BMW was purchased from Goldhawk Motors, a used-car lot in West London, for three thousand five hundred pounds. Hassan paid cash. Now are you happy that we've got the situation well in hand?"

"I told Samantha we had," Tayfield said and relaxed.

"By the way, while you're here I want you to have your physical. They're expecting you this evening."

"Physical?" Tayfield did not understand. "Why?"

Rosen smiled, eager to placate his agent's concern. "This is your first trip home in almost a year. You're due for a physical just like everyone else. That's one of the benefits of working for the government—good medical care."

Tayfield did not appear happy at the prospect. The Mossad, like every other government agency in every other country, functioned on bureaucracy. If there was a regulation that stated every field agent had to undergo a physical examination once a year then—by damn!—he had better comply. "I feel fine," he protested. "Why should I waste time having doctors stick things in me when I could be with my family?" The flush started again and he could feel his heartbeat increase.

"You know the rules and regulations as well as I do."

"But I'm telling you I'm all right." The objection was half-hearted.

75

Tayfield did not feel at all well. He had never been a man who possessed tremendous energy; taking life easy was his style. But lately everything had seemed to be such an effort. When he did start to rush, when he felt the tension start, that was when his heart sounded like a cavalry charge, his face burned and his arms sometimes went numb.

His own optimistic diagnosis had been anemia. That would account for the sluggishness. He had gone on a vitamin splurge—A, C, even iron supplement, everything he could think of until he was certain he rattled when he walked. He had kept it from Samantha, of course, like the time he had turned away from her and looked out of the farmhouse window. She did not have to know.

"When did *you* last have a physical?" he challenged Rosen in a final attempt to delay the inevitable.

"You don't have to worry about me. I'm not in the field." Rosen stood up to signify that the meeting was over and he expected no more arguments from Tayfield. "I'll be in touch before you go back."

That evening, like a man walking the last mile, Tayfield entered the room where the medical staff waited. He took off his clothes and donned a white gown. There was nothing he could do except surrender with a degree of grace. The sooner he got this over with, the sooner he would be reunited with his family.

Tayfield slept that night in the Mossad safe house. The following afternoon he was driven to Ben-Gurion Airport with his two suitcases and taken through to the arrivals area to mix with the passengers disembarking from the New York El Al flight.

Suppressing his impatience, he waited to pass through the checkpoints. He did not even feel indignant when the attractive woman customs officer demanded payment on the gifts he had brought from America. Around him other passengers argued about the duty. Not Tayfield. He had neither the time nor the inclination. He handed over the money and took the receipt.

As he cleared customs, an excited shout assaulted his ears. His daughter, Ilana, came rushing forward from the waiting crowd to throw her arms around his neck and hug him. He dropped the two cases and held onto her tightly, unable to believe that almost a year had passed since he had last seen her. Finally he let go and stepped back, marveling at the resemblance to his late wife, the same chestnut hair and hazel eyes which had bewitched him a lifetime earlier.

Beyond Ilana he could see Avi Spiegler, his son-in-law. Avi was holding the hands of his young son and daughter, Yosef and Danielle—Tayfield's grandchildren. To Tayfield's biting disappointment the children regarded him uncertainly, not recognizing the man who paid them such infrequent visits.

Never mind, Tayfield thought. In one short week he would change all that. He stepped forward to kiss his son-in-law, and then lifted both children into his arms. "Do you know who I am?"

"Grandpa Gershon?" the little girl whispered uncertainly.

"That's right—Grandpa Gershon." Tayfield felt tears beginning to burn in his eyes.

It was good, so good, to be home again.

At the exact moment that Alan Tayfield was rushing into the welcoming arms of his family at Ben-Gurion Airport, Salim Maazi was only a short distance to the north: in Southern Lebanon, sitting in a hut in the Rashidieh refugee camp, south of Tyre and close to the Lebanese village of Azziye. Gone were the expensive Harris Tweed sport coat and fine cashmere sweater he had worn to visit Samantha's farm in Somerset. Like the two men sitting with him at the table, Maazi wore a brown-and-green camouflage uniform and heavy brown boots. Gone also was the soft exterior; the raw, simmering power that Reynard had seen had bubbled to the surface.

"You are certain that the spy George Tokvarian transmitted no message before you captured him?" Maazi demanded of the two men.

Ahmed el-Shafri, the older of the two men, shook his head. "He didn't have the time, Salim, be assured of that. Yussuf and I broke into his apartment while he was assembling the transmitter." El-Shafri did not dare tell Maazi that the transmitter had been assembled, that a message might have gone out; he just prayed that it had not. "Tokvarian was wounded when we entered the apartment. We had fired first through the locked door."

"Is that so?" Maazi looked carefully at Yussuf Torbuk.

"It is as Ahmed says. We were right on his heels."

"I hope you were," Maazi said with a dangerous softness. Then he slammed the table with his open hand and yelled: "Two years! Why did it take you two years to find him out? Just because I am working in Europe, does that mean you can relax? How much information did he send out in those two years? How many lives did he cost?"

"But—" el-Shafri started to interject.

"Shut up!" Maazi roared and hammered the table with his hand again. "I expect excuses only from women. From my men I want swift action, not stupidity." Two years! he cursed silently. No wonder the Israelis knew where every rifle, every damned rocket and round of ammunition was located. The Palestinians had more Israelis on their payroll than the entire Tel Aviv Water Board! Jordan's King Hussein had certainly got his facts right when he made that sneering comment.

Yussuf Torbuk watched Maazi carefully, judging when the moment of temper was safely past. "Just be grateful that we caught him when we did, before he could pass anything of real value on to the *Yehudis.*"

"But you failed to find out what he had already learned about us, eh?" Maazi asked Torbuk.

Torbuk's smooth, unlined face, that would have seemed more natural on a boy of sixteen than on a man of thirty-four, turned sad as he recalled the two fruitless hours he had spent with the spy. He had been a hard case, that one. Even when they had attached the electrodes to him, the black-haired Israeli agent had spit in their faces and cursed them. "If he knew anything at all, he would have begged us to listen, Salim," Torbuk answered. "My powers of persuasion are too skillful to be ignored."

"Pray that you're right," Maazi said in an ominously quiet tone. "Because if the Israelis know of the rebirth of Black September—and the purpose for which it is being reactivated—you will be the first casualty." For a few seconds an atmosphere of tension linked the two men as Maazi allowed Torbuk to reflect on the threat; then Maazi said, "So when you couldn't use him anymore, you chopped him up and sent him to the Israeli embassy in Rome. That was not clever, Yussuf."

"Why not?" Torbuk asked, dispelling the momentary dread aroused by Maazi's warning. "Is it wrong to let them know that we have caught one of their spies?"

"It is sometimes better to let them worry about what has happened to their people. No news at all can be far more psychologically devastating than even the worst possible news." But Maazi did not really expect Torbuk and el-Shafri to appreciate that view. Both men were reliable lieutenants. Give them orders and they would carry them out faithfully. They had little imagination, though; no initiative of their own. Perhaps it was better that way. In every unit there was room for only one strategist. That one man was Maazi. He had been chosen to lead Black September once more into battle because he possessed vision as well as daring. And what a battle—the opportunity to write history, and to use for ink the blood of the Israelis, the blood of all those who would betray Palestine.

The two men tried to hold Maazi's gaze as he stared at them. El-Shafri, his graying hair cut so short that the scalp gleamed sweatily through, the watery, pale brown eyes, the patchy week-old beard. And Torbuk with his child's face, the innocent brown eyes that reflected none of the passion that flowed within him. He was like Dorian Gray, Maazi thought. Did Torbuk keep a portrait hidden somewhere, an image that was as ravaged and bitter as his own face was clean and wholesome? Torbuk must have enjoyed questioning the Israeli spy. There was a wide streak of sadism in the baby-faced man. Too much, maybe. He became carried away with his job when often a gentler touch would work. Or he killed a man before he could break, just for the sheer pleasure of killing him.

"What news is there of the English actress?" el-Shafri asked.

"Everything is well in hand." Maazi produced a clipping from *Variety*. "She will be arriving in approximately four weeks. I am working on the script she will use."

"At which camp will you film her?"

Maazi tapped the floor with his foot. "We will begin here, at Rashidieh."

"Rashidieh?" El-Shafri was shocked by the answer. "But—"

"Again with a but!" Maazi glared angrily at el-Shafri. "She will see a windswept refugee camp populated by thousands of suffering Palestinians. A camp that is under the constant threat of Israeli guns—a camp that is pounded mercilessly by Israeli aircraft."

"They only attack Rashidieh because they know the *fedayeen* use it as a base," el-Shafri protested.

"So what? This woman believes in us. She accepts that we are soldiers fighting for our liberty. She supports our struggle." A cynical smile slipped across Maazi's dark face as an idea occurred to him. "Perhaps we might even arrange something special for her visit. A strike across the border so that the Israelis will hit back. Think what propaganda we could make from that. Samantha Sutcliffe, the English rose, diving for cover in a stinking refugee camp that is being bombed. Imagine the expression of horror on that beautiful, delicate face when she sees the shattered bodies the Israelis will leave behind, the blood of innocent children soaking into the sand."

El-Shafri and Torbuk listened in awe as Maazi hatched the scheme, fleshing it out as he went along. To those who knew him intimately, Maazi was a legend. A supreme planner, the grand master of terror. Among his credits were the letter-bomb war of 1972 against the supporters of Israel, and a year later the takeover of the Saudi Arabian embassy in Khartoum during a party for an American diplomat. But his towering achievement had been planning for the Munich Olympic Games mission. And, unlike Ali Hassan Salameh, who had finally fallen to the Mossad, Maazi's role had remained undetected.

Maazi accepted the respect of the two men as his rightful due. It was good to be back in action again. Those last years—lying low as an information officer—had dulled his spirit. It had been a prison sentence passed by Arafat upon one of his favorite brothers, exiling a man of action because the time for creating a peaceful image had arrived. Loyal to Arafat and the Palestinian cause, Maazi had performed his work well, gaining sympathy for the struggle, pitting himself enthusiastically and skillfully against the massive Israeli propaganda machine. But all the time he had yearned for the real battle. For combat, where he could fill with pride his flourishing Palestinian identity and try to wash away the disgrace his father had brought upon the family name by settling for comfort in Kuwait instead of joining in the fight. Now, Maazi's time had come again.

"The woman could be killed in such a raid," el-Shafri eventually pointed out. "Even you, Salim, cannot control exactly where the Israelis will drop their bombs."

Maazi shook his head. "Leave that to me. I'll ensure no harm comes to her." Or—would he? For an instant the notion of having Samantha killed during an Israeli raid tantalized him. Then he dismissed it. Selfishly. He wanted Samantha for himself. Only after she had served him fully, would he consider sacrificing her.

"Will the woman be alone?" Torbuk asked.

"No. Her manager"—Maazi's lips curled in a sneer as he said the word —"will accompany her because he is frightened to let his valuable property out of his sight. At this very moment he is in New York, cringing before Jewish film producers, begging on his hands and knees for their dollars, begging them to forgive him for what Samantha said in Paris." Maazi smiled as he pictured the scene. "Pierre Reynard, the French journalist, will also be here. He will chronicle Samantha Sutcliffe's work to assure us of an even larger audience."

"How long will she be here?"

"Two weeks." He got up from the table and walked to a corner of the hut where three weapons rested against the wall. His own was a Beretta Model 12 submachine gun which he gripped lightly in his right hand as he walked outside into the bright sunlight. The air was perfectly clear and

80

in the distance he could see the ancient Crusaders' fortress of Tyre. It was a memento of when wars had been simple affairs. Then, the fortress had been impregnable. Now, war was different. Buckets of Greek fire tipped over the battlements solved nothing any more.

He glanced around the refugee camp. Children played, women worked and men—both young and old—sat in groups, smoking and talking. The sight depressed Maazi. He knew that if these human sweepings from the camps ever did return to Palestine they would carry on just as they were doing now. They were good for nothing. The camps were just an excuse for them to remain idle and waste away their lives.

"*Maktoub*," Maazi muttered derisively, the word that would forever explain Arab complacency. *Maktoub*—it is written—and therefore it must be and will always be. Pierre Reynard, the writer, the intellectual, must be able to recognize traits deep within these helpless people that Maazi could never see. Otherwise, how could the Frenchman pen such sympathetic, eloquent stories about them? Maazi wanted Palestine for himself, for men like himself, men who were strong and unafraid to take what was rightfully theirs. He did not want these apathetic camp dwellers to share the country with him. He despised their laziness almost as much as he hated the Israelis who had stolen his birthright.

He climbed into a jeep and drove around the camp. Suddenly his mood brightened as he spotted a squad of young boys between the ages of nine and fifteen, taking military training. The boys were dressed like himself, in combat uniforms and red berets, and they were shouldering mock Kalashnikovs as they marched proudly. Maazi stopped the jeep and got out to watch. At the instructor's command the boys snapped to a halt, facing Maazi. They stood at attention and gave him an open-handed salute. Maazi returned the salute and then, his heart bursting with pride, joined in with the boys as they sang *"Biladi, Biladi"*—"My Country, My Country," the Palestinian anthem.

When he started the jeep again and headed north toward Beirut, Maazi was in a happier frame of mind. The squad of young boys singing *"Biladi, Biladi"* more than compensated for the listless good-for-nothings who thronged the camps.

Maazi's journey ended in front of an apartment building on the Rue Ayoub Tabet in the western section of Beirut. Heavily armed Palestinian commandos in front of a long-closed dress shop that took up the bottom floor of the building waved Maazi to a halt. One guard took his subma-

81

chine gun. Two more guards accompanied him to the second floor, jogging alongside in tight formation as they swiftly climbed the stairs.

The door to one of the apartments was open. Inside were more guards and the tall, thin uniformed figure of Dr. Mohammed Nasser, once a dentist and now Fatah's chief of operations. "My brother, it is good to see you again," Nasser exclaimed when Maazi was shown in. "Welcome home from Europe. You have done well in your work there."

Maazi acknowledged the praise of the older man. "My work there was important, but not as momentous as that which must now be accomplished." He looked around the apartment, expecting to see someone else. "Where is the Russian, Vlasov?"

"He will be here soon. Come, sit down, talk to me. Too long has passed since we last spoke." He led Maazi to a couch. When they were seated he snapped his slender, well-manicured fingers at one of the guards. The man brought over two cups of thick Turkish coffee. "You have achieved a remarkable coup with the Sutcliffe woman," Nasser complimented Maazi. "The chairman is delighted. Our voice will be heard. Our plight will receive great sympathy throughout the world."

"My brother," Maazi replied, "I may not have been totally happy doing such pedestrian work, but nonetheless I did the very best I could."

Nasser's hawklike face broke into a smile. "And you are being rewarded by this opportunity to return to action. This is what you have been waiting for, eh?"

Maazi nodded, gratified that the leaders of the struggle appreciated where his strongest talents lay. He lit a cigarette and sipped the coffee, fighting down impatience as he awaited the arrival of Pavel Vlasov, the Russian whose network of information was so crucial to the Palestinians' plans.

Fifteen minutes later Vlasov was shown into the apartment. A short, stout man with cropped blond hair, a round jolly face and bulging brown eyes, he wore a pale gray business suit in which he sweated profusely. Dark patches showed under his arms and across the back of the jacket, and the trousers clung wetly to his legs and crotch. He shook Nasser's hand, nodded when Maazi was introduced to him and then flopped wearily onto the couch.

"I have definite news at last," Vlasov said breathlessly; the journey up the stairs had debilitated him and he needed time to regain his strength. "The American diplomat Robert Shea has bewitched the Jordanians into agreeing to meet with the Israelis and the Egyptians. Shea has told the

Jordanians that the Israelis are willing to offer Palestinians on the West Bank and Gaza full autonomy. Not independence and self-rule, but the right to govern themselves, their own police, everything, while the Israelis maintain a low-profile military presence. The Jordanians told Shea that they find this an acceptable basis for further negotiations."

"How did you find this out?" Maazi asked.

Vlasov regarded Maazi with a mixture of amusement and contempt. "I have heard from Dr. Nasser that you are a brave soldier who will use my information wisely. But it is no business of yours how I secure that information. Be satisfied that we support you."

Maazi bit his tongue. He had as much love for the Russians as he had for the Americans. Either side would use you and then discard you if they felt they could make a better deal elsewhere.

Vlasov waited for the rebuke to sink in; then he continued talking. "The king told Shea that he is tired of war, that his country cannot afford to keep its military budget so high. Of course, the Americans also dangled billions of dollars of financial aid under the king's nose, just to make sure. Royalty!" He pretended to spit on the floor.

Maazi raged silently as he listened. Like the Egyptians, the Jordanians were prepared to sell out the Palestinians for American dollars. "We will never accept a settlement imposed upon us by other states," he told Vlasov. "We will accept nothing less than the return of our entire country. There is no room for Palestinians and Israelis to live side by side. And we, the Palestine Liberation Organization, are the sole representatives of the Palestinian people . . . not those weak-willed moderates, those traitors on the West Bank and Gaza, who would talk to the Israelis."

"Of course, of course," Vlasov hurriedly agreed. Again that cynical smile spread itself across the jolly round face.

Maazi gazed stonily at the Russian, resentful of Vlasov's patronizing stance, realizing that if his government suddenly decided they wanted peace in the Middle East—a peace that did not include justice for the Palestinians—they too would desert them. Then the PLO would have to fight the entire world.

"What about Shea's dealings with the Saudis?" Nasser asked.

Vlasov grimaced. "Who is capable of knowing what those incestuous desert princes ever think? Who can read their unfathomable minds? Shea is working hard on them. He flies from country to country, offering promises, proposals, counter proposals. He is a messenger boy. And, above all, he plays on the Saudi fear of communism. 'If we don't help you,' he threatens them, 'you will fall prey to the Communists. Your wealth will be confiscated. You will become paupers in the land you once ruled. And we will not help you unless you help us. We do not need your oil, we just need your cooperation,' he tells them."

"But *your* government would like access to their oil," Maazi cut in.

"I did not think we were discussing my government," Vlasov retorted. "This business would run far smoother if you kept your mind on it and did not worry so much about what my government is or is not doing. We helped to put you into operation in 1970, after the Jordanians drove you out. We supply you with arms and intelligence. That is all you need to worry about."

"How do we act?" Nasser asked quietly. "Do we strike now or do we wait patiently until this American, Shea, has aligned everyone?"

Vlasov pondered the question carefully. The decision was his and he savored it. Moscow Center had given him complete control of the case, total responsibility. He could choose whatever avenue he thought best, as long as the end result was the destruction of any American initiative to bring peace to the Middle East and to establish a multinational force to combat Soviet penetration. Peace was not on Moscow's agenda.

Vlasov understood that after twenty-four years of unquestioning service, he could have ascended high within the KGB apparatus, perhaps even to directorate level. He had offended no man—at least, no man who still wielded power. Such grandeur did not interest him, though. He preferred the field, the covert operations he had enjoyed turning from mundane work into a fine art. Moscow's reward for his faithful service had been to allow him to continue in the field, within Department Five—the executive action branch of the First Chief Directorate, where the *wet* affairs were planned.

It was almost a game to Vlasov, a sport—chess on an international scale, where neither player had the courtesy of seeing what his opposition was planning. Vlasov considered himself to be an excellent player, adaptable, resilient, always ready to improvise. He was perfectly at home in a dozen Soviet embassies around the world, just as he was at ease in the back streets of Buenos Aires or Baghdad.

"How do we act?" Nasser asked again.

Vlasov held up a hand while he continued thinking. He could order the Palestinians to strike immediately. At the Israelis themselves . . . or at the Jordanians and Saudis to persuade them not to become further involved in the American scheme. Such action would prove nothing, though, he realized with regret. It would be just another blood-soaked operation which would serve only to alienate world opinion. Something more sophisticated was needed this time. An act so daring, so audacious, that the whole world would gape in wonderment and admiration when the Palestinians struck—just as it always seemed to gape when those damned *Zhidi* got away with something like Entebbe.

"You will wait," Vlasov replied at last, sitting back on the couch and clasping pudgy hands across his stomach. He was taking full enjoyment from this moment, choreographing the actions of a group that had struck terror throughout the West and, very soon, would do so again. Black September had never been a grass-roots movement springing up from the seething mass of bitter discontent within the refugee camps. From the very start it had been KGB-inspired, working to disrupt the West. It had been dissolved when the Russians decided it was time for the Palestinians to show a more diplomatic approach but now, with Vlasov as the new puppet master, it would rise again. He, Pavel Vlasov, would orchestrate a strike that would destroy forever American endeavors to build upon their Camp David betrayal of the Palestinians. "You will allow the American, Shea, to bring this scheme to full fruition. And then you will demonstrate that Palestinian destiny is not to be trifled with as if it were stocks and shares being bargained on Wall Street. The United States *must* be discredited in the eyes of the Arab masses. You must demonstrate that Washington's ploy in the Middle East is to divide the Arab nations and thereby conquer them on behalf of their Israeli protégés."

"Where is Shea now?" Maazi asked.

"In Riyadh," Vlasov pulled himself up from the couch. "When I have further news I will contact you."

Nasser motioned for one of the guards to escort Vlasov from the apartment; then he turned to Maazi. "Why do you antagonize him so?"

"Because he's using us. We are Palestinians, proud people, fighting to regain what was stolen from us. We are not the tools of the KGB," Maazi answered angrily. "Vlasov lets us think we are fighting to regain our homeland, when in reality we are proxy troops of the Russians, fighting and dying for their benefit."

Nasser gazed thoughtfully at his hands while he mulled over Maazi's words. "It is true, Salim, but in a world that has been conditioned for so long to look upon us with loathing, we must accept whoever will be our friend without questioning his motives," he said philosophically. "What are your plans now?"

"I will make them only when we receive the final word from that fat Russian pig. At the moment, my men are organized. They wait upon my command."

"You trust all of these men?"

"Absolutely. They have all worked for me before in Black September —before I was shunted aside to do public relations work in Europe."

Nasser smiled bleakly at the undisguised distaste in Maazi's voice. "Go, my brother," he said, holding Maazi and kissing him on the cheek. "*Filastin* awaits your bravery."

Maazi returned to Rashidieh late that night. Light showed from the hut. He opened the door and entered. Inside were Ahmed el-Shafri and Yussuf Torbuk, drinking coffee and smoking while a small transistor radio played jazz music from an Israeli station.

"How was your meeting?" el-Shafri asked as he poured coffee for Maazi.

"The Jordanians are betraying us again. Soon the Saudis will follow the same path." Maazi ignored the proffered cup of coffee and walked over to a steel file cabinet set against the wall. He leafed through hanging folders until he found what he sought. It was a United States Information Service black-and-white photograph of Robert Shea, the American government's special envoy to the Middle East. Maazi gazed at the photograph, taking in Shea's perfectly groomed short gray hair, the impeccably knotted tie, the detestably earnest all-American look of the man.

"Irishman!" Maazi muttered vehemently. "How dare you seek to dictate to us when you cannot even bring peace to your own country?"

From the photograph Maazi turned his attention to the biography which rested in the file cabinet. Robert Shea had been born in 1928 in the Back Bay section of Boston. Upon graduation from Boston College, he had served for two years in the army, seeing action in Korea. Afterwards he had worked as an economist before deciding to enter the diplomatic service. His initial assignments in the late fifties and early sixties had been as an economic assistant at the American embassies in Paris and London. Upon his return to the United States he had been a part of the Johnson administration's economic team where he had displayed a diplomatic flair for negotiating settlements in industrial disputes. The Nixon and Ford administrations had retained his services, but in 1976 he had returned to private practice before the present administration had recalled him to the fold as special envoy to the Middle East.

At the very bottom of the biography, almost like a postscript, was mentioned the fact that Shea was married, with two daughters and a baby grandson.

"Here is the man who seeks to turn our fellow Arabs against us," Maazi said, dropping the photograph of Robert Shea onto the table between Torbuk and el-Shafri. "Look well upon his likeness and remember it."

As the two men studied the photograph, Maazi left the hut, climbed into the jeep and drove a short distance to the beach. He stood for a while, listening to the waves lap quietly onto the shore, gurgling as they sucked sand back into the water. Then he sat down, drawing his knees up to his chin as he gazed out at the blackness of the Mediterranean and created a vision of the future.

Under his command Black September would be resurrected as a vengeful spirit to sweep aside those who would betray Palestine. Maazi would wait until Vlasov brought word that the American treachery was complete, and then he would swoop. Like Carlos when he had executed the kidnapping of the OPEC ministers from Vienna, Maazi would spirit away the delegates to this American meeting and hold them hostage until the Arab states concerned pledged themselves to the only true path—that of bitter conflict with Israel until Israel was no more.

And Pierre Reynard, Maazi suddenly decided, would be on hand to witness it all. Yes—Reynard would chronicle the courage and daring of Maazi and his men. The Frenchman would relish the work, to be present as such historical passions erupted, to be present as Black September— almost ten years after writing its most glorious chapter—was reborn.

"Do you have such passions, Pierre, my friend?" Maazi whispered to the dark, empty sea. "Does such hot, violent blood flow within your veins as it cries for justice?"

No, Maazi answered himself—you are a journalist, a cold commentator on life's triumphs and tragedies. With your pen you pare them down to human scale so that little men everywhere can understand.

Pierre, you are like a spectator at a game, enjoying the excitement of clashing bodies from the safe comfort of your seat. Yet when you return home you describe the game as if you had been a part of it.

Maazi understood the Frenchman more fully than any psychologist could have done. The Reynards of the world lived off the backs of the men of action, stole their thrills to enjoy as their own.

The Reynards of the world were parasites. Yet they had their uses.

87

CHAPTER
SEVEN

"I$_{\text{T}}$'s a watched pot, Mrs. Sutcliffe, that never boils," Mrs. Riley said as she spotted Samantha looking through the window of the breakfast room to the road that lay beyond the low stone wall of the farm. "Your gazing through that window won't make your French friend get here any quicker."

"Thank you for your advice, Mrs. Riley," Samantha responded coolly. She turned around to face the Irish housekeeper who was setting dinner plates on the oak table. "I was just seeing what the weather was like."

"I'm sure." The housekeeper set down cutlery noisily, unable to disguise her disapproval of Samantha's relationship with Pierre Reynard. Mixing with all these foreigners would surely lead to no good. Not that Mrs. Riley would ever consider herself a foreigner. She believed the Irish belonged in Britain; they were an integral part of the country. The French did not! How many wars had to be fought to prove that point, for God's sake?

Samantha had been delighted to receive Reynard's totally unexpected telephone call that morning. He was in Yorkshire, he explained, researching a story about the country's conservative economic policies adversely affecting the hard-hit north of England. And while he was in the neighborhood, would Samantha give him the pleasure of having dinner with him that night?

"In the neighborhood?" Samantha had gasped. "Do you realize just how far it is from Yorkshire to Somerset?" Her protests, though, had been halfhearted. If Reynard had been in Aberdeen she would not have objected to his driving all the way south to visit her. She had difficulty reminding herself that his Arab sympathies, unlike her own, were real. In a way, that made him her enemy.

"What time will you be home tonight, Mrs. Sutcliffe?" the housekeeper asked.

"I don't know. But please make sure that David is in bed before nine."

Mrs. Riley nodded. Samantha returned to the window as she heard the sound of a car. A Ford Cortina driven by Reynard turned into the farmyard and Samantha went outside to greet him. Reynard clambered out of the car, took her hand and, as he had done at the Plaza Athenée, kissed it tenderly.

"How was the drive from Yorkshire?" she asked as she led him into the house.

"The miles simply flew by," he replied gallantly. "The return trip will, I fear, take much longer." Seeing Mrs. Riley he nodded politely and asked after her health; then he enquired where David was. Samantha called her son's name and his footsteps sounded loudly on the stairs as he came down from his room.

"How do you do, sir?" David asked Reynard formally, extending his hand.

Reynard smiled as he shook hands with the boy in the short gray flannel trousers, long gray socks and gray shirt that were part of his school uniform. "I have something which I think might be of interest to you." He presented David with a flat envelope which the boy ripped open eagerly, dark brown eyes shining with joy as he recognized complete sets of French, German and Italian stamps.

"What do you say to Mr. Reynard?" Samantha asked. Again she was torn by confusing emotions. Despite his peculiar political sympathies, Reynard was such an attractive man, so kind and considerate. She found herself wanting to sit down with him, to talk, to learn why such a gentle, intelligent man would support vicious murderers. But she knew she could not. To broach that subject would be to destroy her own cover.

Before David could rush back upstairs and begin mounting the stamps in his album, Mrs. Riley ordered him to sit down for dinner.

"Come inside," Samantha invited Reynard. In the living room she offered him a glass of wine, and they sat together on a leather divan in front of a roaring log fire.

"I don't think your housekeeper likes me very much," Reynard ventured apologetically.

"My housekeeper doesn't like many people. I'm sometimes surprised at how well she puts up with David and me." She told Reynard about the housekeeper arriving back at the farm to find the vandals that night. "If there had been only one man, he'd have finished up in hospital."

"I can believe that," Reynard said. "Your Mrs. Riley seems to be half housekeeper and half Irish wolfhound."

Samantha laughed at the description, knowing she could never have phrased it so eloquently herself. And at the same time she knew she had to be very careful. Reynard was so easy to speak to, so comfortable to confide in. "Where's your friend Maazi?" she asked.

"Salim?" Reynard appeared surprised at the question. "He is in Lebanon, making the arrangements for your visit. What of your friend Tayfield?"

"He's also away. In New York."

"Ah!" Reynard's face lit up; behind the glasses his light brown eyes sparkled. "So, our chaperones are absent."

"Stop it, you make me feel like I'm a sixteen-year-old Spanish girl," Samantha protested.

Reynard laughed. "What are we doing for dinner?"

"I made reservations at a country inn near here. Good, wholesome English cooking."

"As a Frenchman I am afraid that I cannot believe there is such a thing as good, wholesome English cooking. Please forgive me." He set down his glass, stood up and waited for Samantha to bring her coat. She took his hand and was surprised at how calloused it was, so out of keeping with the rest of his appearance.

"Is something the matter?" he asked.

"No. Why should there be?" She led him into the breakfast room, where Mrs. Riley and David were eating dinner. Samantha bent to kiss her son. Mrs. Riley, with forced politeness, wished Samantha and Reynard a pleasant evening.

Under Samantha's direction Reynard turned left out of the farm, passed through the village and continued for a further three miles. Finally Samantha instructed him to take a side road. A mile along the road was a wide circular driveway with the brightly lit inn set back almost in the trees. Cars filled the parking lot and Samantha was grateful that she had made reservations.

As Reynard turned into the driveway and headed for a vacant space, the black BMW glided past before stopping a hundred yards further along the road. Wadi Hassan swung the car around and killed the lights and engine. He lit a cigarette and settled down. On the seat next to him was a thermos flask of coffee and a pack of sandwiches. He was well prepared for a long wait.

Miserable whore, he thought. I hope she chokes on her food. The episode with the milk bottles still burned in his memory. Maazi had entrusted him with a job, and he had let this woman make a fool of him.

Or had it been the woman? Had someone else been watching? Someone connected with those people who had fired the barn that night? Had he been delayed long enough so that he would be unable to return to the farm and possibly stop them? The questions made Hassan nervous. Until he remembered, at last, that the Mossad did not use milk bottles. They used bullets.

He unscrewed the top of the thermos flask and poured a cup of coffee. Maazi would want to know about the Frenchman Reynard visiting the woman. Hassan realized Maazi would be furious, the great Palestinian Lothario being stabbed in the back. What would Maazi do? Would he slit Reynard's throat like a chicken? Would he destroy the very man whose influence he manipulated, all because of a weak, stupid woman? Perhaps, Hassan thought as he remembered the milk bottles again, Maazi would slit both their throats. That prospect warmed him even more than the coffee.

"There is an atmosphere here that instills comfort and goodwill," Reynard remarked as he entered the inn and looked over the solid oak beams and ornate brasswork, the blazing fire and leaded windows. "But such decor is an old deception practiced by English restaurants to take your mind off the terrible food."

Samantha smiled good-naturedly. "There's a lot of English people here who don't look so bad on such food," she reminded him, indicating the dozen tables in use.

"I can think of only one," he said, squeezing her hand. "And she more than makes up for all the rest." Only when they were seated at a table by the window did he release her hand, but not before giving it a gentle kiss.

An old man with an apron tied loosely around his waist trudged slowly to their table and set down a basket of home-baked bread. He waited patiently while they decided upon their order. Then, just as slowly, he walked away. "Is he any example of the speed of service?" Reynard whispered.

Samantha held a hand to her mouth as she started to giggle. "I forgot to tell you, he's the cook and dishwasher as well." She felt silly, carefree like a schoolgirl again, without a care in the world.

Every so often the old man visited the table with portions of their order. Between courses Reynard smoked Gitanes, enjoying the leisurely pace of the meal. It was a pleasant change from the perfectly served formal meals to which he was accustomed.

At ten o'clock they left the inn, hand in hand. Reynard opened the passenger door of the Cortina and helped Samantha into her seat. Before closing the door he stooped down, cradled her chin in his hand and kissed her lightly on the lips. "I wanted to do that in Paris."

"Why didn't you?" She tilted her face expectantly.

Reynard kissed her again, this time with more urgency. Then he stood up abruptly. "In Paris I was uncertain whether you were a woman or a film clip." Grinning, he walked around the car and climbed into the driver's seat.

"Here we go again," muttered Wadi Hassan. "Back to the farm and there he screws her. Oh—wait until Maazi hears this," he chuckled gleefully.

He waited until Reynard's Cortina had a quarter-mile lead; then he started the BMW. Hassan wished he could be a fly on the wall, all the better to tell Maazi exactly what had gone on, to tease his rage with intimate details—not that it would need much imagination.

Hassan did not even bother tailing the Cortina closely. He knew where they were going. Where else do you go after wining and dining but to bed? Hell, he could even take the rest of the night off and fill out his report anyway.

Samantha rested her hand on Reynard's as he gripped the steering wheel. She felt so comfortable in the car—the gentle warmth of the heater, the closeness of Reynard beside her—that she did not want the journey to finish. She felt that she could stay in this position forever and be content.

When they were near the farm, she turned on the interior light and pulled down the sun visor as if to check her appearance in the vanity mirror. There was no sign of the BMW's lights. She knew he was back there somewhere, though; the man with the moustache did not give up. She was used to him by now. She was not even afraid anymore. Besides —and the idea momentarily filled her with guilt at enjoying Reynard's company so much—if the tail was the work of the Palestinians, the French journalist possibly knew all about it.

When they reached the farm, Samantha entered the house first and listened carefully. Everything was silent. Telling Reynard to go into the living room, she tiptoed up the stairs. David was fast asleep, one arm outside the covers. Samantha pulled the blanket up to his neck, kissed him on the cheek and then went along the hall. Through the door of Mrs. Riley's room she could hear the housekeeper's rhythmic snoring.

Back downstairs she found that Reynard had stoked up the fire and added logs, and was now stretched out comfortably on the heavy rug in front of the hearth, his back resting against the leather divan. Feeling like a conspirator, Samantha locked the living-room door and joined him on the rug, resting against him, her head on his shoulder. Her entire being was filled with a delicious comfort she had not known since—since those stolen hours with Asher Davidson. Sometimes there had been a fire just like this one to watch; and other times their hotel room had been bare except for some flimsy furniture. Always they had made time to talk. About world affairs. About athletics. About Walt Disney. About them-selves, the future they would share. Talk had been so important.

"What shall we talk about?" Samantha suddenly asked Reynard.

"What would you like to talk about? The work you will do in Leba-non?"

She shook her head and felt his hand brushing the hair back from her face. No—not that. She might forget herself and show her true feelings. Damn! Why did she have to find this Frenchman so attractive? Why could he not have been slimy, repulsive? "Too serious a topic for a fireside chat. Think of something else."

"Why don't you have a dog?" Reynard asked. "What kind of farm doesn't have a dog?"

"You said yourself we've got Mrs. Riley." She snuggled closer, letting her eyelids drop, feeling the heat of the fire through them. "What kind of dog do you think I should have? A Doberman?"

"No." Reynard placed his arms around her shoulders. "Too vicious." He thought for a few seconds. "An English sheepdog."

Samantha pictured one. Back-to-front dogs she had always called them. You never knew whether they were coming or going, or which end to feed.

She giggled again. Was it the two glasses of wine she had drunk with dinner that were making her feel so deliriously happy?

As if in a dream she felt Reynard's hand slide off her shoulder until it rested just above her breasts. Despite his rough skin, the touch of his fingers was tender, just as she had known it would be. She felt the merest trace of stubble as his cheek rubbed hers and found it wildly sensuous.

"Why didn't you stay that night at the Plaza Athénée?" she mumbled as she felt his lips crushing her own, the tip of his tongue penetrating. She opened her teeth a fraction, clamped down playfully, refused to let go as she tantalized him with her own tongue.

Somehow—she did not remember it happening—they were not sitting side by side anymore. Now she was on her back, legs bent so that her tweed skirt rode up above her knees. Reynard's left hand was underneath her. His right hand picked delicately at the tiny buttons of her silk blouse. As the last button yielded, the garment fell away. She gasped as his lips teased her senses, tracing an excruciatingly slow, faint pattern from her stomach to her breasts.

Gradually she became aware of his right hand exploring the inside of her thigh, massaging tenderly, moving higher. Was it Reynard's hand she felt, or was it Asher's touch she was recalling? She could not be certain. Was she fooling herself, protecting herself from her own recriminations by imagining that she was again in Asher's arms?

Since Munich Samantha had been convinced that she would never be able to love again. But now, as she felt the arms of another man around her, she was questioning that conviction. It did not make any sense—not when that other man was Pierre Reynard.

Then, with a primeval cry that she was unable to control, she drove all doubts from her mind and pulled the Frenchman down on top of her.

Slowly the fire dimmed and expired into faintly glowing embers. Reynard awoke to feel a slight chill on his naked body. He reached out to the hearth where he had placed his glasses and slipped them on, thinking how foolish he must appear, wearing only his glasses.

As he looked down at the sleeping figure of Samantha, his eyes traced the contours of her body. She breathed lightly, evenly. Her chest rose and fell with a graceful rhythm. Reynard smiled and leaned over to place the gentlest of kisses on her breasts. She moaned softly and, in her sleep, reached out for him. He took her hands and held them to his mouth, caressing the long, slender fingers with his lips.

At last he stood up, donned his trousers, unlocked the living-room door and walked barefoot to the breakfast room where he recalled seeing a heavy plaid blanket folded over the back of a chair. As he returned to the living room and relocked the door, he saw that Samantha was awake, sitting up on the rug, supporting herself with one hand.

"I thought you might be cold," he said, unfolding the blanket.

"Thank you." She noticed he was wearing trousers. "Are you leaving now to drive back to Yorkshire?"

"Only if you want me to."

Yes, I do! a voice inside her cried. She stilled it by patting the rug next to her. "No, I don't." Reynard slipped out of his trousers and kicked them in an untidy heap on the floor. "What time do you have to leave?" she asked, wrapping her arms around his body. Perhaps those rough hands were not so out of place after all. His body, although Spartanly thin, possessed a sinewy strength.

"What time does your Mrs. Riley wake up?"

"About six."

"I'll be gone before she rises."

This time they made love leisurely. The urgency of their earlier encounter was missing. Each sensation was made to be prolonged, to be treasured. To rush now would be sinful.

Before falling asleep, Samantha asked Reynard to wake her when he was ready to leave.

Reynard watched her drift off into a deep, childlike sleep. With loving care he draped the blanket over her, then kissed her on the forehead. A tiny pulse throbbed gently in her temple and he kissed that, too.

The return journey to Yorkshire would not be so onerous after all, he decided; the memories of this evening would occupy him completely.

Wadi Hassan glanced at the luminous hands of his wristwatch and cursed loudly. Two-thirty! How long was this going to last? Was Reynard staying in the farmhouse forever?

Hassan fished in his pocket for a cigarette and cursed again when he remembered smoking the last one only ten minutes earlier. The night had turned chilly. The coffee and sandwiches were gone. He was cold and miserable and he could not even turn on the car's heater without warming up the engine.

Dare he leave his post and drive into the village, look for cigarettes somewhere? There might be a machine. Reynard and the woman were probably asleep now anyway, sated. He could leave for half an hour.

Hassan got as far as pressing down on the clutch and turning the ignition key. Then he changed his mind. He dare not leave. Maazi would flay him alive if he learned that Hassan had deserted his post. Maazi had let the incident with the milk bottles pass, but if Hassan failed again, Maazi would kill him without a second thought.

But Maazi was in Lebanon, a voice reasoned from the depth of Hassan's mind. How would he ever know?

He would know, Hassan decided glumly. Maazi always found out. That was why he was so feared. Cursing, Hassan resigned himself to further discomfort in the BMW.

Without warning, the driver's door of the BMW was jerked open. Hassan looked up in shock and forgot immediately about the cigarettes, the cold, Maazi.

"*La!*" he screamed in Arabic when he saw the stern, unforgiving face that stared down at him. "No!"

Before Hassan could scramble for the Makarov pistol he wore in a shoulder holster, the silenced Czech-made M52 automatic in Hunovi's right hand belched flame. The high-velocity bullet smashed into Hassan's chest, ripped through his heart and exited from his back before passing clean through the seat and floor of the BMW to bury itself in the earth below.

Immediately Hunovi removed the Makarov and holster from the dead man and pushed the body across the car into the passenger seat. He got behind the wheel himself, started the engine and turned the car around. As he did so, he glanced at the fuel gauge. The tail had been professional enough to keep a full tank, Hunovi saw approvingly.

Two miles away he pulled off the road and drove the BMW bumpily into the woods. When he found a clearing, well hidden from the road, he stopped and got out. From his jacket pocket he took a small rectangular object which he attached to the BMW's fuel tank. He set the timer and walked away quickly.

The police would find a burned-out wreck. Inside would be an incinerated body. All traces of the incendiary device would be destroyed in the eruption of the gas tank. Eventually the police might discover that the dead man had been a Palestinian named Wadi Hassan. If the British authorities bothered to contact the Israelis—which Hunovi doubted strongly—they might even learn that the late Wadi Hassan had once been a suspected member of Black September. Hunovi did not think they would learn much more.

As he put distance between himself and the doomed BMW, Hunovi smiled grimly.

Operation Asher had paid its first dividend.

A small part of Shlomo Berger's debt had been recovered.

And the Wrath of God was functional again.

CHAPTER
EIGHT

"**T**HE Saudis insist that Jerusalem become an international city," American special envoy to the Middle East, Robert Shea, told the Israeli prime minister. "They demand that all Moslems be allowed to pray at the holy places."

"Israel had never stopped a Moslem from praying in Jerusalem," the prime minister replied. "Although the same could not be said for Jews when the Jordanians ruled East Jerusalem. How international do they insist upon it being?"

"They have put forward one proposal," Shea answered. "West Jerusalem to be the capital of Israel and East Jerusalem to be the capital of Palestine—"

"Wait a minute," the prime minister interrupted. "We are talking autonomy while they are insisting upon total self-rule. That's the only way there could be a capital of Palestine—two separate states."

"But at least they're talking," Shea insisted. "Please hear me out. Jerusalem would be an open city with free access for all. The city would be run under a borough system whereby a governing council would be elected by both the Israeli and Palestinian communities. Israeli and Palestinian mayors would alternate every four years. The majority of Palestinians, those whom we know are moderate and only want peace, would happily work for the success of such a scheme."

"Alternating mayors," the prime minister mused.

"They have a similar system in Dublin, you know," Shea added, proud of his Irish heritage. "One term they have a Catholic, the next term they have a Protestant."

"I know. And once they even had a Jew as lord mayor of Dublin. It's a pity your less-enlightened brethren in the north can't come to such an amicable arrangement," the prime minister offered gratuitously.

"Northern Ireland is not on the agenda here," Shea replied stiffly. "We are talking about the Middle East." Often Shea wondered how an Irish-American such as himself had become so heavily embroiled in Middle East affairs. Why had the administration not selected a Jew, or a diplomat with an Arab background, as its special envoy to the Middle East? No, perhaps it was better this way; no one could claim that Shea was influenced by his ethnic background, his personal feelings. In fact, the only feeling he really had about his work was to bang all their heads together until they saw sense. These people were rougher to deal with than anyone he had ever come up against before; they were suspicious to the point of being neurotic. Shea was never even sure what time of day it was anymore, what with all the flying from country to country and the hurried trips back to Washington to report on progress. He had taken to using Kissinger's trick of keeping his watch on Eastern standard time and letting the Middle East leaders see him at his convenience. So what if he slept while the sun was high and tried to hammer out an agreement when the moon glowed? At least he kept his sanity.

"Mr. Prime Minister, the Saudis are tacitly implying that they will afford recognition to the state of Israel if only you will bend. They are agreeing to meet with you. That in itself is a major breakthrough." The words were spaced out, spoken slowly, and Shea's Boston accent became more pronounced as he tried to close the deal.

"They're not asking us to bend. They're asking us to break," the prime minister objected.

"Are you prepared to reject out of hand what could be the final lifeline to this region?" Shea asked.

"I don't want to surrender everything for a stinking promise that might not be worth the paper it's written on. Can't you understand our position, Mr. Shea?"

"Yes, I can. But they are willing to sit down and talk. At least agree to meet with them." Shea knew he should not be so irritated by the prime minister's obstinacy. The Saudis and Jordanians had been just as stubborn. No one wanted to be seen to lose face. And, he supposed, the Israelis did have reasonable qualms about security. Their neuroses were based on bloody history.

"We'll talk," the prime minister said. "Tell them everything is open to discussion." He would discuss anything for the chance to sit down with the people he had fought for half his life. Discussions did not cost anything.

"Good." Shea reached out to shake the prime minister's hand. "I will return to Cairo, then to Amman and Riyadh. Perhaps after this meeting is held, we will have joyful news to give to the world's press. At least to some of the world's press it will be joyful."

The prime minister smiled as he understood the meaning of Shea's last sentence. "You are a very cautious man, Mr. Shea. You play your cards close to your chest." The prime minister admired the way the American special envoy had maintained such a heavy cloak of secrecy over his dealings; he was not prepared to let out a word until he had a triumph to boast about.

"My government has to be cautious," Shea replied, his blue eyes twinkling. "We don't like to count our chickens before they hatch. Unfortunately, we have done that too many times in the past. Good day, Mr. Prime Minister."

Brimming with the satisfaction of a job well done, Shea was driven to his hotel by a young army officer with platinum blond hair and eyes that were a vivid blue. The combination intrigued Shea and he wondered where the young Jew's family had come from originally.

When they reached the hotel Shea clapped the young man on the shoulder. "To peace," he said, smiling.

"To peace," the soldier replied, and stared after the American as if he were mad.

When Shea left Israel the following day to fly first to Egypt and then to Jordan and Saudi Arabia, Alan Tayfield was also at the airport.

The week had passed far too quickly for Tayfield. It seemed that he was only just getting to know his family again when the time was up and he was being driven to Ben-Gurion Airport to catch the El Al flight to New York.

Sadness weighed heavily on Tayfield as he made his farewells. He held onto each member of his family a moment longer than was necessary. As he clasped his grandchildren he wondered miserably whether they would forget him by the time he next came home.

Whenever that would be!

That decided it for Tayfield. The next time, he vowed silently, would be the last. After completing Operation Asher he would return home never to leave again. Either the Mossad could give him a desk job, or he would retire.

The flight was called. Reluctantly Tayfield walked away, blinking back the tears that threatened to spill embarrassingly down his face. As he entered the passenger lounge, he spotted the same agent who had met him a week earlier. Without a word Tayfield followed the man out a side exit and into a car for the short trip to the Mossad safe house.

"How was your week with the family?" Rosen asked conversationally when Tayfield was brought in.

"It wasn't a week. It was only six days," Tayfield answered. "You stole the first day from me."

"So I did. So I did."

"And what did those quacks find out about me?" Tayfield thought Rosen seemed tired, face drawn and haggard as if he had spent a night on the town. Except carousing was not in Rosen's character. Maybe something else was bothering the director of special operations.

Rosen did not answer the question. Instead, he fired back one of his own in a quiet but chilling manner. "Can you think of one good reason why I should not pull you from Operation Asher?"

"What?"

"You heard me. What can you do that no one else can?" Rosen pushed a folder across the table that separated the two men. Tayfield glanced down and saw that it was his medical file. He reached out a hand, then stopped.

"What does it say?"

"Do you want the medical terms or just the plain facts?"

"Give me words I can understand." Tayfield stared in fascination at the folder that contained his future.

"Your blood pressure's dangerously high. Your heart's in worse shape than our economy. You're a walking time bomb that can go bang whenever you feel like lighting the fuse. You have angina, my friend."

"Angina?" Tayfield thought about the tearful parting with his family at Ben-Gurion Airport. He could go back to them now, tell them that he was home for good; he could even explain what he had been doing all those years when he had pretended to be selling electronics. Angina? It was his ticket home. . . . But where would that leave Operation

101

Asher? . . . And, more importantly, where would it leave Samantha?

"Angina's treatable, right?"

"To a degree, the doctors say. Just as long as you stay relaxed." Rosen laid emphasis on the last word, waiting to see how Tayfield would react.

Tayfield seemed puzzled. "How can you relax in the field?"

"Precisely. Like I said before, give me one good reason why I shouldn't pull you."

"Because Samantha and I are already inside, that's why," Tayfield answered with a measured determination that surprised himself. He knew he had just shattered the vision of his homecoming. He would go home, yes—but first he was going to see Operation Asher through to the end. It had been his job from the beginning, and he was not about to quit now. "It'll take you weeks, months, to set something else up. And who knows what can happen in that time? You started Samantha. You can't pull her out now, which means you dare not pull me either. So you're stuck with me whether you like it or not."

Rosen dared not show his relief at Tayfield's response. He had been counting on Tayfield's loyalty to the Mossad, his love of his country, to propel him on this very course. If Tayfield had balked, Rosen would have had no choice but to pull him, and then they would be in the very position that Tayfield had just described.

Thank God he understood human nature, Rosen thought as he mentally congratulated himself. But what if he had been wrong? What if Tayfield had quit on health reasons as he was entitled to . . . as Rosen should have insisted? Where would that have left Operation Asher? All the previous night the director of special operations had stayed in his office to ponder the possibilities raised by the grim results of Tayfield's physical. He had even considered substituting a false, healthy report in the medical file and sending Tayfield on his way in blissful ignorance. The idea had lasted for little more than a second before Rosen quashed it. For two reasons: first, on a personal basis he would not willingly endanger the life of one of his men by such deceit; and second, from a professional viewpoint Tayfield might cause his own death by not knowing that his body was unable to take the punishment it might receive, and in doing so he might wreck the entire mission.

Finally Rosen had chosen to leave the decision up to Tayfield, but to propose it in such a way that Tayfield's pride and loyalty would not allow him to refuse. And Rosen had been right. By doing it this way, with Tayfield knowing exactly what was wrong with him, he might slow down, become excessively cautious for fear of risking his heart. But that was a far better alternative than scrapping the operation altogether and waiting fatalistically for whatever barbarism the Palestinians were hatching.

"You're to take these with you," Rosen said, handing Tayfield a small glass bottle of nitroglycerin tablets; the bottle carried the label of a British chain of chemists. "The directions are there, let them dissolve underneath your tongue if you feel the pain, a tightness in your chest—"

"I know what the pain feels like," Tayfield said.

"I bet you do. What did you think it was all this time? Indigestion? Look, you want to see this thing through and you're perfectly right that we've got to go forward with the original plan. But get this straight: I'm only letting you go on your solemn oath that you will endanger neither yourself nor Samantha Sutcliffe."

"I promise."

"Get whatever information you can and get out. No heroics. Are you going to let Samantha know about this when you see her tomorrow?" Rosen thought that decision was best left to Tayfield; he had to work with Samantha.

"It's better that she doesn't know. She'll have enough on her mind." Tayfield groaned inwardly as he pictured all the flying that loomed ahead. He would take a later plane, one that would get him into New York in the early evening. Then, switching back from Gershon Shual to Alan Tayfield, he would go straight to the TWA terminal for the flight to London.

"All the luck in the world"—Rosen held out a hand which Tayfield shook— "and don't forget, the first sign of trouble and you and Samantha bail out."

"We will." And Tayfield meant it; he wanted to see his family again.

After Tayfield had left the safe house and was on the way back to Ben-Gurion Airport, General Benjamin Avivi entered the room where Rosen sat. Avivi had overheard the entire conversation from the adjacent room.

"Do you think he understands how ill he really is?" Avivi asked.

"I hope to God he does. And yet I can't get over the feeling that maybe I should have yanked him and tried something else."

"What?"

"I'm damned if I know," Rosen replied gloomily. "It's a funny thing, but ever since our earliest days, the Mossad has never regarded an agent as expendable. Never mind about the technology, never mind the money that was paid for equipment . . . our agents were always our most precious assets. I've just broken that tradition, do you understand that, general?"

Avivi regarded Rosen curiously, wondering why his director of special operations was baring his sould like this. Confession? "Go on," he prompted.

"By playing on Tayfield's pride and patriotism and making it seem like it was all his idea, I've just sent a man into the pit."

"You could have substituted him."

"You know damned well I couldn't. You were listening in. Tayfield said it'll take weeks or months to get where he is now. And those were the words of a bloody optimist."

"What about Hunovi?"

"I'll get word to him immediately through Zurich. He has to know about Tayfield's condition."

"Of course. Do you think, Joel, that the woman should be informed of Hunovi's presence?"

Rosen shook his head. "No. It's enough that Tayfield knows. Notwithstanding Samantha Sutcliffe's motivation, and the guidance she'll receive from Tayfield, she can't handle herself anywhere near as professionally as one of us. If she is aware of Hunovi, she might do something stupid to compromise him. If and when Hunovi decides the time is right, he can identify himself to her."

Rosen watched Avivi pick up Tayfield's medical file and scan through it. "Do you know something, general? I've got a premonition that no matter what the outcome of Operation Asher, I'm going to be attending the *shivah* for another Mossad man. And it'll be a *shivah* I could have helped to avoid."

"And that bothers you deeply."

"Of course it does. I'm not an army man like you—I don't relish sending people out to get killed. Sorry," he added quickly as he realized that he had overstepped the mark. "I'm just getting a bit too involved on this one."

"Joel, don't aim too high. Don't let the string out and try to grab everyone. As soon as Tayfield or Hunovi get a whisper, we'll hit their bases with the military."

"Sure." Rosen nodded, then lifted the telephone and put through a call to the number in Zurich that controlled Hunovi. While he waited for the telephone to be answered, he looked up at Avivi. The general was watching him intently.

You know damned well what I'm thinking, don't you? Rosen mused. Call in a military strike—like hell I will! For anything else, maybe. But if it's Black September again, I'm going to let the string run so far that we'll nail every single murdering son of a bitch. And then we'll offer up their rotting corpses as a sacrifice to the memory of Shlomo Berger—and Asher Davidson—and every poor bastard those butchers ever killed.

Rosen started to explore his stomach with his fingertips. Two more kilos had fallen away. Good. He had another premonition—that his return to field fitness would not be wasted.

Damn! He *was* going to be in there at the kill!

CHAPTER
NINE

ANY reservations Samantha had about Mrs. Riley driving her in the Range Rover to Heathrow Airport at six o'clock in the morning disappeared within the first five miles. The Irish housekeeper handled the large, cumbersome vehicle with the skill of a Jackie Stewart. Even her gear changes were smoother than Samantha had ever managed.

"You drive this tank like you're used to it," Samantha complimented the housekeeper.

"Surprised?" Mrs. Riley asked.

"A little. It's three times the size of your Austin."

"Get away with you," Mrs. Riley exclaimed as she double declutched and downshifted evenly for a sharp bend in the narrow road leading to the M4 motorway. "I learned to drive a tractor in Drummod when I was only thirteen. Anything else is a Rolls-Royce by comparison." Then she fell silent as she concentrated on the road.

Samantha grinned and looked back to where David slumbered on the rear seat. He had wanted to come so badly, to wave good-bye at the airport and see the planes. And now he's fast asleep. Not that she could blame him. The farmhouse had been pandemonium until late the previous night as she had packed and unpacked before finally deciding to take only casual clothing, jeans and blouses, a lightweight leather jacket. She was going to Lebanon to work, not to attend social functions. But as an afterthought she included a cotton print dress and one pair of high-heeled shoes.

They drove east, into the dawn. Mrs. Riley lowered the visor to keep the strong glare of the rising sun out of her eyes as she steered in stony silence. Samantha sensed that something was bothering the normally talkative Irishwoman, but it took her half an hour to figure out the reason. "You still don't think I should go to Lebanon, do you, Mrs. Riley?"

"No, Mrs. Sutcliffe, I do not. You're exposing yourself to danger, and for what? So you can try to resolve a problem where even dear sweet Jesus wouldn't know where to start?"

Samantha considered arguing the Palestinian case. She would need practice in that for her arrival at the airport where the press would undoubtedly be waiting for her. She chose not to; nothing would ever change Mrs. Riley's mind once it was firmly made up.

"By the way, don't let David get up to any mischief just because I'm away," she told the housekeeper. "He might try to take a few liberties."

"Don't you worry yourself about him, Mrs. Sutcliffe. I'm not that old and infirm that I can't put him over my knee if he starts playing me up. With your permission, of course."

"Of course," Samantha murmured, surprised that Mrs. Riley had even asked her. She glanced at the strong red hands that gripped the steering wheel and had no doubt that Mrs. Riley would not think twice about putting David across her knee if the occasion demanded it. Or herself, for that matter, she suddenly decided, and squirmed in the seat. Some mother hen.

As they drove through the long tunnel leading to Heathrow Airport, David awoke, disappointed that he had slept throughout the entire journey. Mrs. Riley pulled up in front of Terminal Three and Samantha got out, taking her one suitcase. David followed her and she held him for a few seconds, kissing him and telling him to do whatever Mrs. Riley said. He promised solemnly to be on his best behavior, and demanded in return that Samantha write every day and bring back every Lebanese stamp she could find.

"Good-bye, Mrs. Riley. I'll see you in two weeks."

"God willing," muttered the housekeeper.

Samantha leaned back into the Range Rover to kiss the Irishwoman; then she stood waving farewell as the vehicle moved away. She could see David's face turned sadly toward her until the vehicle was out of sight. Only then did she choke back a tear and wonder when she would see her son again.

Wheeling the case behind her, she crossed the sidewalk and entered the terminal. Alan Tayfield was waiting just inside, already checked through on Middle East Airlines flight 202 that would leave at nine-thirty. With him was a group of reporters and photographers from the national newspapers and press agencies. A flash went off the moment Samantha appeared, and the reporters surged forward to ask questions.

"What do you really hope to accomplish by making this documentary, Miss Sutcliffe?"

"Some justice for the Palestinians," was her instant reply. "Recognition of their plight."

"Do you really think you can change the entire world all by yourself?"

"No." She handed her case and passport to Tayfield to check her onto the flight while she answered the questions. "I just want to change the little corner of the world that I inhabit." She looked at the ring of attentive faces surrounding her, newsmen eager for their story, and decided the time was ripe for really quotable material. "There is so much wrongdoing in the world, so much evil that needs vigorous condemning, yet no one bothers to do anything about it. They always leave it for someone else. Well, I've appointed myself to be that someone else in the case of the Palestinian people. If I show a lead, perhaps others will find the courage to follow in other areas."

"Are you fearful for your life?"

"After what happened at my home when the Zionists tried to *persuade* me to remain silent? I suppose I should be afraid but I'm prepared to take the risk," she answered, with a quick smile to take the bite out of what might otherwise be construed as mock heroics. "After all, the Palestinians' lives are in danger every day. They have the spirit to fight back and so will I." While she spoke, she wondered why the reporters and photographers seemed to be jockeying her into another position, crowding in until she had to move back, and then crowding in again.

"That's it," she heard someone say.

She turned her head as more pictures were taken and saw that she had been placed directly in front of the El Al desk. In any picture the El Al sign would be in the background, along with the airline desk staff who were staring icily at her. Bastards, she thought. Cunning, conniving bastards. She walked away quickly, her face blazing with anger. When the reporters tried to ask more questions, she glared at them and refused to speak.

"Neat trick," Tayfield observed wryly when she rejoined him. "I could see what they were doing but there was nothing I could do to stop it without breaking up the party."

"At least the agency boys won't be able to sell any of their pictures to Arab newspapers," she replied. "Serves them damned well right."

They passed through security and sat waiting in the VIP lounge. "That was very thorough surveillance your people had me under," Samantha said quietly.

"I told you we were thorough."

"And deadly," Samantha added, recalling the excitement two days after Reynard's visit when a farmer searching for a lost cow had discovered the burned-out BMW concealed in the woods two miles from the farm, its driver charred beyond recognition. Only after extensive inquiries had the dead man been identified as a Palestinian named Wadi Hassan who had been vacationing in England. What he had been doing so deep in the woods defied police investigation, although binoculars found among the wreckage had spawned the theory that he might have been an amateur ornithologist. Police had ruled that the probable cause of the fire was a gas tank leaking onto a hot exhaust. An inquest had passed a verdict of death through misadventure, because Hassan had no business being in the woods.

"Did Hassan's death upset you?" Tayfield asked.

Samantha shook her head. "Just one bastard less," she whispered.

Tayfield squeezed her hand. It had upset her, he knew that. Not because Hassan had been killed, but because it had happened so close to the farm. Only one aspect of Operation Asher frightened Samantha— that David, her son, might be somehow drawn into it.

At 8:50 they boarded the Middle East Airlines flight. With a palpable shock, Samantha realized that her feet were no longer touching British soil. The next ground she would walk upon would be in Lebanon. She thought of David staring back at her as the Range Rover pulled away, and of Mrs. Riley's continuing disapproval. What would the housekeeper have to say when Samantha returned and the truth could be told?

But could it ever be told? Samantha had not considered that before. Her role in this could never be made public. For her own safety, for David's. No matter what happened, no matter what information Tayfield learned and reported back to his superiors in the Kiria, Samantha's own role would always remain exactly what it appeared to be—an actress sympathetic to Palestinian ambitions. To a degree, that knowledge saddened her. Like any performer she appreciated recognition, applause; but in this situation she could never afford to accept it. Only she and those people directly involved with Operation Asher would know what she had done. And Asher himself, of course, her dead love. Somehow he would know what had been done to avenge his murder.

The Middle East Airlines flight took off at 9:45. Tayfield read a newspaper while Samantha tried to immerse herself in books on Lebanon which she had acquired from the Lebanese tourist office in Piccadilly. Flight attendants in salmon pink uniforms patrolled the first-class section, pampering their travelers. Once, Samantha caught two of the attractive young women talking quietly while they sent quick glances in her direction. She realized that she must be a celebrity on the flight and resigned herself to being the center of attention.

The aircraft touched down in Beirut at 4:40 P.M., local time, and Samantha gazed curiously through the port windows at the capital city of a country ravaged by a war it never wanted. She was uncertain what to expect. Would she be greeted by bomb sites, huge craters similar to those she had seen in pictures of Europe after the war, whole areas flattened by thousands of tons of high explosives with just a wall or two left standing upright in some grotesque pattern? To her surprise everything seemed normal, at least in the airport. Huge jets were parked in orderly rows. Tanker trucks and small vehicles drove busily around the airport perimeter. Only once, and even then Samantha was uncertain, did she see something out of the ordinary. That was when Tayfield whispered for her to "look at three o'clock." As the airliner swung gently into its final parking position and the engines died, Samantha thought she glimpsed an antiaircraft emplacement.

The plane emptied quickly. Samantha and Tayfield followed the line of passengers into the immigration hall. "Welcome to Lebanon, Miss Sutcliffe," the immigration officer said as he checked her passport. "May your stay be a pleasant one."

"Thank you. I'm sure it will be."

In the Arrivals area, Salim Maazi waited with a group of Lebanese and international journalists. Samantha looked around, expecting to see Pierre Reynard, who had promised to meet her in Lebanon. There was no sign of the Frenchman, and Samantha could not help feeling disappointed. She had neither seen him nor spoken to him since that one night in the farmhouse; all arrangements had been made by Maazi.

For five minutes she patiently answered questions from reporters. She could not help thinking they were more polite than their counterparts at

Heathrow Airport. And there was no El Al desk at Beirut for them to pose her against. Finally Maazi dismissed the reporters and took Samantha's case in one hand and her arm in the other.

"Welcome to my adopted country. One day soon I hope to welcome you to my real home."

"I look forward to it." He seemed different than when she had seen him at the farmhouse with Reynard. He was tighter, harder, more alert.

"I am pleased to welcome you also, Mr. Tayfield. I hope that your opinion of what Samantha is doing has softened since we last met."

"I'll reserve my judgment until I see how this affects her career," Tayfield replied with a stiff coldness that was genuine. He could not help but contrast his present feelings of alienation with the warmth generated by his home country only a few miles to the south.

"Your trip to New York was not a success?"

"It was not what it could have been before La Tour d'Argent and the article in *Variety.*"

Maazi smiled sympathetically. "A person's value in life can be measured in many ways. Only the Jews have money as their sole yardstick."

Tayfield gripped the handle of his suitcase tightly. It was all he could do not to fling it at the smiling Palestinian. Instead he satisfied himself by saying, "I read somewhere that the Palestinian leaders don't live like paupers either. The refugees might—the poor bastards rotting in the camps—but the head honchos pull in the loot." He used American slang purposely, to make the accusation sound even more vulgar.

Maazi's smile turned to ice. "If you wish to believe what the Zionist press writes about us, that is your privilege." Still holding Samantha's arm, he led them out of the terminal to where a white Mercedes waited.

"Like I said, the Palestinian leaders don't live like paupers," Tayfield could not resist saying.

The driver's door of the Mercedes swung back and Ahmed el-Shafri jumped out to open the rear doors for Samantha and Tayfield, and place their baggage in the trunk. Maazi settled himself in the front passenger seat. "Please bear with me," he said without turning around. "We have a little more traveling to do." He reached down and pulled out something from beneath the seat which he tried to hide from the occupants of the back. But Tayfield glimpsed the shining steel of the Beretta submachine gun.

The sight of the weapon jolted Tayfield. All the planning for Operation Asher, the training of Samantha, the final briefing from Rosen in Tel Aviv

114

—all of that dwindled into insignificance compared with the sight of the automatic weapon pulled from beneath the seat. That one action, more than anything else, made Tayfield realize where he now was—in Lebanon, in the power of the Palestinians.

El-Shafri took the Mercedes south along the coastal road, turning on the air conditioning as the inside of the car heated up. Tayfield wished he would open a window instead. In the front passenger seat, Maazi sat warily, offering only the occasional comment as they passed what he considered to be places of interest. He pointed out the Ain al-Helweh and Mieh-Mieh refugee camps, south of Sidon, and both Tayfield and Samantha could not help feeling genuinely sorry for the wretches who were forced to occupy them. From time to time, Maazi would glance back at his two passengers. Once he smiled as he caught Samantha staring at him, and he realized that the gun he had tried to conceal was all too visible. "For your protection," he remarked lightly. "Madmen abound in this country these days."

The sight of Samantha and Tayfield turned Maazi's thoughts to the tag he had ordered on the actress. Obviously, the unfortunate Wadi Hassan had benefited little from the milk-bottle episode. Someone else had surprised him while he maintained his vigil. Never mind what the British police decided, Maazi knew better. Hassan had not been the victim of a freak accident, a faulty gas tank leaking into a hot exhaust. Maazi recognized the signature of the Mossad all too clearly. Someone else had been watching Samantha. But who? Those same men who had vandalized her farm? Why had they bothered to take out Hassan? That was an unnecessary killing, and even Maazi admitted that the Israelis planned their murders most selectively. Or was it on that particular night Hassan had seen something which it was better for Maazi not to know? If so, what . . .?

As they drove even further south, past Tyre, Maazi replaced the gun under his seat. "Here, we are perfectly safe," he declared. "Even the Israelis cannot touch us now."

Don't you bet your last penny on it, Tayfield said to himself. We've been here before and we'll be back if necessary. He knew exactly where el-Shafri was heading—to Rashidieh, a transit camp built by the French in 1936 and enlarged twenty years later by the United Nations Relief and Works Agency. Israeli intelligence described the camp as a guerrilla stronghold and jump-off point for attacks against the Jewish state.

Tayfield looked out of the Mercedes' window with interest. To the right

115

stretched the blue expanse of the Mediterranean; and to the left, land that started to rise toward the mountains. With increasing frequency the Mercedes passed groups of uniformed, armed guerrillas. Tayfield also spotted pieces of medium artillery under heavy camouflage in orange groves. He tried to commit everything to memory. One day it would all come in useful.

"Are you feeling all right, Mr. Tayfield?" Maazi asked.

"Why shouldn't I be?" Tayfield shot back, surprised by the unexpected question.

"Your face has turned very red."

"I'm British, remember? I'm not used to such hot weather. Can't you open a window?"

"The air conditioning will have to suffice, I'm afraid."

Listening to Maazi, Samantha turned to look at Tayfield. His face was violently inflamed. She touched his cheek with her hand. "Alan, what's the matter?"

"It's nothing," he protested. "Just this damned heat and the air conditioning. I hate it." He looked out of the window again, forcing himself to be calm. When he was certain that Samantha had turned away, he slipped a tiny white tablet underneath his tongue.

The Mercedes entered Rashidieh and Samantha studied the cramped, squalid buildings. "How many people live here?"

"About fourteen thousand," Maazi answered. "See?" He pointed through the windshield. "We have schools, a clinic, everything a small town could boast. Everything, that is, except a place that is really home."

"I'd like to meet some of the people."

"You will," Maazi promised.

El-Shafri pulled up outside a low wooden hut, opened the trunk and carried the baggage inside. Samantha, Tayfield and Maazi followed, "Not the Plaza Athenée, I regret to say," Maazi apologized. "I hope you will forgive me."

Samantha looked at Tayfield before answering. The redness had disappeared, now there was a slight smile of encouragement on his face. "I didn't expect the Plaza Athenée. It would be hard to describe authentically the plight of the refugees if I were living in luxury."

The hut was divided into a communal area with a table and four mismatched chairs, while off to one side—separated by flimsy partition walls—were two small bedrooms, one for Samantha and one for Tayfield. Bathing and toilet facilities were communal, and outside. In each bedroom an army bunk had been erected, thin towels had been laid out. On each bunk was a copy of the script Samantha would use for the documentary.

"What do you think of it?" Maazi asked while he watched Samantha skim through the pages. He was proud of the work he had put into the script.

"I like the title—*A Modern Tragedy*. How long do I have to learn this?"

"The camera crew will arrive tomorrow. We would like to be out of Rashidieh and on to the other camps within a couple of days."

"How many camps will we be visiting?" Tayfield asked.

"All of them."

Samantha started to read carefully. The script was skillfully written propaganda, guaranteed to jerk tears from even the most disinterested viewers. It was also, she knew, more invention than truth, including visits to memorials for the innocents murdered in Israeli raids on civilian camps. Samantha had known Tayfield long enough to appreciate the comprehensive intelligence network he represented. And had not she herself seen heavily armed Palestinian soldiers on the journey south from Beirut? But the documentary would work, just as long as the narrator—herself—acted the role perfectly. She would have to, she understood that. She would have to speak for the camera, be the tongue to its eye, as it panned across the pathetic hopelessness etched on the faces of the refugees and tried, in stark comparison, to capture what little charm existed in the volunteer-staffed schoolrooms where children learned and played. "Do you think you're being too heavy in some instances?" she asked Maazi. "Surely you've heard of overkill."

"Where?"

"In these constant references to the terror attacks by Israeli aircraft. Wouldn't just one or two mentions be enough? Why keep on about it? You're liable to turn your viewers off."

Maazi removed the script from Samantha's hands and glanced through it. Like any writer he resented having revisions suggested. "I hope for your sake that you are not in Lebanon long enough to see how true these words are," he replied in a curt dismissal of her objections. "Then you would learn the real meaning of overkill—using napalm on children."

"Do you expect trouble?" Tayfield asked. An uncomfortable vision of Samantha and himself being trapped—injured—even killed!—by the very people who had sent them, started to form in his mind. Surely they must know where he and Samantha were.

"We always expect trouble, Mr. Tayfield. That is the basis—and the success—of our continued existence."

Two surprises awaited Samantha that evening. The first was Maazi's invitation on behalf of one of the Palestinian families for her and Tayfield to share dinner with them. The second surprise was the appearance of Pierre Reynard, who had arrived that day in Lebanon from Paris.

Samantha was in her room preparing for dinner when she heard Reynard's voice calling for her. Feeling her face flush at the prospect of seeing him, she quickly fluffed her hair with her hands and went into the main part of the hut. Reynard was standing by the table, dressed in a short-sleeved cotton shirt and baggy khaki trousers that might have come from an army-surplus store. Somehow the change in appearance suited him. Without the expensive, well-cut clothes Samantha had always seen him wearing, he looked fitter. His arms had a wiry strength, and the short hair covering them was bleached almost white. Remembering how those arms had once held her, she gave way to a faint, delicious shiver.

"Welcome to Lebanon," Reynard greeted her.

"That's the third welcome I've had. From the immigration officer, from Salim and from you."

"Which one did you believe the most?" He took her hand and caressed it gently before lifting it to his lips.

"I believed them all; they all sounded sincere. Instead why don't you ask which welcome I liked the most?"

Reynard smiled, content to let that question remain unasked. "I understand that we have all been invited out to dinner tonight. You, me, your manager, Tayfield. Where is he, by the way?"

Samantha indicated the communal bathing area just outside the hut. "Cooling down. Alan and the heat don't agree. I'm looking forward to dinner, all that *mezze* and *arrack, shish kebab* and *baklava*—"

"I think you might be relying too much on the Lebanese tourist guides," Reynard cut in. "We are eating tonight with a refugee family, not in a restaurant on the Rue Hamra in Beirut. These people survive on handouts from the UNRWA, and whatever their rich Arab cousins decide to let fall from their well-stocked tables."

"I see," Samantha said thoughtfully. "Is that supposed to put me in the right mood for the documentary?"

118

"Samantha, do you remember what I said in Paris? I came here for two reasons. One, because the Palestinians are newsworthy and I am a reporter. Two, because I need to purge my soul of the false values that one picks up living in Paris. To eat like these poor people will very quickly help you to identify with them. Sometimes it is beneficial to learn how the other half of the world lives . . . and starves."

Just then Tayfield entered the hut, rubbing his thinning hair with a towel.

"Samantha was just telling me that you were feeling the effects of the heat. I trust you are better now," Reynard greeted him.

"Yes, thank you." The politeness sounded forced. "Cold water helped."

"If there is anything you need, please do not hesitate to ask."

"I'll remember to do that." Tayfield continued on to his room, still rubbing his head. Reynard took Samantha by the hand and led her outside. They stood in the gathering dusk, looking out over the tin-and-canvas dwellings. The smell of cooking wafted on the air and Samantha tried to identify some of the aromas.

"I think Tayfield is as unhappy to be here as he was at your wanting to come," Reynard ventured. "After a few hours he cannot wait to leave. Your being here distresses him. He cannot stand the sight of me. And he wishes the entire Palestinian people would simply evaporate."

Samantha was about to say something in Tayfield's defense but Reynard continued speaking. "He is one of the majority, a perfectly normal, self-centered man who just wishes the Palestinians would go away so that their life-and-death problems would have no effect on his orderly life. You and I—we share something, Samantha. We care."

"Alan also cares. For me. I don't think he really gives a damn about how much commission he might lose if I antagonize film people because of my involvement here. He just worries about my well-being."

"What time is Maazi calling for us?" Tayfield asked as he joined them outside the hut. He looked suspiciously from Samantha to Reynard as if he had interrupted something.

Reynard checked his watch. "At nine. Ten minutes from now."

"Who's the family we're eating with?"

"The man's name is Hassan Bakri. He is an old, very well-respected member of the Palestinian community. More than thirty years ago his father was the mayor of a village in Palestine called Tarshiha. The Israelis renamed the village Maalot after they drove the Palestinians out in 1948."

119

"So now the rest of the family's still waiting to get back in and change the name to Tarshiha again, eh?" Tayfield asked. All he knew about Maalot was that terrorists of the Popular Democratic Front had attacked an Israeli school there several years earlier, killing helpless children.

"They have nothing else to wait for," Reynard replied.

Salim Maazi was wearing a fatigue uniform when he arrived in the white Mercedes. He drove Samantha, Reynard and Tayfield out of the camp to a nearby village, pulling up in front of a two-room stone house. "Hassan Bakri is one of the elders of the Palestinian community," he explained. "He is allowed a degree of luxury."

Inside the house, sitting on a chair while he listened to a radio on the table next to him, was a man who, Samantha guessed, was in his seventies. While many of the people she had so far seen wore western-style dress, the old man was robed in traditional Arab garments and wore a kaffiyeh. His face was a deep brown and seamed with numerous lines, yet his eyes were sharp and inquisitive.

"*Salaam aleikum,*" Hassan Bakri said as he rose to greet Maazi and his guests. "Welcome to my humble home."

"*Aleikum salaam.*" Maazi introduced the three people with him and the old man beckoned for them to sit down on wooden chairs. In halting, painful English he said, "You do my home an honor by visiting me."

"The honor is entirely ours," Samantha responded quickly.

"Where is Rima?" Maazi asked the old man in Arabic. Then for the benefit of Tayfield and Samantha, he said in English, "The old man lives with his widowed daughter, Rima. Her husband and two young sons were killed in August, 1976."

"By the Israelis?" Samantha asked.

"No. By their allies the Phalangists during the civil war. Hassan's family was at Tel al-Za'atar, near Beirut, when the Christians overran the camp and murdered many of the unarmed survivors. After that, Hassan and his daughter came here. You speak out about the Palestinian tragedy," he added for Samantha's benefit. "Now witness it first hand."

The old man's daughter appeared from the other room. As tall as Samantha, Rima Bakri had short jet black hair, a thin straight nose and deep brown eyes that held a haunting, mystical quality. She wore a uniform similar to Maazi's and greeted him by clasping his shoulders and kissing him on both cheeks. Introductions were made again. Rima spoke

120

far better English than her father, and when Samantha inquired about the uniform, she told the actress that she had been a member of Al Fatah for ten years.

"You're a soldier?" Samantha asked.

"We are all soldiers," Rima answered proudly.

"Except for those of us," Maazi cut in, "who are content just to write about soldiers." He glanced at Reynard and gave the Frenchman a slight smile that was not reciprocated.

"Then how did you manage to escape from Tel al-Za'atar?" Samantha asked Rima. She cast a look at Reynard and saw that his face had reddened under Maazi's snub. He seemed remarkably subdued in Maazi's company, content to keep a low profile. Here, it was clearly Maazi who was the respected leader.

"I am alive because the Christians still sometimes believe in the chivalry they practiced at the time of their Crusades," Rima answered. "They thought twice before killing a woman and an old man like my father, but for my husband and two sons—a boy of seven and a boy of five—they did not have to think at all." She closed her eyes and her face softened as the tragic scene came to mind.

Samantha felt tears start to burn her eyes. She thought of her own son, so safe on the farm in Somerset with Mrs. Riley to look after him.

Maazi noticed the way Samantha wiped her eyes and he experienced an inner glow of triumph. No acting skill could substitute for the genuine pain Samantha would feel when she began shooting the documentary the following day.

But Maazi failed to guess the one question that Samantha asked herself to kill her growing sympathy: what did the murder of Asher and his comrades have to do with any of this?

At eleven that night, immediately after Samantha had retired, Ahmed el-Shafri, Yussuf Torbuk and Rima Bakri led two other guerrillas from the Rashidieh camp. Armed with automatic weapons they drove by jeep to a border area not policed by the United Nations. From there they went by foot, sneaking quickly past the sentries who slackly guarded the Christian-held buffer zone. At the Israeli border, barbed wire fences blocked further progress. Using bolt cutters, they snipped the bottom two strands and stealthily crossed over into Israel.

Half a mile inside the border they came to a road and waited. After ten minutes the sound of a vehicle reached them. A jeep on regular patrol approached. The five Palestinians stood up and opened a withering fire on the three soldiers in the vehicle, killing them instantly. Torbuk, el-Shafri and Rima searched swiftly among the dead soldiers for weapons. Then, without warning, they turned the Israeli Uzis on the two guerrillas who had accompanied them from Rashidieh, leaving their bodies at the scene of the ambush. Before departing they dropped the Uzis by the bodies of the dead Israeli soldiers.

As stealthily as they had crossed into Israel, they left. At seven in the morning they were back at Rashidieh while, at the site of the ambush, Israeli soldiers were searching the two dead guerrillas who, they believed, had been killed in the skirmish. On one of them the Israelis found evidence that he came from Rashidieh.

If Salim Maazi had not waked Samantha at six-thirty in the morning she would have quite happily overslept, tired after the previous day's long journey from London. She dressed quickly in jeans and a cotton blouse and joined Tayfield, Maazi and Reynard for breakfast in the main section of the hut.

As they lingered over coffee, and Maazi and Reynard smoked, three more people entered the hut. Samantha had already met Rima Bakri and Ahmed el-Shafri. The smooth-faced Yussuf Torbuk was introduced. The three newcomers helped themselves to coffee and stood around while Maazi explained the day's activities.

"We start with the school. Our hopes for the future lie with our children, but how can they grow up free of bitterness when they are forced to learn in such adverse conditions?"

"I still think you're pushing that point too hard," Samantha told him, realizing that Maazi was using words almost identical to the script he had prepared.

"We shall see." Maazi favored Rima, Torbuk and el-Shafri with a quick, knowing glance that meant nothing to either Samantha or Tayfield.

After breakfast Maazi accompanied Samantha to the school that was housed in a large prefabricated hut with a metal roof. Reynard followed behind, aloof and distant. Almost fifty children between the ages of eight and eleven were already seated behind flimsy wooden desks, and Samantha was surprised to see Rima standing at the raised platform reserved for the teacher.

"Does that shock you?" Maazi asked. "Rima has a Ph.D from the

American University of Beirut. Just because a woman is willing to give her life for freedom does not mean that she is uneducated."

"Doesn't her uniform have an effect on the children?" From her own schooldays Samantha recalled that women teachers dressed in tweed skirts.

"I sincerely hope that it does," Maazi replied. "As well as educating our children, Rima instills them with pride."

"Surely that's as disconcerting to their childhood as being under the constant threat of bombardment?"

Maazi regarded Samantha quizzically. "Do you suddenly disapprove of us, Samantha? Was it all right for you to plead our cause when you were safe in Europe, where you could exploit our misfortune to gain attention and publicity for yourself? But now that you are among us, do you have second thoughts?"

"No, of course not," she said as she turned away, unable to fully comprehend the hate—or pride, as Maazi insisted on calling it—that was being drummed into such gullible young souls.

Floodlights had been erected in the schoolroom. Turned on, they bathed everything in an artificial brightness. The children sat attentively, as if ready for a special treat. From the platform Rima introduced Samantha, and there was a well-rehearsed round of applause. Unable to do anything but smile in response, Samantha stood beside Rima, feeling inadequate next to this powerful woman who had suffered so much . . . until she remembered how she, too, had suffered after Munich.

"Thank you very much," she told the children, waiting while Rima translated into Arabic. "What we are doing here today will, I hope, enable you in the very near future to have proper classes in a proper school in your own country." She realized from the spontaneous applause that greeted her statement that the children were as politically motivated as the adults; before they learned the three Rs, they were taught to hate. She stepped back as the cameraman began to film the class in session.

When the lens turned to her, with the children and Rima in the background, Samantha spoke the opening words of Maazi's script: "The hopes and dreams of every civilization throughout history have rested with their children. The Palestinians are no different, although in the thirty-some years which have passed since they were exiled from their own land, the children have grown into parents and then into grandparents. But even now, the newest generation of children represents those same hopes

123

for tomorrow. Always," she added with special emphasis, "with the fervent dream that one day, tomorrow will really be tomorrow."

Behind her she could sense the children torn between paying attention to Rima and hamming for the camera.

"These children here in the Rashidieh camp in Southern Lebanon might seem like any other children in any other school throughout the world. But there is one major difference. Beneath this building is a bomb shelter, and before these children learn to read and write, add and subtract, they are taught how to file in an orderly fashion into that shelter. Because at any moment they know that Israeli warplanes might attack the camp. They do not understand why, but sudden, unprovoked attacks against these helpless refugees are unhappy facts of—"

A siren began to wail mournfully across the camp. Rima rapped out orders and the children stood up, left their desks and walked quickly to the bomb-shelter entrance.

"Is this a drill?" Samantha asked Maazi, unnerved by the siren and the subsequent activity. Had he thrown this in for good measure?

"No! It's the real thing! See—you questioned my script. Now do you believe me?" he snapped at Samantha. "Join the children! Quickly!" The entire scene could not have been better orchestrated if Maazi had ordered the air raid for that very moment. By instructing Rima, el-Shafri and Torbuk to leave the two dead guerrillas with evidence linking them to Rashidieh, he had ensured a retaliatory strike against the camp, but he could have only prayed that the Israelis would respond so swiftly.

"I'm not going down there!" Samantha spun around and saw that the cameraman was already heading for the door leading outside. Maazi and Reynard followed him. As Samantha moved after them, Tayfield stopped her.

"Down there!" he ordered, pointing to the shelter entrance. "I'm not having you risking your life out there."

"They won't hit a schoolhouse."

"Who knows what the hell they'll hit? The Palestinians hide their arms behind children. They use them as a shield," he added, dropping his voice to an urgent whisper. Damn! Why did the Heyl Ha'avir have to pick this particular morning to attack Rashidieh?

Samantha pushed him aside and ran from the schoolhouse. Maazi was standing outside, bellowing orders. From out of nowhere heavy machine guns appeared, as camouflage was thrown off. El-Shafri and Torbuk ran past Samantha carrying shoulder-launched surface-to-air missiles. Samantha could not believe what she was seeing. Within seconds the pitiful refugee camp was turning into an armed fortress.

"Get down!"

She heard Reynard scream at her. Before she dived to the ground, covering her head with her hands, she saw straight ahead—coming in at almost ground level from the Mediterranean—four Phantom jets.

She closed her eyes and prayed.

CHAPTER
TEN

*T*HE ground trembled and swayed beneath Samantha. She felt her eardrums throb with such excruciating force that she was certain they must burst when the Israeli Phantoms flew low overhead in a tight finger-four formation. From close by, a heavy machine gun barked defiance as the four aircraft roared off into the distance. Unable to believe that the fighters could have overflown the camp without launching an attack, Samantha lifted her head cautiously and looked around.

She was just in time to see the formation of Phantoms break up like a flower in instantaneous bloom. The lead aircraft climbed sharply, swung around in a hard, fast turn and then barreled back toward the camp, its nose pointed directly at the very spot where Samantha lay.

Someone grabbed her roughly under the arms and tried to drag her to shelter. She heard Reynard's voice urging her to run, but her legs refused to work. Dazed by the deafening roar of the aircraft, she stood up and looked around wildly. Tayfield was only a few yards away, pressing himself into the sand in the shelter of the school. Nearby, Maazi was organizing a machine-gun emplacement, screaming at the gunners not to desert their posts, exhorting them to accuracy. Yussuf Torbuk and Ahmed el-Shafri were also close by, ready to fire surface-to-air missiles at the approaching jets. Only figures in uniform were now visible. The other inhabitants of the camp had disappeared, hiding inside their vulnerable little huts like ostriches with their heads in the sand; what they could not see could not harm them. And in the middle of all this chaos stood the cameraman, his legs spread wide apart, camera balanced on his shoulder, wild ambition conquering fear as he prepared to record every moment of the attack.

Cannon fire erupted, eclipsing all other sound, blasting a swathe through the camp. Screams of agony played a vivid counterpoint to the roar of the aircraft. Pieces of tin from battered huts sang through the air like deadly shrapnel. Samantha watched, hypnotized with terror, as the lead Phantom rocketed overhead and seemed to give birth. Two small pods fell away to tumble down toward the far edge of the camp, slowing as their stabilizing fins opened. Then a double explosion ripped across the camp. Even from a mile away Samantha could feel the blast. From within the cloud of raging flame another detonation occurred, a gigantic booming blast that dwarfed the explosions of the smart bombs, and Samantha knew that the lead Phantom had zeroed in directly on an ammunition dump. The air raid—for whatever reasons the Israelis had chosen this particular moment—was not as criminally slapdash as Maazi would have the world believe.

A muted, swooshing roar from close by startled Samantha. The surface-to-air missile from Yussuf Torbuk's hand-held launcher sliced through space as the second Phantom started its attack run. The pilot jinked the plane left and right, and the missile soared past harmlessly. Instead of following his flight leader, though, the pilot of the second Phantom selected the origin of the missile as his point of attack. Cannon fire ripped through the flimsy schoolhouse, barely missing Tayfield, and then marched across the sand with heavy, lethal steps. Samantha saw a uniformed guerrilla only five yards away raise his Kalashnikov pathetically into the sky. He was bowled over like a ninepin. Blood streamed from his mangled neck where a cannon shell had ripped his head clean off. Without thinking Samantha ran across and picked up the rifle, raised it to her shoulder and fired blindly as the second Phantom flashed overhead. Instead of the one round she had expected, the Kalashnikov spat out six. The unforeseen recoil jarred her shoulder brutally and knocked her flat on her back, but not before the alert cameraman had swung in her direction.

As swiftly as it had materialized, the air raid was over. With the sun winking merrily off their wings, the four Phantoms flew west over the Mediterranean in perfect formation, then banked south toward their home base. Behind they left fires raging throughout the camp. Where the ammunition dump had been, men tried valiantly to douse the blaze. Finally they were forced to retreat as more ordnance exploded to send fragments of steel showering across the camp. The man whose rifle

Samantha had taken lay sprawled on the ground like a butchered steer, his torn neck leaking blood into the parched sand.

"Are you all right?" Reynard was the first to reach Samantha and help her to stand up.

"I think so." She dusted herself down and found that she had torn her jeans and scraped her knees.

"For someone who has never handled a rifle before, you acquitted yourself admirably," Reynard commended her. "But you have to watch out for the kick."

"I didn't think you knew much about guns, either." She looked past Reynard to where Tayfield was climbing slowly to his feet. She feared for him when she saw his red face and the way he seemed to be struggling for breath. Reynard also noticed, and he ran across to Tayfield to see that the older man was all right.

"I'm too old for this," Tayfield protested. He shook off Reynard's helping hand. To Samantha's relief he seemed to be all right; the flush paled and his breathing became more regular. "You and I have no business here," he told Samantha. "If he"—Tayfield jerked a thumb at Reynard —"believes a front-page story is worth risking his life for, he's welcome to this infernal place." While he spoke, he fought down a touch of pride as he recalled how the Phantoms had selected the ammunition dump. How close it had been, though, he reflected, pressing a hand to his chest to slow his heartbeat. All because Torbuk had opened up with the missile launcher, he and Samantha had almost been killed.

Maazi came loping across to see that his guests were unharmed. "Now do you see what I mean?"

"What did they use the bombs on?" Tayfield wanted to know. "Something over there went up with a hell of a big bang."

"A gasoline-storage dump," Maazi lied. He turned to Samantha and a warm smile illuminated his dusty, sweat-stained face. "I apologize for doubting you before. You are indeed a very courageous woman."

"I did it without thinking." She picked up the rifle she had fired and looked at it. Blood from its original owner was still wet upon the stock. When she noticed that some of the blood had smeared her hands, she had to fight down the urge to be violently sick. "I didn't realize it would go off in one long burst like that," she managed to say.

"I think that you should undergo some weapons training with our people," Maazi suggested. "Then you might even hit what you were aiming at. Not that you could ever hope to down a jet plane with a rifle."

128

Samantha glanced inquisitively at Tayfield. He offered her that brief encouraging smile again; she was playing her part perfectly, even if fate had assisted with the raid. "Do you think I'd make a sharpshooter, Salim?"

"Anyone can learn to fire a weapon accurately. Whether one can fire that same weapon to take life is another matter. There, conscience and determination come to the fore."

"Could you?"

"You saw me just now, didn't you?" Maazi asked in return, referring to his work at the machine-gun emplacement.

"And what about you?" Samantha turned on Reynard. "Could you fire a gun to kill?" She did not understand why she was trying to antagonize the Frenchman. Was it because of her disappointment the previous night when he had allowed himself to be the butt of Maazi's cynical humor? Or perhaps because she could not help but notice the difference between Maazi's cool, commanding presence and Reynard's subsidiary, almost inconsequential role?

Reynard did not get the opportunity to answer. Maazi broke in with a loud laugh. "Pierre? Fire a gun? My friend Pierre fashions bullets from his typewriter keys. Unfortunately, those bullets cannot bring down a plane."

As the all clear sounded across the camp, Rima Bakri emerged from the school and joined the group. The children spilled out behind her, gazing around in frightened fascination at the chaos.

"Is everything all right, Rima?" Maazi asked.

"See for yourself." Tight-faced and trembling slightly, Rima led Maazi and the others into the school. Jagged holes were torn through the roof and one wall; desks were shattered by cannon fire; wood splinters littered the floor like sawdust. The floodlights had been smashed to powder. Samantha felt herself shivering as she surveyed the damage and pictured for an instant the same thing happening to her son's classroom. Only vaguely was she aware of the cameraman who had followed them into the building and was now opening his lens wide to compensate for the gloom.

"Did the Israelis know this was a school populated by young children?" Samantha asked.

"What would they care?" Rima shot back. She was crying openly now, tears rolling down her cheeks to fall unchecked onto the shirt of her uniform. "All the Israelis are interested in is that this is a building which Palestinians use. Therefore, in their eyes, it is a legitimate target."

Samantha nodded numbly, unable to rid herself of the image she had created moments earlier. David! If something like that had happened to David! Christ—she wanted to scream. But at the back of her mind grew the indisputable knowledge that if Yussuf Torbuk had not fired the missile from the vicinity of the school, the pilot of the second Phantom would never have chosen the area of the building as his target. It was not the Israelis who didn't give a damn who got hurt—it was the bloody Palestinians!

"Today you have become a hero from the Palestinian cause," Maazi remarked. His voice was gentle and he laid a reassuring hand on her shoulder as if he understood her fears about her son. "Now you can stand side by side with Rima."

Samantha managed a wan smile at the compliment. She looked at Rima and thought she saw an expression of anger flicker quickly across the Palestinian woman's face. Was it jealousy that mixed with the tears?

"Is this the front-page story that you're willing to risk your neck for?" Tayfield asked Reynard.

"And what a front-page story," Reynard replied, grinning. "The only thing that could have made it better was for Samantha to have hit that damned plane." He left the school and jogged toward the hut where he was billeted, eager to reach his typewriter.

"Thank God she didn't get hold of a damned missile launcher!" General Benjamin Avivi exclaimed angrily to Joel Rosen two days later as they sat looking at newspapers carrying Reynard's account of the Israeli attack on Rashidieh. "Will you look at these pictures?" He jammed a finger at the stills made from the cameraman's movie reel. "Look at her face! The determination there! She wanted to hit that Phantom more than anything else in the world!"

"She's an actress, what do you expect her to look like?"

"Do me a favor, Joel. There are no actresses in air raids. Only the frightened and the furious. Which category does she look like she belongs to?"

"Whose damned idea was it to have the attack just then?"

Avivi glared at Rosen. "If you'd reported that she was at Rashidieh, we could have stopped the Heyl Ha'avir from hitting the camp."

"I didn't know she was there. I just knew she was in Lebanon, that's all." Rosen stood up and began to pace around Avivi's office in the Kiria. "The instructions I gave our people were not to contact us until they had a definite lead on what was being planned. They were not to risk exposure just to call in their itinerary. Anyway, if you want my opinion, the whole damned episode was a set-up. We were set up and so were Samantha and Tayfield."

"How do you mean?" Avivi asked.

"Since when do the *fedayeen* go around carrying documents to indicate their home base?"

"A double bluff," Avivi mused.

"That's right, a double bluff. We get to show everyone that at least two guerrillas operate out of Rashidieh, and they get this!" Rosen picked up one of the newspapers, rolled it tightly and brandished it like a club. "Every goddamned newspaper in the world, every goddamned television station—all showing poor Samantha Sutcliffe in danger as the wicked Israelis bomb the living shit out of her. Those bastards set a trap for us. Who knows—they might even have sacrificed those two *fedayeen* as the finishing touch."

"Is special operations slipping a little, Joel?"

"Not while I'm running it. Just wait a minute and think. They might have overreached themselves with this. Fine—they got their publicity, their precious propaganda. But the way Samantha picked up that rifle and squeezed off a few rounds at the plane—"

"And fell flat on her lovely English ass doing it."

"It doesn't matter what position she finished up in. The important thing is that her cover has been strengthened a thousandfold by the raid and her behavior during it."

"And her life was placed at tremendous risk, not to mention the danger posed to Tayfield with his particular problem," Avivi countered. "The prime minister was going through the roof when I spoke to him earlier."

"That was not our fault."

"Of course it was our fault, Joel! Even if the woman gets injured or— God forbid—killed in a legitimate automobile accident while she's in Lebanon, it's our fault. Because we sent her there. You!" he jabbed an accusing finger at Rosen. "You sent her there. She's your responsibility."

No matter what arguments he could muster, what rationalizations he could make in his own defense, Rosen knew the *memuneh* was right. Whatever happened to Samantha in Lebanon would rest with him, and he would have to accept it.

131

When Samantha left Rashidieh after spending three days in the refugee camp, she was sent off with a hero's accolade. A line of cheering commandos hoisted rifles into the air and fired off salutory shots as she and Tayfield were driven from the camp by Salim Maazi. Following the white Mercedes was a closed jeep containing Torbuk, el-Shafri and two other heavily armed Palestinians. They were going north, first to Beirut where Samantha would be presented to Palestinian leaders, and then on to the refugee camp at Nahr al-Bard where the filming would continue.

"See, you came to Rashidieh as a mere actress, yet you leave as a queen of all the people," Maazi remarked to Samantha, who sat next to him in the front of the Mercedes. After the air raid, buoyed up by her own high popularity among the Palestinians, Samantha had discarded her designer jeans for a commando's uniform, complete with the red beret which she wore pinned to her long hair. Maazi never missed an opportunity to compliment her on the new look.

"Do I have the Israelis to thank for choreographing my coronation? Should I send them a note of gratitude?" She looked at the row of faces which grinned at the passing car, the rifles brandished in her honor. All this energy expended—and for what? For hate. It was a mob scene, men and women whose emotions were manipulated to fever pitch, and Samantha was frightened by it.

Maazi laughed delightedly at her questions. "I doubt if they would be able to appreciate your gratitude."

"Graditude for what? For almost being killed?" asked Tayfield, sitting alone in the rear of the Mercedes. "Samantha came to this country to help your cause, and you pay her back by placing both our lives in peril. As far as I'm concerned, you can drop us both off at the airport when we reach Beirut. I've had enough of your crap!"

Samantha was uncertain whether Tayfield was putting on an act or whether his rage was genuine. "Alan, I wasn't hurt," she said, turning around to look at Tayfield. "No harm came from it."

"Hurt!" She was responding marvelously, he thought. Tayfield had no reason to ingratiate himself with Maazi—the Palestinian regarded him as a crusty pest who was only in Lebanon at Samantha's insistence—but it was crucial that Samantha continued to court Maazi's favor. "You could have been killed! Especially when that baby-faced lunatic Torbuk fired off that missile."

"Yussuf would not like to hear himself called that," Maazi said in a warning tone.

"No? He hides behind children—takes cover behind their school—to make war. What would you call him?"

"That was an accident. Contrary to what the Israelis claim, we do not fight in that fashion. Yussuf happened to be in that spot when the aircraft came within range. Believe me, our children are the legacy we will leave to the world. We would not place them in danger deliberately."

"I believe you," Samantha said, remembering how Rima Bakri had shepherded the children into the bomb shelter at the first sound of the siren, and the tears that had rolled down her cheeks after the raid.

"Is there any danger of more raids?" Tayfield asked.

"There will be no trouble at Nahr al-Bard, I promise you," Maazi replied. He glanced at Samantha and wondered whether she would stay on if Tayfield left. She had come this far; surely she was no longer tied so strongly to her manager. Maazi wished that Tayfield would leave. The little man annoyed him with his constant surliness.

Tayfield sat back, apparently mollified by Maazi's pledge. He knew of Nahr al-Bard, "Cold River." Eight miles north of Tripoli on the main highway to Syria, the camp had once been the main headquarters of the Popular Front for the Liberation of Palestine and the Popular Democratic Front. Attacked frequently by Israeli aircraft, the camp had suffered a devastating blow as a military base in 1973 when Israeli troops had staged a seaborne invasion to capture and take back leading guerrillas for trial in Israel.

"Where is Pierre?" Samantha asked. "Isn't he accompanying us to Beirut and then on to Nahr al-Bard?" Reynard had maintained his aloofness, after his initial greeting, and Samantha, despite her disappointment in discovering his passive side, still nursed some affection for him.

"Do you miss our French friend?"

"I'm just used to having him around, I guess."

"Like a familiar piece of furniture, eh?" Maazi laughed. "Pierre will meet us in Beirut. He left Rashidieh very early this morning to visit some villages. He is a journalist and therefore considers himself a free spirit, unrestrained by the disciplines of a soldier."

Samantha mulled over the answer before asking, "You're not very fond of Pierre, are you? You capitalize on his influence, yet you dislike him. Why?"

Maazi glanced in the mirror at Tayfield who appeared to have fallen asleep, head against the door, eyes closed, lips trembling slightly as he breathed. Beyond Tayfield, through the rear window, Maazi could see the

133

jeep following closely. "Samantha, before Rashidieh I thought that you and Pierre were very similar. Indeed, it would not have surprised me in the least to find out that you were attracted to each other. I would have been disappointed, perhaps, but not surprised. You both supported us with words. Pierre writes them; you speak them. But in Rashidieh, when you picked up that rifle from the dead man and fired at the Israeli plane, you crossed the bridge from words to action. I think that deep down Pierre also wants to cross that bridge, but he lacks your courage."

"It wasn't courage that made me grab that rifle, it was anger."

"Believe me, Samantha, it was courage as well. I understand these things."

"But Pierre tried to drag me to safety. I heard his voice yelling, felt his hands pull me upright."

"So in panic he tried to save you as well as himself. I was half-right—he is attracted to you although you do not find him appealing."

Samantha returned Maazi's querying stare. She wondered whether Maazi was testing her. "No, I don't," she finally answered.

"I didn't think so," Maazi said. He knew the kind of men who would appeal to Samantha—men of action, such as himself. She had once been an athlete, a woman who stretched her body to the limits to achieve a goal. When she sought a man, she would undoubtedly look for similar qualities. He decided to press his advantage.

"Reynard is a parasite. He uses our struggle, our bravery, to carve a name for himself. By witnessing what we do, describing it, he might even believe that he possesses our strength. But I find him useful. He reminds the outside world of our plight. Occasionally he even conjures up a good idea, although it might need someone with real blood in his veins to see it through."

"Such as?"

"You, for instance. Recruiting you for a documentary was Reynard's idea. Probably his best."

"So I was recruited, was I?" Samantha feigned offense. "And all this time I thought I had volunteered. Tell me something, Salim. What is Rima Bakri to you?"

"Rima?" Maazi smiled as he spoke her name. "What would you have her to be?"

"Is she your lover?"

"She has been," Maazi answered, enjoying the turn the conversation was taking. Samantha asking such questions about Rima could only mean that she was evaluating the competition. "No doubt she will be again. Unfortunately our paths do not always cross and we experience long separations."

"Tell me about Rima," Samantha was curious. She remembered what she had thought was jealousy flashing across the Palestinian woman's face.

"One day Rima will go down in Palestinian legend as a saint. She has given everything for us, her husband and two sons, and still she believes that she has not given enough. Like me, she is prepared to sacrifice her own life for our ultimate victory."

"Will you eventually marry her?"

"That is not something to think about at the present time. Marriage is a luxury soldiers cannot afford in time of war."

"What about an information officer then? Can he afford to think about marriage?"

Maazi chuckled at the question. "Perhaps one day, Samantha, I will tell you the real reason that a soldier of *Filastin* worked as an information officer." He removed his right hand from the steering wheel and rested it gently on Samantha's thigh. This time, unlike the episode at the farm, she did not resist. Forcing down her own hatred for Maazi, she placed her hand over his.

Steering with just one hand, Maazi relaxed completely. He felt totally at one with the world, sharing the car with this elegant English actress who had adapted so swiftly to his ideals. Now if only that Russian pig Vlasov would bring final news of the American treachery—then Maazi's contentment would be complete.

Only when Maazi noticed Tayfield's open eyes staring at him in the mirror did he replace his right hand on the steering wheel. He had to get Tayfield out of the way so that he could be truly alone with Samantha. He decided to give Reynard the task of sidetracking Tayfield. The two men hated each other like poison; it would be amusing to force them on each other.

And it would be even more entertaining to use Reynard, who, Maazi knew, wanted so much to be with Samantha, to create the privacy for Maazi to enjoy her.

Maazi could not remember the last time he had seen the chairman of the Palestine Liberation Organization in such high spirits. Yasir Arafat practically danced around Samantha when she was introduced to him, complimenting her upon her bravery under fire and her worthy decision

135

to participate actively in the battle. The chairman insisted on having his photograph taken with her at least a dozen times, and he gave Reynard garrulous statements in English, French and Arabic about Samantha's courage, to be used in the Frenchman's article.

While all this was taking place, Tayfield stood off to one side, underneath a photograph of Iran's Ayatollah Khomeini, memorizing every detail of the meeting. They were on the second floor of a building on the Rue de Ghazir in the western section of Beirut, close to the American University. Tayfield doubted that the small apartment was Arafat's permanent headquarters—probably just a safe house. Undoubtedly the chairman had many, constantly moving from one to another to outwit those he believed would harm him. And he most certainly numbers us at the top of that list, Tayfield decided wryly. He should only know that he has a Mossad man standing just five yards from him.

"Alan! Come over here!" Samantha called out. "Let's have a group picture, something that we can hang up at home!"

Feeling foolish, Tayfield ambled over. Samantha was throwing herself body and soul into the charade, and he wondered what kind of an emotional hangover she would have when Operation Asher was over and she had the time to reflect upon her deeds.

The chairman of the Palestine Liberation Organization stood between Samantha and Tayfield, his arms around their shoulders. Tayfield grinned blankly into the camera; the only thought that came to his mind was that someone in the group did not use a deodorant often enough. It was not himself, and it certainly was not Samantha. Mentally he ticked off another reason to loathe Arafat. He tried to think of something else. His family in Petah Tiqva came to mind. What would be their reaction if they ever saw this photograph?

All too late he realized that this picture might just be the one which newspapers would pick up—actress and manager with the chairman of the PLO. Certainly the Arab newspapers might use it. He tried to disengage himself from the group but he was not quick enough. The flash popped and his image was frozen onto the film with Samantha and Arafat. Then Tayfield's plastic smile for the camera turned genuine as he realized his fears were groundless. This was his last mission. Even if his heart was not bad, the Mossad would have no further use for a field agent known in Israel whose picture had been taken with Arafat. Tayfield suddenly decided to ask for a copy of the photograph to hang in his study at home.

Hell—he would even get Arafat to autograph it just to prove it was not a fake.

A final picture remained to be taken. From a small silk-lined box Arafat took a silver medal on a red and green ribbon. "For you," he said to Samantha. He draped the ribbon around her neck and stood back while the flash popped again. Samantha glanced down. In Arabic and English was the inscription: Hero of the Palestinian People. She wondered if the medal had been struck especially for her.

After the final picture the chairman left the apartment surrounded by a contingent of guards. A minute later the sound of car and motorcycle engines drifted up to the street.

"Congratulations," Maazi said as he inspected the medal.

While Reynard stared at the medal admiringly, Tayfield looked into Samantha's eyes. They were like two orbs of shining blue glass and he understood how much she wanted to rip the medal from her neck and fling it to the floor. Maybe when this was all over, she would get it melted down and donate the silver to an orphans' fund in Israel.

Maazi drew Samantha aside, out of earshot of the others. "I think that tonight we should celebrate your commendation. Lebanon has much Western civilization that you might appreciate."

"I wouldn't mind a break," she replied honestly, not even caring that it was Maazi who was offering the diversion. "What do you have in mind?"

"The Casino du Liban in Maameltein. Reynard and Tayfield can continue on together to Nahr al-Bard and we'll catch up with them later."

Alone with Maazi? Samantha's eager anticipation of a brief vacation from all this detestable madness changed abruptly to anxiety. Would she be able to handle it? It would be hard to get out of it now. She fingered the medal while she forced herself to face what might lie ahead. "I can't go looking like this."

"No," Maazi agreed. "You most certainly cannot. The people who control that section of the country around Maameltein do not regard these uniforms with love. Do you have other clothes, apart from jeans?"

"One dress and one pair of high-heeled shoes."

"I'm certain you'll look delightful in them." He swung around, spotted Reynard and called him over. "You will accompany Mr. Tayfield to Nahr al-Bard. Take Ahmed, Yussuf and the others with you. Samantha and I will rejoin you tomorrow."

Reynard started visibly at the order before looking curiously at Samantha. She held his gaze for a moment; then she looked down at the medal and ignored his attempt at communication. Was he perhaps a bit jealous now? Or would he be content to allow Maazi to command here too? At any rate there seemed little he could do at this point, no matter what his feelings.

Maazi went downstairs to bring up their luggage from the Mercedes. Using the apartment's one bedroom, Maazi changed first. When he emerged wearing a plain gray suit, white shirt and red patterned tie, Samantha entered the room. Once the door was closed she ripped off the medal and uniform and flung them to the floor. She stared at the discarded uniform with hate, able at last to give vent to her true feelings.

This was not acting a role. This was letting herself sink so low that she questioned whether she would ever be able to regain her self-respect. How could she face David after all that had happened? Embraced by the chairman of the PLO. Awarded a medal that read Hero of the Palestinian People. Propositioned by Maazi . . . was that not what his invitation to the casino had been? It was all part of a seduction routine—the hand on her thigh during the journey from Rashidieh, the visit to the casino, the opportunity to let her hair down in the middle of all this stress. And she had to play along; she understood that. Tayfield was convinced that their key to learning information was Maazi. Samantha had to draw it out of him. But, God!—how could she allow herself to do it?

The moment passed and Samantha recovered her composure. She stepped into the light brown cotton dress, slipped on the high-heeled shoes and made believe she was preparing to go out for the evening. Trying to insulate herself from the task at hand, she began to fantasize. Who would make a wonderful beau for an enjoyable evening? Pierre Reynard's name came reluctantly to mind. She recalled that night in the farmhouse and tried to equate the Frenchman with the man who let himself be abused by Maazi. He was like two characters in one. Schizophrenic—she came up with the word she wanted. Out of Maazi's shadow he was his own man, charming, sensitive, yet strong and definite in all his actions. But with the Palestinian . . .

She gave up trying to form a suitable comparison. Instead she decided to make believe she was going out with Asher. It would not be Maazi who kept her company that night; it would be Asher.

As dusk fell Maazi and Samantha traveled in the Mercedes along the coastal road north of Beirut. Beyond Jounieh, Maazi pointed to the battery of bright lights which lay directly ahead, shining onto the sea.

"That cliff on which the casino stands—Lebanese legend has it that the gods lived there once."

"Don't they live there anymore?"

"Only the God of Luck, and then just for a select few."

"Are you one of them?"

Maazi tapped the steering wheel with the heel of his hand, keeping time with the music from the radio. "I think that tonight I shall be. My English rose will bring me good fortune. Which day of the month is your birthday?"

"The eleventh."

"Then eleven black it shall be."

Outside the casino he parked the Mercedes and locked the doors, but not before depositing the fully loaded Beretta in the trunk. Samantha recalled once seeing a film where a distraught gambler had left a casino after losing all his money and had then shot himself. The thought of Maazi doing the same brightened Samantha's mood immeasurably.

Inside the casino Maazi went to the cashier's window and changed a check drawn on a Zurich bank for ten thousand dollars. Then he stood at one of the roulette tables, keenly observing the run of play.

"You're going to risk all of that on my birthday?" Samantha asked.

"It's the only certain way to find out whether you were born under a lucky star." After he had watched for ten minutes, Maazi started to place his bets. Samantha stood next to him, trying to feign interest. This was not her idea of relaxation. The gambling did not last long, though. Within six spins of the wheel, Maazi was down to his last five hundred dollars. He placed it on the "evens" square. When twenty-three red came up, he muttered *"C'est la vie"* for the benefit of those watching, took Samantha's hand and led her from the gaming tables to the Salles des Ambassadeurs, where the floor show was shortly to start.

Samantha sat down with a drink, and for the first time that evening she started to enjoy herself. She divorced her mind from Maazi's presence and concentrated solely on the extravagant entertainment. The quality of the show, the stage machinery and technology were equal to, if not better than, anything she had ever seen in Europe, and she applauded each turn enthusiastically. And at the same time she questioned how all this could be happening in a country beset by war.

Schizophrenic—the word she had used to describe Pierre Reynard came to mind again. Lebanon was also schizophrenic, she decided philosophically after her fourth drink. Had she had four drinks already? Maybe a good psychiatrist could help the country. Yes, that was it—group therapy on a gargantuan scale.

"Show's over," Maazi said softly as he caught Samantha deep in thought. For a moment he had believed she was asleep.

"I'm sorry. I was somewhere else."

"Shall we dance?"

She allowed him to lead her to the Baccarat nightclub, melting into his arms as he held her tightly on the dance floor. The music was slow, soulful. Other couples brushed past but Samantha did not seem to notice them. Now she understood why she had drunk so much. The alcohol took her mind out of her body, made it easier for her to believe that she had turned back the clock and was in Asher's arms.

Only once had she ever danced with Asher, one night in Brussels when they had decided to risk being seen together. They had gone to a workmen's bar near the railway station where the music had been provided by a juke box into which they had fed francs for two hours while the bar's other patrons had good-naturedly cheered them on. And when their supply of francs had eventually been depleted, Asher had been too embarrassed to let her go, frightened that the telltale bulge in his trousers would be seen by the bar's customers.

Samantha could feel that erection now. Only it was not Asher's. It was Maazi's erection pressing into her stomach as he clung tightly. She felt his warm breath on her neck and she wanted the music to stop. The drinks no longer helped. She could not—would not—dream anymore. "Let's sit down, please," she whispered. "I feel tired."

"By all means." Maazi pulled his jacket straight to conceal the swelling and followed Samantha to an empty table. "Would you like another drink?"

"Yes, please." That was what she needed, more alcohol to rekindle the numbness.

A shadow loomed threateningly across the table. Maazi and Samantha looked up simultaneously. Two men in tuxedoes stood there. One was in his fifties, gray-haired, a lined face; the other much younger, like father and son. Maazi tensed.

"Miss Sutcliffe, we would appreciate it if you and your escort would leave," the older man said in perfect English.

"Leave? Why?"

"We do not like your company. We do not like being in the same building with you. The sight of you spoils our evening."

"Just wait a minute—" Maazi cut in.

"That is precisely what you have. One minute. Otherwise we will gladly assist you to leave." Without another word, the two men walked away.

"Who were they?" Samantha asked slowly, trying to understand what had just happened. Why would two perfect strangers demand that she leave?

"Phalangists," Maazi answered simply.

"Was it because of me? Those pictures in the paper?"

"Perhaps. And perhaps it was not so wise to come here after all. It's like spitting in their faces and seeing what they'll do. We'll leave."

"We will?" Samantha gasped without realizing what she was saying. "You'll run away from them?"

"Would you prefer to stay?" Maazi asked with a cynical smile. "So that we may both be beaten to a pulp or shot?"

Samantha's next words wiped the vaguely amused expression from the Palestinian's face. "What's the matter, Salim? Don't you fight when there are no small children to hide behind?" The drinks had gotten to her more than she had realized. They had lowered her guard completely. Her real thoughts were spilling out, Christ help her!

Maazi's swarthy face turned to rock. He grabbed Samantha by the wrist, jerked her roughly to her feet and dragged her from the nightclub. "Don't you ever dare say anything like that to me again!"

"I'm sorry," she gasped as she tried to keep pace with his rapid exit from the nightclub. His grip hurt, her arm felt like it was being pulled from her shoulder. "I'm sorry—it's just that I—I expected you to stand up to them."

"Do you think I am a coward like Pierre Reynard?" he shot back. "Is that what you believe? That I hide behind words like him?"

"No—no, of course not." She began to cry, in confusion. What the hell was the matter with her? Why was she acting like this? The whole veneer she had labored so carefully to build up was starting to crumble.

"Get in the car!" Maazi yanked open the passenger door of the Mercedes and flung Samantha into the vehicle. He opened the trunk to retrieve the Beretta submachine gun and climbed into the driver's seat.

"Salim, I'm sorry. I didn't mean what I said back there."

Maazi said nothing. He placed the Beretta under his seat, started the car and got back onto the coastal road, driving north. Less than five

141

minutes later, he pulled off the road, killed the engine and cut the lights. When he turned to her, the hardness had left his face. "I apologize for my actions before," he said softly as he rubbed his fingers gently against her cheek, "but my pride will not allow me to be called a coward; can you understand that?"

"Yes, I can," Samantha replied, having used the short journey to regain some control over her emotions. She could handle the situation now.

"I ran only because it was wise to do so, not because I am a coward. This area is a Phalangist stronghold. I do not wish to give up my life foolishly." His fingers began to comb through her hair, his face moved closer.

"Is it wise to stay here now?" Samantha asked, trying to put off what she recognized as inevitable. Here, in this Mercedes, Maazi would take her—and if she wanted to help Tayfield, if she wanted revenge on the people who had murdered Asher Davidson, she would have to submit. Not only submit, but act as if she were enjoying it.

"We are no longer in the nightclub. On the road we are just a man and a woman looking at the nighttime Mediterranean." He pressed his lips against hers, started to probe with the tip of his tongue.

She forced herself to relax—pictured herself with Asher—once more with Asher.

And then the driver's door opened silently on well-oiled hinges and a man's voice said, "Filthy Palestinian pig."

Maazi and Samantha froze. Samantha gazed wide-eyed over the Palestinian's shoulder to see the two men from the nightclub, the white shirts contrasting so vividly with the black tuxedoes. Then a gasp of terror escaped from her lips when she saw the pistol clutched in the hand of the older man.

"Filthy Palestinian pig," the older man said again as his finger tightened imperceptibly on the trigger, and in the fraction of time it took him to utter those three words Maazi dived to the floor of the car, snatched the Beretta from underneath the seat and, in one fluid motion, threw it up and squeezed the trigger.

The inside of the Mercedes exploded with ear-shattering noise. Glass splintered and metal buckled as the wild spray of 9-millimeter bullets gouged into the door and window. The man with the pistol staggered back as bright red stains blossomed grotesquely across the front of his pristine white shirt. The younger man turned and ran blindly toward a large American car parked fifty yards behind the Mercedes. Maazi jumped to the ground and squeezed off another burst, hitting the younger man squarely in the back. He sprawled on the road, twitching spasmodically.

Samantha screamed. Dropping the Beretta onto the floor of the car, Maazi slapped her across the face, then held her head close to his chest. "It's all right, it's all right." When he tried to shut the door, he found it would not fit. Holding the door closed with his left hand, he started the engine, thrust the transmission into drive and steered with his right hand. Beside him Samantha shivered uncontrollably.

"Get hold of yourself," Maazi kept repeating while he concentrated simultaneously on driving and keeping the door closed. "Get hold of yourself."

Slowly Samantha settled down. When she looked at Maazi, she saw a savage expression on his face. His mouth was a thin line curving upward as if a grin were cemented there. His eyes were gleaming. Was this what killing did for him? Would it do the same for her when the time came?

South of Tripoli he pulled off the road again. "How do you feel?"

"I'll be a lot better when I've had the chance to clean up." The look on his face scared her. His eyes still shone and he was sweating. With a sickening feeling she realized that killing those two men had stimulated him sexually. She had insulted his manhood earlier when he had retreated from the Phalangists' threat. Now he would show her what kind of man he really was.

Without warning he thrust himself on her, smothering her face, driving open her mouth with his tongue. The back of the seat went down as Maazi feverishly worked the control. His hand ripped at her dress and she thought wildly that he possessed none of Reynard's gentleness. Maazi's approach to sex was a reflection of the man himself. Hard, domineering, conquering. A soldier's approach, the direct lunge. She was grateful that enough alcohol remained in her bloodstream to deaden the loathsome sensation, as Maazi drove roughly into her.

But the sensation of Maazi filling her sobered Samantha completely. She wanted to fight against him, to claw at his face, anything to drive him off. It was hateful, detestable, being made love to by a man who had helped to kill Asher. Yet there was nothing she could do about it. She had known this was going to happen. She had drunk to fortify herself. But— God!—to know that she was being used by a man who had heightened his sexual desire by slaughter!

She heard Maazi cry out as he reached orgasm quickly, and Samantha felt relieved that she had experienced no sensation whatsoever. Nothing.

It was as though she had been injected with Novocain. She lay back, eyes closed, senses numb, as Maazi slid off her. He adjusted his clothes. Only when he started the engine did she sit up and straighten her dress.

They reached Nahr al-Bard just after three. Reynard was awake and he rushed out of a hut at the sound of the Mercedes' engine. He saw the damage to the car but made no comment. Nor did he say anything about Samantha's disheveled appearance.

And Samantha forgot all about Maazi making love to her—all about the experience at Maameltein—when Reynard blurted out that Tayfield had been taken ill.

CHAPTER
ELEVEN

"**F**OR crying out loud, I keep telling this quack that there's nothing wrong with me, but he won't listen!" Tayfield protested vehemently to Samantha when she visited him in the clinic at Nahr al-Bard. "He's trying to make a big case out of nothing; probably wants to pad his bill."

Samantha looked at the white-clad Palestinian doctor who stood by Tayfield's bed. "Well?"

The doctor, a bald man with a thick moustache, gave his answer, not to Samantha, but to Tayfield. "If you consider angina pectoris to be nothing wrong, Mr. Tayfield, then you are in excellent physical health."

"Angina? The hell I have! I had a complete physical examination only a few weeks ago. The doctor went over me from head to foot. He would have noticed something like angina," Tayfield lied. More than anything, he did not want Samantha to know how ill he really was. Additionally he was frightened that the Palestinians would insist that he return to England. If he had risked this much, he certainly was not going to quit now.

"Where did you have this physical examination?" the doctor asked.

"In London. Harley Street, where else? I have one every year."

"Harley Street, eh? Then I would respectfully suggest that you have managed to locate the one fool there," the Palestinian remarked acidly. "Any doctor who pronounced you physically fit during the past year is criminally negligent. Now you'd better get some rest." The doctor motioned for Samantha to leave, accompanying her to the clinic door.

"How serious is it?" Samantha asked anxiously.

"Angina is always serious, expecially without the correct attitude on the part of the patient—"

"And Alan doesn't have the correct attitude?"

"How would you describe his attitude, Miss Sutcliffe? He claims there is nothing wrong with him, yet while the nurse was undressing him, she found these." The doctor held out the small glass bottle with the label of a British chemist's chain. Inside were tiny white pills. "Nitroglycerin, for angina."

"I see." She stared at the pills, fascinated. How long had he been this ill, and why had he not told her?

"Above all he needs to rest, Miss Sutcliffe. Ideally I would like to have him flown home to England, away from the pressures of this country, but he refuses to leave while you are here."

"Can he continue with the tour, though?" Samantha asked, aware that her reasons for the question were purely selfish. What would she be without Tayfield there to guide and protect her?

The doctor stroked his moustache thoughtfully. "If he doesn't exert himself, I would say yes. But from what I gathered from speaking to Monsieur Reynard, Mr. Tayfield is unhappy about your being here. The air raid at Rashidieh probably brought this attack on. Further aggravation can do him nothing but harm."

"You mean a heart attack."

"Precisely." The doctor turned away to continue his rounds, clutching the bottle of nitroglycerin pills.

Outside the clinic Samantha found Maazi and Reynard waiting. Reynard appeared agitated, constantly moving from one foot to the other, while Maazi was perfectly calm, completely recovered from the incident at Maameltein. Only when Samantha noticed that he was wearing the pale gray suit did she realize that she was still wearing her dress and high-heeled shoes; how out of place they both must seem amidst all this wretched poverty. Suddenly the scene in the Mercedes rushed to her mind. Maazi had made love to her—violent, dramatic love—only moments after the bloody encounter with the two Phalangists. She had forgotten all about his body pressing against her, the foul sensation of his swollen manhood inside her, the sound of his cry as he achieved orgasm. She had let it all be pushed into the nethermost regions of her memory by the discovery that Tayfield—her perilously fragile lifeline to the real world of David and Mrs. Riley and the farm in Somerset—was seriously ill.

"How is he?" Maazi asked.

"He needs to rest." Samantha thought about Tayfield's family in Israel. Sick like this, alone and cut off in a hostile land. His daughter and son-in-law could not even know. She remembered him once mentioning that he had a brother as well, younger by a few years. What if—heaven forbid!—Tayfield died? Who would tell his family—his daughter, his brother—what had really happened? And who—again that selfish question—would guide and care for Samantha?

"Too bad about his being taken ill like this," Reynard said. "But you're not going to let this stop your work, are you? You're willing to carry on with the documentary, surely."

Samantha stared at the Frenchman with wide-eyed disbelief. Was this why he seemed so concerned? Just when she thought he was genuinely worried about Tayfield's health, it turned out that his anxiety was only for the damned documentary! "How can you even think of something like that?" she snapped, momentarily forgetting her own self-centered thoughts. "Alan means more to me than your propaganda—than all of this!" She made a wide sweeping gesture with her hand to encompass the entire camp.

Maazi took her by the arm and led her gently toward a large tent. "Sleep," he said softly. "Get some sleep; you've been through a trying time." He wondered how much of her hysteria was directly attributable to Tayfield's illness and how much was due to the gunfight and the intensity of his own lovemaking. "Your manager will be perfectly all right, believe me. Our medical staff is very competent."

Samantha nodded weakly. "Salim . . ."

"Yes." He held open the tent door for her to enter. Inside was her suitcase which he had taken from the Mercedes.

"The doctor said that the air raid at Rashidieh probably contributed to Alan being taken ill. If we are exposed to any more danger, any more risk, you're going to lose your narrator. I'll walk out on you, do you understand?"

"I will guard you like royalty," he promised. He cupped her chin in his hand, but when he tried to kiss her on the lips she turned aside to present him with her cheek.

Tayfield was up and walking around the camp the following morning, feeling better as he watched the continuation of the filming. In his pocket was the bottle of nitroglycerin tablets the doctor had returned to him, and

Tayfield smiled to himself as he appreciated the irony of the situation—the Palestinians were giving medical treatment to an Israeli agent, keeping him well so that he could work against them. Damn! He *was* going to look after himself carefully. He would not let anything upset him. He would just do his work and make sure that he lived long enough to enjoy looking at that signed photograph of Yasir Arafat and explaining to his family and friends how he had come by it.

"I'm glad to see you up and about, Mr. Tayfield." Maazi appeared next to Tayfield as the Mossad agent sat on a chair watching Samantha describe the work done in the camp's clinic. "How are you feeling?"

"A damned sight better than I did yesterday, that's for sure," Tayfield answered politely as he recalled his resolution.

"You know you were very foolish to hide something like this," Maazi chided him. "Is that your method of proving your manhood, to scorn medical aid and doctors?" Maazi sat down cross-legged on the sand beside Tayfield's chair. "You have to keep well, you realize that, don't you? Samantha would not stay here if she thought it would harm you."

"Really?" Tayfield appeared amused by the Palestinian's claim. "I think you might be selling yourself short there, Maazi."

"Pardon?"

Tayfield continued to watch Samantha as she explained how the clinics in the refugee camps were free to anyone from any background. With the uniform she seemed to really belong. "You've struck a more powerful chord with Samantha than I've ever done."

"Do you really think so?" Maazi gave a brief smile as he thought about the scene in the Mercedes. Watching him kill had sharpened Samantha's senses. Like Reynard she was attracted to the aura of dangerous excitement that surrounded him. Tayfield was correct, of course. Samantha's questions about Rima Bakri showed Maazi all too clearly where the English actress's feelings lay.

"Sure I think so. Your being a soldier doesn't appeal to her as such, but you're fighting for a cause she sympathizes with strongly. And that's what counts."

"And you don't sympathize with us? Even now?"

"I'd be a liar if I said I did. Sorry, Maazi, but you and your cause don't do anything for me. I'm only here for Samantha's sake. Otherwise, a pox on both you and the Israelis because your bloody dirty little war keeps raising the price of my petrol."

"Stay well, Mr. Tayfield," Maazi said as he stood up. For the first time he found himself liking Tayfield, if only for his disarming honesty. "I would not like to see Samantha more worried about you than she is already."

Tayfield watched Maazi walk away. Playing on the Palestinian's vanity was the quickest way to his heart. Now if only Samantha could find out what filth nested there.

That evening Samantha walked slowly with Tayfield around the camp. A couple of times she stopped to play with young children and Tayfield stood by, watching indulgently. Once it crossed his mind that these children might grow up to be the *fedayeen* of the next generation—the Palestinian terrorists his own grandchildren would have to fight. Please God, let this lousy situation be resolved by then, he prayed.

Certain at last that they were by themselves, Samantha told Tayfield exactly what had happened between Beirut and Nahr al-Bard. "It wasn't as though I was there, can you understand that, Alan?" she said, referring to making love with Maazi. "I'd had a few drinks, my defenses were down, I suppose. I had even accused him of backing out of that fight earlier in the nightclub. I asked him if he was afraid to fight when there were no children to hide behind."

Tayfield's first instinct was to tell Samantha that she had suffered—sacrificed—enough, that it was time to pull up stakes and clear out. The feeling must have shown on his face because Samantha shook her head with a slow determination. "I'm not leaving here until I've paid them back for Asher," she said quietly. "I won't leave."

Tayfield nodded in understanding. "Samantha, you've got to keep at him, draw him out, make him talk more about himself. We've been here five days already and we've learned nothing. In another nine days we're due to go home. We can't live in the hope that something will break. We don't have that kind of time. Maazi's one of the keys to this thing, I'm sure of it. We're certain he was tied in to Black September, and if those bastards are making a comeback, he'll be involved."

"I'll find out everything about him," she promised. She tried to force a smile on her face to hide her trepidation from Tayfield. Maazi had said he would see her that evening. The last time the Palestinian had made love to her she had been drunk, almost hysterical. What would it be like —how loathsome would Maazi's touch be—when she was totally sober and horrifyingly aware of his every action?

149

Samantha sat alone in her tent, elbows on her knees, eyes closed, her head rested in her hands. Pictures of David kept flashing into her mind —the sad expression on his face as the Range Rover pulled away at Heathrow Airport, the time he had tracked mud into the farmhouse when Reynard and Maazi had visited, and the hasty, embarrassed way he kissed her good-bye when she drove him to school.

Reluctantly she pushed the thoughts of David and home from her mind. She concentrated hard, seeking from somewhere in her own past the experiences she could capture and use for her next role, that of Salim Maazi's willing lover.

A golden day in Munich appeared, a vast stadium under a strong September sun and a clear blue sky, the phalanx of police officers resplendent in dress blue uniforms, speeches from dignitaries, lowered flags rippling sadly in the gentle breeze. And in the middle of it all, eleven starkly empty chairs to signify the murdered members of the Israeli Olympic team—and a twelfth chair waiting off in the wings for Asher Davidson to die six weeks later.

Samantha had not possessed the courage to visit Israel to see Asher in the hospital. It was an episode in her life that she regretted deeply, hated herself for. She had needed strength of character at that moment and had been unable to find it. By not visiting Asher, she had betrayed their love.

Now she needed that strength again. And this time she would not fail.

Maazi came to the tent shortly after eleven o'clock that night. He stood in the doorway for several seconds, staring at Samantha as he compared her with Rima Bakri back in Rashidieh. In just a few days Samantha seemed to have gained the strength that Rima possessed. Her skin had darkened under the Lebanese sun and she looked perfectly at ease in the guerrilla uniform. Her eyes had also changed; they were a deeper, darker, more sensuous blue. Had it been the air raid that had worked this transformation, the act of enjoying her own righteous fury as she fired at the Israeli Phantom? Or had it been Maameltein, living through that short but dramatically bloody fight with the two Phalangists?

He let the door swing closed and held out his arms toward Samantha. His mouth fastened hungrily on hers, crushed her lips in a brutal, bruising kiss that left her breathless. She turned out the light and led him to the bunk, feeling that she was on a movie set. The man in the tent with her could be any one of a hundred actors, and when she spoke it would be from well-memorized lines. She had to think this way. To fully comprehend what she was really doing might drive her instantly insane.

But when she unfastened his webbed belt and started to slip her hand inside his trousers, Maazi said, "No."

He gripped her hand and Samantha realized that she had made a mistake. The woman did not lead. In Maazi's world, man was superior. Samantha lay back on the bunk, feeling Maazi's hands exploring her body. She closed her eyes, not in ecstasy but to avoid seeing the swarthy face that loomed over her in the dim light that filtered into the tent from outside.

There was no subtlety in Maazi's manner. She had thought that in the privacy of the tent, far removed from the hectic rush of the night in the Mercedes, he would be more caring. He was not. He used her as he would use a prostitute.

"Was I as pleasing as Rima?" she asked.

"Why do you ask about Rima?" Maazi made room on the narrow bunk to lie beside her, staring up at the canvas roof of the tent.

"Because I want to know all about you. And about her."

"Are you envious of Rima?" When Samantha did not answer, Maazi chuckled deeply. "What could a poor Palestinian woman possibly have to arouse such deep jealousy in an English actress who can have whatever she desires?"

Samantha rolled on the bunk until her mouth was close to Maazi's ear. "She has you."

Maazi's chuckle turned to a low, delighted laugh. "You and Rima might have been born thousands of miles apart—in two different worlds —but you are still sisters under the skin. You are both enviously possessive of something you want, but I do not think that your emotions would prompt you to kill as I know Rima's would."

"She would kill for you?"

Maazi turned to face Samantha. His moustache brushed against her face as he kissed her. "Does that frighten you?"

"Of course."

"Would you kill for me, Samantha?"

She ignored the question. "Would Rima kill any woman you looked at?"

"No." Again he laughed as if he found the entire conversation enter-

151

taining. "She would only kill those who looked at me with longing, as you do. Rima understands that a man has needs. But if she thought that a woman was trying to steal me away . . ." Purposely, he left the sentence unfinished.

"Has she killed?"

"Rima is a soldier. Of course she has killed. With Yussuf and Ahmed she has crossed the border into Israel to ambush Israeli soldiers."

Samantha forgot her role-playing for an instant as a shiver coursed through her body. Torbuk and el-Shafri—yes, she could understand that. But Rima? A woman who taught small children, guarded them so lovingly, anguished over the damage done to the school—could that same woman slip across an international border and cold-bloodedly murder? "And you also kill, Salim?"

"You witnessed that for yourself. Remember, Samantha, if it had not been for my actions you would never return to England. Just imagine for a moment—what if it had been Pierre Reynard with you at Maameltein? What do you think would have happened? Would Pierre have had the courage to shoot it out—the skill and determination to emerge victorious against heavy odds and surprise?"

"No," she answered. She was unable to picture Reynard shooting anyone in that manner, responding with the split-second timing of a trained killer. They would both have died in the Mercedes. She ran her fingers through the thick mat of black hair covering Maazi's chest. "What do you think about when you kill, Salim? What do you feel?"

"Why do you want to know?"

"I'm curious, that's all. I'm trying to understand you."

"I feel a joy," he answered. "A savage joy that rips right through me because in that moment I am almost a god. Perhaps I cannot create life, but I can destroy it."

"How many people have you killed?" She felt his hand slide between her legs and knew that killing excited him; even the talk of killing excited him.

"I have killed many times," he replied quietly. "And in many different ways."

"Even as—as an information officer?"

"So, you bring up that subject again?"

"I knew there was more to you when you came with Pierre to my farm. You just didn't strike me as a public relations man trying to promote a product."

Maazi was flattered, as Samantha had intended him to be. "I was playing a role," he explained. "You should be able to appreciate that. But it was a role that had been forced upon me far too long."

"Go on." She squeezed his hands encouragingly with her thighs, massaged his chest, traced patterns across his stomach with her fingernails. This time he did not reject her advances. Slowly he became erect, and as he grew stronger, the words came more easily.

"The Israelis had wiped out many of my associates. It was time to be a chameleon, to pretend to be a meek little man who would grow old behind a desk."

"Associates?"

He took her hand and guided it down. "Does the name of Black September strike terror into you as it once did to the entire world?"

"No." She forced out the single word. Mention of Black September did not strike terror into her; it created loathing.

"Why not?" Maazi failed to hide his disappointment at Samantha's answer.

"Because I know you, Salim. I am not your enemy. I don't think you'd harm me."

"But Rima would if she could see you at this moment."

"Rima, too, was in Black September?"

"And Yussuf, and Ahmed. There are many of us. The Israelis believe we have disappeared—they want to believe that—and all the time we have just been hiding, waiting to rise again and cover the world with a cleansing flame."

From somewhere deep within herself, Samantha found the courage to laugh. "I don't know whether to believe you or not."

Maazi found nothing amusing. "Samantha, to call me a liar is as hateful to my ears as being called a coward."

"I'm sorry, it's just that to a woman from a small, peaceful English village all this seems so unreal. It just doesn't seem possible."

"Well, woman from a small, peaceful English village"—Maazi smiled at Samantha's description of herself—"do you remember ten years ago when the letter bombs started to arrive at the homes and businesses of prominent Zionist sympathizers in Britain and Europe?"

Samantha reached back into her memory and recalled the flood of X-ray machines that had been installed by large corporations to check their mail. "Was that you?"

"I helped to organize it." Maazi hesitated, "And a close friend of mine

153

organized one of our finest moments of bravery, one which you witnessed."

"Munich?"

"Munich," Maazi repeated. "You cried at the memorial service for the Israelis, but you were also crying for my comrades."

"Pierre! Did he tell you I said that?" How could Reynard have gossiped about their conversation that night?

"He told me everything you said that night. Those were the instructions I gave him."

A lackey, that's all Reynard was; even his loving had probably been part of a plan. The strength he showed in his writing was nothing more than a pretense, a cover-up behind which he hid. "Will I meet your friend?"

"Unfortunately, no. Ali Hassan Salameh was murdered by the Israelis in Beirut three years ago. The pigs from their Mossad fixed a transmitter to his car. When he drove by a parked Volkswagen loaded with explosives, the transmitter set them off. Thirteen people died. Soon the Israelis will pay for that atrocity."

Atrocity! Samantha reeled in shock at his use of the word. And what your friend did in Munich was not an atrocity? Slaying innocent athletes to promote your own murderous cause. Had his friend been alone? Or was Maazi protecting himself? Was it caution holding him back from admitting his own role in Munich? Tayfield and the Mossad believed he had been involved. So, too, did Samantha.

When Maazi opened the tent door just before dawn, Samantha asked sleepily where he was going. "To Beirut," he replied. "I will return tomorrow, and then we shall move back to the southern camps."

"Be careful," she whispered, while she wondered if he remembered anything of what he had told her the previous night.

"I am always careful. Act well today and gain many new friends for our struggle, woman from a small and peaceful English village."

Samantha lay back on the pillow. The scene was over at last and she could allow revulsion to run unchecked through her entire being. Her body was soiled by Maazi's touch, his scent, his essence. She should rise and bathe, rid herself of the stink of the Palestinian. But she was too exhausted to move. She had just performed the most powerful scene of her life. Her muscles ached intolerably as if she had swum four dozen lengths.

Would she ever swim again? she asked herself. Would she ever leave this stinking hellhole and enjoy the tranquility of a beach in Devon or Cornwall, where Israeli aircraft did not streak overhead?

As her strength returned, she climbed off the bunk and walked barefooted around the tent. First she would bathe, and then, when she was rid of Maazi's loathsome touch, she would tell Tayfield all she had learned. He would find a way to relay the information to Tel Aviv.

Salim Maazi sat at a table in the apartment on the Rue Ayoub Tabet. Facing him were Fatah operations chief Doctor Mohammed Nasser and Pavel Vlasov. Two young commandos with rifles guarded the apartment door.

"The American treachery is complete," Nasser said. "With the assistance of our loyal Arab brethren, the United States has stabbed the Palestinians in the back once too often."

Maazi looked at Vlasov; he was just in time to catch the KGB officer picking his nose. Quickly Vlasov pulled his hand down to his lap. "Shea's work is done," Vlasov said. "He met with the Saudis for the final time two days ago. They instructed him to inform the American government that they accept Shea's proposals."

"Which were?"

"For the Saudis, Jordanians, Egyptians and Israelis to meet at a delegate level. Once a firm basis for negotiations has been established, top-level meetings could conceivably take place."

"I wish I knew how you gathered your information, Vlasov," Maazi said.

"I told you once before; it's none of your business."

"I just want to know how trustworthy it is."

"It is reliable information."

"What other details do you have?" Nasser cut in quickly, anxious to stop what he considered Maazi's unnecessary baiting of the Russian.

"The summit meeting will take place at an American military establishment somewhere in Europe," Vlasov answered. "The exact location has yet to be decided upon."

"Why Europe?" Maazi was puzzled. "And why a military base?" It made no sense to him; why did the Americans not simply fly all the delegates into Washington?

"Obviously a neutral country is required. And because these sensitive negotiations are being held in such high secrecy, except, of course, that we know"—Vlasov's face widened in a grin—"a military base would make it relatively simple for the Americans to establish security without appearing to be doing anything out of the ordinary."

Now Maazi understood. Very clever, he thought; he had never credited the Americans with possessing that much subtlety. A thousand rifles and machine guns, and no one would be any the wiser. "What about a date?"

"The final week of May has been put forward. Just a few weeks from now. You will have to work quickly."

"We will, once you let us know where the meeting will be held."

"I'll let you know in good time," Vlasov assured him. "There is one more thing, a small repayment for the services we have given you."

"What?" Maazi and Nasser asked together.

"No matter what happens to the delegates—and personally, we couldn't care less how you dispose of them—Robert Shea, the American negotiator, is to be killed," Vlasov said. "Do you understand me? Robert Shea is to be eliminated."

"Eliminated," Maazi repeated, suddenly smiling. "Why?"

Vlasov got up from the chair and pulled his sweat-soaked jacket away from his back. "In Moscow we value the Palestinians as men of action. Do not make the perilous mistake of trying to think for yourselves. You're not very good at it." He walked away slowly to the door, waited for one of the guards to open it for him and descended the stairs to the street. A Fiat awaited him, driven by another Russian. Vlasov got into the back seat and the driver pulled away, heading toward the Russian embassy on the Rue Mar Elias B'Tina.

Less than two hundred yards away, Hunovi rewound the film in a Nikon camera, opened the back and popped the exposed roll into his pocket. He straightened up and stretched his arms, feeling sore after crouching over the tripod-mounted camera with its 500-millimeter lens for more than three hours. From the secure shadows of a third-floor apartment which was rented permanently in the name of one of the Mossad's agents in Beirut—just as the Mossad maintained surveillance posts near all known Fatah safe houses—Hunovi had gone through four rolls of film, catching everyone entering and leaving the building from which the stout man with the short blond hair and bulging brown eyes had just emerged. Through the viewfinder, Hunovi had recognized some of his subjects—Salim Maazi and Dr. Mohammed Nasser. Others, like the blond-haired man, could, Hunovi supposed, be innocent tenants of the building, caught up in all this madness just because Fatah had decided to establish a safe house there.

Hunovi inserted another roll of film, lit a cigarette and focused on the building entrance again. He would wait another hour. After that he would leave the exposed rolls of film at a drop site near the Banque Centrale on the Rue Michel Chiha where they would be collected by a Mossad agent and forwarded to Joel Rosen in the Kiria for study. The photographs, though, were of secondary importance to Hunovi. He needed to contact Rosen urgently. A note accompanying the rolls of film would not suffice; it would not enable Rosen to reply. And Hunovi desperately wanted a reply to the request he had to make. He decided to contact his Zurich control the moment he had made the drop.

A flurry of activity in front of the building caught his attention. He dropped the cigarette and pressed the shutter release button on the Nikon as Maazi and Nasser came out. If only Joel says yes, Hunovi thought as he wound on the film, the next time I see that bastard Maazi's face, it'll be split by the cross-hairs of a telescopic sight.

He continued to expose film as Maazi entered the bullet-damaged Mercedes while Nasser waited for one of his guards to open the door of an old Cadillac. The meeting, for whatever purpose it had been called, was over.

Hunovi waited fifteen minutes, removed the last roll of film from the Nikon and left the apartment. The local Mossad agent could take care of the camera equipment when he returned, and that would not be until after Hunovi had contacted him. For even here, in Beirut, the Mossad people did not know Hunovi by sight. They took his orders over the telephone, made preparations for him and cleaned up after he had finished his work.

CHAPTER
TWELVE

JOEL Rosen was pouring himself a cup of tea from the thermos flask when the direct-line telephone rang. He forgot all about the tea and grabbed at the phone. The caller was the woman in Zurich who controlled Hunovi.

"He contacted me less than five minutes ago and asked me to relay information to you," she told Rosen.

"Hold on just a minute." Rosen picked up the other telephone and rang through to General Avivi's office. The Mossad head came quickly and listened in on the extension to the direct line. "Okay, go ahead," Rosen told the woman in Zurich.

"There is film on the way to you of a meeting which the information officer attended. Also present was the opposition's chief of operations. You should receive the film tomorrow. Hunovi wants you to identify whoever you can."

"Is that all?" Rosen could not help the impatient disbelief in his voice. A call about some lousy film when a note left at the drop would have sufficed!

"No." The woman's voice remained calm. "Hunovi wants your permission to send the information officer on a permanent vacation."

"Why?"

"He believes the information officer is the mainspring of their extreme activities."

"What about our old friends? Did he learn nothing definite?"

"Not yet," Zurich answered. "But Hunovi says that if they are setting up shop again, he is convinced that the information officer will manage it."

Avivi held a hand over the extension mouthpiece while he whispered to Rosen. "What do you think, Joel? Should we give him the green light to hit Maazi?"

Rosen shook his head. "Tell Hunovi that we are on top of the situation," he said to Zurich. "If we sent the information officer away now, someone else will take his place and we'll be no better off. We have to let it run."

"That's right, let it run," Avivi broke in. Despite his earlier reservations about letting the string out, he knew that Rosen was correct. If Hunovi took Maazi out now, where would that leave them? The worm would have lost its head but it would still be capable of wriggling. They had to be patient until the entire body could be crushed.

"Hunovi is calling back within an hour to hear your reply," Zurich said. "I'll contact you after that."

Rosen replaced the receiver and looked at Avivi. "Not a damned word on Tayfield, nothing on Samantha Sutcliffe," he said. "Just a request for an elimination."

"Which means that Hunovi hasn't found out a thing," Avivi muttered. "What if this documentary gets finished and Tayfield and Samantha return to England? We'll be no better off than we were before."

Both men lapsed into a gloomy silence as they realized that they might have used a good combination to no avail; all that time and effort spent priming Samantha just flushed down the drain.

Forty minutes later the direct line rang again. "Hunovi says he does not like your disapproval," Zurich reported. "He says that this is not the kind of matter that can wait indefinitely."

Rosen felt himself becoming angry. Despite his deep friendship with Hunovi, he would not accept dissension. "Tell him that we're not interested in what he does or does not like. He will obey instructions."

"I'll tell him word for word. He also mentioned a favor."

"What?"

"He wants a watch on the farm. There is too much at stake to leave that unguarded. He says that if the information officer is not sent away, the boy might be in danger."

Rosen did not understand the connection, but the request was easy enough to fill. "Is that all?"

"No. He wants you at the farm, Joel. No one else."

"He wants Joel?" Avivi glanced concernedly at Rosen. "Why? He's needed here."

Rosen knew the answer to that even before Zurich supplied it. "Hunovi said that Lillehammer was before your time, but it was not before his and Joel's. He wants Joel there because he is the only person who can be trusted. There is no room on this operation for the bungling fools of Lillehammer."

"Tell him I'll go once I've checked over the film," Rosen said just before he hung up.

"You can't!" Avivi exclaimed.

"Can't I? You just watch me."

"I'm ordering you to stay here," the general said. "Your responsibility is to this office, not to your personal friends."

"You'll order me to do nothing!" Rosen fired back angrily. "If I want to, I can write out my resignation effective immediately and then travel to England as a private citizen." He stood up, walked to the filing cabinet and pulled out the volume on Operation Asher.

Mrs. Riley—that was the housekeeper's name, the elderly Irishwoman who had been left trussed up like a Christmas turkey in the farmhouse garage on the night the barn had been destroyed. The information on Mrs. Riley read that she was fiercely loyal to Samantha Sutcliffe, yet at the same time she questioned the actress's allegedly deep commitment to the Palestinian cause. Rosen knew he would be able to capitalize on that.

"Joel, you would resign, wouldn't you?" Avivi asked quietly.

"Damned right. I would if I thought it would help Hunovi close out this case."

"You know something, Joel, that weight you lost suits you."

"Huh?"

"Who do you think you've been fooling?" Avivi asked. "I've noticed the weight dropping off you. I know all about the workouts in the gym, the sudden infatuation with target shooting on the range. You had planned all along to return to the field."

"So? Are you still going to try to stop me?"

"No. But I implore you again not to let revenge cloud your better judgment."

Hunovi's work in Beirut amounted to one hundred and fifty-eight black-and-white photographs which were blown up into eight-by-tens. Rosen and Avivi sat sifting through the still-wet prints, eliminating duplicates, putting names to recognizable faces. Less than an hour later, they were left with a pile of sixteen photographs which had defied immediate identification. Among the pile were legitimate tenants of the apartment building on the Rue Ayoub Tabet, and a short stocky man with blond hair who sweated profusely in a suit.

"I'll get these over to Records, see if they can match up any of these faces," Rosen said. "Then I'm off to London."

"You'll keep in touch with the resident at the embassy, of course," Avivi reminded Rosen.

"Naturally. I've already contacted him to make arrangements for me at Heathrow Airport. Although for the life of me I still can't see why Hunovi reckons that Samantha's boy could be in danger."

"Very well, Joel. If we receive news from Tayfield, I'll let you know immediately."

"Sure. Only I've got that nasty feeling"—Rosen took the false South African passport from his desk drawer—"that I'll still be at the farm when Tayfield and Samantha return to England."

"Do you think Fatah could have fed Berger misinformation, knowing he belonged to us?" Avivi asked. "Then, when he had transmitted, they killed him."

That was the one possibility which Rosen did not want to consider. Because if it were true, his friend would have died for no reason at all.

Joel Rosen arrived at Heathrow Airport late that night and passed through British immigration with the South African passport. At the car-rental desk the keys to an Austin were waiting for him in the name of Roy Chappell. At one-thirty in the morning, he arrived at the farmhouse.

After his second knock, a light flared on the second floor. A minute later the front door was opened by Mrs. Riley. Wearing an old-fashioned red woollen dressing gown, she stared angrily at the stranger who had dared to disturb her sleep.

"Mrs. Riley, my name is Joel Rosen and it is imperative that I talk to you." Without waiting for an invitation to enter, he pushed his way gently past the surprised housekeeper and stood inside.

"What's the meaning—"

"Shussh!" Rosen held a finger warningly to his lips. "Do you want to wake little David up?"

Mrs. Riley's annoyance turned to fearful interest on learning that this stranger knew of David. "Who are you, Mr. Rosen?"

"I am a friend of Samantha Sutcliffe. Now will you talk to me?"

Mrs. Riley showed him into the breakfast room and he sat down at the oak table. "Is something the matter with Mrs. Sutcliffe?" Mrs. Riley asked. She had been worried sick on seeing the photograph in English newspapers of Samantha firing the rifle at the Phantom.

"I hope not." Rosen smiled as he tried to put the housekeeper at ease. "And I'd like to keep it that way."

"I'm listening to you, Mr. Rosen."

"Do you remember that night you were locked in the garage?"

"Do I remember?" Mrs. Riley's eyes blazed. "How could I ever forget what those hooligans did to me—"

"Hooligans, Mrs. Riley? Do you really think that hooligans would have treated you with such respect?"

Mrs. Riley's mouth dropped open as she stared at Rosen. How did he know how they had treated her—and how could he possibly understand what her thoughts had been after the incident? "Are you with them?"

Rosen let the question pass. "You're not very happy about the work Samantha Sutcliffe is doing for the Palestinians, are you, Mrs. Riley?"

"I don't approve of *foreigners*, Mr. Rosen."

"Does that title include me?" Rosen found himself warming to the housekeeper. He would not want her as an enemy, that was for sure.

"I don't know you yet. You speak English like an Australian—"

"South African," Rosen corrected her. "I was born in South Africa. By choice I am an Israeli."

"What would an Israeli care about keeping Mrs. Sutcliffe safe?"

"Mrs. Riley, Samantha Sutcliffe and those two men who tied you up that night have something in common. They all work for me."

"For you?" Mrs. Riley began to feel weak. Her stomach churned uncomfortably and her head felt light. "Do you mean to tell me that—"

"Precisely, Mrs. Riley. Samantha is working, not for the Palestinians, but for the Israelis."

"But why? How?"

"Do you know who David's father was?"

"Was?"

"He's dead. His name was Asher Davidson, an Israeli athlete who died from wounds he received at the Munich Olympics. Now do you understand why Samantha works for me?"

"Well, I never," Mrs. Riley said in a bemused manner. "I would never have guessed."

"And if you had known, would you disapprove of her actions as strongly as you disapproved of them when you thought she genuinely sympathized with the Palestinians?"

"I don't know. This is all too sudden for me to really understand. So many things have happened in the past few weeks that I'm not certain what's going on anymore. And you should have been here when young David saw his mother's picture in the newspaper, firing at that Israeli plane. Wait a minute—if she works for you, why would she have done that?"

"Because the opportunity was there. She could never have hoped to hit a jet fighter with a rifle, but she had the opportunity to strengthen her cover considerably."

"This is all far above the head of a simple Irishwoman," Mrs. Riley confessed. "What do you want from me?"

"I want to stay here in the farmhouse so that I can keep an eye on David and you."

"Do you think something might happen?"

Rosen smiled at the question, at all the concern it contained, not for Mrs. Riley's own safety but for the boy's. "Mrs. Riley, we are very good at our work only because we plan for every possible contingency."

"I bet you do," Mrs. Riley agreed as she thought back to the burning of the barn. "You know, we once had a Jewish lord mayor of Dublin."

"So I heard. Robert Briscoe."

"That's him," Mrs. Riley said, enormously pleased that Rosen knew of Briscoe. Those two other foreigners who had visited Samantha—the wog and the frog—she'd wager they'd never heard of Robert Briscoe. Suddenly she raised a hand as footsteps sounded unsteadily on the stairs. "David," she whispered. "He must have woken up."

Rosen turned around as the footsteps changed to the shuffling sound of slippers dragging across the floor. David entered the breakfast room, his pajamas awry, rubbing sleep from his eyes.

"Who's this?"

"David, I want you to meet a cousin of mine from Johannesburg," Mrs. Riley said proudly, naming the first South African city that came into her mind. "He's staying with us for a week or two while he's on holiday." She wrapped a beefy arm around Rosen and hugged him warmly.

"Hello, David," Rosen said to the boy. "I'm Roy Chappell. I'm sorry

163

if I woke you up but my plane was late." He put his own arm around Mrs. Riley's waist and gave her a fond squeeze. The Irish housekeeper was nowhere near as simple as she would have liked him to believe.

It seemed to Rosen that he had hardly settled in at the farm under the guise of being Mrs. Riley's South African cousin when he received a call just before lunchtime the following day from the Mossad's resident agent in London, a man named Dov Karpinsky who worked out of the Israeli embassy. Karpinsky was brief and to the point: he wanted an immediate meeting with Rosen.

"I have to go out," Rosen said to Mrs. Riley.

"Oh, dear, David will be disappointed," the housekeeper said. "He was so looking forward to showing you over the farm." Then she added in a worried tone, "It's not bad news about Mrs. Sutcliffe, is it?"

"No," Rosen answered, smiling at her anxiety. "Tell David I'll go twice around the farm with him when I return."

As he left the house and started the car, he saw David running toward him from the cowshed. "Where are you going, Mr. Chappell?"

"I have to visit a friend in London."

"Can I come with you for the ride?"

"Sorry, not this time," Rosen replied. He regretted the disappointed expression on David's face. The boy had accepted him immediately as Mrs. Riley's cousin from Johannesburg and now Rosen felt he was cheating him. Looking into the young face, Rosen tried to recall photographs he had seen of Asher Davidson. Had the Olympic runner possessed such thick curly black hair? "When I return I'll take you for a ride, all right?" He reached through the open window to tousle the boy's hair, then drove off.

Halfway to London it started to rain. Rosen turned on the windshield wipers and lowered his speed accordingly. He completed the journey in a little more than two and a half hours, and when he reached St. John's Wood in northwest London the rain was still falling steadily.

On the northeast corner of the junction between the Edgware Road and Hall Road, Rosen spotted the tall, black-haired Karpinsky, holding up an umbrella in his left hand while his right hand beat a steady tattoo with a rolled up newspaper against his leg. Rosen honked twice as he passed Karpinsky before driving completely around the block and stopping twenty yards away from the London resident. After another five minutes of standing in the rain, Karpinsky hailed a cab. Rosen pulled in two cars behind the cab and followed it for three miles into the heart of the West End. When the cab let Karpinsky off at Piccadilly Circus, with the start of the rush hour traffic swirling around him, Rosen was confident that the London resident had not been followed. He pulled alongside, pushed open the passenger door and Karpinsky jumped in.

"We could have chosen a better day for this," Karpinsky said, jamming the dripping umbrella between his legs while he unbuttoned his raincoat. "I'm soaked right through, waiting for you."

"Never mind about the weather. What do you want?"

"A message from the Kiria. Records identified some of the mystery people in the photographs of the Rue Ayoub Tabet."

"Who?"

Karpinsky reeled off a list of names and positions, all minor officials within Fatah. Rosen listened and dismissed them as of no importance.

"There was one other man," Karpinsky said.

"Who?" Rosen asked a second time.

"The short fat man with the light hair. The photograph on file is old, but Records is convinced that it was Pavel Vlasov who came out of the apartment building and was driven away in the Fiat."

"Who's Vlasov?" Rosen wished Karpinsky would get to the point.

"KGB."

"What's so odd about that? Fatah relies heavily on KGB assistance."

"Pavel Vlasov's not a regular field agent," Karpinsky explained. "He's strictly top drawer, kind of a minister without portfolio used by Moscow, we believe, on special missions as the need arises. He's a troubleshooter, with Department Five."

"Go on." Rosen stopped for the red light at the junction of Charing Cross Road and Oxford Street. He looked into the rearview mirror to check whether any car had been behind him for too long. All he could see was a herd of glistening black taxis, wipers swishing in unison. The light changed to green and Rosen led the northbound charge up Tottenham Court Road.

"General Avivi believes that Vlasov's presence in the same building as Salim Maazi and Dr. Nasser might have something to do with Operation Asher. It's the first time Vlasov's been spotted in Beirut. Usually he works out of Soviet embassies in Europe or South America."

"What's Avivi doing about it?"

"He wants you to return to Tel Aviv immediately. He'll make other arrangements for guarding the Sutcliffe farm."

"Can't," Rosen said and realized how the single word of rejection made him sound like some petulant schoolchild. "Tell Avivi to organize an alternative. Tell him"—he braked sharply as one of the black taxis swerved abruptly in front of him to pick up a fare—"tell him to put a team on this Vlasov. Wherever he goes, whomever he meets, I want to know. But I'm staying right here."

"You'd better come back to the embassy with me and contact him yourself," Karpinsky said.

"Are you crazy? I'm not going to be seen walking within a mile of Palace Gardens. I'll call him from Heathrow Airport on the way back to the Sutcliffe farm."

"Good luck when you do," Karpinsky said. "Drop me off here. I'll walk up to Warren Street Station."

"I'll drop you off right at the station."

"No. I want to get some cigarettes first."

"Suit yourself." Rosen stopped and waited for Karpinsky to get out. The London resident slammed the door, opened his umbrella and walked hastily toward a tobacconist's shop. Rosen started to pull away and then stared curiously into the mirror. The spot at the curb he had just vacated had been taken immediately by a taxi. A man jumped out, thrust some money at the driver and, without waiting for change, started to walk toward the tobacconist's shop. Instead of entering it, though, he pulled up the collar of his coat and stared into the window of an adjacent store, apparently interested in the display of stereo equipment.

Dividing his attention between what lay ahead of the car and what was taking place in the mirror, Rosen could just discern the figure of Karpinsky leaving the tobacconist's shop and walking north toward Warren Street Station. The man from the taxi fell into step twenty yards behind him.

One question sprang immediately to Rosen's mind as, without signaling his intention, he swung the car left down the closest side street, turned off the engine and jumped out. Why, on a day when the rain is bucketing down with monsoonlike force, would a man without an umbrella leave the comfort of a taxi to walk?

The answer was simple. Rosen had not been thorough enough. Karpinsky *was* being followed.

Rosen waited in the side street until Karpinsky walked by on the main road on his way to Warren Street Station. When the second man passed, Rosen followed at a distance of ten yards, one of the many hundreds of office workers streaming toward the station at the end of the business day.

166

Was the tail an Arab? Rosen questioned. No . . . he did not have Middle Eastern features. He was about thirty, tall, with broad shoulders and an athletic gait to his stride. His dark hair was flattened to his head by the rain, and his face, the time Rosen had seen him in profile, was like a boxer's—a fat upturned nose and a square powerful chin.

What then? British? Now that was a possibility. Karpinsky was working in Britain, attached to the Israeli embassy but engaged in covert activities. Such men were considered spies. Did some wild logic make the British believe that the Israelis were working against Britain—possibly for Argentina with that trouble in the South Atlantic? Again Rosen dismissed the notion. It made no sense at all for the British to be tailing Karpinsky. Upon the request of the British government, Israel had stopped arms sales to Argentina. Besides, when it suited their purpose the Mossad even helped the British to combat the Irish Republican Army.

Karpinsky turned into Warren Street Station and joined the line at the ticket window. The man from the taxi went straight to a ticket machine and purchased the most expensive ticket available. Very smart, Rosen thought, doing the same at another machine. No matter where the tail got off he would not get stuck explaining to an inspector why he had underpaid.

Russian, Rosen eventually decided. That was the only selection to make any kind of sense. The Soviets expended enormous energy and time to learn about the agents of every nation in every country in which they were diplomatically represented. Had Karpinsky given himself away somehow? Had he done something to tip off the Soviets about the true nature of his work at the Israeli embassy? If that was the situation, now the Soviets wanted to see whom he might lead them to, and on what kind of cases he was working.

More importantly, if the tail on Karpinsky was a Russian, he would have seen the London resident with Rosen. Perhaps he could not have seen Rosen clearly enough in the car to put together an accurate description, but he would have the license-plate number. The car had been rented in the name of Roy Chappell. Other people—the woman at the car rental counter at Heathrow, for instance—would be able to help with a description. Eventually the investigation might lead all the way to the Sutcliffe farm in Somerset. The Chappell identity would be shot . . . and so would Rosen's cover. He would no longer be a small-time bureaucrat, a forgettable face. He did not need an encyclopedia to know what came next. His description, his alias, perhaps even his true identity, would be logged on the KGB files in Moscow, and from there the information would be forwarded to the Palestinians. And Samantha would be tied in with the Mossad.

There was no way Rosen was going to permit any of this to happen. If the man following Karpinsky was a Russian agent, the moment he had stepped out of that taxi on Tottenham Court Road he had signed his own death warrant.

Karpinsky took the escalator down to the Victoria Line platform and waited for a southbound train. The man from the taxi stood on the edge of the platform five yards away. A train had just pulled out and could be heard rattling away in the tunnel. For a moment the platform was virtually empty; then a new wave of passengers streamed down from the street. Rosen joined the new wave and let himself be swept along until he stood close to the man from the taxi. He saw Karpinsky look up and down the platform. The London resident's eyes opened a fraction in surprised recognition, and Rosen prayed that Karpinsky's training and experience would hold. Karpinsky turned away to study the advertisements pasted on the wall across the track.

Gradually Rosen edged even nearer to the man from the taxi. He was willing to bet that the tail was so intent on Karpinsky that he was vulnerable elsewhere. It was the only chance Rosen had.

"Kogda poezd dolzhen pribit?" Rosen asked, utilizing the little Russian he knew. "When is the train due?"

The man turned around and stared at Rosen with vacant blue eyes. *"Izvinite, ya ne znayu,"* he replied instantly. "I'm sorry, I don't know." As the last word was spoken, the empty eyes turned sharp and the Russian backed away as he realized the simple trap into which he had blundered. He turned and shoved his way through the steadily increasing crowd. Rosen went after him. Karpinsky, catching on to the action in a flash, joined in the chase.

"What happened?" Karpinsky asked Rosen as they walked briskly along the platform. Ahead, the Russian broke into a run and both men kept pace.

"You were being followed. You're finished here—you're known."

"Who?"

"Ivan."

Ahead of Rosen and Karpinsky the Russian turned down a narrow passageway which he guessed to be an exit. Ten yards behind he could hear the twin hammering of running feet on concrete. But instead of leading to an escalator that would take him to street level, the passage continued through to the northbound platform of the Victoria Line. At the end of the passage he could see a crowd massed in expectation of a train. He put on a final burst of speed, eager to lose himself, to find safety in numbers.

"Excuse me, excuse me," the Russian panted as he pushed his way through the crowd toward the front of the platform. No longer could he hear the sounds of pursuit. A greater noise was coming from his left, from the mouth of the tunnel where the lights of a train grew brighter. The crowd backed away automatically from the platform's edge at the approach of the train, and the Russian pushed through. Seeing the rails, and feeling the crowd close in behind him, he relaxed a fraction.

With a thunderous roar the silver train burst out of the tunnel, slowing down as the motorman began to apply the brakes. A chill ran down the Russian's back as he felt the crowd pressing against him and saw the shiny rails beckoning from beyond the edge of the platform. He pushed back and turned his head to see Rosen standing behind him, a grim expression etched on his face. The Russian's mouth opened to scream. The noise was cut off as Rosen placed the flat of his hand in the man's back and shoved.

A woman's horrified shriek rose high above the roar of the train as the Russian toppled over the edge of the platform, arms flailing like a berserk windmill as he attempted to stop himself from falling. He crashed onto the live rail. Current surged through his body, boiling his blood, making his eyes bulge. In the cab of the train the motorman blasted his horn as if the warning would somehow make the electrocuted man rise from the tracks. And then a loud gasp, shock mingled with excitement, arose from the crowded platform as the train passed over the Russian's body amid the rumbling noise of steel on steel.

Rosen was already at the back of the crowd, running down a passageway toward the escalator. He slowed his step and Karpinsky caught up with him. Both men walked quickly up the escalator, thrust their unused tickets at the collector, muttered something about changing their minds and exited into the rain on Tottenham Court Road.

"You'd better get out tonight," Rosen said. "You're known." He turned around as pandemonium broke loose in the station entrance. Two police constables sheltering from the rain galvanized themselves into action and ran toward the escalator.

"I'll call Tel Aviv when I get back to the embassy," Karpinsky said.

"Better not take a train from that station," Rosen said. "We've wrecked their timetable for the day."

"What are you going to do?"

"I'll call Tel Aviv from the airport in an hour or so, give you time to get through and let them know what's happened."

"Okay." Karpinsky saw a taxi with its yellow light glowing and waved it down. Rosen watched the taxi move away, then he returned to where he had hurriedly parked the car. Under the windshield wiper, protected from the rain in a plastic bag, was a parking ticket. He shoved it into his pocket.

By the time he reached Heathrow Airport on the way back to Somerset, the rain had stopped. He drove to Terminal Three, parked the car and went inside to the international telephones.

"Joel, we got word from Karpinsky twenty minutes ago." General Avivi's voice sounded as clear as if he were speaking from the next booth. "Are you all right?"

"I'm fine." Lucky Karpinsky, Rosen thought; he had the signal room and the code books at the embassy to work by. Rosen had nothing. He had to play it off the cuff. "Karpinsky and I weren't careful enough. We'll have to change our London operation."

"It's not just London, Joel," Avivi said. "We're getting information that a similar situation is developing in Paris, Rome, Bonn, everywhere. Wherever we've got representatives, the competition's backers are taking an unhealthy interest in them."

"What's going on? Are they frightened that we'll butt into a major promotion their clients are putting together?"

"Could be."

"What do you think it is?" Rosen asked. "Something to do with those snapshots we looked at together?"

"That seems the likely answer. All we have to do now is find out what. Incidentally, I countermanded your order to Karpinsky. He's to stay put. If he runs now, the backers might figure out that we know something's in the wind. Our representatives everywhere are to carry on as normal." There was a long pause, then Avivi added, "Karpinsky said you weren't coming home."

"That's right. I'm also staying put. If the backers are this heavily involved, it's imperative that I stay on at the farm. There's been no other word, eh?"

"Nothing."

"What about that character in the snapshots? What are you going to do about him?"

"Exactly what you told Karpinsky. Copies of the picture have been sent to all stations. We've put extra strength into the field. We're covering everything."

"Good. I'll keep in touch." Rosen left the terminal, returned to his car and continued the journey west. He started to think about the Russian he had killed—stupid bastard, giving himself away like that, a trick any novice should have been able to avoid. But how many agents had gone down by similar guile? Rosen could think of at least one Mossad operation that had gone bust because of a mistake equally stupid.

He found himself feeling sorry for the motorman. Poor devil had been in the wrong place at the wrong time. Now he would have to live with that vision of the Russian falling under the train for the rest of his life.

Rosen flicked on the radio and tuned into a news station. After five minutes the announcer mentioned a tragedy at Warren Street Station during the evening rush hour. Rosen turned up the volume.

" . . . the dead man has been identified as Eugen Kaminov, a press officer with the Russian embassy in London. Police believe that the accident was caused by the overcrowded platform."

A woman's voice, speaking in a broad cockney accent, came on the air, describing how Kaminov had pushed his way past her to the front of the platform. "Then he just seemed to fall," she said. "It was horrible."

I bet it was, Rosen thought as he turned down the volume. At least the police had it pegged as an accident. No one had seen him push Kaminov. And no doubt the coroner, when recording his verdict, would add a rider that in future such accidents could be avoided if London Transport would take better safety measures.

Finally Rosen's thoughts turned to the cryptic conversation with Avivi. What the hell were the Palestinians up to with the aid of their ever-faithful backers, the Russians? For the KGB to tag suspected Mossad agents in a dozen different countries signified something colossal. But what? It was like an ever-decreasing spiral, Rosen decided. The Russians following the Israelis who were now keeping an eye on one man, a Russian named Pavel Vlasov. If everything went according to logic they would all eventually disappear up Vlasov's asshole.

And maybe only then would they learn what was really going on!

171

CHAPTER
THIRTEEN

$\mathbb{A}$LAN Tayfield could not believe how swiftly time had passed. Almost two weeks had been spent among the enemy, traveling from Rashidieh to Nahr al-Bard and then down south again to the refugee camps around Sidon, and he had been unable to pick up one single piece of worthwhile information.

"What a bloody waste of time," he muttered in disgust to Samantha as they stood watching Ahmed el-Shafri load their baggage into the trunk of the white Mercedes; the shattered windows and driver's door had been replaced, and the car bore no evidence of the battle at Maameltein.

"Do you feel well enough to travel, Alan?" Samantha asked. She could always tell when Tayfield was genuinely upset: he switched from American to British profanity, and the lilting accent picked up as a boy from the Swansea soldier became more pronounced.

"Of course I feel all right. What do you think I am, a blasted cripple?"

"You were doing your utmost to turn yourself into one, hiding how ill you were."

"Don't start that again," Tayfield grumbled. "You've been watching over me like that bloody Irishwoman watches over you and David. You're too young and pretty to be a possessive housekeeper."

Samantha could not help laughing as she was compared with Mrs. Riley. "Seriously, Alan, do you feel all right?"

"Seriously, Samantha, yes, I feel fine," he replied. "How far do we have to go? Just down to Rashidieh for the grand finale of this award-winning masterpiece, and then back to Beirut Airport. After that, jolly old England

172

—without a damned thing to make this whole trip worthwhile. Except, of course," he added bitterly, "that they really believe you're their bosom buddy now." He eyed the commando uniform Samantha wore; it seemed to Tayfield that she had never been without it. God alone knew how many pictures Pierre Reynard had sent out over the wire of Samantha dressed in that damned uniform. Two in particular galled Tayfield: the first where she was being chaired enthusiastically on the shoulders of a group of *fedayeen;* and the second, where she was lying prone on a rifle range, learning how to fire the AK-47.

"Could we have done any better?" Samantha asked.

"*You* couldn't have done any better, that's for sure. I feel lousy for what you've been through. Me neither, I suppose. Christ, even when I was lying in that bloody clinic my ears were wide open."

"Have there been false leads before?"

"Sure. They crop up now and again. Anyway, we won't go home completely empty-handed."

"How do you mean?"

"We'll get one last crack at Rashidieh. I want that place fresh in my mind when I make my report. Then the air force can blast every weapon, every round of ammunition." He fell silent as footsteps sounded close by.

"Are you ready to move out?" Salim Maazi asked.

"What about Reynard?" Tayfield queried, looking around. "Surely we're not going anywhere without our French friend."

"He'll join up with us later," Maazi answered, smiling. Tayfield and Reynard had not grown to like each other at all. "Early this morning he left for Beirut, to file a story."

"More of his bullshit about Samantha?"

"You're entitled to your opinion." Maazi took Samantha's arm and guided her toward the Mercedes.

Ahmed el-Shafri drove south with Maazi in the front passenger seat and Samantha and Tayfield in the back. To Samantha it seemed that nothing had changed since she had first sat in this car two weeks earlier, traveling south along this same coastal road, with the Mediterranean on her right, to her left the orange groves, the hills and Syria, Israel straight ahead, and behind the Mercedes the jeep full of armed commandoes. Most importantly, she and Tayfield were still seeking that first, evasive clue . . .

She reached into her bag and pulled out the script. Although she knew the final scene by heart, looking at it would distract her from the journey. The final scene called for a visit to old Hassan Bakri's home, a reminder

173

of the important man he had once been and the pitiful refugee he was now—with his daughter Rima, who had lost everything, prepared to offer even her life so that her people could again live with dignity. Samantha decided it was a good choice for an ending—the two generations, the legacy left by one to the other. Besides, she would like to see Rima again. Something about the Palestinian woman fascinated Samantha. Samantha wondered if she, herself, could be so strong? Or was *fanatical* the word she really wanted? She would do well to study the Palestinian woman during this final encounter; one day, perhaps, she would be able to use something she learned.

They arrived at Rashidieh in the early afternoon. While Tayfield said he needed to stretch his legs, Maazi took Samantha to the schoolhouse. The building had been repaired since the Israeli air raid. The jagged holes punched in the tin roof by cannon fire had been beaten flat, and the damaged furniture had been replaced. Rima Bakri walked around the class, stopping occasionally to help the youngsters with their work. When the door opened and Maazi entered, the Palestinian woman's eyes warmed in welcome; the expression froze into place the moment she recognized Samantha behind Maazi.

"I'm glad to see you return safely to Rashidieh," Rima greeted the English actress.

"Thank you. I was looking forward to meeting you again." Samantha took the outstretched hand, totally aware of the forced courtesy.

Rima turned to the class and told the children to continue with their work, then she led Samantha and Maazi outside. "What have you learned in your time here?" she asked Samantha.

"About the Palestinians?"

"Of course. That was why you came to Lebanon, wasn't it? To learn about us, to help us?" Rima studied Samantha carefully. Like Maazi before her, she noticed the transformation Samantha had undergone. Was it the exposure to action, or was it something deeper, more sinister? Like the joy a woman experiences when she steals the love of another?

"Samantha learned that she is truly one of us," Maazi broke in. "By an accident of birth, she is English. But deep in her heart, in her conscience, she is a Palestinian."

"Then," Rima smiled slyly, "perhaps you would consider staying on with us?"

Samantha shook her head. "I don't think so. I achieve more for Palestinian justice outside of this country than in it."

"If your sentiments on our behalf manage to achieve anything at all," Rima responded, and a bitter smile crept across her face.

"Do you doubt the value of this documentary?"

"No, not at all. But I question your sincerity, your value to our struggle."

"Rima! Stop this kind of talk at once," Maazi said, stepping in before the sparring between the two women got out of hand. "Samantha is a true friend of the Palestinians, Rima."

"I am a Palestinian," Rima shot back, "and this woman is not my true friend. My friends fight, they do not talk."

"I'm sorry if my visit here causes you distress," Samantha offered, "but I am your friend, believe me."

"No, Samantha," Maazi interrupted. "It is I who must apologize. For Rima's behavior."

"It's all right, Salim," Samantha said, aware that Rima was watching intently, as if angry about even this short conversation between Maazi and Samantha. "I think I understand how Rima feels."

"How could you possibly understand my feelings?" Rima demanded.

"I can understand, as a woman."

"How? Have you ever lost anyone close to you? Your own flesh and blood? Have you ever seen the man you love ripped away from you, slaughtered?"

Samantha's face whitened, and for one dreadful moment she thought that her true reason for being in Lebanon had been discovered.

"Well?" Rima pressed. "Have you?"

Slowly Samantha shook her head. "No."

"Then how can you possibly understand how I feel?" Rima stared at Samantha for a few seconds as if expecting a reply. Then she swung around and walked proudly back to the school.

The final scene of the documentary was filmed at Hassan Bakri's home. While the old man sat at the table eating, as if the camera were not there, Rima brought out photographs of her children and husband. The camera moved from the old man, panned across the photographs in clumsy wooden frames, rested for a moment on Rima's face. Then the lens widened to take in the entire room, with Samantha standing in the foreground.

"Before May, 1948, Hassan Bakri was an important member of the Palestinian community in the village of Tarshiha," Samantha said. "Tarshiha ceased to exist in 1948; in its place is the Israeli town of Maalot. Hassan Bakri is now in his seventies and he understands that he is close to death. His one wish before he dies is to return to his native village so that he may be buried alongside his ancestors."

Samantha stole a glance at Rima and was amazed that the woman's face was now so soft, so gentle. How could such bitterness and hate live behind that tender mask? Despite herself, she began to feel a twinge of sympathy for the Palestinian woman. Both of their loves had been casualities in the same struggle. But Rima's husband had been killed in battle, while Asher had been murdered, butchered by Rima's comrades. Samantha recalled Maazi's talk about Rima crossing the border to participate in ambushes on Israeli troops, and her sympathy vanished. Only pity reserved for the camera lens remained.

"Hassan's daughter, Rima, is a teacher here at Rashidieh, a molder of young children. Yet always at the back of her mind is the poignant memory of her own children, killed with her husband in the bitter civil war that tore Lebanon apart just a few years ago. The Lebanese Christians —that's right, the followers of Jesus Christ—did not want the Palestinians in Lebanon; so they attacked them. Just as the Syrians, the Jordanians and the Egyptians have also attacked them. In truth, and this might seem a strange analogy"—she caught herself thinking of Tayfield; had he discovered anything of value in this, his final opportunity?—"the Palestinians are the modern-day Jews, spat upon, reviled, murdered for the simple crime of being alive. What makes the plight of the Palestinians even sadder is that those same Jews who were once so savagely persecuted are responsible for oppressing the Palestinians as they were once oppressed themselves."

"Rima Bakri," Samantha concluded, "is a teacher, yet she carries a gun which she is perfectly capable of using—and which she is perfectly willing to use. That in itself is the saddest commentary of all upon this modern tragedy."

Samantha allowed her hands to fall to her side, her head to drop. She was exhausted. No role had ever sapped her like this.

Maazi came forward and held her by the shoulders. "Congratulations. The finale was masterful."

"Your script." She tried to smile at him.

"My script was nothing. Your interpretation was what really mattered." He held out a hand for Rima. "Do you still question Samantha's sincerity?"

176

"When my father and I are back in Tarshiha I will question no longer."

Samantha considered asking Rima what would happen to the Jews if —heaven forbid!—the Palestinians ever returned. Instead she broke away from Maazi's grip and left Hassan Bakri's home. She wanted to leave this damned place. She wanted to go home, to see David again, to hold him in her arms and let his closeness wash from her memory this infernal country and the murderers who infested it.

"I'm sorry that I missed the end of the filming," a man's voice said. Samantha looked up, surprised to see Reynard's face. "I've just returned from Beirut."

Reynard was the last person Samantha wanted to see. He represented all the disappointment she felt at the failure of the mission and reminded her of a love that could never be hers again. When she had come to Lebanon, some of her trepidation had been calmed by the knowledge that she would see Reynard. And what she had seen of him had made her wonder how she could ever have welcomed him at the farm, allowed him —no, encouraged him!—to make love to her. He was a spineless man who used—she recalled Maazi's words—the Palestinian struggle to carve a name for himself. He was a parasite who covered his own shortcomings with a glib manner and Gallic charm. Mrs. Riley had been right about distrusting frogs.

"Too bad," she replied. "You'll just have to wait until it gets on television then, won't you?" She walked away quickly and stood by Maazi's white Mercedes, waiting for the ride back to the refugee camp.

In the breakfast room of the farm, Joel Rosen was playing chess with David. From the kitchen wafted the appetizing aroma of the roast Mrs. Riley was cooking, and Rosen found himself eagerly anticipating dinner.

"Can't do that, David," he told the boy. "You'll expose yourself to check." He grinned and pointed out the mistake. David replaced the piece and looked for another move. Rosen sat back, feeling vaguely guilty that he should be enjoying himself so much. He was supposed to be working, yet here he was helping David to improve his game and looking forward to eating like a king. Maybe he had missed something all these years by not getting married and raising a family of his own.

He heard the telephone give one double ring before it went silent. Looking up from the chess board, he called out, "Leave it, Mrs. Riley!" A minute later the telephone rang again. Rosen stood up and started to

177

slip on his jacket. Another minute passed before the telephone gave a final double ring.

"We'll continue the game tomorrow, David. I have to go out now." He reached across the table to run his fingers through the boy's curly hair; then he walked into the kitchen where he told Mrs. Riley that he was going out.

"When will you be back?"

"Three, four hours."

"Is it to do with Mrs. Sutcliffe?"

"I doubt it. You worry too much." Instinctively, he leaned forward and kissed the elderly housekeeper on the cheek. Mrs. Riley's dedication to her family inspired fondness—and he was family now, too. He was Mrs. Riley's cousin from Johannesburg.

Rosen drove east on the motorway for an hour before pulling off at a rest stop. He climbed out of the car and entered the cafeteria, bought a cup of tea and a plastic-wrapped cheese sandwich and sat down next to a man who was engrossed in the *Times* crossword.

"Samantha and Tayfield are confirmed tomorrow on Middle East Airlines flight two-oh-one which leaves Beirut at thirteen-thirty local time and arrives at Heathrow at sixteen thirty-five," the man said without looking up from the crossword.

"Any other news?" Rosen stirred the tea and unwrapped the sandwich. Looking at the meager portion of thinly sliced cheese he put the sandwich aside; the roast which Mrs. Riley had been cooking had spoiled him. He hoped she would warm some up for him when he returned to the farm.

"No. Tel Aviv had contact with Zurich. Nothing to report." The man penned in a clue. When Rosen looked closer he saw that the man had written in meaningless letters just to fill in the spaces. Rosen grinned.

"What about Vlasov?"

"Back in Moscow."

Rosen sipped his tea, disappointed. But what else had he expected? That Vlasov would give himself away immediately? No, patience was needed, just like always. "What else did Tel Aviv say?"

"They want to know whether you'll return home once Tayfield and the woman are back in England."

Rosen nodded. "I'll be at Heathrow Airport when their plane lands. I'll see Tayfield there, arrange to debrief him as he comes through and take any information back with me."

"Good. We'll make arrangements for you on a flight that leaves shortly after MEA two-oh-one arrives. Your ticket will be waiting at the British Airways counter in the name of Roy Chappell."

"Thanks." Rosen pushed away the cup and looked down one more time at the crossword. The man had just filled in another clue with a jumble of odd letters. "That's Carmarthenshire," Rosen said.

"Huh?" For the first time the man looked up.

"That clue you just pretended to fill in—automobile shop has chickens for rent in Wales. Car-Mart-Hens-Hire . . . Carmarthenshire; it's a place in Wales."

"Thanks," the man said, but Rosen was already up and walking away.

On the return journey to the farm, Rosen thought about Mrs. Riley and young David. They would not miss him, not when Samantha would be coming home. But he would miss them. Between them, they had provided him with a brief but warm respite from the pressures of his job.

Had he wasted his time by coming to England? Not really. Thanks to the meeting with Dov Karpinsky—and the deadly encounter with a KGB man named Eugen Kaminov—Rosen knew now that the Soviets were keeping tabs on suspected Mossad agents, doing it as a service to their clients, the Palestinians. Which, to Rosen's way of thinking, meant that whatever the Palestinians were up to, the Russians, as usual, were backing them all the way.

Samantha rose very early the following morning, eager to be on her way home. She washed and dressed in the jeans, blouse and lightweight leather jacket she had worn for the outward journey, and looked around the makeshift bedroom to be sure she had left nothing. Across the back of a chair lay the uniform Maazi had given her. It would stay there; she had no need for such a gruesome souvenir of her visit.

By eight in the morning, the party was ready to leave for the drive north to Beirut. The baggage was loaded in the trunk of the Mercedes. Ahmed el-Shafri sat behind the wheel, pressing his foot down on the accelerator every few seconds to race the engine. Tayfield, Maazi and Reynard stood by the car, waiting for Samantha.

Samantha appeared in the doorway of the hut, holding her jacket and blinking in the strong sunlight. It was almost over, she told herself. A ride in the car, the last detestable moments of Salim Maazi's company, and then she would be sitting on the plane, pampered by the young women in their salmon pink uniforms. And soon she would see David and Mrs. Riley again. Thank God.

179

She started to walk across the baked sand toward the Mercedes, stopping and smiling when a young girl in traditional Arab dress ran up to her, holding a scroll of paper. Samantha unrolled the paper and saw a childish painting of a woman holding a gun, firing into the air. Rima—Samantha thought with a shudder. This is what Rima teaches these children. Where David painted pictures of men kicking a ball or driving a train, Rima taught these children to draw pictures of a woman shooting at an Israeli aircraft. She shook her head sadly and felt tears forming in her eyes.

"Come on, Samantha, we've got a plane to catch!" Tayfield called out. He was as anxious to be on the way as she was.

Samantha bent down to kiss the young girl. Then she carefully rolled the sheet of paper and continued on toward the Mercedes. This she would keep. It would be a constant reminder to her of a portion of hell on earth where the devil, instead of prodding his victims with a flaming pitchfork, poisoned their minds.

Tayfield was the first to hear the faint whisper of the jet engine. He cocked his head inquisitively and looked into the air. Seeing nothing but the clear blue sky he lowered his gaze. The whisper grew louder, became a soft pulsating roar, and Tayfield looked west. Coming in low from the Mediterranean was a lone Israeli Kfir.

"Samantha!" Tayfield yelled out.

Samantha heard Tayfield's frenzied shout and the sound of the approaching aircraft simultaneously. She froze, completely exposed in the open ground between the hut and the Mercedes. The young girl ran away, screaming wildly in a conditioned reaction of fear at the sound of the jet.

Tayfield started to run toward Samantha. Reynard grabbed him by the arm. "No attack!" the Frenchman shouted. "Just one plane! No attack! Reconnaissance!"

Tayfield did not seem to hear. All he could understand was that Samantha was in danger. Maazi flung himself forward and tried to grip Tayfield's other arm. From somewhere, Tayfield found the strength to rip himself free from both men. He ran toward Samantha, painfully aware of the increasing noise of the Kfir as it swooped low toward the refugee camp. God!—not now! Not when they were leaving! Bastards! What were those crazy bastards trying to do? Hadn't they almost killed Samantha and himself once? Why now? For God's sake—why now?

The roar grew even louder, screaming toward a pounding crescendo as the Kfir flashed overhead. Its sleek shape momentarily blotted out the sun and cast a fleeting shadow across the sand where Samantha stood transfixed with terror. She jammed her hands over her ears and looked up at the belly of the aircraft, saw in minute detail its auxiliary fuel tanks, its bomb and missile racks, even the meticulously straight lines of rivets. Then a crushing blow knocked her to the ground as Tayfield dragged her down, pressed her into the sand with his own body, offered himself as a shield against the bullets and bombs he was certain were coming.

The shadow passed. The Kfir blasted across the refugee camp, went into a tight climbing turn and headed west. Moments later it had disappeared into the horizon.

Samantha struggled to free herself of Tayfield's protective weight. The force of his rush had knocked the breath out of her body. She gasped in fright and pain as she tried to slide out from underneath him. She heard herself screaming, "I'm all right, Alan! I'm all right! Please let me up!"

Boots implanted themselves in front of her eyes. At last she felt Tayfield move, the burden on her body lighten. Reynard reached down to lift her to her feet. Her head was swimming and she reached out to the Frenchman for support.

"It was a reconnaissance flight, that was all," Reynard said soothingly. "There was nothing to be worried about."

Samantha turned to look at Tayfield. He was standing up but his legs were trembling as if they could not carry his weight. His face was white, his breath bursting from his mouth in ragged gasps. He started to cough and clutch at his chest. And then his mouth turned up at the corners as if he were smiling, because in that moment he understood that he was not fated to sit in his den at home and admire the photograph taken in Beirut with Samantha and Yasir Arafat.

"Alan!" Before Samantha's horrified eyes, Tayfield slumped slowly to his knees, both hands pressing against his chest, spittle oozing from the still-smiling mouth. "Alan!"

Reynard spun around, pushed Samantha into Maazi's arms and knelt beside Tayfield. "Get a doctor!" he snapped at Maazi. "Quickly!"

Maazi swung toward the Mercedes and rapped out orders to el-Shafri, while Reynard gently stretched Tayfield out on the sand, ripped open his shirt collar and raised his feet.

"What is it?" Samantha asked. "His heart?"

Forgetting her own terror of moments earlier, Samantha knelt down on the sand. Tayfield's eyes were open, bulging out from their sockets. He was having difficulty in breathing, and a vein on the right side of his forehead played a dramatic, throbbing tattoo.

El-Shafri returned with two men carrying a stretcher onto which they loaded the semiconscious Tayfield. Samantha jogged alongside, holding Tayfield's hand until they reached the clinic where a doctor gently told her she could go no further. She watched helplessly as the stretcher was carried inside. The door closed and she felt totally alone.

"Come with me," Maazi said. "You can do nothing for him now."

Numbly Samantha allowed herself to be led away. Outside the clinic a crowd had gathered, attracted by the excitement. Maazi shouted at the people to disperse before leading Samantha back to the hut she had just vacated. There Reynard brought her coffee. She sat on the edge of the bunk, holding the coffee and gazing at the commando uniform she had left draped across the back of the chair.

"Samantha, have faith," Reynard whispered. "The medical staff will do all they can for him." Once again Reynard seemed to be the sympathetic figure she had first met.

"But what can they do?" she wanted to know. "This place is a wilderness. How can they cope with something serious?" She recalled those terrifying thoughts which had occurred to her upon first learning he was ill—who would tell his family if he died? His daughter and brother. What hope did Tayfield have of recovery? In a modern hospital, perhaps; there he would receive proper treatment. But what would the Rashidieh clinic —that Salim Maazi was so proud of—be able to offer?

"They will find a way to cope," Reynard insisted. He gazed intently into her eyes and Samantha recognized the man she had dined with at the Plaza Athénée, the man who had made love to her in front of a fire at the farmhouse. It was as if from crisis Reynard drew his strength. Or did he look upon it as another opportunity for a story?

Thirty minutes later, a man in a white coat entered the hut. Samantha recognized the doctor who had separated her from Tayfield. Had something happened? Fearing the worst, she stood up. The doctor ignored her. Instead, he drew Maazi off to one side, out of Samantha's and Reynard's hearing, and a hushed torrent of Arabic ensued.

"What's the matter?" Samantha asked, moving toward the two men. "Has something—?"

Maazi turned around to smile reassuringly at her. "It's nothing. I have to leave for a few minutes." He crooked a finger at Reynard. "You, come with us."

"What is it?" Reynard asked as the three men walked quickly toward the clinic.

"Tell him what you just told me," Maazi ordered the doctor.

"The patient Tayfield has slipped into a coma," the doctor explained. "His heart is so weak that it cannot pump sufficient blood to his brain; therefore the brain tissues have deteriorated."

"A coma? Will he come out of it?"

Maazi regarded Reynard with a curious gaze. Was there concern in the Frenchman's voice? Was he worried about the fate of a man who could not stand the sight of him?

The doctor shrugged his shoulders in response to the question. "Perhaps. If we could risk moving him to Beirut—"

"Get to the important part," Maazi interrupted impatiently as they reached the clinic. The crowd of curiosity seekers was still clustered around the entrance and Maazi shoved his way through roughly.

Inside the clinic, the doctor led the way to a small room that had been transformed into a private ward. Tayfield lay on a bed, dressed in a white gown. Attached to his arm was an intravenous drip. His breathing was very shallow, his eyes closed. Only when Reynard stared hard could he see the sick man's chest rise and fall.

"Before he lapsed into the coma," the doctor said quietly, "he spoke as if in his sleep. He rambled. He seemed delirious."

"So?" Reynard took hold of Tayfield's wrist. The pulse rate was deathly slow.

"He spoke about Rashidieh," the doctor said. "About the *fedayeen*, about their arms, about their ammunition caches."

Continuing to hold Tayfield's wrist, Reynard did not seem to hear. Suddenly Maazi grabbed him by the shoulder and swung him around. "When he spoke about Rashidieh, he spoke in Hebrew!"

"What?" Abruptly, Reynard let go of Tayfield's wrist. "Are you sure it was Hebrew?" he asked the doctor.

"Of course I'm sure. I speak the language."

"Do you know what that means?" Maazi demanded. "Do you understand what you've done? You—yes, you!—introduced an Israeli spy into our midst!"

"That's impossible!" Reynard protested. "Tayfield's a Welshman. You can check that out easily enough. How can he be an Israeli spy?"

"The same way that a Syrian-Armenian named George Tokvarian was an Israeli spy. We caught him a few months ago. Now we catch another."

"Tokvarian—?" Reynard's light brown eyes narrowed and Maazi recognized confusion there.

183

"Yes, Tokvarian. Yussuf Torbuk and Ahmed el-Shafri caught him trying to send a message from his apartment in Beirut. And now the Israelis use you to replace him."

"Then what does that make Samantha?"

"Yes—what does that make Samantha?" Maazi's brain was reeling from the abrupt turn of events. He could barely bring himself to accept that Tayfield—that weak, inconsequential little leech of a man—could be a spy. But Samantha as well? That would mean that not only Reynard had been duped; it would mean that Maazi had been fooled also. "You interviewed her for me. What do you think?"

Reynard shook his head in disbelief. "You know her as well as I do, Salim. Do you think she could have been this convincing?"

"She is an actress."

"And is he?" Reynard pointed to Tayfield.

"I don't know. I'm not sure about anything anymore. But I hope for your sake, Pierre, that Samantha Sutcliffe is not a spy." Maazi strode out of the clinic with Reynard close behind. He called for el-Shafri and told the gray-haired Palestinian to fetch Rima from the school.

"Return to the hut and stay with Samantha," Maazi instructed Reynard. "Tell her Tayfield is all right—tell her whatever you like, just keep her calm."

"What if she wants to see him?"

"She can, later on, after Rima gets here."

When Rima returned with el-Shafri, Maazi explained quickly what had transpired, from Tayfield's panicky attempt to protect Samantha to his ramblings in Hebrew. Rima's face flushed with a mixture of confusion and anger.

"The English rose you were so fond of—an Israeli?"

A tight expression hardened Maazi's face as he recognized the mocking bitterness in Rima's voice. "We don't know yet. We have to check. In the meantime I want you to stay with her."

"To guard her?"

"Yes, but in such a way that she will not know she is under guard. Do you understand me?" Maazi waited for Rima to nod in agreement before he continued. "You will be her companion. She will stay here as long as Tayfield is in the clinic, and he will remain there until I know exactly what has taken place."

He watched Rima walk toward the hut, then he delivered his final orders to Ahmed el-Shafri. "Take Yussuf with you. Go to Paris immediately. By tonight I want you to have located the producer of Samantha Sutcliffe's last film, *La Maquisarde*. When you find him, I want you to learn why he chose Samantha Sutcliffe for that role."

"Do you think the producer could be part of this?"

"You and Yussuf will find out for me."

Driving the rented Austin, Rosen followed Mrs. Riley and David in the Range Rover to Heathrow Airport to meet Middle East Airlines flight 201 from Beirut. If the flight was on time, Rosen estimated that he would have two hours to talk with Tayfield before his own British Airways flight to Frankfurt left. At Frankfurt he would hook up with a flight to Tel Aviv.

The Beirut flight landed ten minutes ahead of schedule at four twenty-five in the afternoon. By five-twenty the last of the passengers had come through customs and still Rosen waited. He could see Mrs. Riley fidgeting anxiously. David was nowhere in sight and Rosen assumed he had become bored with the wait and had wandered off.

A Middle East Airlines flight attendant walked past, and Rosen asked if there were any more passengers. The young woman shook her head.

Anxious now, he walked over to the information desk and told the clerk on duty that the two passengers he was waiting for had not arrived. When he gave the names, the clerk lifted a telephone and called the Middle East Airlines office.

"I'm sorry, sir, but there seems to have been a misunderstanding."

"What kind of a misunderstanding?" Rosen asked nervously.

"Passengers Tayfield and Sutcliffe confirmed their reservations well in advance, but they didn't make the flight."

"Thank you." Rosen walked back to Mrs. Riley. David came running from a book shop to join them. "They missed the flight." Rosen said with a forced lightness. "Maybe they'll be home tomorrow."

David seemed disappointed but Mrs. Riley's face reflected skepticism. She did not believe Rosen for a moment. He shrugged his shoulders helplessly.

While Mrs. Riley took David back to the Range Rover, Rosen went to the car-rental desk and took out another vehicle. Then he hastened to a telephone. He did not have the time to call General Avivi directly. Instead he placed a call to the Israeli embassy and spoke to Karpinsky.

"Relay the information to the *memuneh* that they haven't shown up," he ordered the London resident. "And tell him that I'm staying put until they do."

CHAPTER
FOURTEEN

I T was shortly after seven in the evening when Paul Hechter left his office. Leaden skies and a driving rain greeted him as he stepped onto the sidewalk, pulled up the collar of his raincoat and looked optimistically along the Rue Marbeuf for a taxi. He was late for dinner already. His wife, Gabrielle, allowed their four-year-old daughter to stay up on Friday night for the Sabbath dinner, and Hechter always tried to be home by six-thirty. Tonight, though, he had been unavoidably detained by a last minute appointment.

A black Renault rolled slowly toward him, wipers sweeping a clear swathe across the windshield, tires spilling water from the flooded gutter onto the sidewalk. Hechter's hopes brightened. Could the driver of the Renault be someone he knew, a good Samaritan? His anticipation grew when the rear door of the Renault swung open as the car drew level.

And then Paul Hechter found himself staring down the barrel of a submachine gun held unwaveringly by Yussuf Torbuk.

"Get in," Torbuk said in French.

Hechter looked around nervously. People walked by under umbrellas, others scurried past with bowed heads; all were totally oblivious to the drama taking place.

"Get in," Torbuk repeated.

Hechter climbed into the back seat. Maintaining a grip on the gun with one hand, Torbuk reached across Hechter to slam the door. Immediately, Ahmed el-Shafri pulled away from the curb and headed toward the junction with the Champs-Élysées.

"What do you want from me?" Hechter asked.

"Turn out your pockets," Torbuk answered.

Constantly aware of the gun pointed at his side, Hechter emptied his pockets. The thick bundle of cash he carried was examined by Torbuk. With a laugh, the smooth-faced Palestinian rolled down the window and scattered the banknotes onto the wet street. "Sorry, Hechter," he said regretfully. "You don't carry enough cash to bother about." He turned his attention to the wallet, scattered documents onto the floor of the car until he found a driving license. "Rue Danou," he called out to el-Shafri.

"Where is that?"

"Answer him," Torbuk commanded, prodding Hechter with the gun.

"Off the Boulevard des Capucines, near the Opera House."

El-Shafri turned right onto the Champs-Élysées and joined the heavy flow of Friday-night traffic.

"Who is at your home?" Torbuk asked. Hechter was slow to answer and Torbuk rammed the muzzle of the gun viciously into his side. Hechter gasped in pain. "Who is at your home?"

"My family. My wife, Gabrielle, and my daughter, Tanya."

"No one else?"

"No one."

"That's better," Torbuk crooned. "See how much easier it is when you cooperate with us."

Hechter fought down the pain in his side and tried to think what these men could want. Not money; they had demonstrated that already. He attempted to place their accents. They spoke French well enough but it was not the language of Paris. And they had known his name even before going through his wallet. "What do you want from my family?"

"You'll find out soon enough. But if you do as we say, no harm will befall them."

"Do you have a doorman at your apartment?" el-Shafri asked as he stopped for a red light.

For a moment Hechter considered opening the door and leaping out. No, that was hopeless. A dozen bullets would rip into him before he landed on the street. And even if he did escape, what then? These two men had his address from the driving license. They would go straight there. Even before he could call the police these men would exact their revenge upon his family. He resigned himself to cooperating. "Yes, there is a doorman."

"You will act like we are your friends, then," said el-Shafri. "You would rather have us as friends than as enemies, right?"

When they reached the apartment building on the Rue Danou, el-Shafri got out first and held open the rear door for Torbuk to exit. Torbuk gripped the submachine gun under the cover of his coat while he waited for Hechter to get out. The uniformed doorman greeted Hechter with a polite little half salute. Hechter nodded in response.

"This way," Hechter said to el-Shafri and Torbuk, leading them to the elevator.

"Which floor?" Torbuk asked.

"Three."

Torbuk pulled the door closed and pressed the button. At the third floor they got out and walked along a narrow, carpeted hallway. Hechter produced a key and unlocked the door to his apartment.

"Paul, is that you? You're late," a woman's voice called out.

"Answer her!" Torbuk hissed as he pushed Hechter into the apartment and kicked the door shut. The submachine gun was in plain sight now, and a pistol had appeared in el-Shafri's right hand.

"I had to work late, darling. I'm sorry."

There was the sound of footsteps, the light racing ones of Tanya, and the heavier, measured tread of Gabrielle Hechter, swollen in her seventh month of pregnancy.

"Paul!" Grabrielle gasped as she saw the two armed men with her husband. Her dark brown eyes opened wide in fright. "What—"

"Shut up!" Torbuk snapped. He pushed Hechter toward his family. "Inside, all of you!"

They entered the dining room where the table was set for Friday-night dinner. Candles in silver holders waited to be lit. There was a bottle of wine and a silver goblet, the Sabbath *hallah*. "Sit down at the table," Torbuk ordered.

Obediently, Hechter took his place at the head of the table; Gabrielle sat on his left with Tanya opposite. While Torbuk stood in the doorway from where he could survey the entire room, el-Shafri took up a position next to Hechter. "We have some questions to ask you. If you answer them to our satisfaction, no one will be harmed."

"What kind of questions?" Gabrielle asked.

"Do you see how worried your wife is, Hechter?" el-Shafri said. "She wants to live long enough to enjoy the child she is carrying. And that depends on you."

"What is it you want to know?"

"The film you made, *La Maquisarde.*"

"What about it?"

"Why did you give the part to Samantha Sutcliffe?"

Suddenly Hechter knew who these men were, why their accents were not those of Paris. "I gave her the role because she was best suited for it."

El-Shafri asked again. "Why did you give the part to Samantha Sutcliffe?"

"I just told you. Why does any producer give an actress a certain role?"

El-Shafri moved quickly. His free hand snaked out to grab Tanya's long black hair and pull her head back. The girl started to scream in terror and el-Shafri jerked her clean out of the chair.

"Paul!" Gabrielle cried out. "Tell them whatever it is they want to know! For God's sake!"

"I just did." Conflicting loyalties ripped through Hechter. Did his deal with the Mossad include this, being forced to watch while his daughter was assaulted, his family destroyed?

El-Shafri pressed the muzzle of the pistol against Tanya's temple. "Make no mistake, Hechter, the bullet from this gun will smash through your child's head like an egg," he said softly. "And I will have no hesitation in pulling the trigger. Now, for the last time, why did you give that role to Samantha Sutcliffe?"

Unable to tear his eyes away from his daughter's chalk white face and the angry patch of red where the muzzle of the gun pressed, Hechter answered: "I was asked to, as a favor."

"A favor to whom?"

"To—" Again, Hechter faltered.

"A favor to her manager, Alan Tayfield?" el-Shafri prompted.

"How—"

"We know everything, Hechter. We just want to hear it from your lips." El-Shafri released the girl's hair abruptly and she collapsed onto the floor, crying hysterically. Ignoring the weapons held by the two Palestinians, Gabrielle rose from her chair and went to her daughter, holding her tightly.

"Who does Tayfield work for?" el-Shafri asked.

"Do you promise that nothing will happen to my family?"

"We promise."

"He works for the Israelis. He is Israeli."

189

"Is he with the Mossad?"

"I believe so."

"Is Alan Tayfield his real name?"

"No. It's Gershon Shual."

"Did he tell you why he wanted Samantha Sutcliffe to have that particular role?"

A belated loyalty to Tayfield tore at Hechter and he shook his head. It was obvious that these men knew all about Tayfield—perhaps he was dead already—but they were uncertain about Samantha. While seeming to give them everything he knew, Hechter could still protect her.

"What about the woman? Is she working with Tayfield? Or is he just using her?"

"I don't know," Hechter lied.

"The truth!"

"That is the truth." The panic in Hechter's voice was genuine and he was glad of its presence; it made him more confident that his altered version would be accepted. "Tayfield only told me he needed a role for Samantha that would arouse controversy. I had just signed for *La Maquisarde*. We tested Samantha for the role and she was perfect."

El-Shafri was satisfied. No man lied when guns were pointed at his wife and daughter. He walked away from the table and approached the stereo system that rested on a stand by the wall. Working quickly, he leafed through the records, finally selecting the *1812 Overture*. He placed the record on the turntable, dropped the arm toward the end of the piece and turned up the volume. Cannon fire and the ringing of bells filled the room, echoing distortedly off the walls.

Hechter sensed what was about to happen. He stood up, clutching the edge of the table as he stared at el-Shafri. "You promised that you would not harm my family—"

"Promises to Zionists?" Torbuk said from the doorway, and laughed as he opened fire with the submachine gun. The staccato burst was drowned out by the clamor of battle from the loudspeakers.

Hechter was the first to die as three bullets stitched a bloody pattern across his chest. Gabrielle was next, clasping her hands in front of her swollen belly as if to protect her unborn child. Finally, Tobruk pointed the hot weapon at the tiny figure of Tanya, still lying on the floor. For a moment he hesitated, as if debating whether to spare her young life. Hatred drowned out any spark of sympathy as he glimpsed the silver goblet, the candlesticks, the bottle of wine, the Sabbath *hallah*, all miraculously undisturbed by the hail of bullets. He squeezed the trigger in a short, savage burst.

The ringing sound of the climax to the *1812 Overture* stayed with the two Palestinians as they walked briskly along the hallway, down the stairs and out of the building to their car.

By the following evening, el-Shafri and Torbuk were back at Rashidieh, reporting on their mission to Salim Maazi.

Maazi listened expressionlessly. It was good that they had killed the producer and his family; it was a lesson from which others might take heed. But, he questioned, could they have learned more? Had Hechter fooled them as Tokvarian had once fooled them? And as Tayfield would have fooled them had he not panicked when the Israeli Kfir had overflown the refugee camp?

"He knew nothing more than he told us," Torbuk said as he sensed Maazi's doubts. "He was a family man, his wife and daughter were his treasures. He would have done anything to avoid harming them."

"Then why did he become involved in this scheme?"

"Because he was a Zionist," el-Shafri answered. "When Tayfield asked the favor, Hechter could never have known that one day it would come back to him. Believe me, Salim, if Hechter had known about Samantha, he would have begged us to listen."

"How is Tayfield?" Torbuk asked.

"Still in a coma."

"Is there any hope of his recovering?"

Maazi shook his head. "The doctor says he's slipping."

"And the Sutcliffe woman?"

"She sits on her bed with Rima for company." For the first time Maazi's face showed some emotion, a grim smile as he considered the scenario he had created. Out of sheer jealousy Rima would happily kill Samantha, who had everything the Palestinian woman could possibly want: wealth, fame, a healthy son. Now, if it were true that Samantha was also a spy, Rima would tear her apart slowly, exact her own cruel revenge upon the fair-skinned Englishwoman for what the Phalangists had done to her husband and children at Tel al-Za'atar. But until Maazi knew for certain, Rima was being forced to play the sympathetic figure. Rima was a far better actress than Samantha could ever hope to be, Maazi decided. "Find Reynard for me," he told Torbuk and el-Shafri. "Bring him here right away."

191

While he waited for the French journalist, Maazi carefully considered his options. He could decide arbitrarily that Samantha was a spy, and he could dispose of her accordingly. She would just disappear, along with Tayfield—two victims of the Lebanese turmoil; such tragedies happened all the time. But if she was not a spy . . .

That intrigued Maazi the most. If Samantha had been used as an unwitting tool, as the key—if her sympathies for the Palestinians were genuine and had been cleverly exploited by the Israelis—she could become a most dangerous weapon in Maazi's hands. He had to know the truth!

"You wanted me?" Reynard asked as he entered the room where Maazi sat thinking.

"Sit down." Maazi gazed coolly at Reynard, trying to judge how the Frenchman would react to the news he was about to receive. "Ahmed and Yussuf have just returned from Paris. They interviewed the producer of Samantha Sutcliffe's last film."

"Paul Hechter?" Reynard asked without hesitation. He remembered Hechter well from the press conference at La Tour d'Argent. If ever Reynard had seen a man totally shattered by an unexpected turn of events, it had been the producer.

"That's right, Paul Hechter. He's dead now."

"Dead?" Reynard blinked in surprise.

"His wife and daughter are also dead," Maazi said evenly. "It was regrettable but necessary."

Reynard was chilled by the news, the callous manner in which Maazi spoke about the deaths of three people. "Why? What are you talking about?"

"Alan Tayfield and Paul Hechter worked together, Pierre."

"Hechter—" Reynard closed and opened his mouth like a fish out of water. "Hechter was an Israeli agent?"

"He was sympathetic. Tayfield needed a controversial platform for Samantha Sutcliffe, a role where her alleged sympathies for our struggle would receive enormous exposure. Tayfield asked Hechter for a favor,.to cast Samantha in that role, and Hechter complied."

"Samantha, too? Another Israeli?"

"I don't know yet. All I do know is that they used you to bring Samantha to me, with Tayfield clinging to her like a leech."

"Wait a minute—" Reynard protested when he saw the blame being shifted onto himself.

192

Maazi reached down underneath his chair and brought up the Beretta submachine gun. The words died on Reynard's lips as Maazi cocked the weapon and pointed it squarely at the Frenchman's chest. "Why should I not kill you now, Pierre?"

Reynard looked from the muzzle of the gun into Maazi's eyes. They were cold, like twin points of ice fixed on Reynard's face. "Because you know damned well you'd be a fool if you did. And I don't think you want to appear a fool in front of your people. You won't pull that trigger, Salim. I'm more use to you alive than dead."

"If I had killed you three months ago, before you interviewed that damned woman and suggested using her in a documentary, we would not have been infiltrated by the Israelis. Would that have made me look a fool?"

Reynard felt sweat dripping down the side of his nose and knew he was only moments from death. "What did the Israelis learn?"

"Nothing."

"Then what harm was done? If anything, you're the winner because you've eliminated one of them. That makes two of their people you've caught in the last couple of months. Tayfield and that Armenian—"

"Tokvarian."

"That's him. You're beating them, Salim, can't you see that?"

The door swung back with a crash. Maazi turned around and Reynard closed his eyes in an involuntary flinching motion. The crash of the door could so easily have been the sound of the submachine gun. El-Shafri stood in the doorway, his face red from the exertion of running. "Come quickly!" he gasped. "The clinic! Tayfield!"

Gripping the Beretta tightly in his right hand, Maazi followed el-Shafri. Reynard kept pace with him. In the clinic they found two doctors standing by Tayfield's bed. One was removing the intravenous drip; the other turned the sheet over Tayfield's face.

"What happened?" Maazi asked.

"He died. A few minutes ago."

"Did he ever regain consciousness?" The question came from Reynard as he lifted the sheet and placed his hand on Tayfield's forehead; it was still warm to the touch.

"No. His heart just ceased to function."

Reynard let his hand rest on Tayfield's head for a few seconds; then he drew Maazi away from the bed, out of the doctor's hearing. "Salim, there is a way to learn if Samantha Sutcliffe is a spy."

"How?" Maazi's gaze flickered from Reynard to Tayfield and back. Was Reynard trying to demonstrate how valuable he was? Did he understand how close he had come to death? How, if it had not been for el-Shafri's urgent summons, the trigger might have been pressed all the way?

"Listen carefully."

As Reynard spoke, Maazi began to smile. El-Shafri's summons had been a timely omen not to kill the Frenchman, for now Reynard was demonstrating how valuable his intellect and imagination could be.

Sometimes, even Maazi had to admit, wisdom was as powerful a weapon as courage.

Sitting up straight on a collapsible canvas chair, Rima Bakri stared at the figure of Samantha stretched out on the bed. Now that Samantha was asleep, emotionally exhausted after more than a day of worrying about Tayfield, Rima could release herself from the role Maazi had told her to adopt. She was enjoying this moment, this opportunity to gloat over the plight of the English actress who had taken the Palestinians by storm, the idealist who had fired so bravely—and so ineffectively—at the Israeli Phantom; the scheming witch who had seduced Salim Maazi.

How weak and pitiful Samantha seemed now, Rima rejoiced as she remembered her own reactions after Tel al-Za'atar. She had not broken down and wept like this. No—she had straightened her back and, with her elderly father, had left the smoking ruins of the refugee camp to journey south where she would be able to continue the struggle. Her sacrifices had made her stronger.

Rima hoped that Maazi would somehow find proof to incriminate Samantha. Nothing would please the Palestinian woman more than to witness this aloof English bitch beg in vain for her life. And then her precious son—so safe in England—would be struck by the same grief that Rima had once borne.

Samantha stirred, began to wake. Immediately, Rima resumed her act, slipping on a mask of sympathy. "How do you feel?" she asked solicitously.

"How long was I asleep?" Samantha rubbed her red-rimmed eyes with her hands. No matter what happened now she felt sure she would be unable to cry anymore; her tear ducts had run dry.

"Almost an hour."

"Has there been any news?"

"None. I would have waked you if there had been. Would you like something to eat?"

"I'm not hungry, thank you." Gnawing pains bit into her stomach. She had not eaten for more than a day but she knew she would be unable to keep anything down. All she wanted was for Tayfield to recover, for both of them to leave—and that would take a miracle. Goddamn that bastard Israeli pilot! If it had not been for him, she and Tayfield would be away from here by now, back in the comfortable security of England. And what of David and Mrs. Riley? Had they gone to meet the plane she and Tayfield were supposed to have been on? What were they thinking now?

Rima turned away from Samantha as the door was pushed back. Maazi and Reynard entered.

"How do you feel?" Maazi asked Samantha.

"Drained," she replied. "I'll only feel better when Alan is well and we can leave."

"I'm sorry to say that might be a little while yet. Has Rima been looking after you properly?"

"She's been wonderful," Samantha answered, surprised by the rush of warmth she suddenly felt for the Palestinian woman. Rima had cared for her like a mother would nurse a sick child.

Maazi squatted on his haunches next to the bed. "Samantha, I have something to tell you which might come as a shock."

"What?" Samantha looked nervously from Maazi to Reynard, and finally to Rima who continued to sit in the chair.

"Your manager, Alan Tayfield—he is an Israeli named Gershon Shual."

Samantha's mouth dropped open; nothing could have prepared her for this.

"Tayfield is a spy, Samantha," Reynard added unnecessarily. "An Israeli spy."

Five seconds passed while Samantha struggled to regain her composure. Then she exploded in a furious denial. "That's impossible! I've known Alan for years! He's managed my career! He's a Welshman, not an Israeli!"

"No, Samantha," Reynard countered. "He is an Israeli."

"How on earth did you manage to reach this preposterous conclusion?"

"Yesterday, after he suffered his attack. While in the clinic he spoke deliriously—and he spoke in Hebrew."

"Hebrew?" She gave a brittle laugh. "Are you too stupid to recognize the difference between Hebrew and Welsh?"

195

"The doctor who overheard him understands Hebrew perfectly," Maazi said. "Tayfield spoke about our people, about Rashidieh, the weapons he had seen, troop strength."

"No!" Samantha shook her head and the thick brown hair flew about wildly, lashing her face. "It can't be! It can't be!" She heaved herself off the bed and began to walk around the room. By Rima's chair she stopped. "Did you know anything about this?"

"Yes." Rima looked up at Samantha, a slight smile playing around her mouth.

"Then why wasn't I told?" she snapped, swinging back to Maazi. "Why am I the last one to know?"

"We had to make certain," Maazi replied.

"And how did you do that? Did you call the Israelis and ask them?"

Maazi ignored the sarcasm. "We talked to the producer of your last film in Paris."

"To Paul Hechter? And he confirmed this lunacy? He said that Alan works for the Israelis?"

"Not voluntarily." Maazi smiled and shrugged his shoulders. "We had to jog his memory a fraction. Eventually he told us that Tayfield approached him to give you a role that would raise controversy."

"Samantha, the Israelis exploited your sympathies for the Palestinian people so that they could turn you into their Trojan horse," Reynard tried to explain. "They hid behind you."

"I already told you, it's impossible. For two years I've been as close to Alan as—as—" In her excited attempt to disprove their allegations she failed to find a suitable analogy. "Do you think I wouldn't have seen through him? Do you think I'm stupid?"

"Perhaps not," Maazi said. "Perhaps you are very clever, Samantha, in which case there is only one alternative: if you were not used by Tayfield, then you were in this thing with him."

Samantha stared in horror at Maazi as the charge was leveled.

"Have you ever been to Israel?" Maazi asked.

"Never!" She spat out the word. "What is this, an inquisition? Am I on trial here?"

Reynard raised a hand to stop any further questions from Maazi. "Samantha, if you are truly what you say you are—a friend of the Palestinian people—then the only emotion you should be feeling right now is outrage. Not at us, but at Tayfield and the Israelis. We have concrete proof that Tayfield is a spy. His reports to Israel bring their bombs down upon the heads of Palestinian children. Think of that and tell us what you feel."

Samantha breathed out heavily. She understood why Reynard was pressing her so hard. He had led her to Maazi, suggested using her in the documentary. Reynard had been the first to be fooled, and his enthusiasm had helped to convert others. Now Maazi was blaming him. Reynard's own head was on the chopping block.

"Well?" he prompted impatiently. "What do you feel?"

"Outrage," she replied in a hushed voice, using the very word that Reynard had suggested. "I feel outraged."

"Because you and your convictions were exploited by the Israelis?"

She nodded.

"But how can we believe that?" Reynard asked with sudden sharpness.

"How can you not?" Samantha cried out. "You ask me a question and then you dare to doubt my answer!"

"A test—we need a test," Maazi broke in, looking to Reynard. "Like the biblical wise king of Israel, Solomon, we need a foolproof test." He laughed at the odd comparison he had formed and looked around the room to see who would share the joke. Then, from the holster on his waist, he removed a Makarov pistol and worked the operating mechanism with a menacing snap. Samantha flinched at the crisp noise.

"Samantha, I want you to prove to us how outraged you are. By . . . killing . . . Alan . . . Tayfield."

Samantha spun around as a muted laugh broke the shocked silence of the room. Belatedly Rima held a hand over her mouth to disguise the obvious enjoyment she was finding in the drama.

"Here is the gun, Samantha," Maazi said. "One shot is all you will need. One shot, the *coup de grace*, and you will prove your good faith in our eyes."

"My good faith was never in doubt," she replied, eyes swinging back to Maazi, transfixed by the pistol he held out, butt first, to her.

"Samantha, there is no other way we can believe you." The soft-spoken words came from Reynard. "No other way."

"You bastard," she swore at him. "You stinking, hypocritical bastard." In that moment she hated the French journalist more than she had ever hated any man.

Rima stood up, gripped Samantha by the arm and pushed her roughly toward the door. "You fired many bullets at a plane," she reminded the actress. "Surely it will not be difficult for you to fire just one bullet at a sick man. Remember your anger of that day and use it again."

As a group they walked to the clinic, Samantha still held by Rima, with Maazi and Reynard bringing up the rear. In Tayfield's room, a doctor was checking the level of the drip. Maazi motioned for him to leave. Samantha stared down at the bed. Tayfield lay on his back. The sheet was up to his neck but his left arm was exposed to accept the drip. His eyes were closed, his face sickeningly pale, and he did not appear to be breathing. In the coma he looked as he might in death.

"Take the gun, Samantha," Maazi said. He held her hand and pressed the butt of the Makarov into it. "Do what you have to do."

As if in a trance, Samantha clenched her hand around the butt. She knew she had to squeeze the trigger. Her own life—the chance of seeing David again—depended on her ability to line up the weapon on Tayfield's chest and squeeze that damned trigger. Tayfield was as good as dead already. The heart attack, the lack of proper medical attention, the coma. It was just a matter of time—days, hours, maybe even minutes. It would be a mercy killing; no one would blame her. All she would be doing would be hastening the process, aiding nature. Could that possibly be called murder?

Of course it was murder! a voice inside her screamed. And she loathed herself for even thinking about killing him.

"Samantha, pull the trigger," Reynard urged softly. "Pull the trigger and prove your innocence."

Her hand felt like a lead weight as she raised the gun. The sight of the Makarov split Tayfield's chest. Just a couple of pounds of pressure, that was all. A couple of pounds of pressure on the curved metal trigger and her own safety would be assured. She would see David again, return to England, be away from all this madness.

She started to squeeze, willing herself to carry through the action. The minute amount of slack in the trigger was taken up.

Then she froze. She could not go on.

One more time Reynard urged her. "Pull the trigger, Samantha."

She swung around, the Makarov raised to face height, arm held out straight in front of her eyes. First the sight crossed Reynard's face, eyes startled now behind the glasses, then Rima's. Finally it split Maazi's face.

"May you rot in hell, you bastard!"

Maazi gazed into the muzzle of the Makarov, so close to his eyes that the rifling of the barrel was startlingly clear. He did not move. He only smiled. Samantha squeezed the trigger.

"Click!"

The hammer dropped onto an empty chamber. The gun had been unloaded. They had tested her with trickery and she had failed.

Maazi leaped forward, knocked the gun aside with one hand and slapped Samantha hard across the face. She staggered back and would have fallen had not Reynard caught her. The Makarov dropped to the floor.

"Israeli whore!" Maazi yelled. He strode to the other side of the bed and yanked the tube from Tayfield's arm. He took the bottle from the stand and flung it at Samantha's feet, showering her with liquid and broken glass.

"Stop it!" Samantha screamed. "You'll kill him!"

"Kill him?" Maazi gave a blood-chilling laugh as he bent down, placed both hands under the mattress and tipped Tayfield's body onto the floor. "Your fellow spy died half an hour ago, Israeli whore! And you're going to wish you'd died with him!"

"Rima—take her away and find out everything she knows!"

"So you feel the Palestinians deserve justice, do you? You love us because we're downtrodden, eh?" Rima taunted with a mocking gentleness as Ahmed el-Shafri and Yussuf Torbuk tied Samantha's wrists and ankles to the bunk in the hut which had been her accommodation. Stretched out and totally defenseless, Samantha could only watch as the dark face of the Palestinian woman came closer, her mouth curving in a thin, sadistic expression of pleasure.

"Very soon the Palestinians will love you in return. Ahmed will make love to you, so will Yussuf."

Samantha's eyes flicked to the faces of the two men. El-Shafri's face was covered in sweat as if he found the simple task of binding her ankles strenuous; or was it the anticipation of fondling her body that prompted the perspiration? Yet it was Torbuk's unlined face that terrified Samantha the most; he looked so innocent, so unworn by life, but those deep brown eyes blazed with a murderous passion.

"Which one would you like to have first?" Rima asked. "Or perhaps you'd like to have both Ahmed and Yussuf together?"

Samantha coughed hoarsely, hawked up a piece of phlegm and spit it into Rima's face. The Palestinian woman jumped back, wiping frantically

199

at her cheek with her hand. She looked in disgust at her hand before balling it into a hard, tight fist and slamming it like a hammer against Samantha's right breast.

Samantha's agonized scream filled the room before she clamped her mouth shut, determined to rob her tormentors of the satisfaction of her cries. Tears sprang to her eyes, flooded down her cheeks. She felt a viselike grip on her hair, dragging her head up from the bed. Her head rocked back and forth as Rima slapped her from side to side, swift stinging blows that numbed her cheeks and rattled her teeth.

"Why are you here?" Another two slaps and Samantha's ears rang with the force of the blows. "Why are you here?"

"Go to hell, you murdering bitch!" Samantha managed to spit out. She was no longer frightened. How could they do anything more to her than they had already done?

Rima let go of Samantha's hair and stepped back, motioning to Torbuk. With two hands he ripped Samantha's blouse, leaving it in tatters. Rima held out a hand and Torbuk passed her a bone-handled, slim-bladed knife. She set the cold steel flat against Samantha's stomach. While Samantha shivered at the touch of the metal and watched in helpless fascination, Rima cut upwards with a swift, deft motion. Samantha's white brassiere fell open and the sharp edge of the knife rested gently against the underside of her right breast.

"Why . . . are . . . you here?"

Samantha could feel the blade pressing into her skin. She closed her eyes, gritted her teeth and pressed her lips together. Could she hold her breath long enough to suffocate, bring about her own death and cheat Rima?

The blade was so sharp that Samantha barely felt it move. Nothing more than an instant of pressure; then she was aware of a warm wetness spilling across her stomach. Rima's hand grabbed her hair again, lifted her up.

"Look!"

Samantha opened her eyes to see the two-inch cut below her right breast, the blood that flowed steadily.

"Why were you sent here? What is your mission?" Rima brushed her hand across the open wound and smeared the warm blood around Samantha's mouth. "Did you breast-feed your son as I breast-fed my children? How would you like us to mail your breasts to your son?"

The sight of the crimson stain on the Palestinian woman's hand

200

snapped something deep within Samantha's mind. Her strong resolve to deny them anything disappeared as she licked her lips and tasted the sweetness of her own blood. "Black September!" she screamed.

"What about Black September!" Rima teased the open wound with the blade of the knife.

"Reactivation—I came to learn about Black September's reactivation!"

Rima cursed and opened her hands to let Samantha's head fall back. She swung around to el-Shafri and Torbuk. "You fools! They know!" Then, still clutching the blood-smeared knife, she raced from the hut to find Maazi.

Pierre Reynard watched Maazi supervise the removal from the clinic of Alan Tayfield's corpse, rolled up in a dirty tarpaulin. "What are you going to do with him?"

"Bury him. The sands will take care of the matter for us. Ideally"— he placed a hand on Reynard's shoulder as the bulky tarpaulin was loaded unceremoniously into the back of a jeep—"I would like to send his body back to his masters in Israel as a little memento of how efficient we Palestinians are. But it is a luxury I cannot afford at this time. It is better that their man just disappears."

"And their woman?"

Maazi signaled to the jeep driver, and the vehicle moved away in a growling low gear, carrying Tayfield's body on its final journey to the outskirts of Rashidieh. He turned back to Reynard and surprised himself by feeling a touch of genuine warmth for the Frenchman, so much in contrast to the fury he had felt earlier, when he had pointed the submachine gun at Reynard's chest, fully prepared to pull the trigger. "Pierre, the credit for exposing Samantha Sutcliffe rests with you. What would you suggest we do with her?"

"Salim, I am a Frenchman. Moreover, I am a Parisian. To me, a thing of beauty is to be treasured—"

"And you feel that Samantha Sutcliffe is too beautiful to die, even as a spy, eh?" Maazi asked, chuckling. "Remember," he added, "you once warned me about letting my *couilles* rule my head."

"I remember, but it would still seem a tragic waste," Reynard said. He looked around as he heard Maazi's name being called. Fifty yards away, Rima stood gesturing urgently with the hand that still held the knife. Maazi and Reynard ran toward her.

"She knows!" Rima gasped. "The Englishwoman knows!"

"Knows what?" Maazi snapped.

"She was sent here to learn about the reactivation of Black September. She knows—the Israelis know—about the mission!"

"Impossible! They cannot!" Maazi raced past Rima toward the hut. Inside he found el-Shafri standing by the bunk while Yussuf Torbuk sat on a chair, staring as if mesmerized at the wound below Samantha's right breast. Following Maazi and Rima into the hut, Reynard gulped when he saw the cut and the blood that continued to flow out.

Maazi spun around to confront Torbuk, and a swift backhanded slap knocked the smooth-faced guerrilla out of the chair, onto the floor. "Liar!" Maazi screamed accusingly. "You told me Tokvarian got no message out before you killed him! You were right on his heels, you said! Liar!" He turned on el-Shafri, kicking out wildly at the gray-haired Palestinian. El-Shafri made no attempt to defend himself.

"Salim!" Rima's voice rose sharply above Maazi's yelling as if she were trying to quell a class of noisy schoolchildren. "Now is not the time! What about her?"

Maazi blinked as he tried to control his anger and direct it against Samantha. He took the knife from Rima and pressed it against Samantha's throat. A tiny spot of blood welled up where the point penetrated the skin. "Why do you work for the Israelis?" He wanted to drive the knife right through, until the point pierced the bunk below. Only that way could he salve the shame he felt. He had made love to this woman, told her those secrets of which he was so proud, and all the time she had been working against him, trying to destroy him. "What do the Israelis know? Tell me!"

Samantha stared at Maazi's brown hand, only inches from her chin where it held the knife. She knew now that she was going to die. Perhaps she had known it all along, from the very moment she had set foot on the Lebanese airliner at Heathrow. She and Tayfield had been condemned. But she would be damned forever if she gave Maazi the satisfaction of learning her reason for hating him—for hating all Palestinians—all Arabs. No, she would not furnish Maazi the extra joy of knowing how much he had cost her already. That decision gave her the strength to die with dignity. Slowly, a serene smile spread across her face as she waited for the final thrust that would join her again with Asher.

"What do the Israelis know?" Maazi screamed as he saw that calm smile and recognized its meaning. "Who controls you? Who do you report to?"

Around the room the others watched, hypnotized. Torbuk rose slowly from the floor until he rested in a half crouch. El-Shafri nursed his left leg where Maazi's kick had landed. Rima gazed raptly at the point of the knife pressing into Samantha's throat. No one moved.

Except Pierre Reynard. Without warning he leaped forward to grasp Maazi's arm, swung him around and pulled him away from the bunk. Maazi's eyes opened wide in disbelief, and then he lunged furiously with the knife, carving a huge circle toward the Frenchman's stomach.

If the blow had landed with the extreme force that Maazi put into it, Reynard would have been cut in half. But at the last moment, as the arc of gleaming silver was almost complete, he jumped back. The knife passed harmlessly and Maazi, failing to meet the resistance he had anticipated, lost his balance and slipped awkwardly to the floor. Reynard stepped forward instantly and pressed his foot down on Maazi's wrist with just enough force to pin him.

"Drop the knife!"

Maazi looked up and recognized the determination stamped on Reynard's face. He loosened his hold on the knife. "Remember the *couilles*," he whispered.

Reynard lifted his foot from Maazi's wrist and helped the Palestinian to stand, aware that both Rima and Torbuk were pointing guns uncertainly at him. For the moment Samantha had been forgotten. "This has nothing to do with the *couilles*, Salim. I'd just hate to see you throw away the best insurance policy you're ever likely to have."

Maazi looked from Reynard to Samantha. He noticed neither the cut Rima had made nor the tiny spot of blood that painted a harsh counterpoint to the whiteness of Samantha's throat; all he could see were her breasts. With difficulty he tore his eyes away and turned back to Reynard. "Insurance? I would be throwing nothing away. The Israelis never negotiate."

"This time they will negotiate. Somehow they have managed to convince a famous British actress to work for them. They cannot afford to let her die."

Maazi massaged his wrist while Rima picked up the knife. "Come with me," he told Reynard. When both men were standing outside the hut, Maazi said, "You should not have done what you did in there. I could have you killed. Like Tayfield you could just disappear."

"I was trying to save you from yourself, Salim."

Why was the Frenchman so unafraid? That question bothered Maazi.

203

"You are a strange man, Pierre," Maazi said. "Just when I think I know you perfectly, you confound me."

"I confounded myself as well when I made you drop that knife."

Now Maazi thought he understood. "You want to cross that bridge very desperately, don't you?"

"What bridge?"

"The bridge from writing about men of action to becoming one yourself. Twice today you have shown how important you are to me. First, by suggesting the way to expose Samantha; and now, by saving her from my fury, by keeping her as a valuable bargaining tool."

"I was only concerned that something might go wrong with your mission."

"What do you know of the mission?" Maazi asked suspiciously.

"Do you think I am deaf, Salim? Do you take me for an idiot? What did Rima scream before when she came running from the hut?"

"You tell me—what did she scream?"

"About the reactivation of Black September. About the mission."

"So?" Maazi made no effort to help Reynard.

"Salim, I have worked with you; I have been your friend for a long time. I am not blind. I have seen how you command these people, how you have the respect of the Palestinian leaders."

"And now you think I am planning this—this mission?"

"It would take a fool not to realize that."

"So, because of the privileged position you enjoy within my circle, you would like me to tell you what? No, Pierre, I learned a long time ago to tell journalists only what I want them to know. To give them other information is dangerous; they do not respect confidences."

"You do me an injustice."

"Your support for us would override your professional greed?"

"My support for your cause is my reason for being here."

Maazi walked away, staring at the shantytown of huts and tents that comprised Rashidieh. Should he tell Reynard that long ago he had considered including the French journalist in the operation as his personal chronicler? More importantly, had Reynard crossed enough of the bridge to be capable of carrying his own weight? Maazi could not afford to take Reynard along just for the ride, to ensure his own glorification. The occasion might arise where Reynard would need to use a gun, to kill. Would he have the courage for that?

And—considering the little that Reynard did know—could Maazi afford not to include him?

Maazi turned back to Reynard who stood waiting expectantly. "Pierre, if Tayfield had been alive and I had ordered you to dispose of him, would you have done so?"

"Yes." The answer came immediately.

"Good." Maazi waited a couple of seconds and then said, "Take my pistol, return to the hut and kill Samantha Sutcliffe."

"Are you trying to use the same method of trial for me that I suggested for Samantha?"

"Hoisting you with your own petard?"

"I believe that is the expression." Without hesitation Reynard held out his hand for the gun.

Maazi placed his hand on the holster, then shook his head and laughed delightedly. "I believe you would, Pierre. I really do believe that you would overcome your Parisian love of beauty and kill our insurance policy."

"I would willingly do whatever is necessary to prove myself to you."

"Perhaps you will have the opportunity later on. But first, we will keep her to bargain with. Afterward—when this mission you talk of is history and we have no further need to protect spies—you might be the one to kill her."

Then, as he did to those he loved and trusted, Maazi clasped Reynard's shoulders and kissed him on the cheek.

Late that night, while el-Shafri and Torbuk guarded Samantha in Rashidieh, Maazi met with Rima at her father's house in the nearby village. Speaking quietly for fear of waking old Hassan Bakri who slept soundly in the back room, Maazi and Rima discussed Samantha's exposure, and the knowledge that the Israelis were aware of Black September's reactivation.

A cloud on the horizon was the way Maazi described it to Rima. "But it is a cloud with a silver lining. We know now that the Israelis have heard about Black September's reactivation. But because of the tremendous cloak of secrecy that the American Robert Shea has cast over the negotiations, the Israelis can have no idea of what we are planning. Never would they dream that Shea's secret is not so sacred after all. And we will be even more cautious."

"Do you trust Reynard enough to include him?"

"Right now I trust him more than Yussuf and Ahmed after those fools lied to me about Tokvarian getting out a message before they captured him. I tell you, Rima, if I did not need them so much now—and if they had not served me so faithfully in the past—I would kill them."

Maazi's loyalty to his comrades from Black September's first incarnation—powerful enough to allow him to forgive them for errors that should cost their lives—stirred a chord within Rima. He was a man who was ruled by loyalty—to the cause he served and to those who served him. And that same loyalty included Rima. No matter what other women he found—whether in Europe where he had worked so long for the Palestinian struggle, or in Lebanon where the Zionist English witch had thrown herself upon him to discover his secrets—Rima knew he would always return to her. They shared too much to be separated.

"And Reynard's idea?" Rima asked. "To keep the woman in case something should go wrong?"

"Pierre has the ability to recognize many things that sometimes we cannot see," Maazi answered. "Before, I was so blinded by rage that I could see nothing. I would have killed the woman and she knew it. She was waiting for death with a smile on her face, exulting in the knowledge that she would be cheating me by denying me any information she knew. Now, thanks to Pierre, she will serve a purpose. He is right when he says that the Israelis will do anything to obtain Samantha Sutcliffe's release. They are afraid of world opinion; if they were not, they would have launched a war of genocide against the Palestinians many years ago. So they cannot afford to have the woman harmed while spying for them. One of their own people they would risk, but not this actress. If something should go wrong, and we use Samantha Sutcliffe as a hostage, the Israelis will go a long way to secure her release."

Rima left her own chair and crouched next to Maazi. He ran his fingers through her thick black hair, down her neck and under the rough fabric of her uniform shirt. She scorned the use of a brassiere. Her breasts were firmer, stronger, than Samantha's. Maazi recalled the vision of Samantha tied to the bunk, the blood glistening from the cut below her right breast. Never would he have imagined her possessing such strength of character as to defy him, to be prepared to die. What was the secret she guarded that gave her such determination?

"Salim, make love to me," Rima whispered.

Slowly he stood up and pulled Rima to her feet. Moving quietly, he led her to the rug in the center of the room. He knelt down and began to unbutton her shirt, peeling it back like a skin. Her full breasts bounced free and he kissed them, feeling the nipples harden under the caress of his tongue. Rima's hands pressed against the back of his head, pushing him down.

"Am I as good as your English actress?" she whispered. "Are her fair skin and blue eyes more desirable than what I have for you?"

"What makes you think I have enjoyed her as I enjoy you?"

"The truth shone in her eyes. Without saying a word she wanted me to know that she had stolen you. But I always knew you would come back."

Afterward they lay together on the rug, listening to the sounds of the night. Maazi's arm was pinned under Rima as she slept peacefully, and he could feel the numbness creeping into his hand. When he moved she stirred and turned toward him. Suddenly he laughed.

"What is it?" Rima asked, instantly alert.

"Perhaps Pierre is only half-right."

"What do you mean?"

Maazi laughed again and buried his face in Rima's neck to stifle the noise before it could wake old Hassan Bakri. "If the Israelis will go to great lengths to ensure Samantha Sutcliffe's safety should we need her as a hostage, for the actress *and* her son they would go to the ends of the earth."

CHAPTER
FIFTEEN

T HROUGH Pavel Vlasov, Salim Maazi
knew that the American-sponsored summit meeting would take place at
a yet-to-be-named United States military base in Europe. One country
came immediately to mind—Germany, where American strength was
greatest. Therefore, he wanted David Sutcliffe to be held in Germany, in
case the situation demanded hostages.

The instructions Maazi gave to three of his men—Wasim Jibril, Ali
Hushi and Hashim Zeira—before they traveled from Lebanon to Libya
and from there to England, were precise. They were to abduct David from
the farm in Somerset and transfer him to a safe house in Munich, inhab-
ited by Palestinians living in Germany.

In the early evening the three men passed through the checkpoints at
Heathrow Airport. The immigration officer glanced at the diplomatic
passports furnished by the Libyan government and quickly compared the
photographs: Jibril, black-haired with a long, flowing moustache; Hushi,
almost bald with a high-domed head and a large hooked nose; and
the short, plump Zeira with horn-rimmed glasses and a scruffy Arafat
beard.

A Cadillac from the Libyan embassy awaited the three men. Instead
of going into central London where the embassy was located, the driver
immediately headed west on the motorway toward Somerset. "Once you
have taken the boy, we will handle the matter," he told the three Palestinians.

"When can we expect to be in Germany?" Jibril asked. Befitting his position as leader of the kidnap operation, he occupied the front passenger seat of the Cadillac, while Hushi and Zeira sat in the back.

"Tomorrow evening," the driver replied. "You will be flown into Bonn as part of our diplomatic mission. From there you will be driven to your destination in Munich; it is a long journey by car." He reached across Jibril and opened the spacious glove compartment. Inside were three small automatic pistols. Jibril took one and passed the others back to Hushi and Zeira. "The instructions from my embassy are that there will be no unnecessary shooting. The British are still upset with us over retributive measures we took against Libyan dissidents living in this country." The driver laughed and the three Palestinians joined in.

"Who is in the house with the boy?" Hushi asked.

"As far as we have been able to ascertain, just the housekeeper, an elderly woman called Eileen Riley, and her cousin from South Africa, a middle-aged man named Roy Chappell."

"No one else?" Jibril wanted to know.

"No one."

"When did you check?"

"Yesterday. After we received word from Rashidieh that you would be coming, we asked questions around the village, pretended we represented a Saudi family desiring to purchase a typical English farm."

"This Roy Chappell—what is he like?"

"I already told you, middle-aged." The driver sensed concern in Jibril's voice. "Are you afraid of an old woman and a middle-aged man?"

"We have already lost one man there," Jibril said. "Wadi Hassan."

"I remember. His car burned."

"That's what the inquest conveniently decided."

"You think it was otherwise?"

"We don't think. We know."

The driver smiled darkly. "Then you'd better be extra careful, hadn't you?"

Jibril made an inspection of the small automatic and slipped it into his pocket. Then he leaned back to watch the English countryside slip by.

David had just gone to bed. Rosen sat alone in the living room, gazing without interest at figures that flitted across the television screen while Mrs. Riley worked in the kitchen.

"Would you like a cup of tea?" Mrs. Riley asked, opening the living-room door and poking her head inside.

"No, thanks." Rosen smiled, stood up and turned off the television. All this forced inactivity was driving him insane. He had already called Karpinsky at the embassy twice today; each time the news had been the same —no word of either Samantha or Tayfield, nor had Hunovi called in. "I'm going out," Rosen said.

"To the village again?" Mrs. Riley asked. She knew he used the public telephone to make his calls; heaven only knew what the Post Office would make of it when they learned of all those calls made from the village to the Israeli embassy.

"I'll be back in about twenty minutes or so. Maybe they've heard something by now."

"I hope so," the housekeeper said. "I can't keep telling David that his mother will be home the day after tomorrow. Eventually I'm going to run out of days."

Rosen patted the Irishwoman on the shoulder as he passed her. She felt terrible about Samantha—but he felt worse. After all, he had sent Samantha on Operation Asher. Each time Rosen saw David, he asked himself whether he had signed the death warrant for the boy's mother.

He climbed into his car and drove slowly toward the village.

When Mrs. Riley heard the sound of a car engine fifteen minutes later, she decided Rosen had returned so quickly because he had good news.

But when she opened the door, instead of Rosen's car she saw an enormous Cadillac and three strange men who walked menacingly toward her. She started to swing the door closed but one of the men with a long flowing moustache leaped forward and kicked it wide open.

"Where is the boy?" Wasim Jibril demanded, brandishing a gun in Mrs. Riley's face.

There was no need for Mrs. Riley to answer. Dressed in blue pajamas, David appeared on the stairs, attracted by the sudden outburst of noise. When he saw a gun in the hand of each man, David raised his own hands very slowly above his head, as he had seen men do on television.

"Where's Chappell, your cousin?" Jibril asked Mrs. Riley.

"Out!" the housekeeper replied belligerently. She did not need Jibril's accent—so similar to that of the dark-skinned man with the thinning hair who had visited the farm with Pierre Reynard—to know these men were Palestinians.

"Where did he go?"

210

"To London," she lied.

"When will he return?"

"Not until late," Mrs. Riley answered, and prayed that Rosen would come back soon. These were the men Rosen was guarding against and they had chosen this particular moment to attack. Had they watched him leave? It did not matter. If they were not expecting Rosen to return soon, he might just surprise them enough to turn the tables.

Hashim Zeira grabbed the boy and started to drag him toward the front door and the waiting Cadillac.

"Leave him alone!" Mrs. Riley shouted. "You harm one hair on his head and I'll break your bloody wog neck if it's the last thing I do!"

Jibril silenced the housekeeper by cracking her across the face with the barrel of his pistol. The glancing blow lacerated the Irishwoman's cheek but it was only powerful enough to momentarily stun. Jibril pondered the wisdom of shooting the elderly housekeeper until he remembered his instructions—no unnecessary bloodshed. "Take her as well!" he ordered Ali Hushi.

"We have no orders to take her."

"Don't question me! We can get rid of her later, but we can't leave her here as a witness." He watched the bald figure of Hushi grapple with the housekeeper and try to drag her out of the house; the struggle became more violent as the effects of the blow wore off and Mrs. Riley regained her strength. Jibril closed the front door softly, satisfied that the inside of the house had not been disturbed. When the housekeeper's South African cousin returned, he would never realize that visitors had been there. It would appear as if the Irishwoman and the boy had simply disappeared.

Rosen took the return trip from the village slowly, feeling even more disgruntled than when he had left the farmhouse. Dov Karpinsky had not been at the embassy, nor had there been a message from him. Rosen knew he would have to contact General Avivi soon and admit defeat. He could not stay on in England indefinitely. Reluctantly he would have to acknowledge that Samantha and Tayfield were lost, and concentrate on other avenues to learn the target of Black September.

Would the Israeli government pay a pension to Samantha's son? Rosen questioned. Would David be eligible for the same benefits given to other children orphaned through hostile action? Rosen was disgusted. We persuade his mother to become involved in a fight which is really none of her concern, and then we let her disappear. Damn! The prime minister had been right: it was a mistake to use an illegal, an outsider.

An idea swept through Rosen's mind, a way to forestall the Palestinians whatever their plan. Should the Israelis confront the Soviets with the photographs Hunovi had taken in Beirut, the evidence that linked Pavel Vlasov with Salim Maazi and Dr. Mohammed Nasser? For a few seconds the notion intrigued Rosen. Tell the bastards that we know they're up to something and unless they get the Palestinians to back off, we'll splash the photographs across the front pages of the world's press. But he quickly had to admit to himself that publicizing the photographs would prove nothing. The Russians would simply deny all knowledge of the chubby man with cropped blond hair and bulging eyes. Nothing ever embarrassed those sons of bitches!

A truck approached Rosen as he neared the farm entrance. He signaled, waited for the truck to pass and then swung right. He entered the farmyard, still deep in thought as his headlights suddenly illuminated the Cadillac. Its doors were open, lights off. A pudgy man with glasses was bundling a small figure dressed in blue pajamas into the back of the Cadillac. David! And a bald man was struggling with the housekeeper, forcing her from the farmhouse to the Cadillac.

Rosen jammed on the brakes, threw open the door and rolled out onto the ground as the first gunshot sounded from the vicinity of the Cadillac. A bullet shattered the windshield of his car and he scampered away in the darkness toward the gate, fingers tugging at the Czech-made M52 automatic that had been such a favorite weapon among the Wrath of God teams. He threw up the gun and tried to identify a target in the area lit by his headlights. Two of the Cadillac's doors were closed now. He dare not fire blindly at the car for fear of hitting David.

The Cadillac's headlights blazed on, momentarily blinding Rosen. On the fringe of the glare he spotted two figures, the bald man struggling to use Mrs. Riley as a shield while he tried to reach the Cadillac.

Ali Hushi saw the Cadillac's lights come on, heard the engine roar into pulsating life, and he panicked. "Move, damn you!" he yelled at Mrs. Riley. "Move!"

"Move yourself, you filthy wog!" she spat back. She thrust behind her with both elbows and was delighted to hear a surprised grunt of pain from Hushi as the wind was slammed out of him. For an instant his grip eased, and Mrs. Riley broke free of his arms.

"Get out of the way, Mrs. Riley!"

And there, pinpointed for an instant in the Cadillac's headlights, Mrs. Riley saw the crouching figure of Rosen, the pistol held out in front of his face like an extension of his hands. Flame belched from the muzzle. She heard the sharp, angry report, followed immediately by another noise, a muted whimper of pain and shock that was silenced instantly as the bullet from the M52 shattered Hushi's nose and blew away the back of his head.

The Cadillac's engine raced, then slowed as the driver thrust it into gear. Wheels spinning, the big car surged toward the gate and the figure of Rosen. Rosen switched his aim, squinting into the glare of the headlights as he tried to see the wheels. A lucky shot, maybe; one fortunate round to cripple the Cadillac.

At the last moment, just when it seemed that the heavy car must knock him aside like a rag doll, Rosen dived to his right. The car missed him by inches. The gun flew from his grasp. He turned around but he was too late to see the rear license plate as the Cadillac swung perilously fast onto the road and raced away into the night.

"Oh, Mr. Rosen, are you all right?" Mrs. Riley gasped, forgetting about the pain in her cheek, the blood that flowed where Jibril had struck her. As she ran to where Rosen lay, her right foot kicked against something hard and metallic. She bent and picked up the M52, which she handed gingerly to him.

"How many were there?"

"Four, I think. Three came into the house and there was a driver."

"Did they say anything?" he asked as he replaced the pistol in his shoulder holster.

"They asked where you were."

"By name? They asked for Joel Rosen?"

"No, for my cousin Roy Chappell. I told them you'd gone to London and wouldn't be home until late. I was hoping"—she held out her hands in an expressive gesture—"that you'd surprise them."

"Some surprise," he muttered sourly. "Good thinking, anyway." He walked past the housekeeper to where Ali Hushi lay. Rosen turned over the Palestinian with his foot. He was disgusted with himself. He had killed one of the bastards, but the price—losing David as well as his mother—was way too high.

"Shall I call the police?" Mrs. Riley wanted to know.

"For God's sake, no!" he said sharply. Then he reached for her hand.

213

"Sorry, I didn't mean to yell at you. Just leave it with me; I'll get everything cleared up. In the meantime, you'd better see about your face."

Mrs. Riley touched her injured cheek. "I can see what leaving it with you has done already."

"Mrs. Riley, I'm very sorry. Believe me, we'll do everything possible to get David back safe and sound. And his mother."

"If she's still alive."

"I think she is," Rosen said. "Because if she wasn't, they would have no reason to kidnap David." The Palestinians could have abducted the boy out of revenge. But if it was vengeance they were after, they would not have gone to the bother of kidnapping him. They would have killed him outright, along with Mrs. Riley.

"But you knew something like this might happen," the housekeeper pressed. "When you first came here, you told me you people planned for every contingency. Why didn't you have more people guarding the farm?"

"I thought I'd be enough. If we'd moved in any more agents it would have been noticed. By the locals—and by the Palestinians."

"What are you going to do about him?" Mrs. Riley pointed at Ali Hushi.

"Don't worry—I told you I'd take care of it." He walked into the house and picked up the telephone. There was no need for secrecy now. The first call he made was to the embassy in London. "Find Karpinsky and get him to call me immediately." Next he put through a call to Tel Aviv. General Avivi was at home, asleep, and Rosen left the identical message.

Dov Karpinsky was the first to call back, twenty minutes later. "I want a clean-up team down here immediately," Rosen told the London resident. "We've got a cold member of the opposition to get rid of."

"Two hours," Karpinsky said.

"Good enough. And I want to be on a plane home first thing in the morning. Arrange it."

Karpinsky did not even bother to acknowledge the order before hanging up. Ten minutes later the telephone rang again. This time it was Avivi. Choosing his words with care, Rosen described what had happened.

"Do the British know?"

"Not a chance. Karpinsky's putting together a clean-up team. I'm flying home first thing tomorrow. We'll have to sort something out from there." Again he considered confronting the Soviets with the Beirut photographs, and again he rejected the idea. There was nothing to be gained from

214

following that course. The best options were to continue with the surveillance on Vlasov, and to wait for Hunovi to make contact.

"Do you think it might be wise to alert the British?" Avivi suggested. "They could watch all ports."

"No. If they're planning on taking the boy out of the country, they'll have a million ways to do it. Besides, we can't let the Brits know what's been going on under their noses."

"I suppose you're right," Avivi finally agreed. Having roadblocks, searches, checkpoints, would endanger the boy's life even more. As past experience proved, their only hope was to get him back on their own.

A van containing four men from the Israeli embassy arrived shortly before midnight. Rosen watched from behind a curtain, his pistol ready, as the van entered the farmyard and the men climbed out. One of them knocked three times on the front door, then twice, then once. Putting away the pistol, Rosen let them in.

"Where's the body?"

Rosen indicated the garage where he had dragged Hushi's corpse.

Working with a swift professionalism, the four men carried the body into the van and checked by flashlight for further evidence of the battle. One man recovered the spent cartridge from Rosen's M52. Another found the cartridge ejected by a pistol fired from the Cadillac. A hose was hooked up and the entire area was soaked to flush away any signs of blood. Fifteen minutes after they had arrived, the four men were ready to leave.

"Where do you think you're going?" Mrs. Riley demanded when she saw Rosen preparing to enter the van with the men from the embassy.

"Home."

"To Israel?"

He nodded, one foot on the step of the van, all ready to climb aboard.

"Not without me, you're not," the housekeeper told him in a tone that brooked no argument.

"Mrs. Riley, what would you do there?" he asked, uncomfortably aware of the other men watching him. "I can't take you with me."

"And you can't leave me here either."

"And why not?" For some bizarre reason he found himself amused by the confrontation, and God alone knew he had no reason to find anything funny. He had lost David and killed a man; yet the sight of this portly, elderly Irishwoman telling him—the Mossad's director of special operations—what he could or could not do tickled his sense of humor.

"Five minutes after you drive away from here, I'll have every police

215

officer within fifty miles looking for you," Mrs. Riley stated flatly. "And what do you think they're going to say when they find that dead Arab in the back of your van?"

"You would, wouldn't you?" Rosen asked, smiling at her effrontery.

"Too bloody right I would. Thanks to you, I've lost my complete family —Mrs. Sutcliffe, and now, David. If you think after all that you can just fob me off like some piece of dirty laundry, you're very much mistaken."

"Come on, we've got to leave," the van driver called out.

"Do you have a passport, Mrs. Riley?" Rosen asked.

"No." The housekeeper was taken aback by the unexpected question.

"Then that settles it; you can't come." Rosen climbed into the van, satisfied that the argument was over.

"Just a minute, Mr. Rosen." Mrs. Riley grabbed hold of the door before he could close it. "If you're smart enough to arrange all of this, then you can bloody well get me a passport as well."

Rosen sighed as he recognized defeat. "Get yourself ready. I'll give you five minutes."

While Mrs. Riley returned to her room to pack a case, Rosen telephoned Karpinsky and told him to arrange for one more passenger on the flight. "A woman, elderly, Irish nationality, and as bloodyminded as they come. Use one of our diplomatic passports. She'll have a photograph taken when we get to you."

He replaced the receiver and looked up at the ceiling. From above he could hear the sound of the housekeeper's feet clumping on the floor. "Are you ready yet, Mrs. Riley?"

"Coming!" She walked down the stairs carrying a small case. Across her cheek was a patch of pink plaster covering the cut made by Wasim Jibril's pistol. By the hall closet she stopped.

"You can't go like that!" Rosen burst out when he saw what the Irishwoman was removing from the closet. "You'll sweat to death in Israel in those clothes!"

Mrs. Riley took no notice. She handed him her case to carry and then, resplendent in the ancient fur coat and broad-brimmed beige hat with the feather trim, she marched toward the waiting van.

As he helped the housekeeper into the van, Rosen remembered the hired car with the smashed windshield. He gave the keys to one of the men and ordered him to return the car to Heathrow Airport and settle for the damage.

216

While the Mossad clean-up squad was eliminating traces of the fight at the farm, the Cadillac containing Wasim Jibril, Hashim Zeira and the bound-and-gagged figure of David Sutcliffe pulled up outside the embassy of the Libyan Arab Republic in Princes Gate, London.

"Wait here," the driver ordered. He stepped out of the car, looked up and down the empty stretch of street and then rang the embassy bell. The door swung back and the driver gestured for the occupants of the Cadillac to get out. Carrying David between them, Jibril and Zeira ran across the sidewalk and entered the embassy.

"Where is the trunk?" Jibril asked the man who had opened the door.

The staff member led them to a small storage room in the rear of the building. A metal trunk no more than four feet high rested in the center of the floor. Fitted inside the trunk was a low wooden stool and rings for securing wrists and ankles. When David saw the trunk and recognized its purpose, he tried to fight against the ropes that bound his hands and feet. Jibril held him tightly while the embassy man produced a hypodermic syringe, ripped the sleeve of the boy's pajama jacket and plunged the needle into his arm. Within fifteen seconds the drug took effect, and David's futile struggling ceased.

Together Jibril and Zeira untied the ropes that bound the boy and removed the gag. In place of pajamas they dressed him in ill-fitting jeans, a shirt and a pair of sneakers. Then they folded him into the trunk, sat him down on the stool and fastened his wrists and ankles to the rings.

"Will he be able to breathe?" Zeira asked. A dead hostage was no use.

Jibril pointed to air holes as he closed the trunk. Stenciled across the outside in large white letters was the legend: Property of the Libyan Arab Republic.

"Is the flight arranged?" Jibril asked the embassy man.

"A special courier plane leaves for Bonn at eight in the morning. Your own people will meet you in Bonn. Provided there is no trouble on the *autobahn*, you should be in Munich by evening."

"There is no chance of the trunk being opened by either the Germans or the British?"

"None. Diplomatic baggage can be opened only in the presence of the ambassador or his representative. Customs does not normally interfere with diplomatic baggage unless there is cause to suspect something extraordinary. Before you leave for the airport the boy will be drugged again. He will remain unconscious until you are in Germany."

"Good." For the first time that day Jibril relaxed. They had lost Hushi to the Israelis—to the man who had posed as the housekeeper's South African cousin—but they had the boy. It was more than a fair exchange.

When Joel Rosen and Mrs. Riley were brought from the airport to the Kiria, General Avivi stared in amazement as the housekeeper's fur coat and broad-brimmed beige hat.

"Who—or what—the hell is that?" Avivi demanded when he was in his office with Rosen.

"It's a long story."

"Believe me, Joel, I'll find time to listen."

"That's Mrs. Riley, the housekeeper. If I hadn't brought her along, she'd have hollered blue murder."

"Couldn't you—"

"No, I damned well couldn't! And neither could you." Rosen replied. "She's staying here until we get to the bottom of this."

"In God's name, what are we supposed to do with her?"

"Put her somewhere out of the way, some place where we can keep an eye on her."

Shaking his head, Avivi opened his office door and stepped outside. Mrs. Riley had removed the coat and hat and was now sitting stiffly in the anteroom, gazing at a picture on the wall of children playing ball. "Mrs. Riley?"

"Who are you?"

"I'm General Benjamin Avivi. I'll be—" Avivi struggled to find the right words. "I'll be your host during your stay in our country."

"Does that mean you're going to lock me up?"

"We prefer to call it protective custody, Mrs. Riley. You will be treated as an honored guest."

The Irishwoman glared at him, but the stern expression that had cowed lesser men had no effect on Avivi. "What about Mrs. Sutcliffe and David?"

"We are doing everything within our considerable power to find out about them."

"You sound like Joel Rosen."

"We work for the same company."

Mrs. Riley walked up to Avivi to deliver her ultimatum. "General, if Mrs. Sutcliffe and her son are not returned, rescued, or whatever the word is, I am going straight to the newspapers when I return home."

218

"Oh?" Like Rosen, Avivi was amused by the Irishwoman's dogged determination. "And what would you tell them?"

"Exactly what happened."

"And supposing that we did not allow you to return home to tell the newspapers this story? Supposing we decided to extend our hospitality indefinitely? After all, we did not invite you here. You insisted on coming."

"Oh, no, general." A crafty gleam appeared in Mrs. Riley's eyes. "If that was the way you worked, then your Joel Rosen would have left me with that damned wog in the care of his clean-up team."

"We will find your family for you, Mrs. Riley. Rest assured."

Avivi returned to his office, closed the door and told Rosen: "I've just received my orders. We'd better find Samantha and her son, or God help us all."

Salim Maazi clapped his hands together in triumph the moment he received the information that Jibril, Zeira and the boy were in Munich, secure in the Palestinian safe house on Elisabethstrasse, near the Schwabing district. His secondary insurance was in place. All he needed now was to hear from Vlasov and he would finalize his plans.

But Maazi's joy was tempered by the death of Ali Hushi at the hands of the housekeeper's South African cousin. Was the South African the same man who had been guarding the farm that night when Wadi Hassan's BMW had become his funeral pyre? Maazi wanted to find out. When this was all over, he would take revenge for the men he had lost.

He visited the hut where Samantha was confined. Despite the lack of exercise, the meager washing facilities and the ropes that tethered her to the bunk, she had refused to let her imprisonment break her spirit. When she had faced death at the point of Maazi's knife, she had found the strength to accept it. Now nothing could rob her of that fortitude.

Maazi dismissed the single guard. "How do you feel?" he asked Samantha.

She stared at him haughtily, not deigning to answer. The rejection made him smile inwardly; soon that arrogant facade would come crumbling down like a house of cards.

"Did you know that your housekeeper, Mrs. Riley—the Irishwoman who despised me because of my color and my birthright—had a cousin staying with her while you were away?"

Although Samantha still refused to speak, her face betrayed a flicker of interest.

"He was a South African, a man named Roy Chappell."

"Mrs. Riley has no family."

"Then who was Roy Chappell?"

Samantha compressed her lips, wishing she had not answered at all.

"I'll tell you who Roy Chappell was, Samantha. He was a Mossad agent. Perhaps he was even the man who killed Wadi Hassan, a Palestinian I ordered to watch you. Did Chappell kill him?" He waited several seconds, then he said, "The man who killed Wadi Hassan—burned him to death in his car—succeeded in his work. But this alleged South African cousin of your housekeeper was not so successful in protecting your farm."

Samantha's face whitened imperceptibly as she understood what Maazi meant.

"That's right, Samantha. Chappell did not guard your son well. He is with us now."

"What?" She tried to rise from the bunk but her bonds hampered any movement.

"We have David as well as you."

"David? I don't believe you." She could not accept this final blow. "Where is he? I want to see him."

"Soon . . . you will be able to see him soon. For the time being he is in Germany."

"Germany?" Could it be possible? Could her heart be broken twice? Why did Maazi have David in Germany?

Maazi nodded. "He's in Munich. Until I decide what must be done with both of you, I need him there."

"Why is he in Munich, you bastard? Why did you choose Munich?"

Maazi watched her coldly. What the threat of death could not do, the mention of Munich had accomplished. Samantha's facade had been shattered.

"Does something about Munich bother you?"

She turned her head away from him, determined to say no more.

Maazi smiled. Later he would learn more about Munich, why the name of the city should cause such fury . . . such terror . . . "Do you see the trouble you have caused yourself by working for the Israelis?" he asked with a mocking sadness as he prepared to leave. "How foolish you were, Samantha. How foolish."

Outside the hut Maazi met Pierre Reynard, who had just returned from

Beirut where he had bought copies of European newspapers. Reynard was smiling in satisfaction.

"The final chapter to the story," the Frenchman said, offering Maazi a copy of the British *Daily Mirror.*

Maazi glanced at the front page. "Samantha Sutcliffe feared dead in Lebanon," he read aloud from the headline. "With your byline. Congratulations."

"Thanks. All the papers have it," Reynard said. "Samantha Sutcliffe and her manager, Alan Tayfield, are presumed lost in strife-torn Lebanon. There's a side story that the British government, through its embassy in Beirut, has promised to investigate."

"Let them investigate," Maazi replied. "They will find nothing. Why don't you show her the stories . . . and kill that last hope that burns within her that she will be rescued." Laughing, he watched Reynard enter the hut. Perhaps the Frenchman could win the lady now. After all, tied up as she was, she didn't have much choice.

Maazi was certain the guard would look the other way.

Rosen was preparing to leave his office late that evening when the summons came from Avivi. "You'd better come in, Joel. Something might have broken."

Forgetting all about going home, Rosen replaced his jacket over the back of a chair and entered the general's office.

"This just came in from our people in Washington," Avivi held out a decoded message. "What do you make of it?"

Rosen read the first part of the text and whistled softly. "Vlasov's in New York now . . . what the hell is he doing there?"

"He's been appointed to the Soviet Union's delegation to the United Nations, of course," Avivi answered dryly. "One of their agricultural advisers. Read the entire thing."

"Like hell he has." Rosen skipped down the neatly typed page. "That information is about as factual as the name he's using—Andrei Polikov. Wait a minute, our people are quite certain this is Vlasov, aren't they? There couldn't really be an Andrei Polikov working at the United Nations, could there? We haven't got the time to go on a wild goose chase."

"Do you trust our people, Joel?"

Rosen did not need to answer. "I'm going there. Are you coming with me?"

"Even the redoubtable Mrs. Riley would be unable to stop me."

"Shall we tell the Americans? Carrying our war onto British soil is one thing—everyone does that—but there's no point in having the Americans mad at us."

"Like hell we'll tell them," Avivi responded curtly. "They'll only think we're crying wolf again, seeing ghosts in dark rooms."

Rosen warmed to the *memuneh*. Despite his army background, he was an intelligence man at heart. "I've got a better idea. How about we tell them without officially telling them, if you get my drift?"

Avivi did. "Call in a few favors, eh?"

Rosen nodded. "I think it's about that time."

CHAPTER
SIXTEEN

$\mathcal{T}$HE football spiraled lazily through the air and Robert Shea—dressed in shorts, a red-and-black striped rugby shirt and sneakers—made a fine running catch before turning and twisting his way to the edge of the large lawn where he slammed the ball down triumphantly. Breathing heavily and grinning with satisfaction, he turned around to face his son-in-law, Ian Richards, who had made the pass.

"See that reception and touchdown? I'll play for the Patriots yet!" Shea yelled jubilantly across the garden of the house in the Edgartown section of Martha's Vineyard. "I'm a natural athlete."

"Sure you'll play for them, Bob," Richards called back. "When they change their name to the New England Pensioners!"

Laughing, Shea picked up the football, cradled it in his arm and walked toward his son-in-law. "Can you go for a cold beer?"

"Race you to the house," Richards offered.

"You go on ahead." Shea watched affectionately while his son-in-law loped easily toward the house, enjoying the supple gracefulness exhibited by the slim younger man.

Shea took his time, peeling off the rugby shirt and draping it across his shoulders. The spring sun on his bare skin felt great after the long winter, although he had not been forced to bear the brunt of the raw New England winter like the rest of his family had. Trying to hammer out a deal in the Middle East did have advantages after all!

He reached the house and dropped the rugby shirt over the back of a chair. In the kitchen Richards was waiting with two opened bottles of beer. Shea drank gratefully, wiping the back of his hand across his lips after he had emptied half the bottle with one thirst-quenching gulp.

He took a leisurely shower and came out of the bathroom dressed in a terry robe, feeling remarkably refreshed. He was glad he had managed to create the time to spend one weekend with the family at Martha's Vineyard before returning to the Middle East to put the final touches to the summit meeting over which he had labored for so long.

Those last few days in Washington had been grueling. Squabbling between Jews and Arabs over points of protocol he could understand, but their nitpicking had been nothing compared with the dithering among high-ranking State Department officials over where the damned meeting should be held.

In the ground-floor bedroom, Shea changed into fresh shorts and shirt, slipped on a pair of sandals and went out to the patio. The table had been set in his absence, and his family waited for him. His wife, Eunice. His older daughter, Margaret, who had used the winter months to shed all the weight she had put on during her pregnancy. Caroline, his younger daughter, who had come up for the weekend from New York where she worked as a copywriter in an advertising agency. Ian Richards. And Adam, the apple of Shea's eyes, his ten-month-old grandson who sat in a high chair, nodding drowsily under the umbrella that shaded him from the sun.

Shea sat at the top of the trestle table and bowed his head. The others followed suit. "For what we are about to receive, may the Lord make us truly grateful," Shea intoned. Not that he would ever consider himself deeply religious, but saying grace added a nice touch to family mealtimes.

"When are you off to the Middle East again?" Caroline asked as they began to eat.

"A few days. I have to fly down to Washington first. Pass the salad, there's a good girl."

"When are you going to tell us all what you're up to?" Caroline pressed as she handed her father the wooden salad bowl. "I think you're working for the secret service, all this running back and forth."

"Nothing so glamorous, I'm afraid," he laughed.

"What is a special envoy to the Middle East?" Ian Richards wanted to know. "What exactly is he supposed to do?"

"Whatever he's told to do."

"How boring," Margaret ventured. The baby started to cry and she turned to him.

"I wouldn't call it boring," Shea said. "I'm used to following orders.

For almost thirty years now I've been following your mother's orders."

"There's the phone," Caroline said.

"Excuse me." Shea got up from the table and went to the telephone. The conversation lasted for less than twenty seconds. When he returned to the table, some of the fun had disappeared from his face.

"Washington calling?" Eunice asked.

Shea nodded. "I'll have to leave tomorrow." Then he forced a smile on his face and sat down. "What are we all waiting for? The salad's getting warm."

John Lansing looked like a middle-aged bank clerk who had resigned himself long ago to never moving from behind his teller's window. Of average height, average build, with thinning brown hair and cheap prescription glasses, he had the ability to pass unnoticed anywhere. Except for his eyes, which were light blue and as cold and unemotional as glass, he was the man who rode the subway every morning to a thankless job in some anonymous shop or office and would retire at sixty or sixty-five with a gold watch and be forgotten the following day.

Which was why the man was so damned good at his job, General Avivi decided as he sat with Lansing and Rosen in Nathan's on Times Square. Nathan's was crowded with people who resembled John Lansing, insignificant little men spending a Saturday visiting Manhattan, or shop staff gulping down their hot dogs and hamburgers in order to have time to pay a visit to the off-track betting parlor before returning to their mundane jobs.

But Lansing, despite working in an office, was not chained to a soul-destroying nine-to-five job. Sometimes he wished he were. The desk behind which he often spent a hundred hours a week was in Langley, Virginia, at the headquarters of the Central Intelligence Agency; there, he controlled a network of agents in Central and South America.

"Why didn't you go through normal channels on this one?" Lansing asked Rosen and Avivi. "Why did you sort me out?" And what, he wanted to add, is so almighty important that it warrants bringing over the top brass?

"We helped you once in the past," Rosen said quietly. "We saved your life, remember? Isn't that worth a favor in return, without too many questions asked?"

Lansing's last field assignment had been in 1973 in Frankfurt. It was his last field assignment because his cover as a wine shipper had come apart, his name leaked to what was then one of the premier terrorist gangs in Europe—the Baader-Meinhof. Late one night on the way back to his apartment, his car had been ambushed by three men in an ill-lit side street. At the last moment while he crouched helplessly on the floor of the car, wounded in the leg and waiting for his ambushers to fire the final, killing shots, two more cars had screeched into the narrow street, blocking each end. Inside the cars were members of a German antiterrorist unit and a Mossad agent who had been tailing the Baader-Meinhof thugs in the hope of getting a lead on Palestinians working in Germany. By sheer luck they had stumbled on the assassination attempt. In the short but bloody gunfight that had followed, all three Baader-Meinhof terrorists had been killed. Lansing had escaped.

"You guys don't believe in treading softly, do you?" Lansing said.

"Faint heart never won fair lady," Rosen replied.

Lansing swallowed the last of his hot dog. "Before I left Langley I checked into this guy you call Vlasov. The only thing we have on him is that he's a minor KGB operative, one of the many bureaucrats."

"Update your files," Rosen suggested. "Vlasov's with Department Five. He goes where he's needed, when he's needed."

"And you figure he's up to something now with the Palestinians?"

Rosen nodded. "We think he's running them."

"Then what the hell is he doing over here?"

"You tell us."

"You're really sure this guy going under the name of Andrei Polikov is your Pavel Vlasov, aren't you?"

"Dead sure."

"What do you want from me?"

"We want you to organize a tailing system."

"Why don't you do it yourselves? The niceties of international law, of common courtesy between allies, has never bothered the Mossad before," Lansing pointed out with a grin.

"We don't have the time," Avivi explained. "You can set up the apparatus in an hour. Besides, we've got reason to suspect that our field agents, in many cases, are being watched by the Soviets."

"It's that big, eh?" Lansing took a swig of coffee from the cardboard container and grimaced at the taste. "When you contacted me, I took a three-day leave of absence. That's all I'm giving it . . . three days. I reckon that's a fair exchange for saving my life. After that, you can either go through official channels or play by yourselves."

226

"I doubt if it will even take that long," Rosen said. "Vlasov doesn't have time to waste; he's a busy man."

As they stood up, ready to leave, Avivi noticed a mustard spot on Lansing's jacket. Can you really trust a man who eats so sloppily, he wondered?

Pavel Vlasov was picked up outside the Soviet Mission to the United Nations at precisely nine o'clock the following morning by a mission staff member driving a rented 1982 blue Buick Limited.

"Do we go straight there?" the driver asked as Vlasov settled his roly-poly figure into the back seat.

"Just cruise around for a while. I want to see how decrepit this city has become. When I'm ready to go I'll let you know."

He sat back in the plush seat and withdrew a bulky white envelope from his jacket. The envelope's contents were stiff and Vlasov drummed his fingertips against them while he gazed out of the Buick's windows. He had ordered the rented car in preference to using a mission vehicle. Although he was totally confident of his own cover—an agricultural expert attached to the Soviet Mission—he did not want to draw attention to himself. In the Buick he would look like any New Yorker escaping for the day from this cesspool of a city.

The driver took the FDR south, and Vlasov stared across the East River to Queens and Brooklyn and the massive bridges that spanned the water. Wherever he looked was dirt and rubble, broken-down cars that had been stripped as soon as their drivers had abandoned them, piles of garbage stuffed in plastic bags to rot. Vlasov wrinkled his nose distastefully and longed for the clinical cleanliness of Moscow.

Tiring of the view he opened the envelope and withdrew its contents. A picture was always worth a thousand words, especially those he held in his hand. The camera must have been invented with espionage in mind.

With the pictures from the envelope were strips of negatives. Vlasov held a strip up to the light. It seemed a shame to give away the negatives as well, but a deal had been struck and Vlasov prided himself on being a man of his word. Of course, he had never made any promise not to have the target of this piece of blackmail eliminated. That thought made him smile.

He replaced the pictures and negatives in the envelope. "Have you noticed anyone following us?" he asked the driver.

The man glanced in the rearview mirror, past Vlasov's head to the road behind. "Nothing suspicious."

"Good. Keep watching."

They turned off the FDR at Houston Street and Vlasov grabbed at the door as the pitted road bounced him out of his seat. Their roads were just like their city, just like their entire society, eaten away, crumbling. He sighed in relief that his work would be finished today. By tomorrow he would be on his way back to Moscow.

Rosen and Avivi sat in a yellow Volkswagen Rabbit which John Lansing drove across New York's uneven streets with unnerving speed and dexterity. From the radio in the dashboard came a constant babble of noise, strange code names that would mean nothing to anyone who might tune in to that particular frequency by mistake. But Lansing understood. So did Rosen and Avivi.

"Datsun calling Rabbit. Fatso's running west on Houston."

Lansing picked up the mike. "This is Rabbit. Escort take over from Datsun. Chevette move up. Datsun drop back."

"Where do you think Fatso's heading?" Avivi asked. He liked the code name Landing had given Vlasov.

Lansing shrugged. "Maybe he's just sightseeing. Who knows, he might even have some long-lost cousin over here he wants to look up, God forbid!"

"How long are your cars good for?"

"We can go a lot further than that goddamned Buick without getting thirsty," Lansing answered. "That's why we're using these subcompacts. Besides, there are plenty of them on the road; they're too common to warrant a second glance." Traveling west on Fourteenth Street, Lansing was running well to the north of, but parallel to, Vlasov's Buick.

"Escort calling Rabbit. Fatso's turning north on Sixth Avenue."

"Our turn," Lansing said. He picked up the mike again. "This is Rabbit. I'll take it from Fourteenth Street. Escort get ahead of him and then come around behind. Datsun and Chevette maintain positions."

Lansing reached the intersection with Sixth Avenue just in time to see the Escort section of his team race past. Fifty yards behind, accelerating to catch the changing lights, was the blue Buick.

"There goes Fatso," Lansing said, turning right as the light changed to green. "We'll take him for a couple of miles. Stands out like a sore thumb, doesn't he?"

"How do you mean?" Rosen asked. He failed to see anything peculiar about the Buick or its occupants.

"Nobody sits in the back of a car when the front seat's empty. The back seat's only for some pompous jerk in a chauffeured Rolls or Caddy."

By the time the blue Buick had turned north onto the Henry Hudson Parkway at Seventy-ninth Street, and from there to Interstate 95 through the Bronx, all four cars had taken a turn tailing. Rosen had to admire Lansing's system. They would be able to keep this up all day long without anyone in the Buick becoming suspicious.

"Why do you think he headed south first?" Avivi asked.

"May have been looking for a tail. I'd have done the same thing. So would you, I hope."

"I guess."

"Escort calling Rabbit. Fatso's speeding up, going north on Ninety-five."

"Stick with him," Lansing instructed. "I'll get Datsun to spell you in a couple of miles. What's the traffic like?"

"Getting heavy."

"Good. Pray it stays that way."

When the rented Buick finally pulled into a service area on I-95, just over the Rhode Island border from Connecticut, the team in the Chevette was on its tail. "Chevette calling Rabbit. Fatso's driver has got out. Fatso's staying put." There was a pause of two minutes, then Chevette reported that the driver was carrying two containers of coffee from the restaurant to the Buick.

"Fatso doesn't want to get out of the car," Lansing observed. "Lazy Russian bastard."

"I'd sure like to get out of this one," Rosen offered, stretching as much as he could in the cramped back seat of the Rabbit. Like the other noncontact units, they had pulled off the Interstate, waiting for word from Chevette about the Buick moving off. Datsun and Escort were behind, while Rabbit was just ahead, ready to be overtaken by the Buick, at which point it would pick up the tail from the Chevette.

"Chevette calling Rabbit. Fatso's moving out."

Lansing started the engine and returned to the Interstate, cruising gently at fifty miles an hour. Two minutes later he spotted the Buick among a group of cars coming up behind. "This is Rabbit. Chevette overtake Fatso. I'll take it from here."

The Buick and Chevette passed within seconds of each other. As the

229

Buick pulled in after overtaking the Rabbit, the Chevette whipped past and signaled to turn off at the next intersection. From there, the Chevette team would ride along a parallel road and rejoin the Interstate behind the Buick.

"Sweet," Rosen said, voicing his earlier opinion. "You've got this down to a fine art."

"Just think what we could have laid on for you if you'd only given us more notice—*and* made it kind of official," Lansing replied. He allowed the Buick to build up a lead of four hundred yards, then he maintained a speed that varied between sixty and sixty-five miles an hour.

"Oh, shit!" Lansing suddenly cursed. "Look what that goddamned stupid son of a bitch has gone and done!"

Rosen and Avivi craned forward to see. On the hard shoulder a quarter of a mile ahead, red and white lights had begun to flash. The Buick's right-hand indicator was flickering on and off as the driver prepared to pull off the road. Fatso had sailed right into a weekend radar trap.

Quickly Lansing rapped out orders over the radio. "This is Rabbit. Fatso's triggered a radar trap. I'll get him out of it. Datsun be ready to pick him up once he's clear." Lansing slung the mike back on the hook and pressed down hard on the gas pedal. By the time he passed the halted Buick and the young state trooper standing officiously by the driver's door, the Rabbit was touching eighty-five.

The trooper swung around to look, recognizing what was happening all too clearly: one cop was busy so some damned fool motorist was taking advantage of him, giving him the finger while he was out of his car and unable to give chase. The trooper did not need his radar to know that the Rabbit was going at least twenty miles an hour faster than the sixty-three at which he had clocked the Buick. He spun around, dived back into his car and started the engine. Moments later he was back on the road, foot pressed to the floor, siren screaming as he chased after the speeding Rabbit.

"Fatso's going to be thanking some idiot in a yellow Rabbit for saving his skin," Lansing chucked. "And some poor dumb cop is about to get his ass chewed out just because he did his job."

The chase lasted for a mile, the Rabbit speeding along at just below ninety with the police car glued to its back. At last Lansing signaled and touched the brakes gently. The police cruiser dropped back fifty yards and followed the Rabbit onto the hard shoulder. Lansing stopped, turned off the engine, rolled down the window and waited.

The state trooper climbed out of his car, adjusted his hat and walked purposefully toward the Rabbit. "May I see your license and registration please, sir?"

Lansing reached inside his jacket and the state trooper stiffened, his hand dropping nervously toward his holstered gun. Instead of a driving license, Lansing pulled out a small leather case which he flipped open for the trooper to see.

"Listen, sonny, I don't have the time right now to take you by the hand and explain the facts of life. Suffice it to say that you are in monumental danger of fouling up a major intelligence operation."

The state trooper blinked as he stared at Lansing's identification. "Sorry—"

"Shut up and do exactly as you're told. Pretend you're writing me up, do you understand?"

"Sure. But—"

"Just pretend you're giving me a ticket. And keep writing until that blue Buick Limited has gone, all right?"

The trooper took out his ticket book and pretended to write. Two minutes later, when the Buick finally passed—and when Rosen could swear he saw Vlasov laughing at their misfortune—the trooper was still pretending to write.

"Okay, knock it off before you get writer's cramp," Lansing told the trooper.

"Do you want me to put out the word that you guys aren't to be touched? What about the Buick?"

"Don't put out any words at all. Just get back to doing your job." Lansing was certain that the Buick would not get stopped again. One close brush with the police would keep the driver honest.

By two-thirty in the afternoon, the Buick has reached the outskirts of Boston. The Rabbit stayed well back now, acting solely as control for Chevette, Escort and Datsun; the usefulness of Lansing's car as a close-contact tag had diminished following the episode with the state trooper. Vlasov and his driver had been given too good a look at the Rabbit and its three occupants; perhaps later they would be able to join in the chase again.

"Christ," Rosen muttered, "isn't that son of a bitch going to stop for lunch?"

"Fatso carries enough flab around on his body to keep him going from now until Christmas," Lansing said. "Here—all modern conveniences."

He reached down to the floor and brought out a paper bag. "Ham and cheese on rye with mayonnaise. Pickles on the side. Enjoy."

"Thanks." Rosen took the bag and offered it to Avivi. The general hesitated, and Rosen understood why. "Take out the ham and eat the cheese," he suggested in Hebrew. "God'll forgive you this time."

"No foreign languages," Lansing said. "It's impolite."

"I don't eat ham," Avivi explained.

"Sorry, I didn't stop to think."

"Don't worry." Avivi opened his sandwich and, using only the very tips of his finger and thumb, distastefully removed the offending slices of meat. Rosen took them quite happily, stuffing them into his own sandwich. Even if he were religious—and he would be the first to admit that he was most definitely not—he was so hungry that he would have eaten anything.

"Chevette calling Rabbit. It looks like Fatso's headed right into the center of Boston."

Lansing dumped his own half-eaten sandwich onto his lap and picked up the mike. "This is Rabbit. Datsun take over. Escort move into second spot. Chevette drop back. Keep it close now, keep it close. We don't want to lose him." He picked up the sandwich again and steered with one hand. Mayonnaise oozed out of the side of the sandwich to drip onto his trousers. Avivi decided that the mayonnaise stains blended well with the mustard spots that were still on Lansing's jacket from the previous day.

"*Sheebzdik!*" the driver of the Buick hissed as he jammed both feet on the brake pedal to avoid a truck that sailed straight through a red light. "They drive here like madmen."

"Then be extra careful," Vlasov warned. "I don't wish to become a statistic on America's long list of road deaths. You know, I remember reading somewhere that Boston's drivers are among the world's worst; even more dangerous than those Arab fools in Beirut."

"I wouldn't know about that," the driver muttered, moving forward again but with far greater caution.

"America's roots," Vlasov said, adopting a supercilious tone. "They call this network of roads in the center of Boston the Freedom Trail because they pass important historical sites. Can you imagine the founding fathers spinning in their graves as they witness the disaster that has overtaken their dream?"

The driver was too busy watching the road to pay attention to Vlasov's commentary. He drove by the Massachusetts State House, then the Park Street Church. Vlasov gazed out of the window with interest. Despite his apparent knowledge of the city, it was his first time in Boston. And, he thought, probably his last. He might as well enjoy the view.

"We're entering Tremont Street now," the driver said. "There's the Old Granary Burial Ground."

Vlasov leaned forward in the seat to peer through the windshield. The bulky white envelope was in his hand and he could feel himself starting to sweat. Soon the blackmail started more than twenty years earlier would pay its final, shattering dividend.

Lansing stopped the Volkswagen Rabbit close to the State House. "Now we wait," he said simply, turning off the engine.

"Who's on Vlasov now?" Avivi asked.

"Datsun."

"Are you prepared to split your team into two units of two cars if Vlasov meets with someone here?"

"Depends on whether the other guy's worth going after. It also depends on whether Vlasov is really up to something here. Who knows, maybe he just came for the ride, for the chance to immerse himself in our history."

"Like hell he did," Rosen muttered with such vehemence that Lansing laughed.

"Datsun calling Rabbit. Fatso's pulling into a parking lot. We're watching through the glasses."

"How many other cars are there?"

"Quite a few. Wait, he's stopped a couple of yards from a white Cadillac Seville, '81 model, I think. Fatso's driver is getting out. He's holding something white, a sheet of paper, an envelope maybe—"

"What about Fatso?"

"He's staying in the Buick. The driver's going over to the white Seville. Registration"—there was a pause while the agent in the Datsun adjusted his powerful binoculars—"Massachusetts I-D-F eight-five-oh."

"Chevette, run that number," Lansing said. "Massachusetts I-D-F eight-five-oh, white Seville."

"Rabbit, this is Datsun. The Caddy's window is open a couple of inches. Fatso's driver is passing the white piece of paper—no, wait, it is an envelope—through the window."

"Can you get a good look at the driver of the Caddy?"

"No. Tinted glass. Can't see a thing. Wait a minute, the driver is

233

getting something in return. A brown envelope. He's put it into his pocket. Now he's returning to the Buick, getting in. The Buick's leaving, pulling out of the parking lot, moving away from you."

"What about the Seville?" Lansing asked as he started the Rabbit.

"He's staying put for the moment. Maybe he wants to give Fatso time to get clear."

"What are you going to do?" Rosen asked Lansing.

Lansing put the Rabbit in gear and started to move slowly toward the parking lot. "Rabbit calling Datsun and Escort. Pick up Fatso's tail. But if you see him heading back toward the Big Apple call it off. I think his turn's over. Chevette, stay with me. I'm closing in on the Caddy."

Pavel Vlasov sat in the back of the Buick as it retraced its path through Boston toward the Interstate. No longer did he look out of the window. He was too interested in ripping open the brown envelope his driver had brought from the Cadillac, pulling out the six-page memorandum it contained.

He chuckled when he saw the top-secret classification stamped across the cover. Nothing in the world was secret anymore. With the camera and the photocopying machine, even the most private information belonged to those who were willing to pay for it, or use blackmail. A few seconds, that was all it required. Just a few measly seconds and the secret that governments had labored over for months was public knowledge.

Cooke Barracks—Göppingen. Where was Göppingen? Vlasov pondered. He had never heard of it. Probably just some flea-bitten town in southern Germany that reveled in a false sense of importance because an American military base was nearby. The townspeople—he could picture them now—probably begged for the American dollars while they spat at the soldiers behind their backs. Vlasov could not blame them; he would also hate having Puerto Rican and *chornyi* soldiers polluting the decency of his home town.

He scanned the memorandum. Cooke Barracks was the headquarters of one of the American armored divisions held in readiness in West Germany. Were armored units stationed there? He read further—no, the only units present were the division headquarters company, a company that handled the division's administration, a signal battalion, the headquarters of the division's military-police battalion and an aviation-maintenance section to service helicopters.

Past the details of the base was the makeup of the five delegations that would be attending from the United States, Egypt, Saudi Arabia, Jordan and Israel. Each delegation would comprise four men and would be headed by a senior official from each country's state department. The American delegation would be led by Robert Shea.

Vlasov replaced the pages neatly in the envelope. Soon the information would be in the hands of the Palestinians. He would supply them with details of this Cooke Barracks, and after that the final dispensation of the problem would be theirs.

There would be no peace—no attempt at creating peace—in the Middle East without Soviet involvement. Who did these Americans think they were?

"Datsun calling Rabbit. Fatso appears to be headed back to New York."

"Stay with him a while longer to be sure. Chevette and I will take the Seville from here. Over and out."

"Why hasn't the Seville moved yet?" Rosen asked Lansing as they sat within binocular range of the parking lot. "Why is he just sitting there?"

"He must be checking through the envelope Vlasov's driver gave him."

"Counting the money?"

"That's right," Lansing said disgustedly. "You may think this sounds funny, but I've never really minded someone selling out his own country for a conviction. I can understand that. What burns my gut is someone doing it for money. I reckon scum like that should be sent on a one-way trip to the dog-meat factory."

Just then the white Seville started to move. It swung out of the parking lot, past the Rabbit and, further along the road, past the Chevette. Like two magnets, the subcompacts turned to follow.

"Chevette calling Rabbit—we've got a make on that Seville."

"Let's hear it. Who is it registered to?"

"A Mrs. Eunice Shea, wife of special envoy to the Middle East, Robert Shea."

CHAPTER
SEVENTEEN

EXCEPT for the sound of the engine and the drumming of radial tires over the road surface, the inside of the Rabbit was as silent as a tomb. Lansing's lips were spread in a thin line, his eyes ice cold behind his glasses as he followed the white Cadillac Seville at a steady one hundred yards. Even the radio was quiet now as the Chevette, too, stayed in visual contact with the quarry.

Lansing was the first to break the stunned silence that had followed identification of the Seville's owner. "I guess that news makes my presence kind of official, huh?" he murmured as they passed south over the Neponset River. "I'm no longer doing you guys a favor. It's our business now as well."

"You're aware of Shea's work?" Avivi saked. "You know what he's trying to do?"

"Of course I do. Damn!" he cursed softly. "I wish to hell I could see through that tinted glass."

"To learn whether a man or a woman is driving?" Rosen ventured.

"You've got it. If it is Shea's wife, then why is she doing it? Why is she taking money from this guy Vlasov who you say is in contact with the Palestinians?"

"Would Shea have been that careless to tell his wife about secret work he was engaged upon?" Avivi asked.

"That's out of character. This is a guy who never tells his left hand what his right hand's doing. Look at some of those labor deals he worked on. Take my word, they were as sensitive as any deal he's working on in the

236

Middle East. You dare not let anything slip with those babies until you're damned sure you've got every single loose end tied up."

"What if it's Shea himself?" Avivi asked.

"Why should he do it? Shea doesn't need money. Look at that god-damned car—and that's only his wife's. They're loaded. They've got a home in Boston and another one out in Martha's Vineyard—" Lansing hammered his fist against the steering wheel. "I bet that's where he's going now. The family must be out there."

"What are you planning to do?" Rosen wanted to know.

"I'm going to take him as soon as I think it's safe." He picked up the mike and rapped out an order to the team in the Chevette. "I'm moving closer. When you see me take the Caddy, back me up. Over and out."

Rosen tried to stretch in the confined space of the Rabbit as Lansing increased speed. He was sticky with sweat and his lower back ached abominably from the hours of sitting. But his discomfort was insignificant when compared with the equation he had conceived. Whoever was in that Cadillac plus Vlasov plus Hunovi's pictures from Beirut meant only one thing: the Palestinians knew all about the American peace initiative. All that remained now—and this was the toughest problem of all, as far as Rosen was concerned—was to figure out how those murdering bastards intended to strike.

Buildings gradually gave way to fields. The traffic thinned. Lansing took a 9-millimeter Browning automatic from a shoulder holster and passed it back to Rosen. "I'm going to pull level with the Caddy. Don't mess around; just stick this cannon out of the window and let him know you want him to pull over."

Rosen took the gun and chambered a round. "Does this mean that the United States government will officially condone having an American citizen fired upon by a Mossad agent while on American soil?"

"Just make sure you don't blow anyone's goddamned head off. Okay, get ready, there's an exit ramp coming up. I want that Cadillac off there." He pressed down on the gas pedal, swung out and started to overtake the Cadillac. Behind, the Chevette kept pace.

"Now!" Lansing yelled.

As the Rabbit passed within a yard of the Cadillac's side, Rosen rolled down the window and shoved the Browning out into the wind. Because of the tinted glass it was impossible to see into the bigger car. He had no idea whether the driver was even aware of the gun pointed at his window. Lansing solved that problem by holding down the horn.

237

"He's speeding up," Avivi said needlessly.

"Do something!" Lansing shouted at Rosen. "We miss this fucking exit and there isn't another one for two miles!"

As the Cadillac gained a few yards, Rosen sighted quickly along the barrel of the Browning and squeezed the trigger. The rear window of the Seville exploded in a shower of glass fragments as the bullet smashed through to exit on the right side.

Lansing jerked at the steering wheel as the Cadillac's rear end whipped sideways before the driver regained control; then he pressed forward to draw level again. Rosen fired a second time and the Seville's rear passenger windows disappeared. Suddenly there was an almighty, grinding crash. Sparks flew as the two vehicles collided broadside. Hubcaps went spinning across the road and the Rabbit's rear bumper was ripped half off. Rosen was flung back into the seat, almost dropping the Browning out of the window.

"For Christ's sake, disable him!" Lansing screamed as he pulled away. "Shoot his fucking tires!"

Rosen pushed the Browning out of the window again and fired three rapid shots at the rear tire that was only a couple of yards away. Pieces of black rubber flew through the air. Thick gray smoke poured from the shredded tire and sparks scattered as the bare rim ground into the road surface. Sagging at the rear end and swerving drunkenly, the Seville slowed down. Lansing guided the Rabbit in front while the Chevette took up a position behind. Lansing signaled right and in a slow, limping line the three cars left the highway and pulled off onto a deserted stretch of road.

Lansing was first out. He grabbed the Browning from Rosen and raced over to the battered driver's door of the Cadillac. It was jammed shut. He ran around to the other side. When he yanked back the front passenger door, a dazed Robert Shea turned a deathly white face toward him.

"Get out!" Lansing ordered.

Very slowly Shea slid across the seat and left the car. Lansing turned him around, spread him across the hood of the Cadillac and went through the State man's pockets. He found the bulky white envelope inside Shea's jacket. Opening it, he found not the money he had expected but the photographs and negatives which Vlasov had carried from New York.

"Jesus Christ," was all he could say when he looked at the photographs. "Jesus Christ."

"What is it?" Rosen joined him. Avivi and the two men from the

Chevette came over to form a tight half circle around the spread-eagled figure of Shea. Lansing reached forward, pulled Shea upright and pushed him into the front passenger seat of the Cadillac. Then he handed the photographs to Rosen and Avivi.

The two Mossad men stared in shock. Their initial reaction was identical: they had caught Robert Shea with nothing more damaging than a dozen black-and-white pornographic photographs. Until they looked closer. Each photograph showed two men on a large bed. One was a teenager with short blond curly hair and a slender girlish body. The other —Rosen tried unsuccessfully to cut off his whistle of surprise—was a much younger Robert Shea.

Lansing took back the photographs and crouched down beside Shea. "You want to talk about these?" He was not surprised to see that the gray-haired man's face was streaked with tears.

"Who are you?" Shea finally asked. "I was promised that . . . that it would be all over after today."

Lansing did not need Shea to tell him what the photographs were, or why he had met with the KGB agent. It was all too evident. But he had to know what Shea had turned over in that brown envelope. "The Russians can't make promises on our behalf," he said softly. "In this game you have to pay two separate pipers."

"Federal—?"

"No."

"CIA?" Shea whispered the name fearfully, and Lansing nodded. "What will happen to me?"

"That depends on you, Mr. Shea," Lansing answered with perfect courtesy. "How long ago were these pictures taken?"

"Nineteen fifty-eight."

"Where?"

"Paris. I was attached to our embassy there."

"What happened? How did they trap you?"

Shea looked up at the ring of faces surrounding him and thought he detected pity in every stare. That defeated him completely. "A young French boy—it had never happened before, believe me . . ."

"How did you meet?"

"In a bar. I—I don't know why I did it. He was so—so friendly, do you understand?"

"Of course." Lansing's voice was soft. "Where did you go?"

"To his apartment. He was a student; he lived on the Rue Pot de Terre on the Left Bank."

"When did they tell you about the photographs?"

"A week later. They threatened to send copies to my wife, to the embassy."

"And what did they ask you to do?"

"Nothing."

"Nothing?"

"Not then. But every six months or so I'd receive a message. They still had the photographs and I should never forget."

"Even when you returned to private practice they hounded you?"

"Even then."

"When did they call in the debt?"

"When I was appointed by the president as his special envoy to the Middle East. I had to report everything."

"Did you?"

Shea nodded miserably. "I was too frightened to do otherwise."

"Exactly what information did you pass?"

"How my negotiations with the Arabs and Israelis were progressing. What we—the United States—were trying to do."

"Did they ever tell you why they wanted this information. What they planned to do with it?"

"Never."

"What did you think it was for?"

Shea just shook his head.

"Did it ever occur to you that every piece of information you gave to the Russians would be channeled straight to the Palestine Liberation Organization, so that they could plan to knock over this meeting?"

Shea remained silent, head lowered.

"What did you give them just now, in the parking lot?"

"The—" Shea stumbled over his words, "I gave them the memorandum concerning the final details of the Arab-Israeli summit meeting."

"What did that include?"

"Date, place, security measures and so on."

Lansing stood up and walked away from the group around the Cadillac, beckoning for Rosen and Avivi to join him. "We've been lucky," he said. "No damage at all. I'll have Vlasov picked up right away and held until after the summit meeting. Whatever plot the Palestinians are hatching will just collapse without that information. End of story."

"What about Shea?" Avivi asked.

Lansing shrugged his shoulders. "Maybe it'll be best to let him resign, avoid the stink."

"Like hell you'll pick Vlasov up," Rosen said, and both men swung around to face him.

"What do you mean by that?" Avivi demanded.

"Aren't you forgetting a couple of minor details like Samantha Sutcliffe and her son?"

Lansing looked from one man to the other, unable to understand what the English actress had to do with Shea.

"Did you read about her being lost in Lebanon, feared dead?" Rosen asked the CIA man.

"Sure I did. With her manager. Serves them both damned well right, getting involved in a dumb stunt like that."

"That dumb stunt was the result of a lot of hard work on our part. Samantha Sutcliffe was working for us. Her manager was a Mossad agent. They were trying to learn what the Palestinians are up to."

Lansing stared incredulously at Rosen. "Oh, shit, you Jews are a fucking devious lot! Why didn't you tell me this before?"

"Because it was none of your business."

"Are you going to tell me now?"

Rosen nodded and brought him up to date, ending with the kidnapping of David Sutcliffe. "That's why I'm convinced that Samantha is still alive."

"Contingency measure," Lansing agreed. "Have you got anyone else out there?"

"One agent, the best."

"When did you last hear from him?"

"More than two weeks ago, when he sent the pictures of Vlasov coming out of that apartment building on the Rue Ayoub Tabet." For the first time it occurred to Rosen that he and Avivi were conducting a top-level Mossad planning meeting on a deserted stretch of road somewhere in Massachusetts.

"So what do you want to do?" Lansing asked.

"Let the string out; carry through the meeting as planned with all the necessary precautions to safeguard the delegates."

"What makes you think you'll be able to get Sutcliffe and her kid back if you follow that course of action?" Lansing asked.

"Time—it'll give us time to find out where they're being held."

Lansing turned around and walked back to Shea. Rosen and Avivi followed. "What's the date and place of this meeting?" Lansing asked Shea.

"May twenty-sixth. We're using an armored division headquarters in Germany, a place called Cooke Barracks near the town of Göppingen; that's a little east of Stuttgart."

"That's Wednesday a week, ten days," Lansing said to Rosen and Avivi. "I'll give you both until next Saturday to come up with a plan acceptable to me; otherwise I'll blow the whistle and have the meeting changed." He swung back to Shea again, a steely toughness concentrated in his unblinking pale blue eyes.

"I've got those photographs now, Shea, and they're just as dangerous in my hands as they ever were when the Russians had them. Do you read me loud and clear?"

Shea nodded.

"What were your plans?"

"I was to return to Washington on Tuesday, and then fly out the following day. First to Riyadh, then to Amman, Cairo and finally to Jerusalem to inform all parties of the meeting arrangements."

"And that's exactly what you're going to do, Shea. But mark my words, one mistake, one tiny slip, and copies of these pictures go straight to your wife, to State, to every goddamned newspaper in the land. Get it?"

"You're as bad as they are."

"You're damned right I am. And you two"—he looked at Rosen and Avivi—"I hope to God that your man comes through with the goods, because after next Saturday it'll be too damned late."

On Wednesday, three days after his meeting in Boston with Robert Shea, Pavel Vlasov returned to Beirut.

At midday the apartment on the Rue Ayoub Tabet was stifling, and Vlasov found himself wishing that he was back in the air-conditioned comfort of the rented Buick, riding around the northeastern United States. He moved uncomfortably on the hard wooden chair, tugging at his trousers where they stuck sweatily to his groin, while he watched Salim Maazi and Dr. Mohammed Nasser read copies of the memorandum.

Tired eventually of watching the two men, Vlasov turned his attention to the opposite wall on which was taped a large-scale map of the town of Göppingen. In the northeast corner of the map was a collection of dark rectangles and squares over which was printed the two-word legend—

Cooke Barracks. South of the military buildings was a large open space titled Flugplatz—the casern's airstrip.

Next to the map of Göppingen was another piece of paper, a hand-drawn layout of Cooke Barracks itself, which Vlasov had obtained through his embassy in West Germany. Penciled in red was a line that led from the gatehouse past the signal battalion headquarters and barracks, past mess halls and offices, past the division's personnel-administration buildings to a large gymnasium. It was in that gymnasium, according to Shea's memorandum, that the summit meeting would be held.

"Well?" Vlasov finally asked. "What have you decided? How will you get on base? There is only one entrance, by the military police checkpoint."

Maazi looked up and gazed pensively at the maps. "Do the Americans produce their own food on the base?" he asked. "Do they raise their own cattle and pigs, till their own land for fresh vegetables, bake their own bread and grow their own wheat for flour?"

"It would hardly seem likely," Vlasov acknowledged, appreciating where Maazi was leading.

"Then that means they bring it in from outside. They buy from the Germans. And knowing the Americans and their fatuous boast of being the world's best-fed army, it's reasonable to assume that deliveries are made daily."

"You plan to hijack a supply truck?" Nasser asked.

Maazi nodded. "What would be simpler? In the next two or three days, our people in Germany will watch the camp." He stood up and walked across to the overall map of Göppingen, pointing to the roads that led to the American base. "They can watch from these three points: where Flugplatz Strasse runs down from Hohenstaufen Strasse; the junction of John F. Kennedy Strasse with Hohenstaufen Strasse; and here, on Rossbach Strasse. They will report back to me on the movements of civilian supply vehicles and their schedules. On the day the meeting starts, we will take over one such vehicle."

"And then what?" Vlasov asked.

Maazi turned to the hand-drawn map of Cooke Barracks. "I think we can safely assume that the deliveries are so regular the gate guards will just wave them through." With a finger he followed the red pencil line. "We will drive straight to the gymnasium. It will take the Americans a minute or so to react to the fact that the truck is not following its normal route to the mess halls or supply centers. And that is all the time we will need."

243

"You are forgetting something, Salim," Nasser pointed out. "That section of the base around the gymnasium will be declared off limits for the duration of the meeting. How will you get the truck there?"

Maazi returned to where he had been sitting and picked up his copy of the memorandum. He found the section Nasser was referring to. The official reason for declaring the gymnasium area off limits was that a meeting of NATO officials was taking place. Only the division's commanding general, the two assistant division commanders and the chief of staff were privy to what was really taking place. "That's right," Maazi agreed with Nasser, "and their own secrecy, their own deviousness, will be the downfall of the Americans. The military police will not be responsible for security. Like the other people on the base, they will not be informed of what is really happening. The American Secret Service will provide security. Their men will be concealed in the area, the security will be very low-key because the Americans are so confident of their secrecy. By the time they will be able to react, a small group of determined, heavily armed men will be inside that gymnasium with the delegates as their hostages. After that, the Americans will be powerless."

"And then you will make your demands," Vlasov finished for Maazi. "The entire Arab world will see how it is being betrayed by the avaricious leaders of Egypt, Jordan and Saudi Arabia. The American peace initiative"—he laughed dryly as he spoke those two words—" and their dream of creating an anti-Soviet multinational force will fall flat on its face."

"And the Russians, of course, will make as much propaganda as possible out of the incident," Maazi remarked.

"It is none of your concern how we claim our payment for the assistance we give you. Just don't forget what I told you when I was last here: one of the delegates is not to be abducted—he is to be killed."

"Shea? No, I won't forget. Just tell me something, Vlasov. How do you Russians deal with people who do *not* cooperate with you?"

"Fail on this mission," Vlasov replied with a sweaty but ice-cold smile, "and you will find out."

Long after Vlasov had left the apartment, Maazi remained with Nasser, talking over a meal brought in by one of the guards.

"When will you move Samantha Sutcliffe to Germany?" Nasser asked.

"When we all go, three days before the operation."

"Isn't that cutting it fine?"

"The less time we all spend in Germany, the more I'll like it," Maazi answered. "The Israelis are too close to the German security agencies; they live in each other's pockets. Wasim Jibril and Hashim Zeira are finding a site we can use as a safe house in the Stuttgart area. The boy will be moved there. The woman will be kept there as well."

"Who will guard them during the operation?"

"Yussuf, Ahmed and Rima. After we have reached Libya with the delegation members, Samantha Sutcliffe and her son will be disposed of quietly." A cruel smile distorted Maazi's swarthy face. "Rima begged me for the privilege of killing the woman—and how could I refuse her?"

"And if—if you fail to take over the meeting? If something should go wrong? If you are trapped?"

"Then the woman and her son will be granted a reprieve. They will become our bargaining tools. But that won't happen," Maazi added quickly, clapping Nasser on the shoulder. "Don't even think of such things. We will succeed because we have justice on our side."

"What about Reynard?"

Maazi had given much thought to the Frenchman. Ever since he had suggested the means by which to expose Samantha—and had then dared to physically challenge Maazi and wrest the knife away from him— Maazi's opinion of the Frenchman had undergone a powerful transformation. But had it changed dramatically enough for him to trust Reynard completely? How would the Frenchman react if bullets started to fly? Would he become the parasite again, searching for a typewriter to hide behind while real men did the fighting? Or would he grab a gun and battle for his life?

"Reynard's greed and ambition are his most reliable qualities," Maazi answered at last. "He uses our struggle to carve his own name, yet his ambition gives him an inbuilt instinct for survival. If necessary, this instinct will make him fight."

"Does he know what the mission entails?"

"No." Maazi lit a cigarette and smiled at Nasser through a cloud of smoke. "His ambition might then betray us. He might file the story before it actually happens."

Nasser emitted a short, sharp laugh; then he became very earnest. "Ten years ago we were planning our Munich operation. Did we think then that we would still be fighting ten years later?"

Maazi crushed out the cigarette after only two puffs. "No. But what was done in Munich will pale into insignificance against what will be done now. We will record the greatest moment in the history of our people."

Nasser nodded. "And I will be in Libya to greet you as a hero."

On Thursday night, Hunovi went home for the first time in more than five years.

It was not the grand homecoming he had always envisaged, where friends would be on hand to welcome and fete him. Instead it was a clandestine trip in total darkness. Like a wraith he slipped from the PLO-controlled area of southern Lebanon into the Phalangist zone, where he surrendered to the first Christian militiaman he saw. Under the guns of suspicious Christians he traveled by jeep the few miles to the border. There he got out and, in a symbolic gesture, walked across into Israel.

"Welcome home," Joel Rosen said, clasping Hunovi in an unabashed display of emotion. "How does it feel?"

"Temporary, unfortunately." Hunovi looked past Rosen to the helicopter that had brought the Mossad director of special operations from Tel Aviv. Beyond the helicopter he could see the shadowy outlines of tanks and armored personnel carriers, a far larger force than was normally held in readiness at the border.

"What has happened to Samantha?" Rosen asked. "Is she—?"

"No. She is being held as a hostage."

Rosen made no attempt to hide his relief. "I knew she wasn't dead when she missed that plane—I just knew it."

"But Tayfield is."

"When?"

"On the day they were supposed to return to England."

"His heart?" Rosen asked, and Hunovi nodded. "He ignored instructions and overexerted himself, eh?"

"With the cooperation of a grandstanding Kfir pilot," Hunovi replied with a cold anger. He explained what had happened. "It was because of Tayfield that the Palestinians trapped Samantha. Tayfield was delirious before he lapsed into a coma. He spoke in Hebrew."

"But why did they kill Hechter and his family?"

"Maazi wanted to learn why Samantha was chosen for the role in Hechter's film. The family was wiped out in revenge."

"Murdering bastards," Rosen murmured. "At least I killed one of them when they kidnapped the boy from the farm."

"He is being held in Munich," Hunovi offered.

246

"Could we get them both out?"

"The boy, perhaps, but never Samantha. The guards have orders to kill her if there is even the slightest threat to Rashidieh. What about those photographs from the Rue Ayoub Tabet?"

"Jackpot," Rosen answered and gave a brief smile. "The short fat man with the light hair—his name's Pavel Vlasov, KGB Department Five. He was holding a sword over Robert Shea's head. They had been blackmailing Shea for more than twenty years. He was stupid enough to be trapped in some sordid homosexual encounter in Paris. He delivered every piece of information about his work in the Middle East into the Russians' hands."

"And they briefed the Palestinians, set them up to hit the final meeting," Hunovi said, nodding in comprehension. "How did you learn about the blackmail?"

Rosen related the story of his visit to the United States with General Avivi, the meeting with John Lansing, the chase through Massachusetts. "Lansing has given us until Saturday to come up with something, otherwise he's going official and will have the meeting changed. The prime minister has given us the same deadline."

"What do you mean?" Hunovi looked puzzled.

"Do you see those tanks?" Rosen asked. "They're part of an invasion force ready to roll at a moment's notice. When the prime minister learned that the Palestinians intended to attack the summit meeting, he ordered immediate mobilization . . . to sweep into Lebanon and crush the Palestinian military structure once and for all."

"Samantha would be killed. We can't let that happen."

"Then come up with an alternative damned quickly."

"We've got to force Maazi into a situation where he has to use Samantha and David as hostages to secure his own escape."

"You mean let the meeting take place . . . ?"

"Listen to Hunovi very carefully, Joel."

Rosen could not help smiling at the abrupt manner in which the agent had slipped into using the third person; he was about to hatch something he found very distasteful.

When Hunovi finished speaking, Rosen was smiling no longer. Hunovi's scheme was complicated. What would Lansing say to it? The CIA man had already described the Jews as a "fucking devious lot." What would be his reaction when presented with Hunovi's plan? And how would the prime minister respond? Would he hold back the Israeli invasion of southern Lebanon on the mere chance that Hunovi's scheme could succeed?

"Well?" Hunovi asked, watching Rosen intently.

"I'll sell it to the prime minister and to the Americans," Rosen promised at last.

"You'd better." For a moment Hunovi appeared lost as he gazed past Rosen. In the distance, beyond the massed armor ready to roll into southern Lebanon, he could see the lights of Kiriat Shmona, a town in his own country. He could stay here; he deserved it. He could stay and let the armor roll northward in an invasion that would destroy the Palestinians, destroy Maazi and his plan, destroy the reincarnation of Black September.

Then he began to think about Samantha, tied to that bunk in the hut in Rashidieh. He thought about the boy, held captive in Germany. He could not leave them to be killed by the Palestinians.

An Israeli athlete who had loved Samantha—and whom she had loved in return—had been murdered by the Palestinians. Hunovi would not surrender Samantha and her son to the same fate.

Ten minutes later Rosen sadly watched Hunovi reboard the jeep and head back into Lebanon. He climbed onto the helicopter and closed his eyes in thought as the aircraft lifted off and headed south.

First he would tell Avivi what had been decided. The *menumah* could sell it to the prime minister. Then Rosen would contact John Lansing in Virginia and sell it to him.

And finally Rosen would visit the house where Mrs. Riley was being held. Not a day had passed without the Irish housekeeper complaining about the accommodation, the cooking, the cleanliness of the safe house. Perhaps now—when she understood that Samantha and her son were alive and that measures were being taken to rescue them—she would stop making Rosen's life an utter misery.

Part Three

CHAPTER
EIGHTEEN

SAMANTHA left Lebanon the same way she had arrived, on a Middle East Airlines flight. But the aircraft went to Frankfurt, not London, and she traveled on a false French passport made out in the name of Louise Mayer. Her hair had been cut very short and tinted jet black by Rima. Dark glasses shaded her eyes. She bore no resemblance whatever to an English actress named Samantha Sutcliffe.

Rima sat next to Samantha during the entire flight. In the row of seats behind were Maazi and Reynard. Scattered throughout the aircraft was the remainder of the team: Ahmed el-Shafri, Yussuf Torbuk and three more Palestinians from Rashidieh who had worked with Maazi for Black September—Hussein Badowi, Ismail Kassem and Mahmoud Tretzi. Only Maazi and Reynard traveled on their own passports. The other members of the team used diplomatic documents supplied by the Libyan government which acted, in this instance, as a supply clearinghouse. The weapons that awaited the Palestinians in Germany came from the same sympathetic source.

Samantha had no idea why she was being taken to Germany, but any thought she might have harbored about trying to escape when they left the aircraft at Frankfurt, passed through immigration and changed to an internal flight bound for Stuttgart was quashed by Rima's constant gloating reminder that David was in their power. His safety depended on Samantha's total compliance with their orders. Not that Samantha believed for a moment that the Palestinians would ever release her and David willingly. Instead, she nurtured a faith that the Israelis would not allow them to die. They always rescued their people, she kept telling herself. Remember Entebbe. This time would be no different.

They reached Stuttgart as dusk fell. Wasim Jibril waited with a Volkswagen bus for Maazi's party. Samantha bent carefully to enter the vehicle in order to avoid putting pressure on the cut below her right breast. Although it had almost healed it was still sore; and the center of her throat bore a minute scab where Maazi had penetrated with the knife point.

"When will I be able to see my son?" Samantha asked as Rima took the seat next to her.

The mask that Rima had worn throughout the long journey from Beirut slipped as she understood that in the privacy of the Volkswagen bus there was no longer any need for pretense. "I will never see my children again. Why should you be allowed to see your son?"

"I did not willingly place my child in a war zone!" Samantha fired back, taking the bait that Rima offered. "I did not have a child solely for the purpose of martyring him!"

Rima's face flared dangerously. "When you agreed to work for the Israelis you placed your son in peril. Whatever happens to him, you will have no one to blame but yourself. Do you think you will be able to bear your loss as well as I bear mine?" She laughed at the horror that twisted Samantha's face.

"Enough!" Maazi cried out from the front of the vehicle where he sat with Wasim Jibril. "Silence!"

Rima dropped her voice to a vicious whisper. "What I did to you in Rashidieh with the knife will be nothing to what I will do to you. And to your precious son." She leaned closer and jabbed Samantha hard in the stomach with straightened fingers. Samantha gasped and fell forward. Tears sprang to her eyes as she strained for breath.

"How easily you cry," Rima mocked. "I hope you do not die so easily. I would hate to be robbed of the pleasure of killing you slowly."

A handkerchief was held out to Samantha. Surprised by this single act of kindness she looked up and saw Reynard's face. "Keep it!" she hissed. "I hope you die with the rest of these bastards!"

Samantha sat quite still, unable to stem the tears that ran down her cheeks. Rima continued to watch, enjoying the sight of those tears. The other men in the bus, who had flown from Lebanon, looked away. Once Samantha caught Reynard giving her a furtive glance. She forced herself to think about the Frenchman, to take her mind off David for a moment. Did a spark of decency still exist deep under the layer of slime he had so willingly assumed; a memory, perhaps, of that one night they had shared? But when she met his gaze, he lowered his eyes quickly.

Darkness had fallen when Jibril drove the Volkswagen bus to a small, sleepy village five miles west of Stuttgart that looked untouched by the centuries. He doused the headlights and pulled off the main road to follow a tree-flanked track barely wide enough for the bus. Without lights it was slow going. Branches scraped the sides of the bus as it moved deeper into the wood. After about a mile Jibril swung the bus into a long driveway. In the moonlight Samantha saw, with a touch of nostalgia, that they were on a farm. But here no cattle lowed as they did in Somerset. No warm lights beckoned from the windows of the stone farmhouse. The farm was deserted, its land untilled, grown over. The only sign of life was an old red Opel parked in front of the farmhouse.

The front door of the farmhouse opened, and the dumpy, bearded figure of Hashim Zeira came out dressed in jeans and a plaid shirt. "Show her where the boy is," Maazi told Zeira.

Zeira grabbed Samantha by the arm and hustled her into the farmhouse. The building smelled of damp and decay. Zeira carried a wide-beamed flashlight and Samantha could see holes in the walls where plaster had fallen away. In the main room there was no furniture, only some wooden packing crates that Samantha assumed served as tables and chairs. Sleeping bags were strewn about the floor. Cans of food and drink were stacked along one wall; used cans had been flattened and dumped in a cardboard box.

"This way." Zeira dragged Samantha to the rear of the farmhouse, unlocked a door and shoved her roughly into a room that was dimly lit by moonlight dancing through a barred window. In the corner of the room, lying on a damp sleeping bag, was her son.

"David!" she cried out.

The boy tried to stand and run toward her. The four-foot length of chain holding him to the wall pulled him up sharply and he fell over. Samantha knelt beside him, cradling his head in her arms. She heard the door close, the lock turn, but she did not look around.

"Mummy—" David's voice was quiet, much softer than Samantha seemed to remember it being. Had it really been almost four weeks since she had seen him? Perhaps his voice had not changed at all; she just could not remember that clearly. "What are they going to do with us?"

"Nothing, darling, I promise you." She ran her fingers through his thick curly hair. It was tangled, greasy. They could not have allowed him to

253

wash since they had kidnapped him, taken him first to Munich and then here. She ran her hands over his body. His jeans and shirt were soiled. He smelled. The entire room stank. She looked around and spotted a metal bucket next to the sleeping bag. Did they empty it every day? Or did they just leave the waste to pile up? Bastards . . .

"Why are they doing this to us?" David asked. He touched his mother's hair curiously, confused by the change in her.

She sat beside him on the floor. A dilemma that had once plagued her was now ready to be confronted. "David, do you remember when you were much younger, how you asked about your father?"

"You told me he'd died and gone to heaven," David replied solemnly.

"That's right. He has." She wondered how often they fed him, and what they fed him. Even as she cuddled him she could swear she felt his bones poking through. "Your father was—he was killed by those men outside."

"Killed?" David's voice was so full of shock that Samantha questioned the wisdom of telling him. "But why? Why did somebody kill my daddy?"

"Your father was a runner, an athlete at the Olympic Games."

Suddenly David found a small spark of enthusiasm. "At the Olympics?" he asked, seeing so clearly now how he could brag about his father at school. A mother *and* a father who had competed in the Olympic Games. "Why didn't you ever tell me he ran for Britain?"

"He didn't, David." A long pause followed before Samantha said quietly, "He ran for Israel."

"Israel?" The boy's enthusiasm turned immediately to bewilderment. "Why did he run for them?"

"Because he was an Israeli."

"My dad was an Israeli?" The boy did not want to believe it. It made no sense at all. His mother, who had swum for the United Kingdom, was a supporter of the Palestinians; he understood enough to know that the Palestinians and the Israelis were like—like Spurs and Arsenal—like Celtics and Rangers. How could his father have been an Israeli?

"Yes, he was an Israeli. His name was Asher Davidson; that's where your name comes from."

"Then why—why were you always saying those terrible things about Israel? Why did you always stick up for the Palestinians?"

"Because—" She started to answer but David cut her off.

"Are you like Mata Hari?"

"That's right, David," she answered softly, with a smile. "I'm like Mata Hari."

The door opened and a flashlight beam cut through the gloom. Zeira entered, grabbed Samantha by the arm and jerked her upright.

"Leave her alone!" David screamed. "You leave my mummy alone!"

"Shut up!" Zeira swung the flashlight at the boy's head. Samantha deflected the blow with her hand and then, without thinking, brought her knee up sharply into the fat Palestinian's groin. He howled in pain and dropped the flashlight as he clutched his groin.

Another figure appeared in the doorway. Rima. In her hand she held a submachine gun. The room rocked with thunder as Rima squeezed the trigger and fired a burst of six bullets into the opposite wall. Plaster flew. David screamed in fright and Samantha threw herself on top of him.

"Get up!" Rima ordered. "Get up or I'll cut you in half."

Only when she was certain that Rima was not going to fire again did Samantha rise. Zeira was leaning against a wall, doubled up in pain, both hands clasped tenderly to his aching testicles. "Fool!" Rima spat at him.

Samantha felt the gun prodding her in the back as she walked out of the room. She touched a hand to her stomach and realized that the cut had opened again; her blouse was wet with blood.

"What was all that about?" Maazi demanded when Samantha was brought into the front room. Blankets had been pinned across the windows, and hurricane lamps cast an eerie glow around the room. There was a rhythmic clicking noise of work as automatic weapons were assembled and checked. Even Reynard was helping. The transformation was complete, Samantha decided; he handled a submachine gun with as much dexterity as he had ever worked a typewriter. How would David react if he knew the man who had given him stamps was now an active member of the cause which had murdered his father?

"Hashim became careless," Rima answered.

"Is he all right?"

"He will be." Rima pushed Samantha into a corner of the room; none of the men working on the weapons paid her any attention. "When he recovers from milady's knee in his groin."

"Samantha"—Maazi moved close to her—"I would suggest that you enjoy what little time you have with your son, because in three days time I will know whether your lives have any further value to me."

"What does that mean?"

"I have a job to do over here. You are my collateral in the unlikely event

255

that something should go wrong. Once my work is complete, you and your son will be expendable."

Samantha knew that she should no longer be frightened. All she had endured over the past four weeks should have numbed her senses. Nonetheless, hearing Maazi speak so openly of murdering not only her, but David as well, chilled her blood. She called upon all her strength, all of her acting experience, to answer him. "You haven't got a chance of getting away with murdering us. Don't you remember what your friend Reynard showed me in the English newspapers? The British embassy is investigating my disappearance. And Alan Tayfield's. They won't leave a stone unturned until they learn exactly what happened."

Maazi allowed her to finish. "I don't think the British embassy would be too interested in Tayfield," he said at last. "After all, he was hardly British, was he? And as for you—" He called Reynard over. "Pierre, tell our wilting English rose what her precious embassy has learned. She still clings to the faint hope that she will be saved by some knight in shining armor."

Reynard nodded, and in that moment Samantha knew that she had been mistaken on the bus. There would be no sympathy here. "The investigation has ended, Samantha. You and Tayfield were last seen leaving Rashidieh in a car bound for Beirut Airport. You never arrived there for your flight. You have become a statistic—one of the regrettable casualties of war."

"Would you like to tell my son that he is also a statistic of war? Do you remember my son—you gave him stamps when you visited my farm —and you told him that cows have calves, not babies? Why do you hide from him? Are you afraid of a child's accusations?"

Reynard tried to walk away but Samantha grabbed him fiercely by the arm. "Are you proud of yourself now, Pierre? You told me once that you supported these conscienceless murderers because their cause was just. Now you are one of them. Does that make you feel more of a man?"

Reynard shook himself free and returned to the task of assembling the weapons, unable to look at Samantha when she tauntingly called his name.

Maazi smiled as he signaled for Rima to return Samantha to the room, for he knew now that the Frenchman was his.

The gymnasium smelled of fresh floor polish and stale sweat. Joel Rosen's heavy wingtip shoes echoed loudly as he walked across the highly varnished basketball court, and he noticed that John Lansing was wearing crepe-soled loafers. It was just as well the special-services sergeant was not present, Rosen thought; he would have a screaming fit if he saw me walking across his precious floor with these clodhoppers.

"The gymnasium was declared off limits as of this morning," Lansing explained as he reached the bleachers on the far side of the court and sat down. "We've got today and tomorrow to set everything up."

Rosen joined the CIA man on the bleachers. "Which means?"

"All of this"—Lansing waved airily at the equipment, the rubber mats, the football and baseball gear, the two indoor soccer goals, the bleachers themselves—"will be coming out of here. We'll use the gym office behind the snack bar as our control."

Rosen looked around and tried to imagine the cluttered gymnasium as a fitting place for a meeting of such international importance. He failed. "I don't see how you're going to do it. No matter what you do, it'll still be a gymnasium."

Lansing grinned. "Where's your imagination, Rosen? State's putting in carpeting right across here, wall-to-wall stuff. Bring in tables, sparkling white cloths, chairs. A coat of paint on all the walls, plasterboard to cover the worst sins like that snack bar. You'd be surprised what a bunch of busy beavers can do with this place in a few hours. By the time we're finished, it'll look better than the White House."

"Where are the delegates going to eat?"

"Meals will be brought in. State's providing a field kitchen that will knock out *cordon bleu* fast food."

The gymnasium's double doors opened and two dozen men wearing army uniforms entered. One man with sergeant's stripes quietly gave orders and the squad started to remove the equipment. Ladders appeared and two men dismantled the basketball hoops and backboards. Rosen and Lansing stood up as four more men began to take down the bleachers.

"Real soldiers?" Rosen asked.

Lansing shook his head. "I told you—this place is off limits now. Besides, did you ever see a real sergeant give his orders in such dulcet tones?" He led the way to the snack bar, close to the double doors, leaning against the counter while he watched equipment being wheeled out. Within half an hour, the gymnasium was bare.

"Come in the office," Lansing invited. Behind the snack bar was a door to the gymnasium office. The room was littered with sneakers and worn athletic equipment. Pictures of divisional sports events dotted the paneled walls. Half a dozen ashtrays were full to the brim with fat cigar butts.

Clearing a space for himself on the desk by the simple procedure of pushing everything onto the floor, Lansing sat down and lit a cigarette.

"Here's how we're going to work it, Rosen. United States Air Force planes will bring each delegation into Rhein-Main Air Base which shares the real estate with Frankfurt am Main International Airport. The delegates will be brought out through the military section; that way, we can avoid taking them through German immigration, etcetera. From Frankfurt they will be flown by helicopters directly to the door of this building. They'll just walk out of the choppers straight into the meeting hall. No one will see them come on base. Hell, no one in their own countries will even know they've left."

"You're certain that Robert Shea will keep his side of the bargain and carry on normally?"

"Shea wouldn't dare to do otherwise, not while I hold those photographs and negatives. He might not give a shit about himself—suicide's probably crossed his mind a dozen times since we nailed him with the goods in Massachusetts—but he cares a lot about his family. He's got my solemn oath that once this thing is finished, I'll turn everything over to him and give him the matches to burn it with. What about you now? Is your little scheme going to work?"

Rosen let his eyes wander around the office before answering. "It'll have to, won't it?"

"Don't hand me that line," Lansing said angrily. "This entire deal's only going through because of you, so I don't want to hear crap like that. My neck is on the block just as much as that Sutcliffe woman's."

"I don't think so, Lansing," Rosen said softly. "I don't think any of our necks are on the block like hers is—or her son's."

"She and the boy mean a lot to your people, eh?"

Rosen nodded. "We never give people up—and we're sure as hell not going to start with her." Rosen did not see any reason to tell Lansing that the Israelis were holding off a massive invasion of southern Lebanon for the chance of rescuing Samantha and the boy.

When they left the office an hour later, the gymnasium's transformation was well under way. Rolls of royal blue carpet were stacked in the center of the basketball court, waiting to be laid down. The scent of floor wax and stale sweat had surrendered to the more powerful smell of fresh paint. The walls, which had been a dull, dirty gray, were now pastel blue. The snack bar by the gymnasium entrance was half-concealed by plasterboard. Only the high ceiling of the gymnasium had not been altered.

"Do these men get paid union rates?" Rosen asked, gazing around in utter fascination. Never had he seen painters and builders work so swiftly; the entire scene reminded him of a theater or opera house between acts, when scenery was shunted around by the stagehands.

"Union rates? Are you kidding?" Lansing laughed. "No one concerned with this operation belongs to any union. Come on, let's get out of here. You've got to catch your flight home. The next time you see this place it'll be for the real thing."

Outside the gymnasium, Rosen watched folding tables being unloaded from army trucks. Chairs followed them. He walked with Lansing past green wooden barriers that had been erected to place the gymnasium off limits. By the helicopter that would take him to Frankfurt for his flight to Israel, he turned for a final look. Fifty yards from the gymnasium, on the other side of the off-limits barriers, soldiers came out of the personnel-services division building without giving a second glance to the activity in the gymnasium. Mechanics in an aviation hangar worked without curiosity on helicopters.

"Congratulations on a perfect set-up," Rosen said to Lansing as he boarded the helicopter.

"Thanks. I hope yours is just as good."

Bright sunlight streamed through the window of the front room in the deserted farmhouse outside Stuttgart. Salim Maazi stood opposite the window, legs spread comfortably apart, eyes narrowed as he faced the strong sun. Around the room, sitting on crates or cross-legged on the dirty floor, were the members of his team. Smoke from half a dozen cigarettes hung motionless in the air like streaky cirrus clouds of gray, moving only when a breeze was created by someone trying to find more comfort.

Clapping his hands for attention, Maazi swung around to face the large sheet of white paper he had taped to the wall. With swift, sure strokes of a thick black pen, he drew a map. A road appeared, splitting up as other roads ran from it. Squares represented buildings. There was a tennis court, an aircraft hangar and one large square that he ringed with a heavy, ugly circle—the gymnasium on Cooke Barracks. The map was a larger, more easily identifiable version of the chart which Pavel Vlasov had obtained for him.

"The participants in this meeting of treachery are scheduled to arrive at nine o'clock on Wednesday morning, two days from now. Our own action will commence at approximately twelve-thirty. At that time the

259

entire base—to use an American slang expression which is particularly appropriate for this situation—will be out to lunch. The mess halls will be full. Off-base personnel will have returned home to eat. It will be a moment when the base is at a low state of readiness.

"According to the reports made out by Wasim Jibril and Hashim Zeira"—he nodded to the two men who had laid the groundwork in Germany while guarding Samantha's son—"there are two trucks which make daily deliveries to the base at about that time. The first truck carries produce from a wholesale vegetable market, but we will discount this particular vehicle because it is open and therefore totally unsuitable to our needs. The other truck, which is a closed vehicle, brings in beer from a local brewery in Eislingen, the next town. On the base, this truck makes deliveries to the Ratskeller, here"—he pointed to a building on the map —"to the Rod and Gun Club, here, and to the Enlisted Men's Club, here. After it makes those stops, the truck leaves the base and makes further deliveries at the Officers' Club and at the NCO Club, neither of which are on post. On Wednesday, the beer drinkers of Cooke Barracks—the officers, the NCOs and the enlisted men alike—will, regrettably, have to go thirsty."

A ripple of laughter echoed around the room and Maazi smiled. Like any commander he knew that he had to generate precisely the right psychological mood in his men. Too much time and seriousness created tension.

He lit a cigarette, inhaled deeply and looked from face to face. They would not let him down. In two days time they would write their own page in the history books, a complete chapter on the Palestinian struggle to regain a homeland. His eyes caught those of Rima. Hers might be a secondary mission; she had not been selected to take part in the raid itself, but she appreciated its importance. The honor of killing the spy and her son once the raid had succeeded would be Rima's; she would avenge herself completely for Tel al-Za'atar.

"On Wednesday morning Rima, Ahmed and Yussuf will stay here to guard the Sutcliffe woman and the boy. The remainder of us will travel to here"—he pointed at the map—"to humiliate those who would betray *Filastin.*"

"Where will we commandeer the brewery truck?" The question came from Hussein Badowi, one of the Palestinians who had traveled from Rashidieh with Maazi.

"The truck travels from Eislingen along Grosseisinger Strasse and then

260

turns into Rossbach Strasse, which leads to Cooke Barracks," Maazi answered. "On Rossbach Strasse there is a cemetery. There we will block the road and take over the truck. The entire operation should take no more than twenty seconds."

"Once we have the truck, the gate guard will just wave us onto the base?" This time it was Reynard who posed the question.

"He is accustomed to the sight of the brewery truck. But to be on the safe side, we will hold the driver until we are past the gate. Now here" —he jabbed his finger on the road leading into the base from the gate— "is where speed counts. We will stop for nothing. I estimate that from the gate to the gymnasium is half a mile at the most. At the gymnasium we will use the truck as a battering ram. The people inside will have no chance. Before they can recover from the shock of the assault, we will be inside."

"What about security?" Reynard asked.

"I have been assured that it will be low key. The Americans cannot afford to let people know the importance of what is really happening by having an entire regiment there. And once the delegates are in our power, even an atom bomb would be useless to the Americans. They dare not risk casualties among these delegates."

Reynard nodded in acceptance of the answer. He took a pack of Gitanes from his pocket, offered one to Rima who sat next to him on the floor. She shook her head. Reynard lit his own and then asked Maazi, "What happens then?"

"Then?" Maazi smiled as he recognized the excitement in the Frenchman's voice. Reynard's calm intellectualism had disappeared completely. He had finally discovered the unmatched thrill of battle. "Then we will play our cards for all they are worth."

The Israeli government had chosen Chaim Lankin to head its delegation to the American-sponsored meeting. A former ambassador to the United Nations, Lankin had been born in Montreal sixty-two years earlier and still spoke English with a distinct Canadian accent, even to the point of finishing the occasional sentence with a querying "Ay?"

The day before Lankin and his party were due to leave from a military air base on the United States Air Force plane to Frankfurt, General Avivi sent for the former ambassador.

"There's been a change of plans," Avivi said simply. "You're including a new man in your party, Joel Rosen. Which of your staff would you like to leave behind?"

"Pardon?" Lankin said.

"It's a security matter. I'm afraid you don't have any choice."

Lankin knew the Mossad chief well enough to understand that he would not make such a demand without good reason. "Do you expect trouble in Germany?"

"When don't we expect trouble?"

"What is Rosen?"

Avivi smiled. "He's a specialist."

"In what area, might I ask?"

"Palestinian affairs. How does that sound?"

"It sounds as if you'd better tell me exactly what is going on," Lankin replied.

"I had always intended to," Avivi said with a thin smile.

The following day, when the U.S. Air Force flight took off, heading west to Germany, Joel Rosen was aboard as the delegation's expert on Palestinian affairs.

CHAPTER
NINETEEN

T HE first helicopter appeared in the overcast sky above Cooke Barracks at five minutes before nine on Wednesday morning, swooping low over the divisional headquarters building at the edge of the airstrip to touch down in front of the gymnasium. Ducking their heads against the dust devils whipped up by whirling rotors, the American delegation, led by Robert Shea, left the helicopter and walked under a newly erected blue-and-white canopy to the gymnasium entrance. The moment they were clear, the helicopter lifted into the air to make room for the next flight, which even now was descending as it approached the army base.

Standing under the canopy were two young men in gray flannel suits. Sunglasses protected their eyes against the dirt flung up by the helicopter. One of the men opened the double doors for the American party to enter. Inside the gymnasium, the first person Shea saw was John Lansing.

"Welcome, Mr. Shea." Lansing extended his right hand. "I wish you good luck in today's work."

"Thank you." Shea stared first at Lansing's shabby suit and then into his cold blue eyes. He looked around the gymnasium. The entire floor was covered in plush blue carpet. The walls sparkled with fresh paint. Tables draped with white linen had been erected in the shape of a large horseshoe. At the top, like a bridal party at a wedding, would sit Shea and the American delegation. The positions of the other delegations were denoted by miniature flags set in black wooden bases. Black-and-white nameplates signified where each man would sit. Along one side of the horseshoe, opposite the double doors, would sit the Jordanian and Saudi Arabian delegations; facing them would be the Egyptian and Israeli representatives. Notebooks, pencils, carafes of ice water, tumblers and ashtrays were set out neatly. Directly in front of each nameplate was a low stack of typewritten documents. From the steel girders in the roof hung the flags of the five nations present.

Shea felt at home immediately. The gymnasium resembled a thousand other places he had chaired meetings. In this familiar environment he would be able to forget for a few hours the sword that Lansing held over his family's head.

"No mistakes, please, Mr. Shea," Lansing uttered quietly as if he could read the State man's thoughts.

"I trust that the same applies to you," Shea responded.

Lansing gave a grim little smile. "We don't make mistakes." He turned and walked to the office behind the boarded-up snack bar.

During the next five minutes, three more helicopters touched down, bringing the Egyptian, Saudi Arabian and Jordanian negotiators. Shea greeted each delegate personally before introducing members of his own team.

The helicopter carrying Chaim Lankin and the Israeli delegation was the last to arrive. Joel Rosen gazed out of the window as the helicopter descended. In the distance he could see Hohenstaufen rising into the low clouds. The helicopter passed over tennis courts and two soccer fields before the airstrip came into view. As the helicopter came down, Rosen could even read the signs that had been erected by the green wooden barriers: Off Limits Except for NATO Staff. He smiled at the Americans' thoroughness; even the most suspicious mind would see nothing odd about a NATO meeting at an army base.

Two olive-drab pickup trucks with army markings were stationed by the wooden barriers. Although Rosen was unable to see into the vehicles, he guessed the men inside would be wearing army uniforms; but they would never draw army pay. They were American secret-service agents, part of the low-level security the State Department had organized for the meeting. The high-level security had been organized by John Lansing, and that was inside the gymnasium.

The same two men in gray flannel suits and sunglasses opened the gymnasium door for Chaim Lankin and his retinue. As they entered and Shea came over to greet them, the buzz of conversation in the gymnasium ceased; all that could be heard was the clattering of the last helicopter as it climbed into the air. Lankin looked over the groups of delegates, aware that they were all staring at him. Old hatreds and distrusts die hard, he reflected; if the Americans can find accord among us, then it is they who are the chosen people and not ourselves.

It was the leader of the Egyptian party, a former army general whom Lankin had met before, who broke the ice. "I am glad that we meet again," Gamal Shamri greeted the Israeli. "And I pray that in this place we will finally make our peace an all-encompassing one."

"That same prayer has passed my lips many times," Lankin replied.

The delegates took their seats. Instinctively Rosen felt uncomfortable with his back to the double doors, but that was the way it had to be. He tried to concentrate on what Shea was saying from his position at the top of the horseshoe.

"On behalf of the United States government, I welcome each of you to this historic meeting. In front of you are the proposals from your respective governments. My own government believes that these proposals offer a firm basis for a lasting peace, an honorable peace, in the Middle East. And it is my fervent belief that when we are finished here, we will have important, joyous news to tell the world."

There was a shuffling of paper as each delegate picked up the stack of typed documents. Shea used the moment to look at Rosen, remembering him from the car chase in Massachusetts. Then he glanced over his shoulder in the direction of the concealed snack bar and wondered what was happening back there.

Through holes drilled in the plasterboard—so minute that they were invisible to the delegates sitting at the tables—John Lansing stared back at Robert Shea. Standing behind the snack-bar counter with Lansing were four other men. Behind them, the wall between the snack bar and the office had been removed. The desk had been shoved to one side. The piles of athletic equipment had disappeared. A communications center had been set up; a technician sat alertly at the equipment.

Resting on the snack-bar counter in front of each man, like weapons lined up at a fairground shooting gallery, was an Israeli-made Uzi submachine gun. But the ammunition inside the Uzi magazines was definitely not Israeli-made. The bullets were of a special low velocity. At close range they had more than enough power to kill a man, but they would not have enough power to rip clean through his body and cause innocent casualties elsewhere in the gymnasium.

Next to Lansing's weapon was a long steel lever. The mechanism it

265

controlled had worked perfectly in the dozen dry runs they had made the previous day. Now, as Lansing rested his left hand gently on the lever and waited for that moment when he would throw it for real, he tried to imagine what thoughts were passing through the mind of Robert Shea. Was the man from State thinking about his family, or would some misguided loyalty to his blackmailers make him tip his hand?

Lansing moved his position so that he could spy on Joel Rosen. Who would have thought that the dapper gray-haired man sitting on Chaim Lankin's left was anything but a diplomat? Dressed in a fawn suit with a crisply knotted tie and highly shined brown shoes, Rosen looked just like a career government official. Which, Lansing supposed with a wry smile, was precisely what he was.

Samantha reached out to hold her son close as she heard the lock being turned. Automatically she assumed it would be one of her jailers come to remove the dirty plates from breakfast, if cold canned sardines and dry black bread could be termed breakfast. Even the water which had accompanied the Spartan meal had tasted brackish, as though it had been drawn from a spring that had long since ceased to be fresh.

The door opened and Samantha recognized Salim Maazi. He was dressed in jeans, Adidas sneakers and a lightweight blouson top. A Beretta submachine gun was slung casually across his chest. "I have come to say farewell, Samantha. Are you going to wish us luck in our venture? *Mazel tov*—isn't that the expression the Jews use?"

"I wouldn't know," she replied. She hugged David tighter. Like his mother he was beyond fear. His entire world had been turned upside down; all he felt now was a fatalistic numbness.

Maazi came into the room, kicked the door closed and crouched down beside Samantha and David. "Before I leave you, there is one thing I want to know. Why did you work for the Israelis?"

The way Maazi phrased the question gave Samantha a brief instant of triumph. Twice the Palestinian had made love to her—once when she was drunk and hysterical, the second time when she thought herself so deeply into the role that it had been an actress Maazi had bedded, not Samantha Sutcliffe—and it galled him that a woman he thought he had known so intimately could have fooled him. "It's driving you crazy, isn't it?"

"Crazy? No—" He smiled at her as if he were a polite and charming stranger. "I'm curious, that's all. Why would a woman as attractive as yourself, as talented and successful, throw away her life and that of her son for such an oppressive cause?"

"You'll go to your grave still wondering," Samantha promised.

"Perhaps," he said fatalistically. He stood up, ready to leave. As he passed through the doorway he looked back for a moment. "It is a great pity, Samantha, that you and I did not meet under different circumstances."

"Yes, it is," she surprised him by agreeing. "Then I would have had the opportunity to hate you all over again."

In front of the farmhouse, Maazi supervised the loading of his squad into the Volkswagen bus. Wasim Jibril sat up front with Hashim Zeira. In the back sat Hussein Badowi, Ismail Kassem, Mahmoud Tretzi and Pierre Reynard. Weapons were concealed under the seats, and all the men wore casual, functional clothing. An air of excitement filled the bus; it could have been carrying a group of friends to a sporting event.

Maazi passed his gun through the open door to Zeira. Then he turned to the three people who would be left behind at the farm: Rima, Yussuf Torbuk and Ahmed el-Shafri. There was no telephone at the farm, no means of communication. Other arrangements had been made. "Listen to the American Armed Forces Network radio station," Maazi reminded them. "When you hear that we have landed safely in Libya with our hostages, kill the woman and the boy. We will all meet again when this is over, as heroes. If something"—he paused, unwilling to even discuss the alternative—"if something should go wrong and we need the woman and the boy, there will be a message on the Armed Forces Network. It will be a record request: for Rima, 'Come Fly With Me.' "

" 'Come Fly With Me,' " Rima repeated. She clutched at Maazi's hand, reluctant to let him leave.

"If you hear that record request, you will take the woman and the boy in the Opel to the airport at Echterdingen." He bent forward to kiss her gently on the lips, and then slapped Torbuk and el-Shafri on the shoulder. "Until we meet again," he said as he climbed into the front of the Volkswagen bus with Jibril and Zeira. He slammed the door, thrust a clenched fist through the window and yelled, *"Biladi, Biladi!"*

As the Volkswagen pulled away, el-Shafri and Torbuk retreated to the farmhouse. Rima stood watching until the vehicle had disappeared. Only when the sound of the engine had been swallowed up by the trees did she follow her two comrades. Already they had the portable radio tuned to Armed Forces Network but Rima paid no attention. She picked up a submachine gun and walked to the room where Samantha and David were imprisoned.

"Salim and his men have left," she said, standing over the two captives. "By tonight he will be in Libya, receiving the hero's welcome he so richly deserves. And you"—she moved the gun for emphasis—"will both be dead." She backed away until she reached the furthest corner of the room where she crouched down on the floor. "I have a problem, deciding which of you I should kill first." She smiled at Samantha as if another woman would be able to sympathize with this particular dilemma.

"David—do you want to see your mother die? Or would you rather I shot you first?"

Samantha clutched David's head, jammed her hands over his ears. "Shut up!" she screamed at the Palestinian woman.

Rima's smile grew wider. "Perhaps I should kill your son first, Samantha. Surely as a good mother who did not raise her child to be a martyr, you would want to spare him the pain of witnessing your death."

Samantha struggled to move toward the taunting Palestinian woman. The chain attached to the wall snapped against her leg, holding her back.

"I know what to do," Rima continued, enjoying the game even more as she watched Samantha's distress increase. "I can let each of you watch the other suffer. I can shoot to wound first of all, in the legs or the arms. Does that sound a fair solution?"

"Shut up, you bloody bitch!"

Rima got up and pushed Samantha roughly away from David. Then she lowered the submachine gun until the muzzle rested against the boy's chained leg. "Ask your mother why she works for the Israelis."

Samantha felt David quivering with terror in her arms. She could stand whatever they did to her—just thinking about Asher gave her strength— but she would do anything to spare her son more suffering. "You murdered Asher Davidson!" she cried out.

"Who?" Surprised by the mention of an unknown name, Rima stepped back a few paces. "Who was Asher Davidson?"

"At Munich in '72. You killed him."

"One of the Israelis? What was he to you?"

"My—" Samantha's head dropped. She had failed to deny the Palestinians this one precious secret.

"Was he your lover?"

When Samantha offered no reply, Rima smiled triumphantly. "Your lover." The words echoed mockingly in the small, damp room. Then

268

Rima's voice turned bitter. "Couldn't you have found an Englishman to love? A lord of something—a duke? Why did you throw yourself on scum like that?"

"Because he was a good man, but you would not understand anything about that. You know nothing of love; all you know is hate."

The bitterness faded from Rima's face for an instant. "Do you really think I don't know what love is? I had a husband and children once, before the friends of the Israelis murdered them. And then you tried to steal Salim from me."

Samantha laughed, a sound so out of context that she was shocked at herself. "Steal him? A murderer? You must be mad! I was using him so that I might help others to destroy him!"

Rima's face turned hard as she opened the door. "I know what to do —I won't shoot either of you." She waited a moment, just long enough for Samantha to understand what she had said, for any hopes that still lived within the English actress to be rekindled. "We'll just leave you and your precious son imprisoned here. You can starve to death!"

She burst out laughing and slammed the door. There would be extra reason for joy when she met with Maazi. She would be able to tell him that Munich had claimed more victims.

Helmut Wunderlicht heaved the last crate of beer into the truck and slammed the cargo door. He was breathing hard from the exertion and his pale blue uniform stuck to his body. He took off his sweat-stained cap and wiped his brow while he waited for the brewery dispatcher to log him out.

"All right, Helmut. Drive carefully," the dispatcher said.

"I always do. *Ade.*" Wunderlicht lit a cigarette, clambered into the high cab and settled himself on the single seat. The engine started at the fourth attempt. It's old like me, Wunderlicht thought; neither of us moves so quickly anymore. Grinding the transmission into first, he drove slowly toward the brewery gate. Perhaps he would be able to stop on the way and empty a couple of bottles. The Americans never counted too closely what they paid for; they were too busy stealing for themselves to worry about two or three missing bottles. Besides—he glanced down at the shriveled stump on the middle finger of his right hand where it rested on the steering wheel—the Amis still owe me for this.

The cigarette burned down and he lit another. He turned down Grosseisinger Strasse heading into Göppingen, and changed down into second gear as he swung the heavy truck right onto Rossbach Strasse. A hundred yards ahead on the deserted road, abreast of the cemetery, a blue-and-white Volkswagen bus seemed to be in trouble. It was pulled off to the side with its engine compartment open. A chubby man with glasses and a wispy beard was staring at the engine, shaking his head in confusion.

Wunderlicht grimaced as he looked at the cemetery. Every day when he drove by this place he felt frighteningly aware of his own age. Then he switched his attention to the man by the Volkswagen.

"Here comes the brewery truck," Zeira said through the open window of the Volkswagen bus to the six men who crouched out of sight.

"Wave him down," Maazi ordered.

Zeira stepped into the middle of the road and held up his hands like a traffic policeman. Inside the truck, Wunderlicht cursed. "Get out of my way, you stupid bastard! I don't have the time to stop for you!"

Zeira stayed put. At the very last moment Wunderlicht stamped on the brake pedal. The crates of beer in the cargo space slid forward with an ominous crash and beer slopped into the driver's cab through the narrow communicating doorway. The truck quivered to a stop two yards from Zeira.

"Are you crazy, man!" Wunderlicht hollered out of the window. "I could have killed you!"

Suddenly the doors of the Volkswagen bus burst open. Men with guns appeared. The right-hand door of the truck flew back and Wunderlicht found himself staring down the muzzles of two submachine guns. Maazi and Jibril jumped into the cab and squatted on the floor, below the level of the window. In the wing mirror, Wunderlicht saw more men running to the back. He heard the rear door being slammed. "All right, let's go!" Zeira yelled.

"Move!" Maazi ordered, jabbing the German in the side with the submachine gun. *"Schnell!"*

Wunderlicht glanced at the guns pointing at him, at the cemetery so conveniently close. He licked his lips nervously, put the truck into gear and continued to the guard post at the entrance to Cooke Barracks. Maazi was more than satisfied. The entire incident had cost them no more than fifteen seconds.

In the back of the truck, Zeira, Reynard, Badowi, Kassem and Tretzi crouched down and braced themselves against the walls to stop from falling as the truck bounced along the uneven road. Beer from the

270

smashed bottles slopped across the floor, soaking through their shoes, filling the confined space with fumes. As the truck reached the end of Rossbach Strasse and turned right to approach the gate, they gripped their weapons tightly.

"What do I do now?" Wunderlicht asked Maazi. He had one eye on the gate, the other on the submachine gun jammed into his side.

"Whatever you normally do. And no mistakes." Maazi answered, crouched out of sight.

Wunderlicht braked to a gentle halt, anxiously watching the military policeman who emerged from the guard post. It was a tall black corporal he had seen many times before.

"*Gruss Gott,*" Wunderlicht greeted the corporal.

"*Gruss Gott* yourself, old man. Bringing us more of that good German beer?"

Wunderlicht understood only enough English to nod and smile stupidly.

The corporal noted the truck's license number on a piece of paper attached to a clipboard and waved Wunderlicht through. After a few seconds, Maazi raised his head cautiously above the level of the windows. They were a hundred yards inside the base. Two cars were approaching from the opposite direction; on the sidewalk, a couple of soldiers walked together, talking.

Maazi waited until the truck had passed the cars and the soldiers; then he reached across Wunderlicht, opened the driver's door and shoved hard. Wunderlicht's startled cry changed to a scream of pain as he bounced onto the road. Maazi slid into the seat, slammed the door shut, grabbed the wheel and stomped hard on the gas pedal. In the mirror he could see the German lying motionless in the road. By the time anyone could react, they would be at the gymnasium.

Ahead the road bent slightly to the right and left before running straight again. The back end of the truck veered perilously as Maazi took the shallow S-bend at thirty-five miles an hour. To his right stretched the airstrip; on its edge he could see the division headquarters with pennants flying proudly from flagpoles. To his left were buildings—the division's personnel-administration offices. And there—directly ahead of the truck—were green wooden barriers with NATO off-limits signs, two olive-drab pickup trucks and the gymnasium with the blue-and-white canopy leading to its entrance.

"Hold tight!" Maazi yelled as he saw men in uniform leap from the pickups. "We're going in!"

The flimsy barriers were smashed aside by the truck. Men jumped out of the way as Maazi steered the truck directly at one of the pickups. There was a loud, jarring crash and the smaller vehicle bounced aside, rocking up and down as its suspension tried to absorb the impact. In the back of the truck, two men slipped on the beer-soaked floor and were helped immediately to their feet by their comrades.

Maazi braked, swung the wide steering wheel to the right, away from the gymnasium.

Then, with a wrenching strain on his arms, he yanked the wheel the other way. The truck responded slowly. "Come on, you stinking beast!" Maazi spat out between clenched teeth. "Come on!"

The truck swung around in a wide arc—body leaning at a steep angle under the force of the turn—until it was pointed directly at the blue-and-white canopy and the gymnasium's double doors.

At the last moment, as the canopy loomed large in the truck's windshield, Maazi took one hand off the wheel and covered his eyes.

John Lansing cocked his head slightly at the sounds of the truck colliding with the pickup and the abrupt, hard revving of an engine. He gripped the cold metal of the lever tightly with his left hand, while his right hand closed on the stock of the Uzi in front of him. The men alongside Lansing braced themselves on the counter of the snack bar as they peered through the spy holes bored into the plasterboard.

The delegates had also noticed the noise, but only two men had reason to think it might signify danger. Robert Shea glanced to his right, at the gymnasium's double doors, and then quickly returned his attention to what the leader of the Saudi Arabian delegation was saying. He could see Chaim Lankin bristling with indignation at the Saudi's words. To Lankin's left, Rosen was moving in his chair as if expecting trouble.

With a noise like thunder, the metal double doors slammed back on their hinges as the front of the truck ripped into them. The main bulk of the truck's body rammed into the portion of the wall above the doors and the entire building shook. Lights flickered before coming on again. Plaster showered inward. The Saudi delegate's words died on his lips as he raised both hands to his face. Several of the men jumped up from their seats in shock and terror.

"Everyone sit down!" Maazi shouted as he and Jibril jumped down from the cab and fought their way past the tangled remains of the canopy which clung to the truck's windshield and doors. Both men opened fire simultaneously over the heads of the delegates. Bullets smashed into the opposite wall as the other members of the raiding party poured out of the truck to join Maazi and Jibril.

"Sit down, I said!" Maazi felt something warm flowing down his cheek. Above his right eye was a deep cut where he had slammed into the windshield at the moment of impact. In the excitement he could not even recall hitting his head.

Gradually the frightened delegates resumed their seats. Some stared with fear at the group of armed men, others with fascination. Chaim Lankin, the head of the Israeli delegation, gazed at them with undisguised contempt; here stood the very reason for his country's hard line, how could you negotiate with savages like these? One of the Saudis closed his eyes in resignation; he had been in Vienna in 1975 when Carlos had hijacked the OPEC ministers.

"You are all prisoners of Black September!" Maazi bellowed. He paused long enough to let the words register. His eyes swept across the stunned faces, and exultation swept through him. Even now, so many years after their last operation, the name Black September still inspired terror. "You will pay the price for the treachery of your governments."

Of all the delegates, Robert Shea seemed the calmest. He stared at Maazi with genuine curiosity. The blood dripping down the Palestinian leader's face had started to congeal on one side of his thick moustache. Shea was fascinated by the sight. So this was the end result of one stupid indiscretion more than twenty years ago.

From outside the gymnasium, a siren wailed. Moments later another joined in to form a mournful chorus. A bullhorn barked: "You inside! The building is surrounded. You cannot excape. Throw out your weapons and come out with your hands raised."

Maazi snapped around to face Shea. Without taking his eyes from the State man he rapped out an order to Reynard. "Go out there; tell them who we are and what we want." Reynard passed his own submachine gun to Wasim Jibril who was staring intently at Joel Rosen; then he walked outside with his hands held high above his head.

Three military-police jeeps were positioned outside the gymnasium. On one of them, a heavy machine gun tracked Reynard as he pushed his way past the destroyed canopy. The secret service agents who had been manning the pickups now leaned across the hoods of their vehicles, automatic weapons in their hands.

"That's far enough!" A blond-haired man in a gray suit came forward to meet Reynard. In one hand he held a Browning automatic, in the other he clutched a radio.

"Are you in charge here?" Reynard asked.

"I am. What's going on in there?"

"The meeting has been taken over by Black September."

"By who?" the secret service agent asked. He had not heard the name for years, and even now he was unsure that he had understood correctly. Reynard repeated the name and the secret service agent asked: "Those shots—is anyone hurt?"

"No. And no one will be hurt as long as our demands are met."

"What are they?" The blond-haired man ran his eyes over Reynard and tried to guess his nationality. Not an Arab. Were they pulling in outside talent, dipping into the pool of international terrorism?

"You'll find out in due time. For now, we need helicopters. Enough to carry all the delegates, six of my comrades and myself to Stuttgart International Airport. There, you will arrange for a fully fueled, crewed, long-haul commercial airliner to be waiting for us."

"Where's your final destination?"

"At the moment that is none of your business." Reynard replied coldly. He looked beyond the blond-haired secret service agent as two more MP jeeps and an army ambulance arrived; so much for the Americans and their penchant for secrecy. Another jeep approached from the direction of the divisional headquarters building. On the front of the vehicle was a bright red plaque with two shining silver stars.

"That's going to take time, arranging all that," the blond-haired man said. "You've got to be patient. Let's all walk away from this, eh?"

Reynard ignored the conciliatory tone. Maazi had chosen the Frenchman to be the spokesman because he was *not* an Arab; he had reasoned that the Americans would be more receptive to a European than to an Arab, but he had given Reynard strict instructions on how to conduct himself during the negotiation process. Reynard was to be curt; he was to ignore any overtures to communication; he was to give orders and then get out. "You have fifteen minutes. If those helicopters are not here by then, we'll send out a body." Without waiting for an answer, he dropped his arms, turned around and walked back into the gymnasium. The blond-haired man spoke urgently into his radio.

Inside the gymnasium time seemed to have stood still. Little had changed. Maazi stood near Shea; the other five men were spaced along one wall.

"How many men are out there?" Maazi asked.

"A lot of army personnel, but the secret service men are in charge. They know they'll get a body if we don't hear from them in fifteen minutes."

"Well done," Maazi said.

Reynard collected his weapon from Jibril, who was still staring intently at Rosen, and took up a position behind the Israeli delegation.

"What do you intend doing with us?" Gamal Shamri, the leader of the Egyptian delegation, asked.

Maazi grinned with delight at the question. He dabbed at the gash on his head and showed the blood to the Egyptian. "Do you know what this is? It's Palestinian blood, the same blood which has been spilled for more than thirty years because you—our Arab brothers!—have betrayed us again and again. No more, we say! No more treachery! No more dealings with—them!" He waved his gun in the direction of the Israelis. "In exchange for your lives we demand that your governments dissociate themselves from this act of betrayal. Only when we are satisfied that your governments have retreated from this treacherous position and are prepared to support the Palestinian struggle for justice will you be released."

"Does that include my government?" asked Chaim Lankin.

"Your government?" Maazi laughed. "An illegal country has no government to act for it. You will be released when my own comrades are released from your stinking jails. Otherwise you will be the first to die."

As Maazi finished speaking, Reynard leaned over Lankin's shoulder and plucked the blue-and-white Israeli flag from its pedestal. With a cold smile he crumpled the flag in his hand, dropped it on the floor and stamped on it. Hashim Zeira sniggered at the action.

Behind the plasterboard, John Lansing listened to Maazi's harangue and calmly reached his decision. If he waited any longer, Maazi's squad might be too spread out; there would be a chance of hitting one of the delegates. Now the Palestinians were at their weakest, fresh from their first triumph. There would never be a better opportunity. He whispered terse, final instructions to the men behind the snack-bar counter, wiped his hand on his trousers to clear the sweat and gripped the steel lever. It felt as cold as ice to his touch.

Lansing pulled back on the lever and a horizontal section of plasterboard dropped clean away to leave an unobstructed field of fire.

The noise of the plasterboard falling on the floor had the same stunning effect on Maazi's men that the truck had had earlier on the delegates. Maazi swung around to see five men aiming weapons into the gymnasium from behind the snack counter. But unlike Maazi and Jibril who had shot into the wall for effect, Lansing's men fired to kill.

Hashim Zeira's snigger was throttled abruptly as two of the low-velocity bullets exploded inside his chest. Wasim Jibril died with blood spurting from between his hands as he clutched his throat in a final, futile gesture; his last thoughts were not those of pain but of puzzlement, unable to understand why the Israeli delegate in the fawn suit looked so familiar. A second later, when the firing ceased on a sharp command from Lansing, only two of the invasion force were left standing—Maazi and Reynard, who dropped their weapons onto the floor and raised their hands.

Lansing yelled at the radio man to signal to the agents waiting outside the gymnasium that the situation was under control. Then he vaulted nimbly over the counter. "Get away from those weapons!" he snapped at the two survivors. "Kick them clear!"

Reynard complied immediately, kicking the submachine gun across the carpeted floor. Maazi looked longingly at his weapon for a moment as he debated his chances of snatching it from the floor and shooting his way out of trouble. He decided against it. Stepping back two paces, he gazed around, taking in the grotesquely sprawled figures of Jibril, Zeira, Badowi, Kassem and Tretzi. Pools of blood stained the blue carpet a dark brown, more Palestinian blood. His eyes moved to Reynard, standing immobile behind the Israeli delegation, frozen with fear by the weapons pointed at him; the flag he had taken from the pedestal lay by his right foot. Maazi had never seen such naked fear in a man. Sadly he concluded that the intellectual was too strongly ingrained in Reynard; the parasitical coward had risen to the surface.

Maazi switched his gaze from Reynard to the delegates who, a minute earlier, had been in his power. Most avoided his eyes as if contact might single them out for some future retribution, but one of the Egyptians sneered at him, glorying in the Palestinian's humiliation. At last, Maazi's eyes met those of Robert Shea, who sat stiffly in his chair at the head of the horseshoe. As he recognized the source of yet another betrayal, the Palestinian's face darkened with fury. The man who had worked for the Russians—and whom the Russians wanted put to death—had delivered Maazi's entire squad into the hands of the Americans.

With a scream of rage bursting from his lips, Maazi leaped upon the gray-haired State man and dragged him off the chair. Shea tried to defend himself against the furious onslaught, the fists that pummeled his face, the hands that gripped his throat and tried to choke the life out of him. Lansing threw himself on top of the two twisting, squirming men, grabbing Maazi by the long hank of hair he combed across his scalp to disguise his baldness.

And then a single gunshot ripped through the air, a bullet smashed into the steel girders supporting the roof to ricochet around until it fell, spent, in the far corner of the gymnasium.

Pierre Reynard had chosen his moment well. When all attention was focused on the struggling figures at the top of the horseshoe, Reynard had grabbed hold of the delegate sitting nearest to him. Now his left arm was locked tightly around that delegate's neck, while his right hand jammed a Czech-made M52 automatic pistol into the man's head. The delegate, whose ears were still ringing from the warning shot fired so close to his head, was Joel Rosen. And as the Mossad director of special operations fought against Reynard's grip, his jacket flapped open to reveal a glaringly empty shoulder holster.

"The next bullet goes into this man's head!" Reynard called out as he dragged Rosen around to form a shield against the weapons held by the men behind the snack bar counter. "Drop those guns at once!"

Lansing climbed slowly to his feet. So did Maazi. Shea remained on the ground, coughing and groaning softly. Maazi shook his head and wiped blood from his face, surprised as anyone else to see the pistol in Reynard's hand. He had underestimated Reynard yet again. The Frenchman had realized that one of the Israelis was armed—a Mossad agent, no doubt— and Reynard had overcome his fear to surprise the man and take his weapon.

One of the men behind the counter raised his weapon threateningly. Lansing spun around. "Put it down!" he yelled, his main concern now for the safety of Joel Rosen and the other delegates. He could not risk casualties in a wild firefight. Reluctantly the man lowered the gun and set it down on the counter.

Maazi stepped away from Lansing and touched his face with his hand. The blood was still dripping steadily from the cut above his right eye, hindering his sight. He wiped roughly at it with his sleeve and then retrieved the Beretta submachine gun he had dropped. His head ached abominably and he felt weak from the attack upon Shea. He breathed in deeply and tried to steady himself.

"Stalemate," Lansing said. He knelt down and helped Shea to his feet. The diplomat collapsed into his chair, holding his face in his hands. "There are only two of you left. Outside there's a battalion. You're not going anywhere. Your lives for the Israeli your pal's holding. I promise you safe passage if you let him go."

"No—not a stalemate," Maazi contradicted the CIA man, beginning to fully comprehend the ramifications of Reynard's attack on Rosen, the way the pendulum had swung again in his favor. "We hold two more hostages."

"Where?" Lansing looked around the gymnasium.

"Near here." Maazi swung around until the submachine gun was pointing at the Israeli delegation. "Mr. Ambassador from an illegal country," he mockingly referred to Chaim Lankin. "Perhaps you would like to inform your fellow delegates about the hostages we hold."

"Two of our people," Lankin replied flatly. He looked up at Joel Rosen. The Mossad man's face was turning scarlet from the pressure of Reynard's arm; veins stood out starkly on his forehead.

"Tell the delegates what kind of people."

"An Israeli agent and her son," Lankin answered.

"An Israeli spy and her son," Maazi said.

The leader of the Jordanian delegation jumped to his feet, eyes blazing. "Are we to be held hostage for Israeli spies?"

"Is it not a worthwhile exchange?" Maazi asked. "You sit down with the Israelis to talk of peace; now you have the opportunity to show how sincere you are. And look what you sit down with." He waved the gun at Rosen. Reynard pulled back the Mossad man's jacket to show the empty holster.

Maazi turned to Lansing. "Listen to me carefully and make no mistakes. Go outside and tell your people that we still want the helicopters, we still want a fully fueled airliner waiting for us at Stuttgart. And now we want something else. A message is to be transmitted immediately over the Armed Forces Network radio: Here is a record requested especially for Rima . . . 'Come Fly With Me.' Do you understand?"

Lansing repeated the instructions word for word.

As Maazi opened his mouth to say more, the figure of Lansing seemed to sway in front of his eyes. Reynard started forward, forcing Rosen ahead of him. "Are you all right?" he asked anxiously.

Maazi gulped and looked to Reynard for help. "My head—I'll be fine in a minute."

Reynard tightened his grip on Rosen's throat. "Bring a radio in here so that we can listen for ourselves," he told Lansing. "The message is a signal for our comrades to meet us at Stuttgart Airport with the other hostages. You and the Germans will accord our comrades every courtesy. No tricks, or everyone dies."

While Reynard spoke, Maazi gazed numbly at the bloody bodies that littered the carpet—his comrades who had given their lives in yet another betrayal. For a moment he considered demanding body bags for the dead men to be flown home in so that they could be laid to rest as heroes. It was a romantic idea, but impractical. They would have to remain here, but they would not be forgotten. He lifted his eyes and stared at the delegates. The sight of them brought home with stunning clarity how he had failed in this, his most important mission since Munich. He had been recalled to action and he had been found wanting. Anger drove the pain from his head and turned his concentration sharp again. He gripped the Beretta with renewed intensity. They would all pay.

"Salim, listen to me," Reynard whispered urgently in Arabic, sensing the direction of his thoughts, "this Israeli, the woman and the boy are enough."

"What do you mean?"

"We are only two now. We cannot handle all of these traitors; the odds are too great."

Maazi nodded. Three hostages were as good as thirty, especially when one of those hostages was Samantha Sutcliffe. With these three hostages he would be able to demand that the Israelis empty their jails of Palestinians. And the Arab world—the people who supported him even if their leaders did not—would still learn how their governments were betraying their ideals by sitting down with the Israelis to talk peace. Maazi turned to Lansing. "When we hear that our comrades and the two hostages they hold are waiting for us at Stuttgart, we will release everyone but this Israeli."

Lansing watched Maazi carefully, trying to gauge his mood. The Palestinian was more dangerous now than at any time. The blow to his head had affected him badly. There was no way of knowing how he would act. It was Lansing's task to keep him calm, to keep everyone alive. "How many helicopters do you want now?"

"One. Just for the three of us. And remember, no tricks, because we can still transform this hall into a slaughterhouse."

"No tricks," Lansing repeated softly. "I'll go outside and arrange everything for you."

Maazi watched Lansing leave the building; then he swung back to cover the entire gymnasium. Although his dark restless eyes swept across the anxious faces of all the delegates, the Beretta remained pointed unwaveringly at Robert Shea.

CHAPTER
TWENTY

A steady rain began to fall from the low clouds, spattering the windows of the farmhouse. Yussuf Torbuk rose from the wooden crate he was using as a seat and looked out, unable to conceal his impatience any longer. The Armed Forces Network one o'clock news had just finished and there had been no mention of the attack.

Surely by now something must have happened, or had it all gone wrong? Had the brewery truck, upon which so much depended, failed to adhere to its normal schedule? Had Maazi's team been unable to get on the American base?

Torbuk turned away from the window and leaned against the wall, watching as Ahmed el-Shafri inspected a submachine gun, dropping out the magazine, working the operating mechanism. It was the fifth time Torbuk had seen the gray-haired man check the weapon in the last fifteen minutes. Only Rima seemed totally undaunted by the creeping tension. She sat on the floor, back against the wall, chin resting on her knees as she stared across the room. On the floor beside her rested another submachine gun and two fragmentation grenades.

"I'm going out to check the car, turn the engine over," Torbuk suddenly said.

El-Shafri did not appear to hear. Only Rima looked up. "Stay where you are," she commanded quietly. "The car works perfectly."

Torbuk slouched against the wall again and lit a cigarette. He would not argue with Rima. Although it was unspoken, the Palestinian woman was Maazi's second-in-command.

From the radio the announcer detailed the remainder of the afternoon programs. Torbuk smoked, taking quick, nervous puffs at the cigarette. El-Shafri reassembled the submachine gun. Rima stood up and walked outside, leaving the door open as she stood in the soft rain, hands on her hips, staring at the trees.

A metallic snap, abnormally loud in the quietness of the room, sounded as el-Shafri replaced the magazine in the weapon. He lifted the gun and, with a satisfied grunt, aimed at some imaginary target on the other side of the room.

"Will you put that down?" Torbuk burst out.

"Relax," el-Shafri advised. "Your life depends on your weapon. You should check yours."

"I've checked it all I need to." Torbuk covered his eyes with his hands and tried to control his frazzled nerves. How much longer were they supposed to stay without any news? The pressure was burning him up. Surely they should have heard something by now. For all they knew there could be a company of German antiterrorist troops concealed in the woods surrounding their hiding place. Maazi might have failed. One of the others, Reynard probably—Torbuk had never liked the idea of including the French journalist on the mission—might have cracked and told the Germans or the Americans where Samantha and her son were being held.

But they would never rescue them alive. He took a few steps toward the room at the back of the farmhouse; he would finish them now.

"Listen!" el-Shafri said urgently as he set down the submachine gun. "The message!"

Torbuk forgot all about Samantha and the boy as he concentrated on what the radio announcer was saying.

". . . for Rima. 'Come Fly With Me.' "

Even before the introduction to the song began, Torbuk was running through the doorway. "Rima! The record request! Salim needs us!"

Rima spun around, her face whitening. "Are you certain?"

"Listen for yourself!"

Rima ran back into the room and bent low over the radio. "Start the car," she ordered Torbuk. "Ahmed, collect all the weapons. I'll get the woman and the boy." She pinned the two grenades to her belt, picked up the submachine gun and ran toward the rear of the house, throwing open the door to the room where Samantha and David were imprisoned.

When Samantha saw the gun clutched tightly in Rima's hand, the wan, frantic expression on her face, she clasped David protectively.

"Unlock yourselves!" Rima threw a key at Samantha.

"Why? Can't you shoot us here?"

"Don't ask questions!" Rima stepped forward as if to attack the English actress. Eager to save his mother from punishment, David scrambled for the key and inserted it into the heavy padlock that secured the leg chains holding himself and Samantha.

"Get up!" Rima ordered. "Quickly!"

David stood first and helped his mother to her feet. When he looked at Rima, an adult hatred burned in his young eyes.

"Come on!" Rima snapped. "Move! We're leaving!"

"Where are we going?" Samantha asked.

"I told you, no questions," Rima answered, pushing Samantha ahead of her, out of the room.

Samantha stopped dead. "Do whatever you've got to do. We're not moving a bloody inch to help you."

Rima jabbed Samantha viciously in the back with the barrel of the gun. Samantha bit back a cry, determined to deny the Palestinian woman the pleasure she would take from such an admission of pain. Instead, it was David who screamed.

"You fucking-bloody-pissing-shitty-cow!" David yelled, running the sentence together in his fury, and exhausting in one breath all the words he knew he should not say. Then he lashed out wildly at Rima with his feet, catching her solidly on the leg.

The kick took Rima completely by surprise. She staggered back, the submachine gun pointing at the ceiling as she squeezed the trigger. Samantha's hand shot out and slammed the barrel of the gun into Rima's face, shoving the Palestinian woman off balance. Now, she thought. Now!

But before Samantha could wrest the weapon from Rima's grip, the strong hands of el-Shafri grasped her from behind. Simultaneously, Torbuk grabbed hold of David's thick black hair and lifted him, screaming in pain and frustration, off the ground.

Rima leaned against the wall, cradling the gun to her breasts as though it was one of her long-dead children. Her nose and mouth were bleeding, and more than anything else she wanted to empty the entire magazine into this English bitch and her son. But she knew she dare not exact such a fitting revenge. Samantha and David represented their ticket to safety,

283

their escape from whatever trap Maazi had fallen into. She would have to wait before exacting vengeance, but there was nothing to stop her from venting a portion of her rage.

"Hold her," she whispered menacingly. With as much force as she could muster, she rammed the gun into Samantha's stomach. Despite el-Shafri's tight grip, Samantha catapulted forward as the breath was driven from her body. Then, gasping and helpless to resist, she was dragged by el-Shafri from the farmhouse, through the rain, to the waiting Opel.

Samantha sat in the back with Torbuk. Seated in front were Rima and el-Shafri, with David squeezed in between them. While el-Shafri drove, Rima kept a pistol pressed into David's neck. Resistance was futile now, Samantha reflected as she cursed herself for not being quick enough to take full advantage of David's fiery bravery—had he *really* learned such obscene language in the genteel village school?

Something had happened to Maazi and the other men. To Reynard as well, Samantha could not help thinking with a savage joy. That was why she and David were being taken from the farmhouse. Rima needed them as hostages. Nonetheless, one move now and Samantha was certain that Rima would have no compunction in blowing David's head off.

In the gymnasium Reynard was growing tired as he continued to hold his arm around Joel Rosen's neck and press the M52 automatic into his head. Forty minutes had passed since the message had gone out over Armed Forces Network radio to Rima and the others in the farmhouse. Surely they should be at the airport by now.

Reynard changed position to give relief to his aching legs. He looked past Rosen at the delegates, sitting quietly, their hands on the table in plain view. Lansing and the CIA sharpshooters who had hidden behind the plasterboard were now lying face down on the floor, hands clasped over their heads. The radio technician had brought his equipment from the back office and had taken Rosen's vacated seat, next to Chaim Lankin. Everyone averted their eyes from the five dead bodies that had been the Palestinian attack team.

Next to Reynard stood Maazi, watching the delegates intently. Every few seconds the Palestinian rubbed his right eye. The bleeding had stopped, the dizziness had passed, but his eye itched annoyingly. The more he rubbed, the worse the irritation became.

To Chaim Lankin's left, the radio technician adjusted his headphones as a message came through. "Your people just arrived at the airport," he told Maazi and Reynard.

"How many?" Maazi asked, instantly suspicious.

The attention of every delegate was riveted on the radio technician as he relayed the question. "Five. Two men, two women and a boy."

"What were they driving?"

Again the question was relayed. "A red Opel."

"That's them," Reynard whispered.

"What about a plane?" Maazi asked.

"Lufthansa has agreed to supply an A300 Airbus, crewed and fully fueled. They want to know your destination so that a flight plan can be organized."

"Tripoli," Maazi replied immediately. He looked sharply at Gamal Shamri. The leader of the Egyptian delegation was nodding sagely, as if he had known all along where this episode would end, and who would be behind it. Maazi waited for the information to be passed; then he asked Lansing, "Is our helicopter outside?"

Lying on the floor Lansing twisted his neck to look at Maazi. "It was there two minutes after you demanded it."

Reynard shifted his grip on Rosen again. "Let the delegates out first," he advised Maazi. "We'll leave after they've gone."

Maazi pondered the suggestion before realizing it was the right one. With the gymnasium empty there would be no one behind their backs when he and Reynard left, taking the Israeli agent with them. "Go outside," Maazi ordered Lansing. "Tell your people that we are freeing the hostages."

Lansing climbed to his feet, dusted himself down and walked outside, arms raised. A minute passed before he returned, clothes wet from the rain. "There'll be no trouble," he promised. "Once the delegates are free you will be flown immediately to Stuttgart to join your comrades."

"Send them out," Maazi told the CIA man.

Lansing stood by the front of the truck where it poked through the double doors. First he sent out his own men. Then, delegation by delegation, he ordered the remaining hostages to leave. Soon the horseshoe of linen-draped tables was empty—except for one man.

"Go on, get out," Lansing told Robert Shea. "What are you waiting for?"

Shea stood up. "It is my duty to remain. I am the senior American-government official present."

Lansing wondered where Shea had got the nerve to call himself that. Where he had even found the courage to stay at all, remembering Maazi's ferocious attack upon the State man. The Palestinian knew who had betrayed him. Shea had more guts—or he was more stupid—than Lansing had ever realized.

Shea's eyes moved from Lansing to Rosen and Reynard. Finally his gaze rested on Maazi. A spark flashed between the two men, and in that instant Lansing understood exactly why Shea had chosen to remain behind—to redeem himself in front of his countrymen who considered him a traitor, and, more importantly, to square accounts with his own conscience.

"Shea—don't!" Lansing yelled, as he recognized what was about to happen. The Palestinian jumped back, swinging his gun around in a wide arc as Shea ran toward him, crouched low like a linebacker charging a quarterback. Explosions boomed back from the walls and high ceiling of the gymnasium. Bullets seared the air above Shea's head as he threw himself in a flying tackle to cut the last few yards.

Maazi took his finger off the trigger and used the gun as he would use a club, to swing wildly at Shea's head. The stubby barrel glanced off the gray hair as Shea wrapped both arms around Maazi and tried to drag him down. The Palestinian drove a knee into Shea's groin and the fury of the assault slackened for an instant. Shea's back curved from the force of the blow, and Maazi used the fraction of a second to jam the muzzle of his gun into the envoy's stomach. Eight bullets remained in the magazine. Maazi held down the trigger until the gun clicked empty.

In slow motion, Shea slid to the floor, hands caressing Maazi's legs. Blood poured from one great, gaping hole in his stomach. The back of his jacket was torn apart where bullets had gone clean through.

Maazi stepped back and kicked himself free. "Go outside!" he ordered Lansing breathlessly, while his fingers fumbled to replace the spent magazine. "Tell your people that everything is all right."

Instead of obeying, Lansing knelt down beside Shea. Blood-flecked saliva bubbled from his lips and he coughed violently. His face was screwed up in pain but the agony did not reach his eyes; they were at peace.

The coughing ceased. Shea's body gave a final, rigid shudder, and then his facial muscles relaxed.

"Go outside!"

This time it was Reynard's voice that barked the order. A single warning shot smacked into the carpet a foot from where Lansing knelt. He

286

stood up slowly, arms above his head once more. The pictures the Russians had taken in Paris were in a safe at the agency. Once this was over, Lansing would burn them personally. Robert Shea had paid his debt.

Lansing walked out into the pouring rain. The military-police jeeps and ambulances had gone. The delegates had been taken away. All that remained was a handful of secret service agents who fingered their weapons nervously at the sound of shooting from inside the gymnasium. "It's all right," Lansing said quietly. "Shea's dead. He was a brave man."

Maazi followed Lansing out of the gymnasium, with Reynard and Rosen bringing up the rear. Twenty yards away was an army helicopter, its blades whirling lazily to lift a fine spray of water from the ground. Lansing started to climb aboard, but Maazi called him back.

"You stay here." The Palestinian motioned for Reynard and Rosen to enter the helicopter. Before he climbed aboard himself, he looked back one last time at the gymnasium, at the brewery truck jammed into the entrance. They would pay, he promised silently. Everyone connected with today's shame would be forced to pay—the Israelis, the Americans, the Arab states that had conspired to stab the Palestinians in the back. By Allah, they would all pay. Shutting the sight from his mind, he climbed aboard.

He sat down and stared across the cabin to where Reynard and Rosen sat. The Frenchman was clutching the M52 so tightly that his knuckles gleamed whitely. Maazi realized he was totally unfamiliar with the weapon. "Hold the gun like this," he said. He took the M52 from Reynard, demonstrating the grip before passing it back. "Firmly, but not too tightly. We don't want to lose our insurance because you accidentally squeezed the trigger."

The helicopter lifted off toward the low cloud and Maazi gazed out of the rain-streaked window. As the craft passed over the divisional headquarters, he saw faces lining the building's windows. More witnesses to his disgrace. He would be back for them as well.

Parked at the very end of the runway at Stuttgart Airport, far away from the curiosity seekers who thronged the terminal, was an A300 Airbus with Lufthansa markings, engines whining, wipers swishing back and forth across the flight-deck windshield. A steep white-painted ramp led up from the ground to the door of the first-class compartment. At the bottom of the ramp, unprotected from the steady, drenching rain, stood a bedraggled group: Samantha, holding David's hand; Torbuk, el-Shafri and Rima

—all gripping submachine guns; and an unarmed Bundeswehr officer. Around the Airbus was a tight ring of gray-painted German army trucks.

Rima looked from one truck to the next, at the faces of the soldiers that stared back through the rain-spattered glass. There was no animosity in those faces, just a simple professionalism. The soldiers had a task to perform, to ensure that these people left German soil as quickly as possible. After that, they would be someone else's worry. And if the Airbus did not return? If it was blown up on some deserted airfield? Well, that was the concern of Lufthansa and Lloyd's of London. The Germans had been through hostage situations before; their country was used as a battlefield by rival Middle East factions. Like a clearing bank for human flesh, they had the hostage situation down to a fine art.

Torbuk touched Rima's arm and pointed skyward. Descending from the clouds was the helicopter. They watched it hover overhead until trucks moved away to make landing room, then it settled gently, scattering a curtain of water across the concrete. Maazi was first out, his back to the Airbus as he pointed his submachine gun into the helicopter's cabin. Rosen came out, hands in the air, with Reynard right behind him. Reynard grabbed the collar of Rosen's jacket, put the gun to his head and forced him toward the Airbus ramp.

"What happened?" Rima asked as she clutched Maazi. She wiped his face tenderly, trying to remove the dry, caked blood.

"There was a trap. The man the Soviets trusted worked both sides of the fence."

"How did you get away?" Rima pressed, too interested in Maazi to notice how David was staring incredulously at the newcomers. During his imprisonment at the farmhouse the boy had not seen Reynard at all. The sight of the Frenchman now, holding a gun, came as a shock—but it was nowhere near as stunning as seeing Joel Rosen as well. Rosen looked back at David and tried to relay a message with his eyes. Not understanding, the boy tugged at Samantha's arm. Rosen turned away.

"We escaped because of Pierre," Maazi answered Rima. He spotted the Bundeswehr officer. "Where is the flight crew, the captain?"

"On board."

Maazi slung his weapon over his shoulder and clambered up the steps into the first-class compartment. The door to the flight deck was open and he burst through. "How long before we take off?"

The captain, a burly black-haired man in his late forties, looked up briefly and continued to check his instruments. Beside him sat the first officer. The forward-facing seat behind the captain, which on some flights carried a second officer, was empty. "Whenever you're ready. We have priority clearance. Nothing leaves here until we do."

"How long is the flight time to Tripoli?"

"Normally about three hours. But today—with this weather—it could be closer to four." The captain shrugged his broad shoulders expressively to show Maazi he had no control over atmospheric conditions. "We have to circumnavigate a major storm system."

"Are you frightened?" Maazi hefted the Beretta. "Of this?"

"Only a fool wouldn't be. Company instructions in this situation are very clear. We are to comply with your demands and not risk the safety of passengers or crew."

Maazi nodded approvingly. "You are a wise man. Heed your company's instructions and you will live to be an old man."

The captain did not think the comment was worth a reply. His job was to fly these terrorists and their hostages to their destination. He was not expected to make polite conversation with them.

"Who sits here?" Maazi indicated the vacant seat behind the captain.

"Engineer/second officer, when one is included in the crew."

"I'll take the seat when we take off."

Maazi returned to the first-class cabin to supervise the loading of the passengers. Rima was standing in the aisle, watching while Samantha and David buckled themselves into the rear seats. Reynard sat across the aisle from Rosen, halfway up the cabin, the gun still clenched in his hand. Torbuk and el-Shafri stood with their backs to the flight deck, alert to everything that went on. Maazi told them to sit down for the takeoff.

The first officer, a man in his thirties with blond hair and clear blue eyes, came down from the flight deck to ensure that the door was properly fastened. He walked around the cabin, checking that all the passengers had their seat belts fastened.

"Would you mind putting your gun away, sir?" he said calmly to the Frenchman. "Aircraft skins are notoriously fragile. They were designed to cut flying weight, not to withstand bullets."

Maazi walked over to where the first officer stood. "Put the gun away," he said quietly in Arabic. "The Israeli's not going anywhere." Reluctantly Reynard pocketed the M52.

On the flight deck the captain received his clearance from the control tower. He waited until the first officer and Maazi had taken their seats, then he proceeded to the takeoff position. A minute later the bulky Airbus was rolling along the runway, lifting into the air. If he did not think about these armed madmen—the one sitting directly behind him, the three men and the woman in the first-class cabin—the captain could believe it was a perfectly normal flight.

"Turn off the no-smoking and seat-belt signs," the captain instructed his first officer when the Airbus reached its cruising altitude and was headed on a southerly course. Below were solid clouds while above the sun shone brightly in a sparkling blue sky. "Then go back and check that everything's all right. Keep them smiling at each other. You know the drill."

"I'll come with you," Maazi said, rising from the seat and removing the earphones from his head.

"Do you think it's safe to leave me alone?" the captain asked.

Maazi smiled at the question. The captain was thawing out, overcoming his initial stiffness, the resentment at being ordered where and how to fly. "Like I said to one of my men in the cabin, where would you go?" Then the smile faded. "Besides, I know some navigation. I can read compasses. Just remember that if you think of changing course."

The blond-haired first officer was relieved to see that Reynard had not brought out the automatic pistol again. The combination of guns and aircraft never failed to frighten him. The submachine guns which the Palestinians held across their laps—even the two grenades pinned to Rima's belt—did not disturb the first officer nearly as much as the nervous manner in which the Frenchman had gripped the gun. Like Maazi, the first officer could guess that Reynard was unaccustomed to handling such a weapon.

"Do my men seem calm enough?" Maazi asked after watching the first officer make his tour of inspection.

"I guess." The first officer swung himself into a seat at the front of the cabin and produced a pack of HB cigarettes. "The old man's a nonsmoker, doesn't like anyone lighting up on the flight deck." He offered the pack to Maazi, furnished him with a light. "We've got a first-aid kit on board if you want to do something about that cut on your head."

Maazi sat down next to the first officer and touched his head. He had forgotten all about the cut. "It can wait until we reach Libya. Where are we now?"

"Somewhere over Germany."

"Still?"

"We've only been airborne fifteen, twenty minutes. If you wanted to get to your destination in no time flat, you should have booked on Concorde."

Maazi managed to smile at the line. The first officer was doing his job admirably, keeping everyone loose, the guns unfired. "I thought the Germans were born without a sense of humor."

Now it was the first officer's turn to smile. "That's a rumor the English created about us." He turned in the seat and jerked his head toward the back of the cabin. "Who are your traveling companions?"

Maazi took refuge in the cigarette, drawing in a lungful of smoke while he debated whether to answer the question. "The woman is a famous English actress," he said at last, enjoying the look of surprise that appeared on the first officer's face. "Samantha Sutcliffe. The boy is—"

"You're joking," the first officer cut in. "I saw her in a film a couple of weeks ago. She didn't look a bit like that." He twisted his neck to look again, wondering if he could have been mistaken. "Wait a minute, I read she was lost in Lebanon, feared dead."

"Take my word for it; she is Samantha Sutcliffe. The boy is her son. What did you think of the film?" he asked.

The man made a face. "I was bored by it, but my wife wanted to see it. Who's the fellow in the brown suit, sitting near the nervous guy in the glasses?"

Maazi felt himself warming to the first officer. "A member of Israeli intelligence."

"Did he have something to do with that business in Göppingen, at the American casern? It was on the radio," he added quickly when he saw Maazi's curious glance. "Six men killed . . ."

"Five of them were my friends—" He broke off as a shadow loomed over the seat. Rima stood in the aisle, having left Samantha and David. The submachine gun was clutched with a loose familiarity in her right hand. "What are you going to do with those three?" she asked Maazi in Arabic.

"I haven't decided yet. We'll see who the Israelis will trade."

"I'll be moving along," the first officer said, rising to his feet and offering the seat to Rima. He walked along the aisle, nodding to Reynard, asking the Frenchman if he needed anything. Reaching the back of the cabin, where Samantha sat with David, the first officer turned around and retraced his steps. On the way back to the flight deck he said to Torbuk and el-Shafri, "Safety catches on?" El-Shafri gazed sullenly while Torbuk

291

turned around to watch the first officer pass through the doorway and resume his seat.

"Salim," Rima said urgently. "I know why the English actress worked for the Israelis."

"What?" Maazi forced himself to concentrate on what Rima was saying. It no longer seemed so important.

"One of the men who died at Munich—he was her lover."

"Her lover?" Maazi swung around to look back at Samantha and David. "One of the Israeli athletes?" He was intrigued by the revelation. After ten years Munich—his greatest triumph, in such stark contrast to today's fiasco—was still creating casualties. No wonder Samantha had gone berserk when he had told her where David was being held. "What was his name?"

"Davidson. Asher Davidson."

"What about the boy? He is nearly nine—could he be the son, the child of that relationship? David? David's son?" Again he looked back. The curly black hair, the dark brown eyes seemed to answer the question for him. Those were not the physical characteristics of an English child.

David saw Maazi staring at him but he paid the Palestinian little attention. His young brain was too busy trying to explain events that he could not understand, and no matter how hard he tried, the answers would not come.

"Mummy—" He pulled Samantha's arm until she turned to him.

"What is it, David?"

"That man who gave me the stamps—"

"Sssh!" Samantha warned as she saw Rima look around at the sound of conversation.

David refused to be hushed. "The man sitting near him in the suit—that's Mrs. Riley's cousin from South Africa. I'm sure of it. Mr. Chappell."

Samantha blinked in amazement. Could David possibly be mistaken? After what he had been through, could he be certain of identifying the Mossad agent who had been sent to guard the farm? She squeezed his arm, pinching with her nails before he could say any more.

"What's going on here?" Rima demanded as she came running back with Maazi.

Rima passed her weapon to Maazi and stooped across Samantha and David, digging roughly with her hands over their bodies, the seats, under the cushions. Satisfied that they were concealing nothing, she stood up, breathing heavily. "Keep quiet. Only speak if you wish to go to the toilet."

"Just like in your school, eh?"

"That's right—just like in my school."

John Lansing supervised the removal from the gymnasium of the six corpses. The five Palestinians would be buried in potter's field, an unknown grave. Better still, he would see they were cremated; nothing would be left of them but ashes. Shea's body would be returned to the United States for disposition by his family.

Lansing thought about Robert Shea and felt a twinge of pity for the State Department man. Poor bastard hadn't had a handle on his own life since he had been foolish enough to fancy a young boy in Paris. Even if the Russians had not called in their marker for twenty years, all that time living with the dread that the pictures—and the shame of his one indiscretion—would surface must have been hell.

Lansing already knew how he would word his report. Once those pictures were gone, there would be no evidence against Shea. He would write that Shea had given his life in a valiant attempt to safeguard one of the Israeli delegates. Ironically the State man would receive a hero's funeral.

Someone tapped Lansing on the arm. He looked around to see the radio operator.

"That Lufthansa Airbus just took off for Tripoli, sir."

"No problems at Stuttgart?"

"No, sir. Everything went smoothly."

"Thank Christ they're out of our hands. What flight number was the aircraft given?"

"Double zero."

Lansing smiled just enough to turn the corners of his mouth, but his eyes remained ice cold. License to kill.

The heavy cloud cover stayed with the Lufthansa Airbus for almost three hours before thinning. When it finally broke completely, the aircraft was clear of land and passing over the Mediterranean.

Sitting in the second officer's position behind the captain, the Beretta slung across his back, Maazi followed the Airbus's course on the chart spread across his knees; every so often he would check the compasses in front of the captain and first officer. "How long before we make our landfall?"

293

"About forty-five minutes," the captain replied.

Maazi folded the chart and stood up. "I'm going back. Let me know the moment you have radio contact with Tripoli." He left the flight deck and entered the first-class cabin. Torbuk and el-Shafri still maintained their vigil, keeping the entire cabin under watch, but Maazi thought that some of their earlier alertness had gone. So close to safety, they were starting to relax and Maazi could not blame them. Reynard stood in the aisle, leaning against a seat back. Rima sat by a window, looking down over the Mediterranean. Rosen appeared to be sleeping, head dropping onto his chest. At the rear of the cabin, Samantha raised a hand and asked if David could use the washroom. Maazi nodded.

"I'll be happy when we touch down," Maazi said to Reynard. He felt in his pockets and pulled out a crushed pack of Winstons. It was empty. Angrily he rolled the pack into a tight ball and dropped it onto the floor.

"Are you still too proud to try one of these?" Reynard offered the Palestinian a pack of Gitanes. Maazi took one and inhaled cautiously. "What are you going to do with the hostages?"

"Offer them in a trade for Palestinian commandos the Israelis hold. You were right when you stopped me from killing the woman, Pierre. Without her who knows what would have happened today? But because we held her, the Israelis negotiated." It was the day's only triumph.

But Reynard's next words took even that away. "No, Salim . . . the Germans and the Americans negotiated. The Israelis had nothing to do with this."

Reynard—damn him!—was right. The Israelis had not negotiated; they had nothing to do with his escape from Germany. "We shall see what happens when we land in Libya. We are free, and that is all that matters." He drew on the Gitanes and coughed as the bitter smoke ripped at his throat and lungs. "What about you . . . what are your plans now?"

Reynard studied the glowing end of his cigarette before replying. "I've been doing a lot of thinking about that during this flight. Before today, I was a journalist. What am I now?"

"A terrorist."

"Is that what I am?" Reynard laughed nervously. "Can I return to my home now, in Paris, and continue where I left off?"

"Come with us to Lebanon."

"What would I do there?"

"Be one of us."

Reynard shook his head and rested a hand on Maazi's shoulder. "But

I am not one of you, Salim. I am a Frenchman; you are Palestinians. I love Paris too much to live in a refugee camp for the remainder of my life."

"We will not always live in refugee camps. Besides, Paris will be dangerous for you now. They will be looking for you. I can think of many men the Israelis have murdered in Paris—Mahmoud Hamshari, Mohammed Boudia, Dr. Al Kubaissi."

Reynard's face paled as Maazi reeled off the names of terrorist leaders who had fallen in Paris.

"I remember when Boudia was killed, the bomb in the car. Perhaps it's better all around if the Israelis do not negotiate," Reynard muttered. "Then we can close three talkative mouths."

The first officer called to Maazi from the flight deck doorway. "We're getting Tripoli Control on the radio. Do you want to listen in?"

"Coming." Leaving Reynard to worry about his future, Maazi stubbed out the cigarette and followed the first officer to the flight deck. He sat down and was about to slip on the earphones when he asked, "How far away is that other aircraft?"

"What other aircraft?" The first officer checked the radar screen and then looked out of the window.

"Over there," Maazi pointed to the port side. Far in the distance, like a shiny silver pin, another aircraft was flying on what seemed to be a parallel course.

"Ten miles, fifteen maybe."

"Where is he headed?"

"How should I know? Maybe the same place we're going. It's a small world and an even smaller sky."

A voice in heavily accented English came through the phones. "Lufthansa zero-zero. This is Tripoli Control. You are not—repeat, not—given clearance for Tripoli. Over."

"What?" Maazi exclaimed. The captain waved at him to keep quiet.

"Tripoli Control. This is Lufthansa zero-zero. Please advise on alternate landing site. Over."

"You will be routed to El Adem Air Force Base. Over."

"Roger." The captain glanced at Maazi who was bursting with questions.

"Why can't we land at Tripoli? That was what we arranged."

"Don't ask me. I don't make the rules," the captain replied. "I have to follow instructions from down there." He glanced out of the window.

The other aircraft was further away now. "Guess he's going somewhere else after all," he murmured.

Maazi was no longer interested in the second aircraft. "I want to speak to Dr. Mohammed Nasser in Tripoli. Get him on the radio."

"Okay, just keep calm. We've come a long way and we don't want any accidents now," the captain said soothingly. "Tripoli Control. This is Lufthansa zero-zero. My passenger wants to speak with Dr. Mohammed Nasser. Please put him on." He waited for confirmation and then turned to Maazi. "They're locating him. It might take a little time."

Ten minutes later, the Fatah chief of operations came on the air. "Why are we not being allowed to land at Tripoli?" Maazi asked in rapid, urgent Arabic.

"Colonel Qadaffi himself issued the order for you to land at El Adem," Nasser replied.

"Why?"

"Because you have disgraced the Palestinian people," Nasser said. "You have failed in your mission. You are not to be received as a hero. Consider yourself fortunate that you are being given permission to land at all."

Maazi slumped back in the seat, stunned, unable to believe that Nasser would speak to him like this. Was this what Nasser—what his own people —really thought? That the sacrifices he and his brave men had made were a disgrace? Did all his previous work count for nothing? "What about our hostages?"

"They are the reasons you are being allowed to land. Without them, we would turn our backs on you."

The captain took over again, waiting for instructions. "Tripoli Control to Lufthansa zero-zero. Contact El Adem on one-twenty-two-point-four." The captain changed frequency to contact the air base and receive new instructions.

Moments later, Maazi felt his stomach churn as the Airbus banked to the east, heading toward the new destination close to the Egyptian border. When he gazed out of the window he noticed that the other aircraft had disappeared completely. The Airbus was now totally alone in the sky.

In the first-class cabin, Reynard checked his watch. They had been airborne for almost four hours. He stood up and stretched his arms above his head. Instead of sitting down again across the aisle from the slumbering Rosen, he walked toward the rear of the cabin as if going to the washroom. As he passed the last row of seats, he glanced down at the two occupants. Samantha avoided his gaze but David stared inquisitively at the Frenchman.

Reynard fished out his wallet and found two Lebanese stamps. Reaching across Samantha to offer the stamps to the boy, he said, "Do you still collect these, David?"

Before David had a chance to react, Samantha leaped from her seat to knock Reynard's hand aside. "Get away from him!" she hissed. "Do you think some lousy stamps can make up for what you've done, you bastard, for what you've helped these other savages to do?" Like talons, Samantha's hands clawed at Reynard's face, nails aiming for the light brown eyes behind the glasses.

Instantly Rima, el-Shafri and Torbuk started forward from their positions. Reynard grabbed hold of Samantha's arms as she lunged at his face and shoved her back into the seat. She kicked out at him, feeling a savage joy as her foot connected solidly with his knee. Reynard grunted in pain and lost his balance. Arms flailing clumsily, he fell across her and the boy.

He felt Samantha's knee drive into his face. His glasses were knocked flying as he grappled blindly with her legs. Again her knee slammed into him, this time in the throat. He pushed himself up. Cursing loudly in French, he dragged the M52 automatic from his pocket and leveled it at Samantha's eyes.

Rima's face was a mask of fury when she reached the rear of the cabin, but el-Shafri and Torbuk were both grinning at the Frenchman's humiliation. "Put that gun away!" Rima yelled. "Do you want us all to die?" She grabbed hold of Reynard's arm and dragged it down.

"My glasses—where are my glasses?"

Samantha spotted them first, on the floor beneath her seat. Spurred on by vindictiveness she stepped on them. Both lenses broke with a sharp crack. Reynard heard the noise and tried to break free of Rima's grasp. "You bitch!"

"I hope you fall over and break your bloody neck," Samantha answered.

Maazi and the captain appeared in the doorway leading to the flight deck. "What the hell is going on out there?" Maazi shouted along the length of the first-class cabin.

"Your friend found the Englishwoman more than a match for him," Rima answered.

"Stay away from her," Maazi warned Reynard. "Just keep an eye on the Israeli."

Reynard pocketed the gun, kicked Samantha's feet aside and knelt down to retrieve the glasses. When he realized that both lenses were broken, he flung the debris angrily at Samantha. Then he resumed his seat across the aisle from Rosen.

Rosen looked around groggily, a man abruptly woken from a deep slumber, and wondered what the commotion had been about. Seeing Reynard massaging his eyes with his fingers, the Mossad man moved gently in the seat and slipped his hand underneath his jacket. His fingers came into reassuring contact with the butt of the Walther PPK he wore in a concealed clip-on holster inside his trousers.

At the back of the cabin, Samantha gripped David's hand tightly. The shattered spectacles lay across her lap and she brushed them away carefully, becoming aware as she did so of a hard, uncomfortable lump beneath her buttocks. She waited until the Palestinians had returned to their positions, then she felt hesitantly underneath the flimsy cushion covering the seat. Her hand touched something cold and metallic, the distinct shape of a handle and trigger guard, a short barrel.

A wave of fear, of stunning revelation, swept over Samantha. Her hand trembled as she lifted the Walther PPK from beneath the cushion and slipped it into the waistband of her jeans.

Reynard!

The offer of stamps to David—the way he had set himself up to be attacked and had then fallen across her.

Before that, at Rashidieh, the way he had stopped Maazi from killing her in his fury at learning he had been duped.

And even before that—at the farmhouse in Somerset—the man with the moustache who had tailed her in the BMW—murdered the very night that Reynard had made love to her in the living room of the farmhouse.

A piece of glass, half of the lens from Reynard's broken glasses, remained on Samantha's jeans, its sharp edges catching in the fibers of the denim. She picked it up, held it between thumb and forefinger and, through it, studied the seat in front. There was no distortion at all. It was plain glass.

She forced herself to be calm. Her hand caressed David's. Soon—so very soon—she would be able to pay these murdering savages back for everything.

Reynard!

Once, when she was trying to understand why he allowed himself to be abused by Maazi, she had thought that Reynard was schizophrenic.

298

But it was not schizophrenia—it was acting. Those two personalities—the intense, charming writer, and the despicable terrorist camp follower—showed a higher acting caliber than Samantha could ever hope to achieve. The way he had so calmly suggested that she shoot Tayfield to prove her innocence . . . !

She stared at the back of Reynard's head, at the sandy hair, and willed him to turn around. Instead it was Rosen who looked back—the man who —Samantha's son had claimed—was Mrs. Riley's cousin from South Africa.

Something like a smile flickered ever so quickly across Rosen's face, as if he understood Samantha's silent questions and was answering, offering her reassurance.

CHAPTER
TWENTY-ONE

MAAZI was on the flight deck, carefully watching the captain and the instruments, when the Lufthansa Airbus made its landfall at an altitude of thirty-seven thousand feet. For the past five minutes a Mirage 5DE had maintained a station off the port wing. Despite the gathering gloom of dusk, Maazi could make out the camouflage colors and the red, white and black markings of the Libyan Air Force. The Mirage's presence both gladdened and troubled him. It was a sign that the journey was almost over, but what lay ahead for him? Was the blistering tirade from the Fatah's chief of operations a harbinger of things to come?

"El Adem. This is Lufthansa zero-zero, flight level three-seven-zero," the captain recited.

"Lufthansa zero-zero, squawk ident on twelve-hundred." There was a pause of a few seconds while the captain indentified the flight through its beacon, then the controller said: "Lufthansa zero-zero, you are radar identified."

Both members of the crew were concentrating hard now. No longer did they have the time to talk to the armed Palestinian who shared the flight deck with them. On the captain's brow had appeared a sheen of perspiration, and Maazi questioned whether the German was always this tense during the final stages of a flight. Was he nervous about landing at night at an unfamiliar military airfield? Or was he concerned about the Mirage that flew escort duty?

"El Adem. This is Lufthansa zero-zero. Request descent."

"Lufthansa zero-zero. You are cleared to maintain flight level two-two-zero."

"You'd better get out there, check everything's okay," the captain told the first officer as he started to descend to twenty-two thousand feet.

Maazi followed the blond-haired crew member into the first-class cabin. The man exhibited none of the friendliness he had shown during the earlier stages of the flight. There were no jokes, no idle conversation designed to calm the passengers. Now he was businesslike, walking up and down the aisle to check that all seat belts were fastened, cigarettes extinguished and seat backs in an upright position. Maazi decided to remain in the cabin, close to his own people. He took a seat near the door. Rima sat next to him. Across the aisle, el-Shafri and Torbuk settled down for the final descent and landing.

Night fell like a dark cloak. Maazi glanced out of the window and saw blackness stretching everywhere, relieved only by an occasional pinpoint of light, a car or a solitary building. The whining noise of the undercarriage being lowered, the solid thump as it locked into position, echoed through the Airbus. And then, as the captain made a final turn, Maazi saw El Adem, a kaleidoscope of approach lights and beacons, a small patch of illuminated civilization like an oasis in the center of a desert. The navigation lights of the escorting Mirage blinked on and off as the fighter banked sharply and soared away.

Guided by the control tower, the Airbus commenced its landing. Slat and full flaps were extended to the limit. A steady glide path took the aircraft over the inner marker, over the approach lights, past a complex of hangars. Then it was rumbling gently along the runway, brakes groaning, thrust reversed to slow its speed.

Maazi gazed out of the window, feeling nothing but relief and a guarded optimism now that the flight was over. On Libyan soil he was as good as home. And if the Israelis *did* decide to negotiate for the safe release of Samantha, her son and the Mossad agent—no matter how worried Reynard was about identification and retribution—then he would have reaped a triumph after all.

The engines died to a muted whisper as the Airbus taxied off the runway and parked close to a brightly lit hangar. Maazi could see a Libyan C-130 transport plane being serviced by a ground crew. He rose from his seat and signaled for the others to stand.

The captain emerged from the flight deck. "You'll have to wait a couple

301

of minutes, let them put up a ramp. Ground control just informed me that a bus is coming out to meet you, to take you and your people in."

"What about you?" Maazi felt a loose kinship with the Airbus captain. For the remainder of their lives, they would share this single experience.

"I hope we'll get refueled immediately and be allowed to fly home."

"Glad to get us out of your hair, eh?"

"It's all part of the job." The captain unlocked the door and peered down. The ramp was being backed into position. A jeep pulled up, disgorging three men in the uniform of the Libyan army, two captains and a colonel.

The Airbus captain was joined by the first officer. Together they stood in the doorway as they might do on a normal flight to thank their passengers for flying Lufthansa.

Maazi was first out, hands gripping the rails as he jogged nimbly down the steep ramp. The Libyan colonel, a middle-aged, slenderly built man with the high forehead of a scholar, stepped forward and extended his right hand formally.

"Colonel Jamil, at your service. I am to be your escort officer while you are in Libya."

Maazi shook the colonel's hand. "Where is Dr. Nasser?"

"He is waiting for you. He arrived only a few minutes ago."

"Why isn't he out here now?" With his feet planted firmly on the soil of an Arab country, Maazi felt confident enough to be angry at the Fatah chief of operations. How dare Nasser say he had disgraced the Palestinians? Who could have done better when beset by such treachery?

"I am a soldier," Colonel Jamil replied with a thin smile. "I do not get involved with politics, either my own country's or those of the Palestinians."

Maazi stood alongside the Libyan colonel and looked up the ramp as Samantha and David left the Airbus, followed by Rosen and Reynard. Rima, Torbuk and el-Shafri were the last to disembark. Reynard moved slowly, negotiating the ramp with great care as if lost without his glasses. As the group gathered on the concrete at the bottom of the ramp, separated into captors and hostages, a rickety green bus drew up alongside the Airbus. Colonel Jamil led the way to the door. "Please board your people," he told Maazi.

Maazi supervised the loading of the hostages on the bus. As Samantha passed, the Libyan colonel smiled down at David and asked in English, "Was that your first ride on an aircraft?" The boy looked up uncertainly and, before Samantha could react, Colonel Jamil scooped David into his arms. "I have a young grandson who looks just like you, with such thick curly black hair and dark brown eyes."

"Leave him alone!" Samantha swung around and nearly pulled the Walther PPK from the waistband of her jeans before Maazi forcefully blocked her way, pushing her toward the bus door with his Beretta.

"Don't worry about your son, Miss Sutcliffe," the colonel said. "No harm will befall him. No matter what our enemies might say about us, we respect children. We do not make war on them." Jamil waited until the bus was loaded; then he passed David to the two captains in the jeep before climbing in himself.

Followed by the bus, the jeep stopped in front of a gigantic hangar a mile away. Leaving the boy in the care of the two captains, Jamil led the way into the building. Maazi stiffened as he entered, automatically raising the Beretta to a ready position, finger curled around the trigger. The damned place reminded him uncannily of the gymnasium in Göppingen, the steep walls, the steel girders supporting the high roof. One set of lights shone down brightly from the center of the room, enough to illuminate the main part of the building but leaving the perimeter in contrasting shadow.

"What is this?" Maazi asked. "Why did you bring us here?"

He held out a hand and dug his feet into the ground, determined to go no further. Taking their cue from Maazi, Rima, el-Shafri and Torbuk gripped their weapons tensely. They understood what troubled their leader. There was no Dr. Mohammed Nasser waiting for them. The huge hangar seemed empty.

From the far side of the hangar a battery of lights blazed on to catch the party in sharp relief. Simultaneously three jeeps pulled up outside the hangar. A dozen heavily armed soldiers piled out of the vehicles to cut off any escape.

"Where—?" Maazi began. The question died on his lips as he saw the pistol that had appeared as if by magic in the right hand of the Libyan colonel.

"Where are you?" General Benjamin Avivi finished the question for Maazi. "You are at Hazor, a Heyl Ha'avir base. Now, very carefully, set your weapons on the ground."

"How—?" Maazi gasped, still unable to fully understand what was happening. His head began to throb again, the dizziness returned. "The German pilot, he was speaking to Tripoli. The compass bearings . . ." He looked around numbly. There was a gun in Rosen's hand as well, a small automatic that was aimed at Rima. And Reynard, who stood with one arm protectively around Samantha, was holding that lethal-looking Czech-made M52, but there was nothing nervous about the way he gripped it now. And, Maazi realized with another shock, the Frenchman was not prepared to use it against the Israelis. He was covering Torbuk and el-Shafri with it.

Reynard—!

"Do you mean the German-speaking Israeli pilot?" Avivi could not contain the smile that accompanied the question. He was enjoying this sweet moment of triumph, the culmination of the plan set forth by Rosen, the end of Operation Asher. "He never spoke to Tripoli. Neither did you. Your aircraft was in permanent radio contact with a second plane."

"That other plane," Maazi whispered. "But—I spoke to Dr. Nasser."

"You spoke to one of our people pretending to be Dr. Nasser."

"And the Mirage?" Slowly, Maazi began to comprehend the enormous confidence trick he had fallen for.

"An Israeli trainer with Libyan markings, the same as the C-One-thirty out there. And those compass bearings you saw were false. While pretending to adjust the navigational compass, the pilot was cranking in variations. You would have done better to check the magnetic compass, but that had also been modified." The smile of victory disappeared from Avivi's face. "Your weapons . . . set them down. We would like to avoid bloodshed."

Maazi let his Beretta hang by the short sling. He stared at Reynard, still unable to fully comprehend the change which had come over the Frenchman. "Why?"

"You spoke of George Tokvarian, do you remember?"

"The spy?" The question came from el-Shafri.

"He was my friend," Reynard said softly.

"And mine," Rosen added.

Suddenly Reynard lashed out with the M52 and caught el-Shafri across the mouth with the barrel. The gray-haired Palestinian staggered back, spitting out two broken teeth from between his smashed lips. Reynard swung on Torbuk and jammed the automatic into his chin. "Did you kill him? Was it you who mutilated him?"

Torbuk's eyes rolled downward, held there by the shiny barrel of the gun.

Maazi raised a hand to his head and fingered the crusted blood that ringed the cut above his right eye. His imagination was not strong enough to accept the transformation that Reynard had undergone. "Pierre," he said softly, "you haven't got the character to kill in cold blood."

"No?" Reynard kept the pistol to Torbuk's chin. A thin, vicious smile Maazi had never seen before appeared on the Frenchman's face. "When you see Wadi Hassan again, he'll tell you differently."

"You? How? What were you doing there?"

"He was spending the night with me," Samantha said. Only now was the truth sinking in. She was not in Libya but in Israel. Ten years too late to square herself with Asher!

"And Hassan saw you?"

"As we saw him."

Rima turned slowly toward Samantha. No expression showed on the Palestinian woman's face to reflect the bitter hatred that burned within her for this English actress. Only a calm, serene smile as she deftly unhooked one of the grenades from her belt, pulled the pin and dropped the grenade onto the concrete floor between herself and Samantha.

"Grenade!" Rosen roared, and dived to the floor.

Samantha grabbed at the PPK in her waistband as Rima leaped at her. She knew exactly what Rima intended—to pull her to the ground and ensure they were both killed by the blast. The gun jumped twice in Samantha's hand as she aimed hurriedly. Both bullets missed. And then the breath was knocked out of her lungs as a body smashed into her. Only it was not Rima who collided with her, but Reynard shoving her to the ground. And as she fell she saw Reynard grab Rima around the waist and force her down, pressing the Palestinian woman's body over the live grenade.

The grenade exploded, tearing Rima's chest and stomach apart and throwing Reynard through the air. Simultaneously Maazi jerked up his Beretta submachine gun and fired haphazardly at the battery of lights on the far side of the hangar. Following suit Torbuk and el-Shafri aimed at the roof lights, plunging the building into near darkness.

"Hold your fire!" Avivi yelled at the squad of soldiers outside the hangar. "You'll hit us!" Crawling on hands and knees, he found Samantha and dragged her toward the door. Once outside she looked around frantically, not even realizing she still held the PPK.

"Where's my son?" she screamed. "Where's David?"

Avivi pushed her out of the way. "He's safe. Keep down!"

Explosions sounded from inside the hangar, the cracks of pistols, the rapid torrent of submachine guns. Flashes of light interrupted the almost total darkness as the three Palestinians fired aimlessly. One of the soldiers started a jeep, flicked the headlights onto high beam and drove forward into the hangar. Immediately, three submachine guns opened fire on him and he toppled out of the jeep, but not before the lights had picked out the crouched figure of el-Shafri.

Reynard and Rosen fired simultaneously. The top of the gray-haired Palestinian's head blew apart as two high-velocity bullets smashed into it.

"Pull out!" Rosen shouted to Reynard.

Using the jeep as cover, the two men slid across the floor to the door. As they reached the outside, a soldier swept the hangar with fire from a jeep-mounted heavy machine gun, disappointed when there was no sound other than the 30-caliber bullets striking the far wall.

"Is there another way out?" Rosen asked Avivi.

"No. They've got to come out the same way they went in."

"What about the men who turned on the lights? They're still in there, for God's sake!"

"The lights were turned on from outside. Only the Palestinians are in there now. Tear gas!" he yelled at the soldiers.

While the machine gunner maintained a withering covering fire, two soldiers began lobbing tear-gas grenades deep into the hangar. Soon even the air outside was filled with acrid fumes, and the assault party was forced to retreat. Jeeps were backed up, their headlights aimed at the hangar entrance. To one side of the main group stood Reynard and Samantha, his arm around her reassuringly. They were only spectators now.

Yussuf Torbuk was the first to yield to the gas. Clutching the submachine gun at waist height, finger pressed down on the trigger, he staggered out of the hangar, half-blinded, coughing violently. The machine gunner cut him in half just above the waist with a long, vicious burst.

"No more! Don't shoot! I'm throwing out my gun!"

The Beretta landed on the concrete in front of the hangar. Maazi stumbled out from the gas-filled building, rubbing his eyes frantically.

"Both hands in the air!" Rosen commanded.

Obediently Maazi raised his arms. Tears were streaming down his face, mixing with blood from the cut that had reopened above his right eye. Rosen, Avivi and the soldiers waited. Reynard tried to turn Samantha's face into his shoulder, to hide the sight from her, but she slipped out of his grasp. Curiously he watched her walk away. Only when he saw the

PPK still gripped tightly in her hand did he realized what she intended to do.

"Samantha! No!" He started to run after her, then slowed his pace. He would let her do what she had to do.

Like a woman under hypnosis Samantha walked between the soldiers, past Rosen and Avivi, until she stood facing Maazi. The gun was held out in front of her, pointed unwaveringly at the Palestinian.

"Salim, look at me."

Maazi blinked back the tears that stung his eyes. As his vision cleared he thought it was Rima facing him. But no . . . it could not be. Rima was inside the hangar, dead, held over the grenade she had activated. "Samantha?" he whispered.

"Did Rima tell you about Asher Davidson?"

"Asher?" Why did that name sound so familiar?

"You helped to kill him, Salim. And you taught me how to fire a gun so that I could kill you."

No one tried to intervene. Reynard joined Rosen and Avivi. This was something Samantha had to do on her own, a part of her life she had to work out for herself.

Samantha looked along the barrel of the PPK at the pathetic figure five yards in front of her. Surely this could not be the same suave Palestinian who had accompanied Reynard to the farmhouse to make the proposition that had resulted in this moment? Could he be the same man who had boasted about his murderous exploits, the times he had killed? The same confident fighter who had so swiftly turned the tables on the two Phalangists in Maameltein? The memory of that particular night—of Maazi's foul body next to her own—strengthened Samantha's resolve.

She squeezed the trigger just as Maazi had taught her when he had given those lessons in Rashidieh; a pressure so even that she would not even realize when the gun was about to fire.

And at that precise moment, Salim Maazi's last vestiges of dignity deserted him. He dropped to his knees, hands outstretched to Samantha in a plea for mercy. Flame blossomed from the muzzle of the PPK. Instead of smashing through Maazi's chest, the bullet ripped high into his left shoulder, knocking him onto his back where he lay moaning in pain.

As Samantha stepped forward slowly and lowered the pistol to administer the *coup de grace* to the stricken Palestinian, the expectant silence was shattered by the roar of an engine. Headlights flashing on and off, a jeep veered past the watching soldiers and squealed to an abrupt halt three yards from where Samantha stood. Driving the jeep was one of the men in Libyan uniform who had taken David to safety. His passenger was a stout, elderly Irishwoman who—despite the warmth of the evening— wore an ancient fur coat and clutched a broad-brimmed beige hat trimmed with feathers to her head.

Samantha's determination eased momentarily as she looked toward the jeep and recognized the woman pushing her way out of the vehicle. Then she swung back to Maazi, the PPK pointed again at his head.

"Mrs. Sutcliffe, I know you hate the sight of this filthy, blackhearted little wog—and you've got every right to, believe me—but don't you think you should leave him for the proper authorities to look after?"

With a tenderness that seemed totally out of place in the crusty old Irishwoman, Mrs. Riley placed an arm around Samantha's shoulders. Her other hand closed around the pistol and she removed it from Samantha's grasp.

"Come on now, Mrs. Sutcliffe. Young David's waiting for you. And really—I don't know how you could have let him get so filthy. It's utterly disgraceful."

An hour later Samantha could scarcely believe the transformation that a lengthy shower and a change of clothes could bring—even if those fresh clothes were only shower shoes and an ill-fitting fatigue uniform, courtesy of the Heyl Ha'avir.

"What on earth are you doing here in Israel?" she asked Mrs. Riley. "You're the very last person I expected to see."

It was General Avivi who answered, now wearing slacks and an open-necked shirt. He sat comfortably behind a desk that was normally occupied by the air base's deputy commander. "Samantha, our entire army could not have kept this good woman away. After the Palestinians took your son, Mrs. Riley returned to Israel with Joel Rosen. And, because we were all so afraid of her, we had to inform her of all our plans to rescue you and David. When I told her that the final act would be played out here, she insisted on being present."

"That's right," Mrs. Riley chimed in. "They brought David to me. I was watching from in here. When I saw you pointing the gun at the wog, I asked to be taken out there."

"Asked?" Avivi exclaimed. "Demanded, Mrs. Riley. You scared my man out of his wits."

Sitting on the other side of the desk, Joel Rosen burst out laughing as

308

he recalled how tenaciously the housekeeper had fought when David had been kidnapped.

"Where is David now?" Samantha asked. She had last seen him in the arms of General Avivi.

"He'll be here in a little while," Avivi answered. "Reynard is getting him cleaned up, finding small clothes. There aren't too many people stationed here his size."

"Is Reynard his real name—Pierre Reynard?"

Avivi's wide forehead creased in thought. "So long has passed since anyone even thought of him by his real name—" He looked to Rosen for assistance.

"We always refer to him by his code name—Hunovi, it means 'the prophet' in Hebrew."

"Will he be going back?" Samantha asked.

"To the field? To Paris?" Rosen shook his head. "His usefulness is finished. Everyone knows that he was in Lebanon with Maazi. The Americans, the other delegates at the meeting in Germany, will be able to identify him. It would look peculiar if he returned and no one else did. When we release details of tonight's incident, Pierre Reynard will be listed as one of the fatalities."

"I see." Samantha supposed she should feel vaguely sad at the demise of Pierre Reynard, but it opened visions of his true identity, an identity she'd like to know better.

The door opened and David, wearing a pair of shorts and a T-shirt, entered the office, tugging at Reynard's hand. The Frenchman let go and David ran to his mother. "That's better," she said approvingly. "You smell clean again."

David sniffed. "So do you," he replied and they both laughed.

"What will happen to Maazi?" Samantha asked Avivi.

"Prison."

"I shouldn't have missed. I could have done you a favor."

"No, Samantha," Reynard said. He came around behind her chair and placed his hands gently on her shoulder. "You exorcised one demon when you defeated Maazi. If you had killed him, you might only have created another for yourself."

"Is it all over now?"

"Not quite. There are still others who were responsible for the PLO strike. Even though they took no physical part in this operation, we hold them just as guilty as those who did."

309

"I see. Will you—"

"Be going out again? Possibly."

Listening to the conversation, David was uncertain that he understood everything that was being said. Only the part about Reynard leaving interested him. He screwed his face into a pout and protested, "You told me you'd take me to a post office and buy all the Israeli stamps, Uncle Pierre."

"And so I will. I promise."

"Uncle Pierre?" Samantha queried, looking up.

"It was your son's idea, not mine. Would you prefer, instead, that he called me Uncle Motti?"

"Is that your real name?"

He nodded. "Motti Shual. It means fox in Hebrew, just like Reynard. It's common practice to have an alias that is related to the real name, just in case the agent should forget the field name."

But Samantha was not listening to the explanation. "Shual? That was Alan Tayfield's name. Is it a common one out here, like Smith or Jones back home?"

"Not that I know of." Reynard rubbed the back of his hand across his eyes. "Gershon Shual—your Alan Tayfield—was my older brother."

"And you—" Samantha gasped.

"He was already dead, Samantha. The living are always more important to us than the dead, no matter how dear the dead might have been. I was hoping to convey to you that he was dead. I tried to make you understand."

"You did, didn't you?" she whispered, as she replayed that terrible scene in her mind. He had urged her time and again to pull the trigger, knowing that the gun was unloaded, knowing that Tayfield was already dead.

The office door opened again and an attractive uniformed young woman entered, pushing a trolley laden with coffee and sandwiches and a sparkling bottle of iced orange juice for David. Reynard took a cup of coffee and sauntered over to the window, motioning for Samantha to join him.

"I'll be away for about a week; then I will return to Israel for good. Will you still be here when I get back?"

"That depends."

"On what?"

"On whether you want me to stay."

310

Reynard took her hand and Samantha could feel her face flush with pleasure. "Of course I do."

"What's the Israeli film industry like?" she asked.

"Small. But you might have sacrificed your career after all, Samantha. There will be lunatics eager to square accounts with Samantha Sutcliffe. The Palestinians are notoriously poor losers."

A shiver ran down Samantha's back—so she and David were not out of danger yet. The peril would remain for the rest of their lives. "I hadn't thought about that. What should I do?"

"At the Plaza Athénée, you told me you could always give swimming lessons," he said with a gentle laugh. "But your best start would be to change your name."

"To what?" She gazed into his light brown eyes, so clear now without the glasses, knowing what she wanted to see there.

"I'll give it deep thought while I'm away." He rested the coffee cup on the window ledge and kissed her.

And to Samantha, it seemed that absolutely nothing had happened between the kiss he gave her now and that parting kiss he had given her when he had left the farmhouse in Somerset so many lifetimes ago.

CHAPTER
TWENTY-TWO

ON Friday, two days after the aborted hijacking of the American-sponsored summit meeting, Pavel Vlasov was back in Beirut. His meeting with Fatah chief of operations, Dr. Mohammed Nasser, in the apartment on the Rue Ayoub Tabet was short. The Russian needed only to know the Palestinians' reasons for the failure of the mission so that he, in turn, could present a report to his superiors that would absolve him of all blame. Covering your rear was important in Moscow.

When the meeting finished, Vlasov walked heavily down the stairs to the street where a Fiat awaited him, driven by a KGB field agent who worked for the Soviet embassy on the Rue Mar Elias B'Tina. Vlasov climbed into the back of the Fiat and sat back, satisfied that the entire responsibility would be placed on the Palestinians. Their men had walked into a trap. No, two traps—one set by the Americans, and one set by the *Zhidi*.

Stupid, useless Arab bastards, every single worthless one of them, Vlasov cursed. For, after all, Vlasov was not to know that Robert Shea had been caught and turned, that the Israelis and Americans had been aware all along of the hijacking attempt and had allowed it to continue for their own purposes.

Nor was Vlasov to know that the white Renault parked a hundred yards along the road—anonymous in the middle of a line of parked cars—had been left there by a man who never intended to drive it again. Vlasov's mind was elsewhere as the Fiat passed along the line of cars.

Watching from the apartment where he had once photographed Vlasov leaving a meeting with Mohammed Nasser and Salim Maazi, Reynard fingered a miniature transmitter. He would have preferred something more sophisticated, a transmitter attached to Vlasov's Fiat that would activate the fifteen kilos of high explosive stored inside the parked white Renault. But there had not been time to be so clever. This would have to do, as would the hasty disguise he had adopted, his sandy hair dyed black, the skin of his face and arms darkened by chemicals, the contact lenses that changed his light brown eyes to dark brown.

As the Fiat drew abreast of the parked Renault, Reynard pressed the button on the transmitter. A massive explosion rocked the street, shook buildings, blew out shop fronts. When the smoke cleared, half a dozen Palestinians who had been in the bomb's killing range lay dead. Cars around the shattered Renault rested at crazy angles. And the Fiat, which had taken the brunt of the blast, was on the opposite side of the street, rocking crazily on its roof.

Reynard watched long enough to be certain that there was no sign of life. Then he left the apartment and raced down the stairs to join others running toward the scene of the terrible accident.

The telephone in Mohammed Nasser's home was busy all night as the Fatah chief of operations tried to gather information about the explosion on the Rue Ayoub Tabet and the deaths of Vlasov and his driver. By eight o'clock on Saturday morning, Nasser was desperately tired, and irritated by the increasing interference on the line. Buzzes, clicks, sometimes even complete cutoffs. He suspected that the telephone was being tapped.

He dialed the number of the telephone company and asked for his phone to be checked. An hour later a uniformed technician arrived to look into the problem. The man took apart the telephone and found nothing. Then, as Nasser watched, he followed the line to the junction box and gave a shout of triumph.

"What is it?" Nasser asked. "What have you found?"

The man held up a minute electronic device. "How long have you noticed trouble on the line?"

"It started during the night."

"This must have begun to malfunction then," the phone company technician explained. "That's why you got the interference."

Nasser wondered who had broken into his family's home to place the bug. The Israelis? The Soviets? How could the Palestinians fight a freedom war when they had to be suspicious of both their enemies *and* their friends. The entire world was arrayed against them.

From then the telephone worked perfectly. At eight o'clock that evening, just as Nasser and his family were finishing dinner, the telephone rang. Nasser's wife answered it.

"Dr. Nasser?" Reynard asked from the apartment on the Rue Ayoub Tabet. Next to him stood the man who had visited Nasser's home as a telephone company technician.

"Just a moment," the woman said. She called her husband to the telephone.

"Is that Dr. Nasser?" Reynard asked. "Dr. Mohammed Nasser?"

"It is. Who is this, please?"

The earpiece of the telephone exploded into the right side of Nasser's head, driving fragments of metal and plastic through his skull and into his brain.

By Sunday evening Reynard was back in Tel Aviv. The skin on his face and arms was still dark, his hair still black. The strangeness of his appearance did not matter to Samantha or David as they sat with him at an outdoor café on Dizengoff Street. All that mattered was that he had returned. Pierre Reynard—Hunovi—they were gone forever. But Motti Shual—Samantha smiled as she tried to become accustomed to that name —had come back.

Munich was now completely avenged. Samantha would never be able to forget Asher. She would not want to. He would always be a part of her. But she understood that she now had the strength to love again, to make a life for herself—and David—with someone else.

Reynard reached across the table and covered her hand with his own. "Are you lost in solemn thoughts of the past?"

"A little," she admitted. While he had been away in Beirut she had visited Asher's grave, and had paid a call on Avi and Ilana Spiegler and their children, Tayfield's family. What had been a duty to pay her respects had finished as a warm and loving meeting, made even more joyous by Samantha's knowledge that soon they would be her family as well.

Samantha smiled. "I was just wondering about something."

She gripped his hand tightly and reached out with her other hand to hold David. "When we go looking for a home, I just hope we can find some place where we'll be able to employ an irascible Irish housekeeper."

314

EPILOGUE

𝑻 HE tanks and armored personnel carriers that had formed the backdrop for the meeting between Joel Rosen and Hunovi in northern Israel went into action a week later, after terrorists had gunned down the Israeli Ambassador to the United Kingdom as he left a London hotel. The terrorists involved in the shooting were apprehended swiftly by Scotland Yard. The arrests were not enough for the Israeli Government which believed firmly that the attack on the ambassador was in retaliation for the destruction of the new Black September cell. In an emergency cabinet meeting, the Israelis decided it was time to deal with the Palestinian threat once and for all.

In a three-pronged ground attack code named Operation Peace for Galilee, and backed by air and sea forces, Israeli troops advanced past Christian militia units to sweep into Lebanon and crush the Palestinian military infrastructure.

One of the first Palestinian strongholds to fall in the savage attack was the Rashidieh refugee camp. While Israeli forces continued north, a helicopter landed just outside Rashidieh. Four soldiers armed with shovels gently moved aside sand until they had uncovered the body of Alan Tayfield, still wrapped in the tarpaulin in which it had been driven from the camp.

When Tayfield's body was interred next to his wife's at a cemetery in Petah Tiqva, Reynard, Samantha and Tayfield's family were joined by Joel Rosen and General Avivi. One by one they moved forward to heap a spadeful of earth on the casket. When they left the cemetery, another funeral party was arriving, comprising relatives and friends of a soldier who had been killed in the fighting in Lebanon. Holding Samantha's hand, Reynard turned around to watch. The tears that had filled his eyes for his brother became tears for the new mourners. Then he managed to create the semblance of a smile.

"There are few of those, thank God," he said quietly to Samantha. "Because of the work done by people like my brother . . . and by you," he added.

"I'd rather have Alan here than see Israeli troops in Beirut," Samantha answered.

"So would I," Reynard said, squeezing her hand gently. "So would I."